Flying Saucers on the moon

By
Harold T Wilkins
Carlos Allende

SAUCERIAN PUBLISHER

ISBN: 978-1-955087-11-7

9 781955 087117

© 2022, Saucerian Publisher

Harold T. Wilkins

Introduction

Harold Tom Wilkins (June 1891 – 1960) was a British journalist known for his books on adventures, fortean research, and historic claims about Atlantis and South America.

In 1931, Wilkins wrote a detailed description of the mystery of the Mary Celeste for the Quarterly Review. It was later reprinted in his book Mysteries Solved and Unsolved. In the 1950s he published books claiming that UFOs are hostile. Wilkins also wrote about White Gods, writing that a vanished white race had occupied the whole of South America in ancient times. Wilkins in his Mysteries of Ancient South America (1945) compiled further accounts of similar sightings of "White Indians" in the Amazon Rainforest from the 16th to 19th century by explorers and Jesuits. Wilkins was also an influence on the hollow earth theory, as he located the descendants of Atlantis to tunnels in South America, especially in Brazil; he also discussed tunnels in other locations such as the Andes.

In 1953, the author published *Flying Saucers on the moon.* In this book, the author recounts recent events at the time of the writing, i.e., Foo Fighters, Maury Island Incident, Kenneth Arnold, and he goes back to history and cites anomalous aerial phenomena from antiquity. The book is aimed at True Believers; however, even the skeptic will enjoy reading it. One neat thing about reading these older books is that they offer the reader a glimpse into the mindset of what was then contemporary times.

The author discussed several aspects of the flying saucers in the chapters on this title that are:

A FOREWORD AND A WARNING; MYSTERIES BETWEEN THE WORLD WARS; THE COMING OF THE FOO FIGHTERS; A VAST BAT-LIKE MACHINE; HAVE THE SAUCER-MEN TERRESTRIAL SPIES? THE MARTIAN CAT AMONG THE PIGEONS; COLOSSAL DEATH RAY AEROFORM; BRITAIN'S NAVY AND AIR FORCE AWAKENED; FLYING SAUCER OF OTHER DAYS; WHAT ON EARTH WAS IT?; SPACE SHIPS, THE MOON, MARS, AND VENUS; HAVE THE FLYING SAUCERS EVER LANDED?; THE SHADOW OF THE UNKNOWN; INTERPLANETARY TRAVEL THE RED LIGHT; APPENDIX; BIBLIOGRAPHY.

Saucerian Publisher was founded with the mission of promoting books in Science Fiction. Our vision is to preserve the legacy of literary history by reprint editions of books which have already been exhausted or are difficult to obtain. Our goal is to help readers, educators, and researchers by bringing back original publications that are difficult to find at a reasonable price while preserving the legacy of universal knowledge. This title is an authentic and exact reproduction (facsimile copy) of the original title printed text in shades of gray. IMPORTANT, although we have attempted to maintain the integrity of the articles accurately, the present reproduction has missing and blurred pages, poor pictures from the original scanned copy. This book have been formatted from its original version for publication. Because this material is culturally important, we have made it available as part of our commitment to protect, preserve and promote knowledge in the world.

Great, but unpretentious, this edition is a rare symbol by itself of what was going in the dawn of the modern UFO phenomena.

Carlos Allende
Editor, 2022

CONTENTS

A FOREWORD AND A WARNING

"... We have learned now that we cannot regard this planet as being fenced in and a secure abiding-place for Man; we can never anticipate the unseen good or evil that can come upon us suddenly out of space ... Before the cylinder fell there was a general persuasion that through all the deep of space no life existed beyond the petty surface of our minute sphere. Now we see further...."

The late H. G. Wells in his War of the Worlds, *who fore-cast that the coming of interplanetary visitors might promote the conception of the commonweal of man, and the abolition of war and world wars, as, perhaps, nothing else can do upon this crazed planet, the Earth.*

"There are many other inhabited worlds ... and on some of them beings exist who are immeasurably beyond our mental level. We should be rash to deny that they can use radiation so penetrating as to convey messages to earth. Probably, such messages come now. When they are first made intelligible a new era in the history of human-ity dawns. At the beginning of the new era, the oppos-ition between those who welcome the new knowledge and those who deem it dangerously subversive may lead to a world war ... But I should like to be living then, when we begin this new era. We might get a true understanding of the beginning of the universe."

The late Bishop Barnes, of Birmingham, England, at the Congress of the British Association for the Advance-ment of Science, at Westminster, London, on September 29, 1931.

It is confidently predicted, in quarters both in Great Britain and on the continent of Europe and, of course, in the U.S.A., that, probably before the present hectic century passes into 2,001 A.D., the first man from earth will have made a landing on the moon. What is he going to find there?

I have before me a cutting from a New York newspaper, perhaps appropriately dated April 1st 1953, which imports that certain optimists have been reading the late H. G. Wells's extremely readable fantasy on the two men who visited the moon in a "degravitated sphere", and one of whom was kept

7

prisoner and eventually put in some sort of lethal chamber
by the Grand Chitinous Lunar, whose brows were sprayed
with a scented fountain after he had been given a long lecture
on Mr. Wells's sociological theories. But it will be recalled
that the man who *did* escape and came back to earth went
away with a big bar of pure gold, stolen from moon-calf herd-
ers, and also noted immense quantities of placer gold lying
around on the lunar crater floor.

It may be, or may not be. But what is the first man to land
on the moon going to find there? No air, no water, no life, a
vaste waste of sand, or scoriae, pitted with lunar craters produced by the bombardment of meteorites falling unbraked on
the lunar shell; a dead world on which, from the beginning of
lunar time, foot of human or humanoid hath never trod? Will
he stand on the vast floor of one of the numerous lunar craters
and contemplate—inside his oxygenated space suit—a lifeless
world on which heaven-topping lunar mountains frown, many
of whose peaks, they say, are at least twice the height of Mount
Everest? No life, or vegetation, on these mountains, only bare,
exposed rock-strata?

Or, as his rocket- or atomic-powered space ship touches the
floor of one of the craters, especially in that north-west quadrant where, as far back as the mid-eighteenth century, English
scientists and members of the Royal Society noted mysterious
lights, will he stand, even more amazed and silent than was
stout Cortes on the peak of Darien, as he, Mr. First-Man-on-
the-Moon, perhaps notes the massive portals which may be the
entrance to great sublunar tunnels? Portals behind which may
stand beings of other unknown worlds in space, who, long
since, anticipated terrestrial man on the moon, and who *may*
have picked up some radio news announcer's story about the
plans of Mr. Richard de Touche-Skadding of Moon Metals
and Minerals' Incorporated, of New York state?

Suppose, as is not very unlikely, that all these suspicious
cosmic anticipators of Mr. First Man, who got to the moon
only in virtue of a science considerably in advance of that of
the earth, stand ready with ray-cannon, electric blast force
guns, paralysing ray-projectors, or variants of Wells's Martian

8

heat ray, or some "degravitator" device that may hold the first terrestrial space ship fast-bound to the floor of the crater, so that there may be no return to earth?

No one, at this time, can answer these fantastic questions; but there may be foreshadowings of portentous answers in what this book reveals of recent mysterious phenomena, not only in U.S.A., but right here in England, in the month between July 21 and August 21, 1953. I have, later in this book, drawn attention to three mysterious incidents on the Cotswold Hills of Gloucestershire, England.

CHAPTER I

MYSTERIES BETWEEN THE WORLD WARS : . . .

I have, for six years, from the end of the second World War, been a close student and earnest investigator, in the U.S.A., and Canada, and, latterly, in the British Isles, of what are probably the most portentous phenomena of this strange century. I refer to the crudely named 'flying saucers', in all their many shapes and sizes. Men and women all over the world say they have seen them in the day and night skies. I, too, have seen them!

On the evening of November 1, 1950, at 6.20 p.m., I was out in the garden of my house at Bexleyheath, Kent, taking a breath of fresh air. The moon had not risen. It was near the last quarter. The night was clear and starry, but in the zenith was a band of cumulus clouds. The night was still. There were no pyrotechnic displays, and no children were letting off fireworks or starting bonfires anywhere in sight or sound. My garden stands on a low hill. I was absently gazing at the stars in the south-eastern quadrant of the sky which, in that region, was clear of any cloud. On a sudden, a round ball of white light appeared flying silently at an angle of about 90 degrees with the ground. It was not moving very quickly. Behind it was no trail of light or sparks. It vanished into the belt of clouds at the zenith, as silently as it had appeared. It did *not* reappear, as would a balloon of any type. I estimate the height of the ball as about 3,000 feet.

It was certainly not a 'shooting star' or meteorite, nor was it a rocket or any sort of pyrotechnical display. Their trajectory is parabolic, whereas the flight of this ball of light was dead level, through the evening sky.

What, then, was it?

I think it was one of the type of phenomena called 'flying saucers'.

Next morning, November 2, when I opened the London 'Daily Telegraph', I read that, at 8.30 p.m., on the preceding night—the night on which I had seen the ball of moving light—a strange orange light, extending through the sky, had been seen by many people on the Herts-Bucks border, some 24 miles, as the crow flies, from the location where I had seen the white ball of light. These people swore they saw an orange light for about 30 seconds, and that it then disappeared. I took the trouble to write, to the editor of the 'Daily Telegraph', a very brief note of what I had seen and drawing his editorial attention to the mysterious orange light seen, about two hours later, some 24 miles away. The letter was neither acknowledged nor published. Probably, it was simply wastepaper basketed by the gentleman on the staff who has the job of editing the letter-to-the-editor column. I hope I do him no injustice when I state that I deem that his pulse would not lose a beat were it reliably reported to him that a dinosaur was at loose in Hyde Park, London, and that the Fellows of the Royal Zoological Society had asked for a battery of howitzers from the arsenal in the Tower of London, to aid them in hunting the monster down. That remarkable American, the late Charles Fort, made the same comment about similar London newspapers of the 1920's.

Now, sixteen days earlier, on the night of 12 October 1950, at 11.15 p.m., a woman cycling homeward from the city of Gloucester to a suburb named Barnwood, was surprised to see four blazing lights, like huge stars apparently stationary in the sky. She said that, in a few moments, these lights started "to go in and out". Two friends told her that they, too, saw these lights on the same night, and that two of the mysterious lights appeared near Churchdown Hill, which is about two miles from Barnwood.

My purpose in drawing attention to these strange balls of light, at the beginning of this book, will soon appear.

A very bright sphere of a similar unknown type, and *not* a meteor, was seen by Mr. Walter Pepperell, manager of a department of the Gloucester Co-operative Society, in *spring* 1910, on a clear and starry evening. He was standing in Market

Parade, in the centre of the town, when he was startled to
see a glowing sphere pass noiselessly across the sky. Its speed
was not great, and certainly it was no meteorite or astronomical phenomenon, nor any sort of balloon. It may also
be noted that another similar mystery of the skies, happening
two years later, in the same part of England, has never been
cleared up. Mention was made of it in the astronomical journal 'Observatory'. According to a Bath, Somerset, newspaper,
residents of Warmley, then a village along the Avon, near
Bath, were, on the evening of March 6, 1912, greatly excited
by the remarkable spectacle of what looked like "a splendidly
illuminated aeroplane passing over the village. The machine
was travelling at a tremendous rate, and came from the direction of Bath and went on towards Gloucester." One editor,
who said in that year, "we are prepared for anything now-
adays", supposed the phenomenon was a "triple-headed fire-
ball, of large size".

I was, myself, in the town of Gloucester, in 1912, and recall
no report of any explosion of this alleged fire-ball. In 1912, it
was accounted a feat that the French aviator, Louis Blériot
had, three years before, flown in what we should now deem a
very primitive aeroplane, across the the English Channel from
France. Neither in England, nor in U.S.A., or anywhere in the
continent of Europe was there any type of aeroform capable
of the speed or performance of the apparition seen over
Warmley, on that March evening.

Since 1945, there has accumulated an immense mass of evidence in the shape of eye-witnesses' reports of day and night
sightings of mysterious objects in the skies. They have been
seen over the snows of Alaska, alike by Eskimos, Indians and
U.S. air pilots and coast guards. They have been seen in the
skies over scientific bases down in the far Antarctic. China and
Peru have seen them; so have England, Wales, Scotland, Ireland, and practically all European countries, including Russia
and her satellites. They have been seen over every sea and
ocean, by liners, freight steamers and warships, and by many
sea and land 'plane pilots. Australia and New Zealand have
seen them; so have remote Islands in the North and South

13

Pacific, east and west of the International Date Line. Every
state in the American Union has seen them. Indeed, the
global range of these reports of sightings is far too wide and
various to be explained, or explained away as mass-hysteria
and mass-hallucinations, or misinterpretation of natural phenomena. Unless, of course, the sceptic is prepared to advance
the theory that the whole planet must be one mass of visionaries and delusional cranks who ought to be having psychiatric
treatment.

Most writers who have looked into this strange phenomenon
have not gone farther back than the year 1946, when the
Wellsian dream of interplanetary contact and travel seemed
to be approaching a dramatic realisation. It was in that year
that there first began to appear on the ticker tape machines,
in newspaper offices and clubs, all over the world, the—as it
seemed—first appearance of strange and shining discs in the
skies of the world, but principally in the U.S.A.

However, I shall show, in a later chapter of this book, that
interplanetary machines and mysterious objects of real and
apparent cosmic, as distinct from terrestrial, origin, are far
from new things in the skies of the earth! This will naturally
startle most people, and certainly most of the orthodox scientists, and astronomers, who have made little or no study of the
history of scientific thought and investigation. It is a fact, by
the way, that specialists seldom study the *history of scientific
progress*. I believe I have traced these cosmic visitants to our
own skies as far back as the year 729 A.D.—back into the dim
and misty ages after the fall of the Roman Empire, when old
England was merely an anarchic welter of warring tribes
striving for hegemony, from the Tyne to the Thames.

At this moment, I will go no farther back than to the year
1931, which will be within the memory of the present generation. In that year, Francis Chichester, well known as an airman and navigator, took off from New South Wales, alone, in
a little Moth airplane which had an open cockpit. He attempted what was then a very dangerous flight of 1,650 miles across
the lonely Tasman Sea to New Zealand. All alone, over this
waste of waters, with not a sign of smoke from any steamer,

14

right across to the horizon, with nothing below his cockpit but the rolling waves, and nothing in the sky save his own airplane, he was startled by sudden flashes, moving mysteriously in the sky. They moved erratically, and came and went at amazing speed. Then, an object which he afterwards described as "like a silver pearl", ranged up to his 'plane. It came in front of the nacelle, and then it suddenly and inexplicably seemed to fade out!

To say he was astonished is to put the matter mildly. He did not suppose that what he was witnessing, over the lonely Tasman Sea, was a vanishing trick denoting, perhaps, command of some cosmic, or unknown ray, rendering an object invisible to terrestrial vision, or the existence of an order of beings whose wave-length, or frequency of "etheric vibration" is very different from that of our own world. Nor did he know that this phenomenon had been seen from the ground, and not in the air, by many sane people, long before the year 1931. Mr. Chichester could offer no explanation of the mysterious affair, but he clearly did not think he had been "seeing things". No doubt, he did not suppose that anyone would believe his story, or regard it as any more than a hallucination induced, perhaps, by mental and physical strain in a very dangerous solo flight of that time, 23 years ago.

He said the mysterious object flashed with the brilliance of a powerful searchlight, or a heliograph. It moved with astonishing velocity, then it slowed down, and again accelerated, to vanish with the speed of lightning, or like the phantasm of a haunted house.

Five years later (October 2, 1936), in the height of the civil war in Franco's Spain, the late Valentine Williams, well known as a novelist and a soldier in the First World War, was motoring with a Spanish bullfighter, Señor Fernandez de Arzabal, and a Mr. Neil O'Malley Keyes, from the headquarters of Franco, at Burgos, to Biarritz. They were about 74 miles from San Sebastian, and in the Basque province of Guipuzcoa, and the car was speeding over a level stretch of road backed by a high mountain saddle. Suddenly, Mr. Williams's two companions uttered a simultaneous exclamation.

15

He turned his head and saw what he at first took to be an airplane flare, or tracer bullet, streaming through the air from the mountain, and speeding on a course at right angles to that of the motor car. The phenomenon was travelling with amazing speed, east of his car and going north.

Said Mr. Williams:

> "It was like a streamer of white smoke, heading earth-wards. As it went, it burst into a bright orange flame. There was no sound or explosion. I cut off the engine of our car, but I heard no drone of an airplane or sound of propellers. The silence was absolute. The surrounding landscape was absolutely deserted. My watch showed the time as 4.18 (or 5.18 British summer time). My two companions, who saw this phenomenon a second before I did, said the white smoke was shot with a 'vivid white light'."

At Biarritz, that evening, Mr. Tom Dupree, of the British Embassy at Hendaye (just over the other side of the international railway bridge, which crosses Wellington's Bidasoa), said he had seen the same thing at San Sebastian, as he stood with his back to the sea on the playa de Onderada. He said the light was green. The Marqués de Casa Calderon saw it as a bright light falling from the sky, as he was walking in Biarritz.

Back home in London, Mr. Williams appealed, in a well known London daily, to any scientific people who could eluci-date the mystery. Of course, he got no answer. If Mr. Valen-tine Williams is now looking back on mundane affairs from the land of shades—he has been dead for some years—his friendly ghost may like to hear that, fifteen years later, one man would like to tell him what he saw that day, on the plain in Guipuzcoa, was a non-exploding or silent satellite disc of some mysterious sort probably linked with an invisible mother craft of cosmic origin, far up in the stratosphere. Both explosive and silent apparitions of this sort have frequently been witnessed in the skies of old England and Western Europe, centuries before the flying saucer phenomenon began to startle America in 1946 and onwards. They have been seen in far days, when long range and controlled terrestrial missiles were still in the womb of the future, and they *were not meteorites*, or other astronomic phenomena.

Certain U.S. pilots, flying their 'planes over the Burma road to China, in the war year, 1943, allege that, on a clear sunny day, their 'planes were "buzzed" and circled by a strange "glittering object". They say its speed was very high, that their ignitions were put out of action, their 'planes held gripped and motionless—as if a ray had been put on them! —and that their instrument panels failed to operate. After some minutes the strange object flew off, when their own motors re-started to function, and also their previously im-mobilised instruments!

In all mysteries, it is a sound principle to look round and see if anything like it has occurred before or since. Here lies some approach towards elucidation, though, as one writes, the core of the mystery still remains.

No one talked of flying saucers on August 5, 1920, when the well known artist, explorer and mystic, Nicholas Roerkh, or Rerikh, was travelling in Mongolia. At 9.30 a.m., on the same day, some of the caravaneers in his expedition were watching a big black eagle flying far above, in the Kokonor region of Mongolia, not far from the Humboldt Chain.

"Several of us," he says, "began to watch this remarkable bird, and, at the same time, one of our caravaneers remarked: 'There is something far above the bird'. He shouted in aston-ishment. We all saw, in a direction north-south, something big and shining, reflecting the sun like a huge oval moving at great speed. Crossing our camp, this thing changed direc-tion from south to south-west. We even had time to take out our field glasses and saw quite distinctly an oval form with shining surface, one side of which was brilliant in the sun."

Remember, this was 1920, and long before the days of V.2 rockets, or terrestrial stratosphere cruiser-liners. Remember, too, that these same gleaming, vast oval machines are among the flying saucer phenomena of 1944-1954! If you, reader, are tempted to think they are ovaloid, secret terrestrial experi-mental machines of some war department of the U.S.A., Brit-ain, or Russia, or emanate from a rocket range in the deserts

17

of Australia, remember that Rerikh saw just such a strange *cosmic craft* in the depths of the Kokonor desert, in Central Asia, *in 1920!* His book relating this incident was published in 1921!

Let us again return to the phenomenon witnessed by the late Valentine Williams, in 1936, in North Spain. Look at the following:

In January 1950, an identical green flame streaked across the sky between Filey, Yorkshire, and Berwick-on-Tweed, but it also carried green and red lights. Nine coastguards saw it and reported that it flashed across the night sky at more than 1,000 miles an hour—that is well above the rate of the speed of sound, namely, 760 miles an hour at sea level. It was like no meteor they had ever seen. Here, too, neither R.A.F. investigators, nor astronomers and physicists from Durham University could throw any light on the mystery, but nobody said that these responsible and sober-minded coastguards were the victims of hallucinations, or mass hysteria!

If the mass of evidence and alleged facts that have come my way since 1946 be considered, it would seem that the mysterious saucers have given our planet a very good (or bad) look over, from "down under" in the Antipodes and Antarctic even unto the northern lights of Alaska, Greenland and the North Pole! More will be said on this, in subsequent chapters, when we detail sightings.

Mrs. Isabella Walmsley, of Christchurch, New Zealand, may have seen a flying saucer as long ago as summer 1935, and she says that one was seen in 1912, by a man in Dunedin, New Zealand. I give her interesting story:

"Everybody, of course, thought this man in Dunedin was a bit 'touched', or crazy, as they say in the States. He must have seen just a meteor, folks said... But I am a light sleeper, a legacy from my days as a nurse, and one night, when we were living in Timaru, New Zealand, I was wakened, suddenly, by a loud, roaring, hissing noise that passed swiftly over the house. It was the year 1935, before there were night-flying 'planes here. When the second world war broke out, I thought it must have been a Jap 'plane, but it did not occur to me to wonder where the base of such a rover could be, with thousands of miles of open sea all round New Zealand! A few days later, I was talking to an old chap who lived in the neighbourhood and was one of those simple souls who are of arrested mental development. He mumbled to me that he had to get up in the night, and when he got outside into the open air, he saw a 'big light like the sun, only moving over your house, missie!' Of course, I had never heard of flying saucers, in 1935; but now I wonder! ... In April, 1952, I spent a week in Dunedin, N.Z., and was similarly wakened by a loud swish overhead. It was still, and about 4 a.m. There was no fading. The noise was there, and then it wasn't! I did not mention it to the people I was living with, there, as I knew how they would regard the story. A few days later, the New Zealand and Australian newspapers were full of flying saucer stories."

CHAPTER II

THE COMING OF THE FOO FIGHTERS

It was in the war year, 1944, when both British and American pilots had singular experiences; but not a word of it has ever appeared in any British newspaper. In that year, the censorship was stringent; but though other mysteries have been revealed since, this one has never had the veil of silence removed from it, so far as Britain is concerned. It is not my business to advance any reason for this silence.

I happen to know that two British war pilots reported to Intelligence officers, after a flight, that strange balls of fire had suddenly appeared while their own 'planes were on high altitude flights. These mysterious balls seemed to indulge in a sort of aerial ballet dance and had, so to speak, pirouetted on the wing tips of the 'planes. When the 'planes went into a power dive, these balls followed them down and outdistanced them, despite the fact that the 'planes were biting into the air with a strident scream at the vertiginous speed they were making. Other pilots reported that they had seen strange balls of blazing light flying in precise formation. The crew of one British bomber reported that 15 to 20 of these balls had followed their bomber at a distance.

This bomber crew said: "We saw a strange flare come from them, and it winkled in and out." (*Vide* page 12, *supra*, on the phenomenon seen over Barnwood, Gloucester, in October 1950).

In the skies of Japan, Nipponese air pilots met these weird balls and took them to be secret and mystifying aerial devices of the Americans, or the Russians. On the other hand, U.S. pilots, equally mystified, and even, at times, frightened, supposed they were a curious device thought out by Japan, or Nazi technicians. It was supposed, in the Far Eastern theatre of the world war, that Japan had invented a last ditch device to stave off the mass-bombing raids of the U.S. Air Force. No doubt, if the Germans saw them, they deemed them to be a hush-hush invention of the British or the American air forces.

One pilot, chatting in a mess of the 415th U.S. Night Fighter squadron, stationed at Dijon, France, spoke to other pilots who had met these balls, and had been derided by Intelligence after their reports had been made. This pilot had a brain wave.

"Let's call the so and so's 'Foo Fighters!'" he said. This nickname was taken up and stuck. It appears that it was suggested by a comic strip in a New York newspaper, at the time. One 'Smokey Stover' said: "Yeah, if there's foo there's fire". Probably the slang word *foo* is a corruption of the French *feu*, or fire.

The 'foo fighters' seem first to have been met with by night pilots flying over the Rhine, north of Strasbourg, and in 1944 and 1945. It will be observed that they were encountered in the sector of the war-time front between Hagenau and Neustadt. Hagenau is in Alsace-Lorraine, 35 miles north of Strasbourg, while Neustadt is in the Bavarian Palatinate, 55 miles due north of Strasbourg. Both places are west of the Rhine.

It was at 10 p.m. on November 23, 1944, when Lieutenant Edward Schlüter, pilot of the U.S. 415th Night Fighter squadron, at Dijon, in south-central France, took off on a routine patrol to intercept German 'planes in the skies, west of the Rhine, between Strasbourg and Mannheim. As the crow flies, he had to go 150 miles on a patrol that would take him east over the Vosges mountains, a very lonely and grim and isolated range buttressing the western approaches to the Rhine. Schlüter is a finely built man, the last word in aeronautical efficiency, and a very experienced night fighter pilot of the second World War. He is a native of Oshkosh, Wisconsin.

With him in the darkened cockpit were the radar observer, Lieut. Donald J. Meiers, and an Intelligence officer, Lieut. F. Ringwald. Nothing happened till their 'plane had crossed the Vosges, and they had sighted the shining waters of the Rhine, rolling rapidly towards Mainz.

22

The sky, that night, was clear, with light clouds, visibility was good, and the moon was in the first quarter. U.S. radar stations, covering all U.S. pilots in that area, had *not* notified them of any other 'plane in the sky. Some way to the east, Schlüter could see the white steam jetted from the smokestack of a German freight locomotive, running in black-out conditions with fire-box door clamped up, and blinded, on one of the strategic railroads constructed, many years ago, on both banks of the Rhine, by order of the famous Graf von Bismarck, the old grim Iron Chancellor of the old German Reich. (I know this region well, myself, having more than once travelled there, on newspaper assignments.)

At this time, in 1944, Germany stood at bay, and the Allies were closing in on her. Some 20 miles north of Strasbourg, Lieut. Ringwald, the U.S. Intelligence officer, glanced to the west, and noticed eight or ten balls of red fire, moving at an amazing velocity. They seemed to be in formation, and they could be seen clearly from the cockpit of the U.S. night fighter 'plane, because the cockpit was unilluminated, to get rid of dazzle.

"Say," said Ringwald to Schlüter, "look over there at the bright lights on those hills, yonder. What are they?"

Schlüter: "Hell, buddy, there are no hills over there! I should say they were stars. You don't need me to tell you that it is not easy to guess at the nature of lights you see on night flights . . . Not when they are distant, as these are."

Ringwald: "Stars, d'ye say? I don't reckon they *are* stars. Why, their speed is terrific!"

Schlüter: "May be, they are just reflections from our own 'plane, as we are going pretty fast."

Ringwald: "I am certain, absolutely sure, that those lights are not reflected from us."

Schlüter, now, gazed hard at the lights. They were, at that moment, off his port wing. He got into radio 'phone contact with one of the ground radar stations.

"There are about ten Heinie night fighters round here, in the sky. Looks as if they are chasing us, and their speed is high. I'll say it is!"

23

U.S. radar station: "You guys must be nuts! Nobody is up there but your own 'plane. Ain't seein' things, are you?"

Meiers, in the 'plane, glanced at the radarscope. "Sure, no enemy 'planes showed up on the screen!" Schlüter now manoeuvred the 'plane for action, and made towards the lights. They were blazing red. *But they seemed to vanish* into invisibility! Two minutes later, they re-appeared, but now a long way off. It looked as if they were aware that they were being chased for attack. Six minutes later, the balls did a glide, levelled out, and vanished.

None of the occupants of the U.S. night fighter 'plane could make out what on earth these red balls were. Schlüter guessed they might be some German experimental devices, like the red, green, blue, and white and yellow rockets that flashed up amid the flak of anti-aircraft batteries when an enemy night bomber raid was on a big scale, and could be heard approaching some way off. I have, myself, seen such rockets when on night patrol in the edge of London, at the time of the big German bomber raids on Central London, or the Thameside dockyards, in 1942, and 1943. The Germans appear to have had these mystery devices, as had the British; but I have never been able to find out what purpose they served.

But the bewildered night fighter pilots of the 415th U.S. Air Force did not let this mystery spoil their stroke. Lieut. Schlüter, that night, heavily bombed eight fast German freight trains on the Rhine railroads.

But, back at the base at Dijon, knowing that they would not be believed by Intelligence higher-ups, and might be charged with hallucinations and war neurosis, Schlüter and the other two did not discuss the matter. They did not wish to be 'grounded', and taken off combat duties. So they made no report to base at Dijon.

On 27 November 1944, another act in the foo fighter drama was staged. Lieut. Henry Giblin, native of Santa Rosa, Calif., was flying a U.S. night fighter 'plane, in the Alsace-Lorraine region, south of Mannheim-am-Rhein. He had with him Lieut. Walter Cleary of Worcester, Mass., as radar-observer.

On a sudden, as they were approaching the German town of Speyer, on the Rhine, south of Mannheim, they got a shock. Some 1,500 feet above their own 'plane, a "hell of a huge fierce, fiery orange light" shot across the night sky at an estimated speed of 250 miles per hour. Again, U.S. ground radar stations reported, when called: "No enemy machines in the vicinity. Only your own 'plane in the sky over there."

Giblin and Cleary decided to say nothing to Intelligence. They, too, feared ridicule from higher quarters. And it is not wise for a war-time flyer to take that risk. "Let some other airman do the reporting!" is his attitude.

No other observations of queer things in the sky came the way of the U.S. 415th Night Fighter squadron until three days before Christmas 1944. On 22 Decr. 1944, Lieut. David McFalls, native of Cliffside, North Carolina, and Lieut. Edward Baker, radar observer—he is a native of Hemat, Calif.— were flying 10,000 feet up, just south of Hagenau, in the old German Reichsland, or Alsace-Lorraine (the German Elsasz-Lothringen). Hagenau is 20 miles north of Strasbourg, and 16 miles west of the Rhine.

Here is the report of U.S. pilot McFall:

> "At 0600 (six p.m.) near Hagenau, at 10,000 feet altitude, two very bright lights climbed towards us from the ground. They levelled off and stayed on the tail of our 'plane. They were huge, bright orange lights. They stayed there for two minutes. On my tail all the time. They *were under perfect control*. Then they turned away from us, and the fire seemed to go out."

On the night of 24 Decr. 1944, McFalls and Baker had another amazing experience. Here is their report:

> "A glowing red ball shot straight up to us. It suddenly changed into an airplane which did a wing over! Then it dived and disappeared."

The reader should note the sudden disappearance of this weird thing in the sky. 'They' would appear to hail from some phenomenal world of a different wave-length of visibility

from our own. 'They'—whoever these 'etherian' beings are—
can operate controlled machines which suddenly appear as
from nowhere, fly at vertiginous speeds, and as suddenly
become invisible. The cosmos seems to become as the dream
of a madman, or a 'mystic visionary'. Yet, in our world of
radiological science, in which we have but touched the thresh-
hold of the unseen rays in the invisible octaves of the solar
spectrum, wherein vast expanses still remain to be explored,
let the physicist pause before he dismisses these stories of
picked men, U.S. war time pilots, as hallucinations. If we
plunge into the even redder hell of World War 3, we *may*,
on this planet, receive a stern lesson about what the cosmos
holds for us in the way of Wellsian terrors. Here is one more
of the cases in which there may be small bliss in wisdom, as
compared with ignorance.

It is true that, in both London and New York, in the late
1920's, a man on a stage was rendered invisible by warping
light rays between rapidly rotating magnetic poles. But
the phenomena of these weird 'foo fighters' are on a scale that
transcends anything we, on this planet, can produce. Invisibility and visibility are produced at lightning speed. They
have no aeroform pattern that any pilot knows.

At this point, one may recall with startling effect the strange
experience of Mr. Kenneth Ehlers, of the Landing Aids Experimental Station at, or near, Arcata, Calif. He, in summer
1948, directed a C.47 pilot to fly to a certain location, in conse-
quence of the appearance on his radarscope of what are tech-
nically called 'discontinuities'. There appeared three of these
signals, denoting that three aircraft were passing over the
airfield at Arcata. Yet, when the pilot reached the spot in the
air, he saw nothing, nor did his instruments record any
electrical reactions.

One is tempted to suppose that *some* of these weird things
—there are, of course, more than a score of types of phenomena called flying saucers—may hail from an Etherian world
that lies all about us in space.

So far, in 1944, the pilots of the 415th squadron had seen
these weird balls at night, and, despite the ridicule of the

higher-ups and the surgical and medical and psychiatric cate-
gories, reports began to be made. In the Pacific theatre, pilots
began to be warned by Intelligence, before starting out on
missions, that, if they met strange phenomena in the sky,
they need not necessarily conclude that they (the pilots), were
suffering from hysteria, war-induced neuroses, or hallucinations.

Pilots, talking war 'shop' in the messes, called the balls
krauts, or *kraut balls*. Two British night fighter pilots, whose
names I have been unable to ascertain—for the British Air
Ministry *ignored my inquiries*—thought the 'foo fighters'
were secret German experimental devices, perhaps intended
to strike fear in a war of nerves. Some U.S. Intelligence officers
supposed the 'foo fighters' were radio-controlled objects sent
up to baffle radar, in the same way that, as I saw in woods
in Kent, England, in 1943, after an all-night raid, thousands
of strips of tin foil were thrown down from enemy 'planes,
approaching the outskirts of the defences of London.

But if they were secret devices, no war department of any
country would have risked sending them over hostile territory, where they might be shot down, or intercepted, and the
secret penetrated—which, of course, applies to flying saucers
had they been secret terrestrial devices seen over U.S.A., England and elsewhere, in the years 1947-1954.

There is the case of a U.S. bomber pilot of the 8th U.S.
Air Force. He reported that he saw fifteen of these 'foo fighters'
following his 'plane at a distance with their lights winking
on and off. The fifteen 'foo fighters' were seen, *by day*, at or
near Neustadt, in the same Rhenish area, some 40 miles west
of the Rhine, and 55 miles due north of Strasbourg, and the
observer was a U.S. pilot flying a P.47 machine.

Here is his report:

"We were flying west of Neustadt when a golden sphere,
which shone with a metallic glitter, appeared, slowly
moving through the sky. The sun was not far above the
sky line, which made it difficult to say whether or no
the sun's rays were reflected from it, or whether the glow
came from within the ball itself."

A second P.47 pilot also saw the same, or another "golden, or phosphorescent ball," which "appeared to be about four or five feet in diameter, and flying 2,000 feet up."

By this time, the higher-ups in the U.S. Air Force had been forced to take notice of the increasing reports of level-headed pilots of both the 415th Night Fighter squadron, and of the 8th Air Force, U.S. bombers. It was no longer enough to wave these reports away with a smile, and half-serious references to hallucinations and combat-neuroses. To pass the 'foo fighters' off as just 'flares' did not carry one-millionth of an inch of conviction to the minds of experienced pilots who had seen lots of flare paths on bombing raids over the German Reich. Whoever saw a flare that behaved as did the 'foo fighters'? Who, too, saw any German, or other jet 'plane, or Nazi V.2 rocket bomb with the remotest resemblance to the red or golden balls?

The final attempt at a refutation came from New York, in January 1945, from scientists who insulted the intelligence of the men of the 415th night squadron. The scientists are surely blood brothers under the skin with the British experts called in by the British Broadcasting Corporation to ridicule observations of flying saucers.

The New York scientist 'classicists' said the men of the 415th and 8th bombers of the U.S. Air Force had been seeing just St. Elmo's lights! It may be noted that St. Elmo's lights are seen on sea and land in times of electrical-meteorological disturbances. They have been seen at the top of Pike's Peak; from a ship's mast-heads in mid-ocean; or from the tops of towers and spires. In the days of Julius Caesar, there was one occasion when these lights flashed from the tops of the spears of his legionaries. In our own day, the old White Star liner 'Germanic', in mid-Atlantic ocean ran into a heavy thunderstorm at 1 a.m. Electrical flames, $1\frac{1}{2}$ inches long, jetted from her foremast truck, and *small balls*, $\frac{1}{2}$ inch to $2\frac{1}{2}$ inches long, ran up and down the mast, but were 'tied' to the mast.

What possible remotest resemblance could there have been between these weird 'foo fighters', under apparent intelligent control, and St. Elmo's lights?

Came 1945, and the 'foo fighters' made their appearance
in the seas of the Far East—the other side of the globe from
the German Rhine—over Japan, and over Truk Lagoon, in
mid-Pacific. Crews of U.S. B.29 bombers reported to Intelligence, after missions, that balls of fire, of mysterious types,
came up from below their 'planes over Japan, hovered over
the tails of their bombers and winked their lights from red
to orange, then back from white to red. Exactly as had happened a few months before on the other side of the globe,
over the Rhine! Here, too, in the Far East, the weird balls
were inoffensive, just 'nosey' and exploratory.

On one occasion, at night, a B.29 flier rose into a cloud
in order to shake off one of these balls of fire. When his 'plane
emerged from the cloudbank, the ball was still following
on behind him! He said it looked to be about $3\frac{1}{2}$ feet wide
and glowed with a strange red phosphorescence. It was spherical, with not a sign of any mechanical appendages such as
wings, fins, or fuselage. It followed his bomber for five or
six miles, and he lost sight of it as the dawn light rose over
the mystic peak of Mount Fujiyama, some 60 miles southerly
of Tokyo. Here, it seemed to vanish; for it became invisible,
exactly like H. G. Well's "Invisible Man"!

The B.29's found that, going all out at top speed, they
could not out-distance these balls of fire. Some 12,000 feet up
over Truk Lagoon, in mid-Pacific, in the Caroline archipelago,
east of Long. 150° East, a pilot of a B.24 Liberator was startled
by the sudden appearance of two glowing red lights that shot
up from below, and for 75 minutes followed on his tail.
One flaming ball turned back, while the other still dogged
his 'plane. It manoeuvred in such a way as to suggest intelligent direction from some remote control. It came abreast of
the Liberator, then it shot ahead, and for 1,500 yards held
the lead. After that, it fell behind. As is the way with flying
saucers, its speed was immensely variable.

As dawn rose over the Pacific, the strange ball climbed some
16,000 feet above him and into the sunshine. In the night
hours, the pilot noticed the changes in the colours of the ball,
which were precisely what had been seen over the Rhine, in

1944. It was just a sphere with no appendages.

The pilot radioed to base, and had the reply: "No, no enemy 'planes are near you. Your own 'plane is the only one up there, as the radarscope shows."

I stated, above, that bewildered Japanese pilots encountered these balls, and assumed they were secret devices of either the Russians or the U.S.A. I can find no report that these balls were ever observed while barrages of anti-aircraft batteries were hurling up flak; and *if* they had been, as they were *not*, German devices to frighten U.S. pilots, they entirely failed in their object. Indeed, neither Germany, nor Japan, had any solution of the riddle of the 'foo fighters'. The 'American Legion Magazine', which carried an excellent article on the 'Foo Fighters' in Decr. 1945, did not suspect that these weird balls were anything but secret devices of the Germans.

Now, while the 'foo fighters' were making their appearance in the Far Eastern theatre of the second World War, they were at *about the same time, in January*, 1945, again sighted by pilots of the 415th Night Fighter squadron. These pilots reported to U.S. Intelligence at the Dijon base, that they had met the blazing balls *solum*—alone—or flying in pairs, and in formations. One pilot said that three formations of these lights, red and white in colour, followed his 'plane. He suddenly reduced speed and apparently took them off their guard. They came on with undiminished speed, and then, to avoid any collision, also reduced speed and fell back, though still dogging him.

From ground radar came the usual reply: "Nothing up there but your own 'plane!"

On another occasion when the queer formation of 'foo fighters' got on the tail of a U.S. night fighter of the 415th squadron, the perplexed and exasperated pilot swung round his 'plane and headed for them, at top speed! As he came, the lights vanished into nothingness, in the fashion of squadrons of 'Etherian' flying machines!

Note what this pilot reported:

> "As I passed where they had been, I'll swear *I felt the propeller backwash of invisible 'planes!*"

Came the reply from derisive ground radar station:

"Are you fellows *all* plum loco? Sure, you *must* be crazy! You're up there all alone!"

The puzzled pilot flew on, and, glancing back, was now startled to see that the balls *had reappeared* about half a mile astern of his 'plane. Said he to himself: "I'll show these spook 'planes a trick!"

The night was starry, but near the zenith was a bank of cumulus cloud. He headed his 'plane at top speed right into the mass of cloud. Then he throttled back, and glided down for about 1,800 feet. He turned the machine round, and headed back from the cloud the way he had entered it, but on a much lower plane. Surely enough, the balls had been surprised! They emerged from the cloud ahead, but now on a course opposite to his own!

It is true that, when the Allies overran Germany, the Russians from south and east, and the British and Americans from the west, no more 'foo fighters' were seen. But then, when secret German experimental stations were seized, and their secrets examined by Intelligence men—and this equally applies to the Nazi station of Peenemunde, more than once badly bombed by the British Royal Air Force 'planes, and, later, seized by the Russians—nothing was found blueprinting plans for blazing balls that can be made visible and invisible in an instant! Why, such a discovery would have been the last word in mid-twentieth century science! It could *not* have been kept secret! Moreover, how can one keep secret a device embodying an amazing discovery that no nation on earth has yet made? *Had* it been made, would not every nerve have been strained by Britain, U.S.A., and the U.S.S.R., in 1944 and 1945, when the war was still raging, to shoot down, or intercept a device embodying one of the most startling and sensational scientific discoveries of the second World War?

The question carries its own answer.

BUT THE 'FOO FIGHTERS', JUST AS OTHER TYPES OF FLYING SAUCERS, HAVE BEEN SEEN IN OTHER DAYS! (I shall give a separate chapter to this startling phase of a mysterious theme.)

31

Look, however, at the following news item which appeared in the *London Sunday Times* newspaper, on *December 8, 1850* —*a century ago*:

SUNDAY TIMES. London. No. 1,470. Dec. 8, 1850.
Price 6d.

REMARKABLE PHENOMENON.—A brilliant purplish meteor (*sic*) with a yellowish-red tail crossed the firmament from north to south, passing over Aberdeen, north Scotland. About midway in its progress, it shot out horizontally, and nearly at right angle to the line of its wake, a *small fiery ball*.

A 'meteor' shoot out a ball of fire in this singular way?

England, alone, in 1950 and 1953, had had a very close look-over by these mysterious visitants, ranging from 'foo fighter balls', and aluminium-like and silvery discs to the sinister fusiform, or cigar-shaped aeroform, coming from none know where, nor what is on board it, but which may have caused fires and even deaths!

More of this disturbing phenomenon, later.

Authority, here, as in the U.S.A., would do better to take its people into its confidence about what it knows, and to remember that, in Britain, the common man and woman endured, for three years, the long agony of nights and days of the hell of enemy bombing, land-mines, and V.1 and V.2 weapons. But Authority, here as in the U.S.A., is all out to 'conventionalise' the phenomena and explain them away, even if the 'explanations' ignore or distort the full facts. The British Broadcasting Corporation which, in spring 1950, refused a script of mine detailing the *facts* about flying saucers, and specially engaged a member of the staff of the Victoria and Albert Museum, London, to give a talk ridiculing those who talk of flying saucers, had, on January 11 1951, hired three men to explain away the phenomena. They were, an expert of aeronautics, a meteorologist, and a physicist, whose line was to prove that things seen in the sky are not what the 'hallucinated' observer supposes, but are misinterpretations, or things that are really not there!

The British Broadcasting Corporation* has deliberately ignored any speaker who may present the case *for* the flying saucers, and as such a talk is usually given at 10 p.m., it is safe to say that comparatively few people will hear it. And those who do will either not take the talk seriously, or draw wrong conclusions from a talk that states *only one side*. All this is sure evidence of the fear of authority, in Britain, exactly as in U.S.A., lest the 'herd' be told the truth—that authority does not know what these things are.

One thing it is safe to say: The derided flying saucers will continue to be seen in the skies of Britain, and in other parts of the world, long after the one-sided talk has been forgotten —as it speedily will be forgotten! No amount of derisive talk or conspiracy of silence can hide the truth.

It was not until January 1 1945, that the U.S. press heard about the 'foo fighters'. In the British press, still heavily censored, nothing appeared till later in the year, when the Reuter ticker tapes began to issue short reports about flying saucers, *but not about 'foo fighters'*. They, however, as I myself noticed when I was handling these tapes in a London newspaper office, soon vanished, and as suddenly as they had appeared. One suspected that the hidden hand of censorship was at work. Very soon, the flying saucers became the theme of the newspaper cartoonists, unfortunate men who have every day to grind out witty or humorous pictures and 'strips', whether or not they are in the mood for it, and who naturally seized, like drowning men at a lifebelt, on what, in Britain, was probably deemed one more case of 'American credulity', of the Orson Welles' radio type, about 'the invasion of Men from Mars.''

On January 1, 1945, Mr. Howard W. Blakeslee, Science Editor of the Associated Press of America, spoke of the phenomena as:

* I refer to the B.B.C. aural, *not* the recently established television branch, some of whose producers seem favourable even to stories alleging that one American met, in 1952, a golden-haired man from Venus, on a ridge in the desert in Arizona, where he had landed from a satellite disc of a Venusian space-craft! But then, the B.B.C. television branch has been 'infected' by the previous example of U.S. contemporaries.

"—the new German foo fighters, balls of fire.. which are only induction or ball lightning, or St. Elmo's fire.. If they are electric, they are something in the air created close to Allied 'planes, not shot like artillery shells; or something afloat in the air to wait for 'planes."

He supposed they might be explained as "induction":

"—because the Allied airmen (*sic*) say they keep up with their 'planes at fixed distances, regardless of the 'planes' speeds, or changes in direction. Radio control from the ground does not explain the marvellous timing of the balls, with the movements of the 'planes. But induction does not explain what happens when a fire ball zooms upwards, leaving its 'plane. The balls fly paths thousands of feet away from the 'planes... Ball lightning is as harmless as the German (*sic*) foo fighters are said to be. The foo balls are said to be red. But if the Germans had devised foo fighters, as a means to stop the ignition of 'planes, they would hardly have disclosed the secret to the Allies."

It seems that, on January 1, 1945, the Washington War Department looked mysterious and refused to talk about the balls. All newspaper men, whether in U.S.A. or Britain, well know that air of mystery shown by Government officials. It is always a cloak for ignorance, or, as Dean Jonathan Swift said, more than 235 years ago: "I do not know. You do not know. But I, *only*, know"—discreetly omitting the words: "just nothing at all!"

The *New York Herald Tribune* gave the official story next day, January 2, 1945, "from a U.S. Night Fighting base (in France)":

"On Decr. 13, 1944, newspaper men were told that the Germans had thrown silvery balls into the air against day raiders. Pilots then reported that they had seen these balls, both individually and in clusters, during forays over the Rhine. Now, it seems the Nazis have thrown something new into the night skies over Germany. It is the weird mysterious 'foo fighter' balls which race alongside the wings of Beaufighters, flying intruder missions over Germany. Pilots have been encountering this eerie

34

weapon for more than a month in their night flights. No one apparently knows what this sky weapon is. The balls of fire appear suddenly and accompany the 'planes for miles. They seem to be radio-controlled from the ground, and manage to keep up with 'planes, flying at 300 miles an hour, so official intelligence reports reveal.

" 'There are three kinds of these lights we call 'foo fighters,' said Lieutenant Donald Meiers, of Chicago. '*One* is a red ball which appears off our wing tips, and flies along with us. *No. 2* is a vertical row of three balls of fire, flying in front of us. *No. 3* is a group of about fifteen lights which appear in the distance, like a Christmas tree up in the air, and flicker on and off . . ."

"The pilots of this night fighter squadron, in operation since Sepr. 1943, find these fiery balls the weirdest thing they have yet met. They are convinced these foo fighters are designed to be a psychological weapon, as well as military; although it is not the nature of the balls to attack a 'plane . . .

" 'A foo fighter picked me up recently, at 700 feet, and chased me 20 miles down the Valley of the Rhine,' says Meiers. 'I turned to starboard, and two balls of fire turned with me. We were going at 260 miles an hour, and the balls were keeping right up with us. On another occasion when a foo fighter picked us up, I dived at 360 miles an hour. It kept right off our wing tips for a while, and then zoomed up into the sky. When I first saw the things off my wing tips, I had the horrible thought that a German, on the ground, was ready to press a button, and explode them. But they don't explode, or attack us. They just seem to follow us like 'wills o' the wisp'."

Any facile theory that these 'foo fighters' were secret experimental devices emanating from Nazi Peenemunde, or, indeed, from any Allied back-room laboratory is dispelled by the fact that Russia, who in 1945 seized the station and laboratories of Peenemunde, in 1950, set up a secret commission to inquire into the mystery of the flying saucers and 'foo fighters'. But the knock-out blow is given to such a theory in the fact that a bright luminous ball of the 'foo fighter' type was seen over Gloucester city, England, on a clear spring night, in 1910; was again seen over Brockworth, three miles from Gloucester, at 10.45 p.m. to 11 p.m. on October 12, 1950, and, by myself, some 3,000 feet up in the sky over the garden of my house at Bexleyheath, Kent, at 6.20 p.m. on November 2, 1950.

Moreover, were the flying saucers, of the score of types seen all over the U.S.A., in the years 1947-1950, and other parts of the globe, ranging from the Antarctic to the Arctic, and from South and Central Africa to the Mediterranean, of U.S. origin, as alleged in February 1951, by Dr. Urner Liddel, chief of the nuclear physics branch of the U.S. Naval Research Office, how is it that the U.S. Air Force spent many thousands of dollars on the Project Saucer investigation, from 1948 onwards? That investigation, by the way, is still going on secretly under another code name, at an Air Force base in Ohio, U.S.A.

It is the fact that none of the Allied radar networks ever picked up the 'foo fighter' type of flying saucer in the war years, 1944 and 1945, when they first appeared to pilots flying on missions. Nor, indeed, were any of the strange discs shot down by anti-aircraft batteries, a most important one of which was the peculiar Fort Churchill, raised high on steel stilts above the sea, which can today be seen by anyone on the front at Felixstowe, on the coast of Suffolk, England, as it stands ten miles out from the beach.

Moreover, none of the experts will agree that, in 1944-45, any experimental station, in or out of Germany, devised any form of long range device of the flying saucer types, which was capable of flying the immense global range from the Rhine region to the Far East, and the mid-Pacific. I think it is pretty certain that, had they been Nazi devices, the German High Command would have found very effective use for them over England, conceived as the brain and heart of the enemy of Nazidom, in its struggle for world hegemony. What is more to the point, as this book will show, is that there is a very long history of these queer visitants in the skies of earth, from 1710 onwards! They are far from new things of the second World War. The Japanese fighters who chased them in their own skies, said: "We thought they were of Russian origin, but they outsped us so that we might have been standing still for all the approach we could make to them!"

A friend of mine who is in the U.S. Air Force, and, therefore, cannot be here named, told me: "The Intelligence Department of our Air Force investigated these 'foo fighters', but explained them as war nerves and visual hallucinations induced by the long drawn-out days and nights of total war." Scientists in New York, as we have seen, spoke of St. Elmo's fire, but did not explain the obvious intelligence shown by these mysterious spheres. When the U.S. pilots in the Rhine area and Austria heard of these silly and too facile theories of armchair folk, they said: "You don't say so? Let some of you come over here and fly a mission with us. We'll show you what are war nerves or St. Elmo's Fire!" Those engaged in Intelligence work connected with radar or the air forces, know that these mysterious balls and lights were seen all through the year 1945, and that Intelligence were baffled in all attempts to solve the mystery. I have already stated the reaction of the ground radar stations, in 1944, when the mystery craft and balls appeared in the skies over Germany and Austria: "You're crazy! Only your own 'planes are in the air!"

All that can be positively stated is that the 'foo fighters' were certainly *not* jet 'planes, long range flying bombs, or rockets, or weather balloons adrift. That is to say, they were *not* of terrestrial origin.

I may, again, draw notice to the fantastic disappearance of the mysterious aeroforms encountered, in 1944, by the two U.S. pilots flying in western Germany. It is reminiscent of the invisible man of that remarkable scientific prophet, the late H. G. Wells. The entities, whoever they are, whatever they are, or whencesoever they come, seem to have control of some unknown and very powerful ray of possible electro-magnetic, or cosmic type. It may be one that can render a big machine invisible in an instant. Or the entities themselves may not be beings of our terrestrial capacity, but of some etheric type living in a cosmos of a quite different range length and wave-frequency than our own earth. Who can say?

As one has noted, in both London and New York, attempts have been made, as in the 1930's, to produce invisibility by warping light rays in an electro-magnetic field. In 1934, in

37

London, there was demonstrated, in a public hall, apparatus which was, perhaps, suggested by the fantasy of the late H. G. Wells's 'Invisible Man'. A young scientist, wearing what he called an 'electro-helmet' and a 'special mantle', went into a cabinet, open at the front, before a brilliantly lit stage, and, with both hands, touched contact gloves, which were over his head. An electric current was switched on, and the man's body gradually vanished, from feet to head! One could step up and touch him, but could not see him. Nor did the camera reveal the secret, for it depicted only what the eye saw. The inventor refused to reveal his secret, which he said was the work of "many years of experiments". All one could see was the development of a cone of light, such as might be projected between the two poles of a powerful transmitter. This cone persisted even when the man could not be seen. The inventor had succeeded in doing on a stage in public what a de-materialising apparition is alleged to do in a haunted house. Whether he developed the powers of some 'new', or previously discovered ray, and created an opaque screen, I am unable to say.

It may be, I may be forgiven for repeating, that, in the case of saucers of the type of the 'foo fighters', and those which appear on radarscopes, as they have done, at U.S. airfields, and are called 'angels' (*Vide* pages 80-2 *infra*), we are in very elusive contact with entities from some unknown world in the vast and wonderful macrocosmos, entities far in advance of our terrestrial scientific knowledge.

A member of the U.S. Air Force, whom I cannot name, told me in June 1952, that, either near the lonely and very wild Jura range—where, in 1950, Swiss folk reported seeing in woods a thing like a dragon!—or in the Swiss Alps, U.S. veterans, *in 1943*, were mystified at seeing on their radarscopes strange objects flying around, very high up in the skies, too far off to be seen by the naked eye. Said one man to me: "We were quite familiar with ionised particles on the radarscope, but this was something quite different." He had seen what, some five years later, were called 'flying saucers'.

On the subject of the existence of invisible worlds, Sir Edward Appleton, the famous physicist, speaking at the meeting

in Liverpool, in September, 1953, of the British Association for
the Advancement of Science, referred to the recently discovered
existence, in the neighbourhood of the constellations of Cygnus and Cassiopeia, of two unknown sources of radio noises.
They had been detected by the radio-telescope.

He asked: "Can it be that there is a duplicate universe
only to be seen with a radio-telescope as distinct from a visual
telescope?"

The stupendous size of the stellar universe was graphically
suggested by Sir Edward when he said that: "The source of
the radio noises in Cygnus was identified with two island
colonies in collision. The distance of this compound group
of stars appears such that it is estimated that it requires 100
million light years for the light and radio waves generated
in it to travel to the earth...We have reached about half-
way (with the 200-inch telescope at Palomar Observatory,
California) towards the hypothetical limits of the expanding
universe.

As it was said about 2,000 years ago, probably by Jessos
in Hindostan: "In my Father's house are many mansions."
Apparently, all of them do not consist of the same order of
matter.

One must, however, make quite clear that the type of flying
saucer which apparently can become alternately visible and
invisible, is *only one* of about a score of these mysterious aeroforms. Among the other types are some which appear to belong to an order of matter like our own. One of them, possibly a mammoth carrier, or space ship which, as photographs
show, may discharge satellite discs within our own atmosphere, is both weird in form and of fantastic size. I have reason
to suppose that this unknown type is definitely hostile to the
earth. Reason based on evidence! There is a third type, taking the form of a vertical column of light, which has been
seen, in England, to discharge a ball of red fire. It has produced serious terrestrial fires. Still another type observed on
the radarscope, in eastern U.S.A., and subjected to radio-
theodolite observations and to ballistical calculation, astounded the staff of an American naval station. They found that

39

not only did it travel at a fantastic speed, but that it was *more than a mile long*! The reader may shrug his shoulders, but he should note that these calculations are not the work of hack writers of scientific fantasy fiction, nor any imagination of mine. I fear that, in this case, too, there may be reason to suppose that, whencesoever this vast aeroform comes, or what it may be, it has caused death to one American airman, even if not disaster in the cases of mysteriously vanished air liners—*British air liners*!

Certain data relating to these unknown visitants will be cited, later, in this book.

It is possible that these mysterious phenomena may ultimately entail consequences that will force the world's crazed rulers to abandon the mounting spiral of demonism, leading to bigger and better hydrogen-tritium, atomic and cobalt bombs, or blood-corpuscle-shattering suprasonic waves. In the class of official scientists whose aim, judged by their *actions*, is: "Let science destroy the world and all that is in it, and let us usher in the third world war", no shadow of hope can be placed. But, whatever the future may hold for us, it is certain that we shall have to face a tremendous re-orientation and revolution of all our ideas of the Great Cosmos and our little planet's place in it. We may also have to realise the stern consequences of the probable fact that our own world is *not* necessarily a unit in a vast cosmos that is friendly to it. It is to be feared that the old statesman's idea that fearful weapons are so dreadful to use that no one, in the end, will use them, is a notion that has not a shadow of any warrant in the history of our times. *But*, if something come on us out of space that may look on us as hooligan children to be whipped with a rod of scorpions, what then? The end will be stranger, if less paradoxical, than anything in Butler's "Erewhon".

CHAPTER III

"A VAST BAT-LIKE MACHINE"

The finger of Fate, moving over the dial of our own planet in the war years of 1944-45, ordained that many apparitions of unknown origin, single, or in disciplinary formations, should soar into the skies of western Europe and the Far East. But, in the following year, 1946, the cosmic spotlight shifted to North America, almost, it would seem, as if that vast continent had some peculiar attraction for these visitants. It might seem that 'they' had observed, far out in space, some grave disturbance to the cosmic equilibrium emanating from dangerous experiments going on in this region of the 'Wart', as the Jupiterians in Mark Twain's 'Captain Stormfield's Visit to Heaven', irreverently called our earth, whose location they had great difficulty in finding on the vast and Brobdingnagian macrocosmic chart in the Heavenly Archive House!

In 1946, the phenomena, whatever they were and are, did not always take the form of balls, orange lights, or glowing spheres, but that of a very strange object "with wings", described by one eye-witness as looking like a "huge bat". It appeared high in the sky over San Diego, Calif., between 7.25 p.m. and 9 p.m. on October 9, 1946. At the time, many people were out on roof tops and the top floors of skyscrapers, watching a shower of meteors. I have reports from sixteen people in San Diego and neighbourhood who say they saw this queer object, and who, not unnaturally, would be most indignant if you suggested that they were suffering from hallucinations or mass-hysteria, or had mis-interpreted some natural and astronomical phenomena, like meteorites, the moon, or the planet Venus.

These eye-witness number seven men, eight women, and a youth. Seven of these eyewitnesses say that the mysterious object had wings. They say it crossed the moon's disc, looked like an extremely long 'plane, carrying two reddish lights,

41

and travelled at an amazing speed. It was bluish-white in
colour.

One woman, whose name and address I have, said:

> "The strange object was certainly no airplane. The
> wings, which moved, were too wide for any bird. Indeed,
> they were rather like the wings of a butterfly. The whole
> object emitted a red glow."

Another woman and a man say the object looked like a
bat, hooked, weird, and very large. One woman saw it from
between two houses, and it took at least 80 seconds to cross
that space; so that, at that time, "—it must have changed
speed from very fast to slow". Two other witnesses who saw
the same weird object from different parts of South California,
say it was stationary for some time. "Then it moved slowly,
accelerated, and left a trail of luminosity behind it. At that
time its motion was very slow." A woman, who is a professional astronomer, took a time exposure of the moon, and
says that the film, when developed, showed a strange effect
of smoke rings, or halations seen on films and plates, as if
fire were coming out of the moon, or as if a passing object
had left a vapour trail.

The sum-total of the eye-witnesses' evidence is that this
strange object, which had the appearance of a space-ship,
remained far overhead all night, considerably varied its rate
of speed, and was alternately brilliantly illuminated and
dark. There was also an occasional emission of a flash of
light, or a luminous jet of gases.

Now, the statement of the bat-like appearance of this
strange object seen high in the sky over San Diego, Calif.,
may be compared with the report made by a Dr. F. B. Harris
in the 1912 issue of 'Popular Astronomy':

> "In the evening of January 27, 1912, I saw an intensely
> black object, like a crow, poised upon the moon. I estim-
> ated it at 250 miles long by 50 miles wide. I cannot but
> think that a very interesting phenomenon happened."

Signor Ricco, of the Observatory at Palermo, Sicily, wrote

that, on November 30, 1880, at 8 a.m., he saw "—winged bodies in two long parallel lines slowly travelling, apparently across the disc of the sun. They looked like large birds, or cranes". *Note*: he meant travelling out in space beyond the earth.

I note, too, that Miss Ella Young, an American authoress, wrote to Mr. Meade Layne, M.A., who has devoted much time to the investigation of these remarkable phenomena, seen at various dates in the western and eastern states of the U.S.A.:

> "I believe I saw a space ship early in 1927, at the Casa Madrona Hotel, Sausalito (Marin county, California). I was, one morning, sitting outside the hotel, thinking of nothing in particular, when I saw a cigar-shaped craft shoot out of a cloud beyond the bay, and across the sky towards Tamalpais. At first, I thought it must be a U.S. airship, but soon changed my mind. It was not shaped like the *Akron* (*N.B.*—A well known U.S. dirigible airship in the 1920's. *Author*). It was long and slender, of yellow colour, and travelling at great speed. As it came opposite me, it seemed to progress by alternately contracting and elongating its body."

One cannot, however, join the lady in her fascinating conjecture—albeit the Project Saucer of the U.S. Air Force says, humorously, that its experts have remotely considered "the possible existence of some strange extra-terrestrial animals, since many of the flying saucer objects described (as seen over American territory) acted more like animals than anything else"—that the strange skyship she saw came from a world fairly close to us, but invisible, and that "they have spirited away . . . whole ships with the crews, and humans, and even dumped a whole cargo of sea serpents and prehistoric animals on our earth". This was the sort of thing so often said, with a wink in his sardonic eye, by the late Charles Fort. In relation to mysteries like that of the *Mary Celeste*, he seemed to enjoy 'guying' his true believers, as, apparently, he deemed that one true believer was worse than ten prophets.

She further adds what is undoubtedly a repetition of other quite true observations made by people in Europe and Amer-

43

ica, both before and long after 1927: "In October 1946, I saw a most brilliant light break out in the sky, soon after sundown. It lasted a few seconds and was not a meteor, nor came from a burning 'plane. Nothing then fell towards the earth." A friend was with her, she adds, when, on December 30, 1946:

"We were on high ground that curves southwards from Morro Bay. The sun had just gone down . . . and the time was 5.35 p.m., when, suddenly, a dark object appeared in the sky. It came forward and grew more distinct. On the golden sky it looked very black. It came forward head-on, and had a bat-like appearance, owing to the curvature of its wings. I am not sure if there were motions at the extreme tip of the wings; but the strange machine seemed to stand still for several minutes, and its form was very distinct. Suddenly, it either lowered itself towards the horizon, or the bank of cloud-mist made an upward movement—maybe, both movements occurred—for the machine passed behind the cloud and did not reappear. Immediately afterwards, a great flush of colour spread over the sea."

The woman with Miss Young, at this time, corroborated the statement that the strange machine hung poised in the air for more than five minutes, and had wings curved like those of a bat.

What was this mysterious object that hung all night in the sky over San Diego? Was it a space ship? Some of the eye-witnesses thought the machine was being navigated, but not in the manner of an airplane. Mr. Mark Probert, who was in company with a youth named Fernando Esevano, when the weird bat-like, winged machine stood high in the sky over San Diego, on the night of October 9, 1946, volunteers a statement which he apparently obtained from some psychic, or 'clairaudient source', in California. The 'source' says the machine comes from "some planet west of the moon"—but how, in outer space, can one orient a planet and speak of spatial compass-points? This is a difficulty of orientation—one of the perplexing problems, by the way, that will, in the years ahead, confront navigators of some type

of rocket, or atomic-power-driven space ship, when it quits
the earth on a voyage to Mars, or Venus, or Jupiter.

Mr. Probert tells us:

> "The strange machine is called the *Kareeta*, or *Cor-rida* ... it is attracted at this time because the earth is
> emitting a column of light which makes it easier of
> approach. The machine is powered by people possessing
> a very advanced knowledge of anti-gravity forces. It has
> 10,000 parts, a small but very powerful motor operating
> by electricity, and moving the wings, and an outer struc-
> ture of light balsam wood, coated with an alloy. The
> people are non-aggressive and have been trying to contact
> the earth for many years. They have very light bodies.
> They fear to land, but would be willing to meet a com-
> mittee of scientists at an isolated spot, or on a mountain
> top."

Again, I presume to offer no comment on the above, or on
the unknown place of origin of this queer winged craft,
vaguely said to come from "some world west of the moon".

But, besides the so-called 'Kareeta', there are alleged to
be abroad in the skies other strange craft of extra-terrestrial
origin. They seem to be connected with the fantastic aircraft
seen by the U.S. pilots over western Germany, in 1944, one
of which came up at an amazing speed, far beyond any type
of aircraft we, here, have been able to build, and in full sight
of the pilots, "did a wing-over and vanished into the air like
aerial phantasms". Before rejecting this story out of hand, I
may warn the reader that, later on in this book, he will be
given a short account of recent radar detections of *invisible
machines in the sky*, which, when a pilot who saw them on
the radarscope, as images of blurs and lines, corresponding to
those a normal aircraft would reflect, went outside to look
for in the sky, he was amazed to discover were *invisible
to the eye!* We may live in a much stranger universe than
the orthodox scientist supposes, and there may be *other* invisible phenomena, besides the filterable virus, electro-magnetic
waves, or ultra violet rays! It does not follow that, because
mysterious objects are not visible to the naked eye, therefore,

they do not exist, and are mere psychological or subjective aberrations.

This type of flying saucer is alleged to be controlled remotely from a mother ship called the *Loka*, alleged to come from an 'Etherian World'. The mother ship is operated by 'screw mechanism and atomically generated power'. It transmits to the smaller discs beams of high frequency from a transmitter panel. The smaller discs automatically send back data of observation which are recorded on the mother ship and the recording discs flame into incandescence and burn out by the operation of wires which set up a white heat. The world from which they come is beyond the normal spectrum of visibility, or any tangibility, or the wave frequencies of colour, or sound as we know them on earth. The satellite discs are small, but the 'brain ship', which directs them, may be up to half-a-mile wide! This 'Etherian World' is alleged to be inhabited by men of very advanced scientific knowledge, and they are alleged to use nuclear energies derived from fissioning the atom by chain reactions. They are said to be *not* hostile, but will attack if they deem themselves menaced.

The mystic quarters in the U.S.A. from whom this information emanates further say:

> "If there is another world war, using nuclear energies, these mysterious cosmic craft may be forced to intervene; for the release of radioactive forces from atomic bomb explosions has rather seriously disturbed the universe. These etherian beings are up to 15 feet tall. Any intervention would be impersonal and impartially directed. No sides would be taken. Why do they now appear in the skies of earth? They come always when a civilisation has reached a peak and seems destined to collapse. Their purpose is to collect, examine and record the achievements of that culture and civilisation, and its scientific discoveries, much as the anthropologist concerns himself with the culture of primitive tribes and vanishing races. All past civilisations on earth have had their day and perished."

Very naturally, rational people, whether they have scientific training or not, may, on reading the above, offer the same

comment that the playwright, Somerset Maugham, makes on
the mystic Asian theme of karma and reincarnation: "It may
be logical, but to me it seems incredible." And, as regards
the alleged existence of 'Etherians', or invisible beings, of
some unseen world of living, thinking and scientific entities
that may lie all about us, the reader must believe it, or not.
All I can myself say is that, at this time, such a theory is
unproved, and perhaps unprovable. It is obvious that, so far
as any objective knowledge of these strange and elusive craft
in our skies is concerned, most folk will rightly demand physical contact with the entities that may be aboard them, or
the capture of a forced-down flying disc that can be examined. But here, one has to make the rather big assumption
that the powers that rule either America or Europe will permit that examination and investigation to be publicly known.

We may, however, consider the parlous case of one of these
alleged entities who may—assuming he can endure and survive the pull of terrestrial gravitation—have been jettisoned
from such a cosmic machine, force-landed, and smashed up
in some remote spot. We may assume that, in the concussion,
he has lost his memory and is found wandering stark naked,
in the dawn of a summer day, in the outskirts of one of our
big cities. Perhaps, the forces let loose in the break-up of
the flying saucer may have had on him the effect suffered
by unfortunate soldiers, in the world wars, who were close
to the concussion and blast of a shell: namely that the *onde
de choc* and the blast had torn away whatever protective gear,
or clothing he had. Weary and entirely disoriented, that entity—one assumes he is humanoid, in accord with the law of
the cosmos—seats himself, say, on the wooden bench of a
public park. Soon, there bears down upon him a policeman,
who scandalised at the sight of a naked man in a public place,
demands to know how he came to be there?

Would not the earth-stranded entity's position be exactly
that of the naked man found, one June dawn, in a Chicago
park? A scandalised policeman asked him who he was and
what he meant by such conduct. The man, raising his arm
solemnly towards the still starry sky, uttered the one word:

47

"Betelgeux," which the policeman naturally wrote down phonetically in his notebook, as 'Beetle Jooce'. Thereafter, the policeman led the previously naked man, whom he had swaddled in a blanket borrowed from a saloon keeper, to a safe place to which three wise physicians were summoned. Both the man and our stranded saucer entity would find grave difficulty in convincing the keepers or the medical superintendent of a mental hospital, that a mistake had been made.

So far, the weight of the evidence is that these weird discs do not desire any close contact with us. They are elusive. We may recall the fate of Wells's Martians and their machines with the great heat ray: What killed these beings with brains and no bowels was not the British Army, or the embattled British Navy, but the pathogenic germs of an evacuated London.

It may also be—how can we yet know?—that these mysterious things may be directed by intelligent organisms not in the shape of man,* and who, in order to communicate with him (if they wish to communicate!) may have to devise some mechanism of radiological type that will do the communicating for them! H. G. Wells once wrote a flesh-creeping story about *saubas*, or ants in Brazil, which, under the leadership of very intelligent ants, overran the whole of that vast country, rendered of no effect the use of artillery and warships against them, and even planned to cross to Europe and Africa! Such a theory may appeal to astronomers like Mr. Howard Shapley, who say that only insects may inhabit Mars. But however fantastic such notions may be, let us remember that more than one fantasy of H. G. Wells was later realised.

---

* In favour of the theory that these entities may be human, or humanoid, is the essential unity of the cosmos. The elder races whose cosmogonical theories are garbled in Genesis, had a perception of the truth when they said that the "Great Unknown made man in His image."

CHAPTER IV

HAVE THE 'SAUCER-MEN'
TERRESTRIAL SPIES?

In summer 1953, a friend of mine who is a pilot in the U.S. Air Force—I cannot give his name, and for obvious reasons—wrote to me that he had heard sensational rumours purporting that the controllers of the U.S. Air Force, which is a branch of the U.S. Army, had had secret reports that mysterious individuals, in the U.S., were known to have had contacts with some of the entities on one type of flying saucer. These individuals were alleged to be meeting flying saucer entities in remote places, in regions of the U.S. that are still unmapped, had taken orders from them, and were going round in parts of the west and middle west on some secret purpose connected with these mysterious aeroforms. Nor, said my friend, did the U.S. Air Force controllers believe that any foreign power was concerned in the matter. It was believed that interplanetary and non-terrestrial aeroforms were concerned.

Naturally, it is impossible to obtain any confirmation of this story; but before the reader dismisses it as mystic nonsense, let us consider certain very strange aspects of the adventure of Mr. Kenneth Arnold, a private airman of Boise, Idaho.

About the time that I, myself, heard from a doctor friend of mine, in Birmingham, England, that, in summer 1947, flying saucers had been seen passing over that city, they—on June 24, 1947—had become sensational news in every American newspaper and radio station. On that day, at 2 p.m., Mr. Arnold, a business man, piloting his private 'plane, took off from Chehalis airport, Washington, west coast, on a flight to Yakima. He delayed an hour, searching for a U.S. Marine Transport 'plane which was missing—supposed crashed on the south-west side of Mount Rainier, Washington.

49

At a height of 9,200 feet, Arnold, flying in crystal-clear weather was startled by a bright flash of light reflected from his 'plane. Looking to the left, and north of Mount Rainier, he saw a chain of nine very peculiar aircraft flying north to south, at an altitude of about 9,500 feet. They seemed to be going in a definite direction, and were approaching Mount Rainier very rapidly. He took them to be jet 'planes. Then he noticed that, at every few seconds, they would dip and slightly change their course. They might have been linked together; for they dipped simultaneously! As they did so, the sun's rays struck them and reflected the light that he had seen from his 'plane and which had startled him.

In a few moments, their outline and contours stood out against the white and glittering snows of Mount Rainier, and now he saw that the queer machines had no tails. But he still thought they might be a secret and new type of jet 'plane. Now, using two observation points on Mounts Rainier and Adams , he clocked their speed. He saw that the strange machines were flying far more closely to the peaks of Mount Rainier than would any ordinary 'plane, or any 'plane he had ever seen. Moreover, their flight was as geese fly, in a sort of diagonal chain. As if they were always linked together, they swerved in and out of the high mountain peaks. He estimated that his own 'plane was 25 miles distant from the strange machines, and he knew, therefore, that they must be of *very large size*. That was so because, though the sky was very clear, he could not otherwise have observed them so closely at such a range. To be seen so clearly 25 miles away, their size *must* be very large. (*Note*: I have emphasised this, because here we are encountering a different type of flying saucer—*Author*).

The first machine passed the crests and summits of the ridge—high and snow-covered—between Mount Rainier and Mount Adams, just as the last one in the chain was entering the northern crest of the ridge. From his topographical knowledge, he estimated that the chain of these saucer-like machines was at *least five miles long*! Their rate of speed was at least 1,000 miles an hour! That may mean that *each machine in the chain was some half a mile long*! (Captain Thos. Mantell, a Kentucky air pilot, who, when ordered by an airfield commandant to pursue a mysterious areoform over Fort Knox, on January 7, 1948, at 3 p.m., was killed and his machine smashed to atoms, radioed, just before he died, that the machine he was pursuing was "metallic, of tremendous size and going too fast for me to overtake".)

The machines kept an almost constant elevation, as no rocket or artillery shell could have done. They were flat, "like a pie-can, and so shiny that they reflected the sun's rays like a mirror".

Unfortunately—and the author of this book sympathises with Mr. Arnold, because *he* had similar luck, 5 July 1949, when he and his brother clearly saw, at 11 a.m. of a bright and sunny day, two 15-feet, ridge-backed saurians with bottle-green heads swimming in the wake of a shoal of marine fish, up the tidal river of East Looe, Cornwall, when the ebb tide was running fast to the bar—Arnold had with him in his 'plane no movie camera with a telephoto lens.

The news spread like a prairie fire, and, before the next night was over, Arnold had telephone calls from all parts of the world; but, not till two weeks later, was he approached by the U.S. Army authorities, or Bureau of Federal Investigation at Washington, D.C.—the equivalent of the Special Branch at Scotland Yard. Now, the hidden hand of the secret U.S. military censorship intervened, and this in a great land whose press violently reacts against any censorship on news. Overnight, saucer stories stopped appearing in the American newspapers. I had letters from friends all over the States who wrote that this was the work of a secret censorship, believed to be operated from certain high officials' departments at Washington, D.C. It was not that any questions of security or defence were involved. But, from that day, all who reported sighting flying saucers were called lunatics and irresponsible visionaries, or men with water on the brain.

Mr. Arnold seemed to have judged that he, too, would be wiser to minimise his estimation of the tremendous size of the singular aircraft he saw passing Mount Rainier. It is clear that, unless the size of the weird craft he saw had been very large, he could *not* have seen the details he had seen, at 25 miles range. Moreover, craft speeding at 1,000 miles or more an hour, would have so blurred the naked eye that a stroboscope would have been needed—unless they were of the colossal dimensions he estimated!

On the same day that Arnold saw these nine discs near Mount Rainier, Lieut.-Governor Donald S. Whitehead, of Idaho, said he spotted a comet-shaped object hanging motionless in the sky of western Idaho. After a time, the strange object seemed to disappear below the horizon, with the rotation of the earth. Dr. Hynek, an astro-physicist on Project Saucer, explained this away as merely the planet Mercury, or Saturn, shining through cirrus clouds. But Governor Whitehead said nothing at all about cirrus, or other clouds, having been near this queer object.

I have before me, as I write, a U.S. official document which, I think, few or no people in England possess. How I obtained it does not matter, except that I may add that I have a friend in one of the U.S. armed services. It would be unwise to say who he is. This document is dated April 22, 1949, and titled:

> "National Military Establishment. Office of Public Information, Washington, 25, D.C. Memorandum. No. M 26 - 49. A digest of the preliminary studies made by Air Material Command, Wright Field, Dayton, Ohio, on 'Flying Saucers'. Project Saucer."

I note in it that the U.S. Aero Medical Laboratory men assured the Project Saucer investigators, that no object travelling at 1,000 miles an hour would be visible to the naked eye. (*Vide*, pages 50-1, *supra*, my remarks on the tremendous size of the objects seen by Kenneth Arnold). But I note they make no suggestion about equipping any of the U.S. pilots, who had orders to stand by ready to chase these weird objects, with a *stroboscope*!

It may also be objected that, if this be so, a meteor, which begins to glow at a height of 80 miles above the earth and becomes visible to the naked eye at 50 miles above the earth, would not be seen by the naked eye of a person on the ground, since the meteor travels at miles per second! Yet we all know it is *visible*!

Then, Professor Josep Hynck, the astro-physicist of Ohio University, and a member of the team of Project Saucer, thought it probable that these flying saucers were aircraft travelling at a speed less than that of sound. Well, that may be possible; but is it probable in relation to the *reports of experienced air pilots*?

A week or so after Arnold made his statement, policemen in Portland, Oregon, the state adjoining Washington, west coast, said they watched a group of discs—three to six—that wobbled, disappeared and reappeared, several times. They added: "They were like shiny chromium hub caps";

> "I was tossing corn to pigeons on a parking lot, when I saw the pigeons becoming quite excited over something. I looked round and up and saw five large objects in the sky, disc-shaped, and of no pronounced colour. They dipped up and down in an oscillating motion at great speed, and vanished quickly. I notified the police radio, and it broadcast an alert to all patrol cars." (*Statement of Patrolman K. McDowell*).

Two other patrolmen and a pilot of a private 'plane, that day in Portland, Oregon, saw: "Three flat round discs that flew at a terrific speed in straight line formation. The last disc fluttered sideways in a sideway arc, very rapidly. What made the things go we don't know. They were soundless and showed no vapour trails. We estimate their height at 40,000 feet."

Hynck's comment is: "These were *not* astronomical and *not* meteors."

The reports of sightings began to snowball! At Muroc—a secret air and U.S. experimental base—in the Mojave Desert, Southern California, a group of Air Force officers said they spotted spherical objects of a disc-like shape whirling through the air at a speed of more than 300 miles an hour. While the police of Portland, Oregon, were radioing alerts to all patrol cars to stand by, three or four deputy sheriffs of Vancouver, Washington, rushed out and saw high in the sky "thirty strange objects that looked like a flight of geese. From them came a vibrant humming sound."

Again, over Boise, the home town of Arnold, and a few days after he told of his sighting the nine strange and large bodies, people watched a queer object, "half-circle in shape, clinging to a cloud and just as bright and silvery as a mirror reflecting the sun's rays". The moving finger shifted to the far north, in Alaska. Here, at Fort Richardson, two officers told of seeing a spherical object, apparently 10 feet in diameter, rushing through the skies at a tremendous speed, and leaving no vapour trail.

Says Project Saucer:

> "Another incident in our Unidentified File took place 5,000 feet above sea level in the Cascade Mountains. A Portland prospector, Fred M. Johnson told authorities he saw a strange reflection in the sky, and, looking up, he grabbed his telescope. He saw six discs about 30 feet in diameter. He watched them for approximately 50 seconds while they banked in the sun. They were round, but with tails, and they made no noise and were not flying in formation."

This seems to be yet another type of saucer: one *with* tails!

Johnson noted a remarkable thing: while the discs were in sight, the hand on his watch-compass dial *weaved wildly*!

There are no magnetic iron ore deposits in this region of the Cascades. Nor any radio or radar stations. Mr. Johnson reported what he had seen to the Project Saucer at Dayton, Ohio, but their experts were evidently baffled. For, in April 1949, they admitted: "These objects seen by Mr. Fred Johnson are still *unidentified* in the official files of Project Saucer."

A few days passed, and then there came a most remarkable story which sounds like a passage out of the late H. G. Wells's 'Men from Mars'. On June 21, 1947, three days before Kenneth Arnold sighted the strange formation of the nine large aircraft over Mount Rainier, a coastguard patrol based on Tacoma, Washington, had an amazing adventure.

It was at 2 p.m., on June 21, 1947, when Harold A. Dahl,

the captain, and a crew of U.S. coastguards were patrolling the southern end of Puget Sound, Washington. In this sound, which extends southward from Juan de Fuca strait, are many islands and fjords. The coastguards' launch put into an eastern bay off a very thinly populated island, Maury Island*, which is about three miles from the mainland. There were low and thundery clouds in the sky, and the sea had a swell. Dahl, who was steering the motor launch, went in close to the shore. On board were two members of the crew and Dahl's fifteen-year-old son, with a dog. Mr. Dahl looked up from the wheel, and was startled to see "six very large doughnut-shaped machines" in the air. He judged them to be 2,000 feet up, almost directly overhead. The strange aircraft were stationary, and silent.

He thought they were balloons, until they began to circle round one machine which seemed to be in trouble. This last machine now descended rapidly, and, as it did so, the five others remained about 200 feet above it. They seemed to be following it downwards. The lowermost machine came to rest almost directly overhead, and about 500 feet above the water. Not one of the six machines had any propellers, or visible means of propulsion. Also, not a sound from them reached the ears of the crew in the launch. They did not seem to have any engines. Dahl estimated that they were 100 feet in diameter. Each had a hole in its centre, which seemed to be about 25 feet in diameter. When light came from the clouds, it was reflected from their metallic surfaces. But there was not *one* brilliance, but *many*, shining from the queer machines. All of them had what looked like large portholes, some six feet in diameter, and equally spaced round the outside of their hulls. They also had what looked like dark and circular windows on the inside and bottoms of their doughnut shapes. Perhaps they were observation windows?

* Maury Island, Washington, is joined to a larger island, called Vashon, by a narrow neck of land. It lies off the eastern end of Vashon Island, and is about 5 miles long and an average of 1 mile wide. The land is rugged, moderately elevated, and has large woods with clearings, where are farms. A few wharves exist which are used by boats from Seattle and Tacoma. Maury Island lies in the south part of Admiralty Inlet, a few miles north of Tacoma. *Au.*

Said Dahl:

"Fearing that the central and lowermost machine was going to crash in the bay, we pulled our boat over to the beach and got out our harbour patrol camera. I took four photos of these balloons, as I still thought they were. All the time, the five were circling round the one which was stationary. Five minutes passed, and then one of the circling machines detached itself from the formation and came right down to the stationary one. It seemed to touch it, and stayed motionless for about four minutes. Then we heard a dull thud, and the central craft spewed out what looked like thousands of newspapers from the inside of its centre! But these falling fragments turned out to be a white type of very light metal that fluttered to earth, and also fell into the bay. The machine then seemed to hail on us in the bay, and over the beach, black and darker type metals, which hit the beach and the bay. All these latter fragments seemed molten. Steam rose when they hit the water. We ran for shelter under a cliff and got behind logs. My son's arm was hit by a falling fragment of metal, and our dog was killed. Then the rain of metal stopped. The strange aircraft silently lifted and went westward towards the Pacific. All the time, the centre one remained in the formation. We found the fallen metal too hot to touch, for some time. But when it cooled, we loaded a large number of pieces into our launch."

When he got aboard the launch, Dahl found something which reminds us of the Oregon prospector, who found that when strange discs were over him in the Cascade Mountains, his watch-compass hand weaved wildly. Dahl found that his *radio was out of action:*

"When I started out on patrol, my radio had been in perfect order. But now, the static was so great, I could not make contact with our shore station! Yet the weather could not have caused all that interference. Our wheelhouse had been hit by the rain of metal, and damaged. I started up the engines and returned to Tacoma, where my boy had to be attended in hospital. I reported the adventure to my superior officer, Mr. Fred. L. Chrisman; but I could see he did not believe me! I gave him the camera and the films and also the metal fragments

we had collected in the island. Later, Chrisman went out
to the island to look for the 20 tons of metal which I
judged had been spewed from the strange machine. When
my films were developed, they showed the strange aircraft, but the negatives were covered with white spots,
as though they had been exposed to some radiation."

According to the report of Project Saucer, Dahl and Chrisman had intended to sell their story to a well known Chicago
magazine, whose editor had asked Kenneth Arnold to fly
over to Tacoma and investigate it. Project Saucer has, however, refrained from saying a word about the *analysis* of the
metal dropped on Maury Island beach. I am told that speci-
mens of it were taken to Chicago University and analysed by
chemical metallurgists, as "metal that had fallen from a great
height in the sky and landed in sand".

I may tell the reader that I had people investigating this
story of Maury Island on the spot, and that it is untrue to
say that this strange alloy thrown down from the machines
may be found, all over that island, as a geological and natural
deposit. My information is that this metal, or alloy, was analysed along with some that had fallen in very similar circumstances from another strange object in the sky, near
Zamalayuca, Mexico.

The analysts reported that the metal was an alloy of calcium, iron, zinc, and titanium, which were the predominant
constituents. Along with these metals were also aluminium,
manganese, copper, magnesium, silicon, nickel, lead, stron-
tium and chromium, with traces of silver, tin and cadmium.
Surely this was a *very* remarkable alloy to be found in a
natural state all over Maury Island!

It may also be added that the content of the calcium was
unusually high and that some very peculiar processing must
have been employed, because the calcium had not oxidised
as it does when heated—in terrrestrial conditions. It was
theorised—*not* by Project Saucer's experts—that the calcium
had been cast onto the hull of the strange machines—what
can they be, but of cosmic origin?—to absorb the lethal cosmic
rays out in space beyond our earth's orbit!

Now, at this point, there comes into this already startling, and, to many folk, incredible story, an element of mystery that baffles any creator of the most thrilling of detective stories. It *seems* to imply, and I do not wish that in hazarding such a conjecture my character as a sober historian of strange events in Britain and America, should be, by hardened sceptics, deemed to be 'demogalised for ever'—it seems, I say, almost as if these mysterious machines, from none knows where, *may have contacts on the earth.* Contacts with mysterious individuals who try by wheedling and dark threats to cover up facts about the strange machines which somebody or something desires should not be known!

On the other hand, those who try to stick to the law of parsimony of evidence may say that, here, we have a lurking saboteur, in the employ of some elusive, or foreign agency, who has for his nefarious object the shooting down of U.S. Navy 'planes and bombers. But, let it be said at once, that, as to the last theory, no evidence of such a saboteur has ever been found by the U.S. Air Force Intelligence, or by the agents of the formidable Federal Bureau of Investigation, at Washington, D.C.

According to Dahl, on the morning after the day of his adventure at Maury Island, a strange man called at Dahl's house to breakfast with him. Some of us know that Quakers, or members of the respectable Society of Friends are partial to meeting folk at breakfast and talking over business, or honest deals with them. But whoever this person was he was no Quaker! Dahl says he—the mystery man—wore a dark suit, seemed to be about 40 years old and had the appearance of 'an insurance agent'. I do not know if this be the sign of infallible or certain depravity! The mystery man drove up in a black Buick car of sedan type. Dahl got out his own car and drove downtown, with the stranger following him in the Buick. Why he did not use the stranger's car for a lift, is not stated. Over breakfast in a hotel, the stranger asked Dahl some curious questions, in fact, pried into Dahl's personal affairs.

Stranger: "Are you happy at your job, and in your family?"

Dahl: "What the blazes are you getting at?"

The stranger gave a peculiar smile. He proceeded to tell the astounded Dahl about what had happened on Maury Island. Dahl, so far, had not made public his adventure. He also knew that no one had been in the island, that afternoon, but himself and his own crew; and he did not think that any of his crew had been talking. If they had, the story could never have reached the ears of an outsider like this man. In any case, the U.S. newspapers had not yet got hold of the story.

"Mr. Dahl," said the stranger, still slowly smiling, "you had better forget what you have seen, and stop talking. Silence is the best thing for you and your family. You have seen what you ought *not* to have seen!"

The stranger then got up from the table and left the hotel. Later, Dahl found that the stranger could not have talked with anyone to whom he (Dahl) had spoken about the Maury Island adventure.

Now arrived on the scene Kenneth Arnold, who had been asked to investigate the strange affair. At the hotel, Arnold was, next morning, called on by Chrisman, Dahl's superior coastguard officer. Chrisman told his own story of singular adventure.

Said he:

> "Two days after Dahl had reported to me about these strange machines over Maury Island, I went out in the patrol launch. It was on the morning of June 23. I looked at some of the tons of metal on the beach. As I did so, one of the strange aircraft suddenly appeared from some-where! It circled the bay, banked at an angle of 10 degrees, and shot up into the centre of a cumulus cloud, high in the sky, I have never seen any aircraft before go into the centre of such a cloud. It is very rough in there. The strange thing looked like a large inner tube, to me. It was not squashed as Dahl had said. It had large portholes round the whole hull, and its brassy, golden metallic surface seemed burled. I noticed, too, an observation window in it. When the sun shone on it, it was unusually brilliant. I picked up a load of the fragments of fallen metal and went back with them in the launch to Tacoma."

Arnold then rang up the U.S. military Intelligence. He asked Lieutenant Frank Brown to fly over to Tacoma, and, on July 31, 1947, Brown and a Captain Dawson called on Mr. Arnold. They said they had flown over in a B.29 bomber. Brown saw fragments of the metal from Maury Island, and sketched for Arnold certain photos that had come to Intelligence, and also a photograph of a strange aerial disc, taken by Wm. A. Rhodes over Phoenix, Arizona, three weeks before. The photos showed a strange vessel like the heel of a shoe—that is, parabolic in shape—with a hole near one of the curves of the strange aircraft. Another photo showed the same strange craft with blurred lines on the film, that seemed to indicate that it was turning edgewise at very high speed, or was in a flat spin. Rhodes had said there were two tails of vapour trailing from the edges of the 'heel'.

Now comes a remarkable picture which Brown showed to Arnold. It was of a strange machine like a *half moon with a tail in it*! Or looking like a half-peak in the centre of the disc. I say remarkable, because, as Mr. Arnold may not know, on March 22, 1870, Captain F. W. Banner of the British barque, 'Lady of the Lake', saw, in mid-ocean off the coast of Liberia, West Africa, a very similar strange craft travelling high in the sky, *against the wind,* and visible half-an-hour! In March 1950, too, an identical body was seen in the sky over St. Matthew, N. Carolina! Mr. Arnold adds, too, another significant remark whose bearing he may not have appreciated: "The peculiar object drawn by Brown had a length one-fourth that of its width, and seemed *bat-like* in the tips of its wings. Here, I remind the reader of the weird machine called the *Kareeta,* seen over San Diego, Calif., in 1946. (*Vide* pages 41-2, *supra*).

Arnold said it gave him a shock; because, when he had observed the nine strange machines flying in formation over Mount Rainier, on June 24, 1947, he had seen that the second one from the bottom looked exactly like the sketch made by Lieutenant Brown!

It looks, therefore, as if a strange machine of this type had been flying over the earth 77 years before Arnold had his own adventure! Later on, my reader will see that we have a long history of the flying saucer, and that it is no new thing of the atomic fission age! Far from new, indeed! But the mystery still remains! We know not whence it comes, nor where it goes.

Brown said he had no time to go out to Maury Island, but was under orders to fly back to Hamilton Field—a U.S. Intelligence depôt—that night. So Arnold helped Brown load a Kellog cornflake box with the fragments of the metal picked up by Chrisman, put them in Brown's car, and saw Brown leave for the airport. Why Brown did not go out to Maury Island is odd. It would seem to have been a very important part of his errand.

Now, again, there intervened a mystery man. This time, he came on the telephone. It transpired that this mystery man had been ringing up a local newspaper, *The Tacoma Times*, and telling them all that was going on at this secret conference at the hotel! He knew so much that he might have been there in the room! Beds were torn apart and the walls and ceiling probed, but no hidden dictaphone or other listening device was found, in that hotel.

"It worried us all. It seemed quite spooky!", said Arnold.

Indeed, it seemed as if the mysterious stranger had command of some long range audio-visual beam, or teleaugmentive beam-ray of a type we do not yet know! He might have been directing it on the hotel, as it seemed. In the morning came news of tragedy. The B.25 bomber, with Brown and Dawson aboard, had crashed 20 minutes after it had left the airport for Hamilton Field. One passenger parachuted to safety. He said that the port engine had suddenly burst into flames. Why, no one knew! It transpired that the 'plane had been under military guard all the time it had waited at Tacoma airport for Brown and Dawson. Sabotage was not suspected. The chief engineer of the bomber reported that the fire extinguisher had also gone out of action. Why, none, again, knew! Both pilot and co-pilot were killed, but the engineer and a passenger had escaped by parachute.

At Kelso, where the crash happened, was an eye-witness, a local sheriff. Said he:

> "I saw the 'plane was flying high when the engine fire occurred. Its wings and tail and fuselage were all intact. It turned and steeply dived for some time, and then crashed into a hillside."

The pilots were first-class men, and yet they had not slowed up the 'plane before the crash. Why? It carried the latest radio devices and yet the pilots had not radioed the base. Why? The two survivors said they had been ordered to strap on parachutes, and had been thrust out of the bomb-door by the pilots, and that the 'plane did not crash till eleven minutes afterwards. During that time, the pilots might have saved themselves. It may be wondered whether, in that last eleven minutes, the pilots threw overboard the metallic fragments from Maury Island, because there was some very urgent need for maintaining secrecy?

All one knows is that nothing has ever been said by the U.S. Air Force about this aspect of the mystery. It is bound to raise the question again: What are the U.S. Air Force, and other U.S. war departments, so carefully hiding from the public?

Yet, again, the mystery man intervened!

Twelve hours before the U.S. Air Intelligence released the news of the crash, he told the press the names of the pilots in the B.25, what they were carrying, where they were bound; and, yet, Mr. Arnold is most emphatic that he had *not* talked with the press, nor said a word about the visit to the hotel, nor what was discussed!

I myself had a friend—graduate of a well-known American university—watching for me at Tacoma. He wrote me:

> "Dear Mr. Wilkins,
> A most unprecedented thing has occurred. Dahl and Chrisman have been shifted overnight. No one knows where they have gone. Nor why. Nor can any letters be forwarded. They have just vanished. It is most unusual in our Coastguard Service."

Of course, the U.S. Air Force—part of the U.S. Army?— sent a search party to the hillside of the crash: but a most minute search of the débris of the crashed 'plane *revealed no trace of the fragments of the Maury Island metal.*

The mystery man intervened a fourth time!

On August 1, he came on the telephone, spoke to a local newspaper office and referred to a U.S. marine 'plane, C.46, that had mysteriously vanished on a flight over the mountains of Washington state, west coast, and which had not been found. He predicted: "The C.46 *will* be found. It crashed on the south-west side of Mount Rainier, where it was shot down because there were people in her who had information 'WE' don't want to get out."

Who are 'WE'? Do 'WE' abduct terrestrials?

As a fact, the C.46 was found 10,000 feet up on the South Tahoma Glacier of Mount Rainier! Eight men climbed and discovered the wreckage. But, here again, is a strange mystery: *None of the bodies of the 32 marines in her were ever found,* and the $5,000 reward, offered by relatives of the lost men, for information, have not from that day to this been claimed! The mystery is insoluble: nor has any evidence of sabotage been found, nor so much as one fragment of bone of the bodies. One cannot resist asking the question, fantastic as it is: *Has this mystery of the lost C.46 any connection with nine queer machines seen by Arnold over this same Mount Rainier?*

Another minor mystery is: what happened to the fragments of Maury Island metal which Chrisman said he had taken to his cabin in the mountains? The mystery of this telephone caller, who may be identical with the stranger who called on Dahl, is a minor aspect of the greater mystery of the nine queer machines whose appearances over Maury Island—twice —seem to follow some sort of pattern. It seems clear that the principles of their construction show an advanced scientific knowledge whose theory is as much beyond us, now, as it transcends anything we can put into aeronautical practice.

We do not know; but the evidence, or data that will be given, later, in this book, about strange spherical or wheel-like machines that have been seen to rise from the ocean several times in the 19th century, and logged by ships' captains and officers, and then seen to soar into the skies may make one wonder—as Mr. Arnold himself has said: whether there be any strange connection between these weird and mysterious amphibious spheres and the vast dumps of furnace slag found on ocean-floors. If there is, then these flying discs may dump and jettison metal elsewhere than in uninhabited islands!

What was the line taken by the U.S. military authorities?

A military intelligence officer called on Mr. Arnold and took away from him every piece of metal he had from Maury Island. Mr. Arnold had planned to make a cigarette ash-tray from the metal. The military man took Mr. Arnold to a smelter's works and pointed out tons of material that, he said, "was exactly like the fragments. It is only smelter's slag that you found in Maury Island," said the officer, smiling.

He did not explain how that could be when there is no smelter's works in this very sparsely populated island, nor is it used as a dumping-place. Further, no reference was made to the curious sixteen constituents of this metal from Maury Island. If what the officer alleged had been true, then smelter's slag must be a most amazing alloy, not to say a shocking waste of valuable metal on the part of any smelter knowing his business.

The absurd 'subterfuge' of the officer was a pointer to the official attitude higher up in the U.S. Air Force. On April 27, 1949—two years later, when the circumstances would not be so fresh in people's minds—Project Saucer's experts administered the knock-out blow:

> "Chrisman and Dahl, under questioning, broke and admitted that the fragments were really unusual rock formations found on Maury Island, and had no connection with the 'flying discs'. They admitted telling the Chicago magazine that the fragments 'could have been remnants of the discs', in order to increase the sale value of their story. During the investigation, Dahl's wife consistently urged him to admit that the entire affair was a hoax, and it is carried as such in Project Saucer's files."

It is likely that Chrisman and Dahl had been badly 'grilled' by the investigators, and warned that their jobs in the Coast

Guard were at stake, unless they recanted, like two modern American Galileos. Some of us are well aware that folk in America and in Britain have often perpetrated hoaxes in the last 80 or more years. The painful craze for publicity and the limelight at any cost account for most of them. Moreover, this alleged recantation would, were it true—and I do not believe it to be true—suggest that both Dahl and Chrisman must have *very* remarkable powers as fictionists.

I have been informed by a friend in Seattle, Washington, that Chrisman and Dahl vigorously denied this allegation of hoaxing. Dahl says: "It is a bald-faced lie for the Air Force to say that I broke under questioning, and admitted that the fragments of the saucers were merely rock formations found in Maury Island. What happened to the fragments of the metal that were in the crashed 'plane? Why have not I and Chrisman been prosecuted if we were such rascals as to have perpetrated a story that led to the death of two U.S. Air Force pilots, and the loss of a 'plane valued at over $150,000?"

Chrisman also points out that, soon after the 'plane had crashed, he was ordered to fly to Alaska in an Army 'plane. Was this likely, had he really been guilty of a hoax that led to so tragic an affair?

I wrote an air mail letter from Bexleyheath, Kent, England, to Chrisman, at Tacoma, on 23 January 1951, pointing out that I was writing a book in which I should deal with the strange Maury Island adventure. Would he be so good as to give me *his* story and a refutation of the libel upon him in the U.S. Air Force release to the press?

It is significant of the censorship that was being applied by the U.S. Army authorities—as, also, was being done in Great Britain, by the various Air Ministries, in 1951—for me to record what did *not* happen in this inquiry!

My letter duly arrived at Tacoma, and was reurned from the Dead Letter Office, at Tacoma, Washington, on March 19, 1951, arriving back at my English address, in Kent, on April 7, 1951. I had endorsed the front of my air letter asking that it be forwarded to Mr. Chrisman's private address, if he were no longer in the U.S. Coastguard Service. Someone at Tacoma

C   65 has written on the letter: 'Not Coast Guard'. The Tacoma postal authorities imprint on it the word: 'Rebuts', and 'Parti' (gone away), and it is returned to me, undelivered. Yet, it is *certain* that someone in the Coast Guard Service at Tacoma knew where Mr. Chrisman had gone, and declined to forward the letter to him. If all Mr. Chrisman's private correspondence be treated in this way by the U.S. authorities at Tacoma, he must suffer considerable inconvenience, if not actual loss.

Why this U.S. official rendering of Mr. Chrisman, who is an honourable man, *incommunicado*? Of what is the U.S. Air Force, a branch of the U.S. Army, afraid? What does it desire to conceal? I have also not been able to make any contact with Mr. Dahl.

I have this letter in my files, and anyone, who is concerned, may inspect it.

A correspondent of mine, Mr. Hardin Ramey, who runs a store at Yukon, Oklahoma, wrote to me, in July 1947:

> "Just had a salesman in here at my store. He tells me he saw, at dusk, on June 21, 1947, six strange objects in the sky overhead. They appeared as large as wash-tubs, and were very high up, flying in formation and travelling at an incredible speed."

Four days later (June 25, 1947), Byron Savage, an air pilot of Oklahoma City, told the local pressmen that, five or six weeks earlier, he and his wife were out in their front yard, at dusk, with the moon rising, and the sun setting on the western horizon. Suddenly, "a fantastic object came over the city. It was about 10,000 feet up, and made no noise. After it vanished, there came the sound of rushing air in its rear. Its speed was fantastic. It was very big and silvery in colour. Far bigger than any aircraft we have."

Nine of the strange speeding objects, racing at a very high altitude, were seen over Kansas City on June 27, 1947. It is curious that both men who saw them report "a sound like that of engines, and vapour trails." Discs like "silver plates" were seen by a housewife to be racing over the Cascade Mountains, not far from where Kenneth Arnold saw his nine weird

machines flying in formation. She said they wavered from side
to side, as they flew, and changed formation. A man at Eugene,
Oregon, also saw silvery objects high in the sky, but going so
fast that his camera would not record them.

Just an envoi here about Mr. Kenneth Arnold, above. I
have been told, by a friend of Mr. Arnold, that the 'Saturday
Evening Post', of Philadelphia, suppressed a remarkable statement made to their staff man, by Mr. Arnold, who said:

> "At my home, I have been visited by unseen entities
> whom I believe to be pilots of these weird discs. They
> were invisible to me and made no attempt to communi-
> cate. But I was aware of their presence because I could
> see my rugs and furniture sink down under their weight,
> as they walked about the room, or sat on various objects
> in the room."

It may be said, of course, that this is talk of spooks, but
assuredly that is *not* the view of Mr. Arnold! Have we, then,
here, beings from some fourth dimensional world of matter
that, so to speak, cuts our own plane, at right angles; or have
we beings of so advanced a science that they make themselves
visible or invisible, in a moment?

I refer my readers to my previous chapter on 'The Foo
Fighters' seen over the Rhine area, in 1944, and manifesting
the same strange and fantastic powers.

CHAPTER V

THE MARTIAN CAT AMONG
THE PIGEONS

In certain mystical and pseudo-mystical circles, both in the U.S.A. and Canada, and, to a lesser extent in Great Britain, there is being foolishly propagated an illusion that *all* the mysterious and elusive entities of the flying saucers, coming whence no one really *knows*, are benevolent super-beings, radiating an unearthly great love and understanding, "like a warm embrace, with a wisdom" that have made a number of gentlemen yearn to follow them, and any "golden-haired man on board Venusian satellite discs, and more beautiful than a woman", even unto the Via Galactea, though he might never return from these abodes of cosmic bliss.

This is a dangerous illusion! A Californian pipe- or opium dream.

It may be true that, so far as has yet appeared, *some* of these cosmic visitants are non-aggressive, and merely exploratory, like Cook's Cosmic Tourists having a look over our planet. BUT—there are others! And, here and there in this book, I shall cite reports of strange and disturbing incidents, not merely in the U.S., but in Great Britain, that convey the unpleasant impression that some of these entities—and I have in mind, particularly, a weird aeroform of cigar-shape held stationary in the centre of a rapidly rotating ring, like Saturn in *his rings*—appear unmistakably hostile to this planet of ours, and show reactions that can by no means be regarded as fear-reactions.

There are saucers, not manned by 'little men', or captained by women, but by entities no one knows, or has even seen, whose irresponsible behaviour takes the form of arson on quite a large and dangerous scale. They seem to have heat-ray projectors recalling those of H. G. Wells's 'Men from Mars', all brains and no bowels, and command of powers conferred by a very advanced science. I may again remind some of the sentimental idealists, who write on this aspect of a new and amazing age, that it does not follow that this planet of ours, which has seen two insane world wars in less than one man's lifetime, necessarily rolls on its solar way in the midst only of other worlds that are friendly to it. Some morning stars may *not* be singing for joy! In this book, my purpose is not to disseminate mystic nonsense and soothing syrup, like some female writer telling the world, for the twentieth time, about the loves of an old priest of Chaldâea, or a young and lovely priestess of Atlantis, and lying on a carpet before a roaring coal fire, in some West End drawing-room displaying her own scanty-skirted charms, to be photographed for the benefit of free advertisement of her new novel, in the columns of a bright morning newspaper.

What appears like unpleasant truth should be told, so far as one may know it, to men and women of courage and intelligence.

Towards the end of the summer of 1947, there were reports that eight mysterious flying saucers had been seen landing in the clearings of a forest of a mountain side, near Ste. Marie, Idaho. It was said to have happened in the broad light of day, and a woman, who said she had seen them landing, was mystified, because she could not see them after they had landed! "They were like washing tubs, and the size of a five-roomed house". A Roman Catholic priest at Grafton, Wisconsin, heard a whirring and swishing sound, followed by a thud and a mild explosion in his parish-yard. He found a sheet-metal disc, some 18 inches long, like a circular saw-blade. It was warm to the touch and weighed five pounds. A hole was in the middle of the disc, and in its opening were "gadgets and some wires". Whether this was what Project Saucer might call a 'prankster's hoax', I am unable to say. The incident was like the case reported, about the same time, by a tobacconist wholesaler, Lloyd Bennet, at Oelwein, Iowa. He said no 'planes were overhead, when an object, shaped like a piece of metal, $6\frac{1}{2}$ inches wide and $\frac{1}{8}$ of an inch thick, "swished through trees and landed" on his lawn.

U.S. military 'planes on patrol, with photo equipment, over the Pacific coast, at this time, November 1947, had no luck, despite sightings of saucers reported from thirty states of the U.S. Yet, in Western Ontario, Canada, many people said they saw *two large formations* of strange discs moving across the sky in a wide arc. These discs were said to have varied in size, from an apparent 8 inches to that of a large, five-roomed house!

Mass-hallucination, mass-hysteria, and faulty observations do *not* seem to explain the queer phenomena seen, at this time, in Sweden. According to the newspaper, the Stockholm *Aftonbladet*, a flying saucer was seen over Stockholm, late on a Sunday night. On that very day, July 7, 1947, a professor of physiology at Sydney University, N.S.W., Australia, told his pupils that flying saucers were "merely illusions created by the red corpuscles passing in front of the retina of the eye, when one stood still and gazed at a fixed point in the sky." Just 'spots in the eye'! But that did not seem to be the explanation for what a man, at this very time, saw at Brighton, Sussex, England. He and his wife were on the beach at 4 p.m., when he saw "something like a moon, only bigger, fly over Black Rock cliffs and out to sea".

Chile now had a turn at the sightings of 'spots in the eye'. A strange object appeared, slowly moving through the sky and discharging white gases. It was seen by scientists at Del Salto Observatory, who said that this "singular meteor" remained visible for a certain time, crossing the horizon at 3,000 miles an hour. (So it could *not* have been a meteor, to have been visible for "a certain time"!) The observatory asked 300 observers in the southern hemisphere to be on the alert, and this was just at the time when reports of saucers came from other parts of Chile, Japan and Holland, and when many people in Naples, Italy, said they had seen "a shining disc fly *slowly* across the sky from east to west, in the night.

Close to the place where the first atomic bomb was tested, a rancher at Roswell, New Mexico, U.S.A., was said, in July 1947, to have found a flying saucer. It landed in his ranch, and was inspected by officers of the 509th atomic bomb group of the 8th U.S. Air Force, who sent it to a 'higher quarter'. This reported find followed a report from D. C. J. Zohn, guided missile expert of the U.S. Naval Laboratory, that he and two other scientists had sighted a flying saucer near White Sands, a proving ground to which public access is prohibited, in New Mexico. Down came U.S. Army authorities who declared this was merely a weather balloon; despite the plain statement of Mr. Ivan B. Tannehill, weather bureau chief forecaster, that it was unlikely that this mysterious object, speeding through the skies at a speed above the rate of transmission of sound waves, could have been a weather balloon. He pointed out that weather balloons have been in use for many years.

At this juncture, when the U.S. Air and Army authorities were talking of balloons, a baffling incident happened, on July 8, 1947, at one of the United States' most secret air bases, that at Muroc, California, where the latest supersonic aircraft are located. At 9.20 p.m., Lieut. J. C. McHenry saw two silver objects, spherical in shape, moving at 300 miles an hour at a height of 8,000 feet. Three other men at the same airport saw them. These objects were *travelling against the wind*, and, so, were neither weather, nor cosmic ray balloons. Earlier the same day, two military engineers had seen a metallic disc diving and oscillating for ten minutes over Muroc Airfield! It would seem that the entities were particularly interested in Muroc Airfield secrets. It is curious that no 'plane took off from the ground to try to intercept them—curious, since, as I say, *orders had been issued for that very purpose.*

Indeed it would seem as if these mysterious discs had a particular interest, in June-July 1947, in Oregon, Washington, California, and ranging a good way inland from the Pacific coast. Some might have said that they were machines of terrestrial origin engaged in mapping these regions of the U.S.A. But this theory would not fit in with the great speed of these machines—far above that of sound-transmission. Also, while some of the discs seemed under intelligent, *direct control,* others, of different shape and size, had the air of being remotely controlled!

For example, there was the silver ball seen at 4 p.m., on

July 30, 1947, by John E. Ostrom, of Nissa, Oregon. He is a 68-year-old man and was, on that day, driving a motor truck along a road near Tamarack, Idaho. He was doing about 45 miles an hour, when, on a sudden, he was startled by a blinding light overhead. Looking up, he saw, with terror and amazement, a silver ball of blinding brilliance slanting down from the sky! It was coming at an angle of 30 degrees, and straight towards his truck. Instinctively, he let go the steering wheel, and cowered down, covering his face with his hands. He felt it must hit his vehicle. It did! It hit the top of his truck and glanced off. Ostrom recovered himself, stopped the engine, and got out. He saw a phenomenon.

Where the ball had hit the truck was a scorched spot the size of a silver dollar. *It had melted the metal and left no hole.* What was peculiar was that, instead of a perforation, as would normally have happened, the scorched spot showed *what looked like a welding* in the original metal of the truck! According to a Seattle newspaper cutting I have, expert welders, who subsequently examined the 'patch', positively affirmed that something must have welded that part of the truck. Mr. Ostrom, however, most emphatically states that no repair, or welding had ever been done to the top, or cab of his truck, and that the singular effect had been produced by the contact of the silver ball. The newspaper adds that there are traces, on that part of the truck, of molten metal *which seems* to have been abraded from the surface of the silver ball which hit the truck. (Why has not this abrasion been chemically and metallurgically examined or analysed?—*Author*)

Was *this* a meteor?

At first sigh., the answer might be *yes* But it happens that, in this very region where Ostrom had his adventure, forest fires of mysterious origin were reported by rangers in this very summer of 1947. And yet, no meteoritic shower was reported over the Cascades at the time. The mystery deepened when another queer thing happened. A Wellsian, Martian phenomenon!

Six days before Mr. Ostrom had his adventure with the silver ball, a man named Bowman, with his wife and niece, were driving along a road towards a part-suspension, part-trestle bridge that spans the Salmon River, in Oregon. The bridge is about 420 feet long, and spans a cañon some 85 feet deep. The Bowmans found that the bridge was aflame from end to end. They halted the car and took photos, for they had cameras with them. Now, a very peculiar feature about this fire struck Mr. Bowman. The day was sunny, no cloud was in the sky, and there was no thunder, or lightning. Yet, not only *one* part of the bridge was on fire. *The whole bridge had been simultaneously set afire!* Oregon road engineers came on the scene and investigated. They found that the steel cables of the bridge had been *melted*. Now, the melting point of steel is more than 2,000 *degrees Fahrenheit*.

I, here, put a question: Had some heat ray from some mysterious cosmic machine, reminiscent of the heat ray of the Martians in H. G. Wells's well known novel, been projected onto the Salmon River gorge bridge by unseen entitities, controlling some radiator in one of the nine immense and unknown machines seen by Arnold, in that very summer of 1947? If the answer to this very disquieting question be *yes*, then, what may happen, in some time to come, to accumulating stockpiles of hydrogen and super-atomic bombs —the hydrogen bomb of which two, simultaneously exploding, can, says a famous nuclear physicist, set the earth off her orbit? I do *not* say that these would be mysteriously exploded, if lunatic terrestrial powers were about to arrange to toss them at each other, but that there might be other unknown ways of de-activation. For consider, *if* there be other inhabited worlds, we share with *them* the solar cosmos, and *they* may not choose to remain inert and hover around while lunatics blast out into space from this earth's orbit terribly dangerous and uncontrollable radio-activities, which may affect other worlds and the central sun. If politicians, masquerading as statesmen, pay no heed to warnings, perhaps the priests of science may, for their own safety, ponder and refrain before it be too late!

Local Oregon forest rangers say that it would have been impossible that burning wood trestles, in this bridge, could

74

have generated a furnace heat capable of melting steel, as did this strange fire. The mystery has never been cleared up. But if that fire were a 'demonstration' from mysterious flying saucers, can it be said that it may be deemed not a token of hostile intent, but a *warning to those who have brains to consider?*

We cannot say! But phenomena like these happened in England, in summer 1953!

I have been told that agents of the U.S. Federal Bureau of Investigation could not solve the mysteries of these Oregon forest fires.*

On July 23, 1947, the editor of an American aviation journal, named John Janssen of Morristown, New Jersey state, reported a weird encounter. He was flying at 6,000 feet when, he says:

"While my eyes played over the horizon, I became aware of a shaft of light that seemed like that of a photographer's flash-bulb. It came from aloft, very high up. It was above that position which, over a 'plane's nose, fliers call 11 o'clock. I at first thought it was merely the reflected sun, bouncing off the sides of an exceedingly high-flying aircraft. I gave it no further thought. Now, the engine of my 'plane *began to perform peculiarly.* It coughed and sputtered spasmodically. I pulled on the carburettor heat and gave it full throttle. This was to blast out accumulated ice from the carburettor at that height. The engine emitted one final wheezing cough and then quit. Now, the nose of my 'plane, instead of dropping to a normal glide, remained .. rigidly .. fixed on the horizon, in its *normal, level flight altitude,* Abruptly, I became aware that my 'plane was now defying its basic law of gravity. I became frightened, and close to panic, at so weird a predicament. I saw the air speed indicator was at zero! There was now an odd prickling, electric-like sensation coursing through my body. I had an eerie sixth sense feeling that I was being watched and examined by

* A mysterious fire broke out in the atomic energy plant at Berkeley, California, in April 1950. Damage to the amount of £53,000 was caused. Sabotage could not be found. Since flying saucers have, on many occasions, shown much interest in Californian bases and experimental stations, had they anything to do with this fire at Berkeley?

something that minutely studied my features, my clothing, and my airplane...with tenacity. I flecked a cold
bead of perspiration from my eyes. *Then I saw it!* Above,
and slightly beyond my left wing-tip, was a strange,
wraith-like craft. One of the flying saucers! Its flanged
and projecting rim was dotted on either side with steamer-
like portholes. It seemed to radiate in a dull metallic hue
that conveyed an impression of structural strength, and
a super-intelligence not of this planet. It was motionless.
Perhaps a quarter of a mile away...beyond, and slightly
higher, I could see another disc, seemingly fixed in the
sky. I assumed that the second strange craft was but waiting for the one nearest to me to complete its examination.
Then I had the most unaccountable urge to reach up
and snap on the magneto switch. I had turned it off when
the engine quit. I switched on both magnetos to the 'on'
position. Slowly, the propeller began to turn...then the
engine burst into its steady rhythmic roar. She nosed into
a stall, picked up air-speed and steadied under control."

That is Mr. Jenssen's story. It must be believed or not! But
it is a fact that U.S. pilots, flying on the Burma road, had this
experience in 1944.

It was in August 1947, that there came one more of those
stories indicating that *some* of these flying saucers may be of
tremendous size. Two pilots, flying on an Alabama line, told
Project Saucer that they spotted a "huge black object in the
sky. It was bigger than a C.64"—a large type of U.S. naval
'plane. "It stood silhouetted against the brilliant evening sky.
We pulled up to avoid any collision. We may have been 1,200
feet distant from it. We now watched it cross our path at right
angles. Then we swung in behind it and followed it at 170
miles an hour, until it outdistanced us and vanished from
sight, four minutes later. It was smooth-surfaced, streamlined,
and had no motors, wings, or visible means of propulsion."

No balloons were reported in the area at the time. Besides,
what balloon would travel at a speed far in excess of 170
miles an hour?

Here, we clearly have a case of some mysterious entities on
an extraordinary machine descending into the lower reaches
of our atmosphere to have a close-up look at a terrestrial air-

plane. To say this weird machine was a terrestrial experimental type involves the dangerous theory that the U.S. would risk a smash-up on an airway, and death and disaster to innocent passengers and pilots. No war department would dare to affront its own public opinion in this way, not even in the U.S.A.! No non-American, or other nation would risk such a secret in a foreign sky!

Project Saucer does not even attempt to explain the occurrence!

Down south, in Mexican territory, south-east of El Paso, on October 10, 1947, a mysterious flaming object exploded in the sky, and left behind it what was described as a "vast cloud of smoke". Whether this was a fire-ball meteor of unusual size cannot be said: but it is very remarkable that, seven hours before this mysterious explosion in the sky over Mexico, five west coast residents reported to the 'San Diego Tribune-Sun' that they had seen the "biggest celestial thing since Halley's comet:

"It soared through the sky about seven hours before the explosion near El Paso. About 12.30, a glowing object was seen in the north-east. It appeared about the size of a four-motor 'plane, viewed from below, and seemed to be 6,000 feet up. Its speed was terrific and it left no trail. It had a strongly fluorescent nucleus, diffused at the outer edge. *It looked like Saturn with a ring round it,* but it was definitely not a meteorite. It travelled in a straight line towards the horizon."

Earlier, on 20 September 1947, the Coast Guard at San Diego, Calif., were told that a flaming object had fallen into the sea off that coast, but no check of airports revealed any missing liner, or 'plane, and the Observatory at Griffith Park did not think it was any sort of meteor. Over Toronto, Canada, on the same day, two people photographed an object like a yellow ball with a trail of streamers. The photos showed an oval white spot trailing two milky lights.

I am told that the U.S. military and naval authorities were so perturbed by these frequent reports that came from responsible people, that orders came from high quarters that every effort should be made to trail these mysterious phenomena. From Japan, came a statement that radar stations had tracked a strange object in the skies that ascended in a *tremendous* burst of speed. Over Labrador, another mysterious object was tracked by radar, and the radar data gave an estimation of speed of *10,000 miles an hour*!

Eye-witnesses, deemed credible, were now asked to sketch what they had seen in the sky. In some cases, their sketches showed strange aerial objects with round noses and tailing into sharp peaks. One, too, seemed to be a sort of flying wing in whose centre was a blob of light. Then a weird blue light was seen glaring *over 250 miles of countryside* in the states of Oregon and Idaho. Airplane pilots said that they had seen the light go out, leaving a trail of flaming particles that gradually formed into a semi-circle, and vanished. No one had been able to form an idea of what this blue light was.

The activity of the flying saucer switched, as it has a habit of doing, to the other side of the globe, as if, once more, to remind us that the whole globe is being looked over by mysterious machines. The Stockholm newspaper 'Aftonbladet' said that mysterious missiles were seen flying very high over the town of Hudiksvall, in north Sweden, in broad day, at noon. This was on October 7, 1947. The objects gave out a noise like that of a motor, and streaks of light came from the tail. "They came from the north, and vanished *at slow speed* in the south-west."

Again, earlier, on August 18, 1947, between 8.15 and 8.55 p.m., Joseph Hofard, of Sorrento, La., saw and photographed about 78 objects like torpedoes, brightly luminous, flying at a "terrific speed over woods and roads. They emitted no sound, but glowed liked phosphor". I have a copy of one of the photos. It shows three of these weird objects flying in formation. I have also a copy of a photo taken by a British visitor, R. Johnson, which shows, high in the sky over a lake in Ontario, a strange circle with a black dot in the centre. From the edges of the circle there jet out rays of light like the spokes of a wheel. and it has a long tail like that of a larg comet. It was seen on September 14, 1950. The time of passage was fifteen seconds, and if this were a meteor, it was a most singular one.

Now, while the U.S. Coast Guards, stationed along the coast of South California, were bemused by the many reports of a strange flaming object that fell into the sea, the captain of a U.S. navy 'ocean ship', oddly called the *Maury*, and three other smaller craft, were rushed from San Francisco Harbour to investigate a queer story about an 'undersea mountain', that had suddenly appeared under the keel of steamers on the sea lanes to San Francisco. This 'reef', or 'submarine mountain', had been detected by several steamships and reported as "a large mass under water, off the Golden Gate". At the same time, puzzled officers and crew of a U.S. Navy survey ship appeared to have discovered a 'phantom reef' 400 miles out in the Pacific, off California.

The charts showed no such reef in the positions named. When the *Maury* arrived at the location, they could find no mountain, shoal, or reef; but, says Captain Hambling of the survey ship, *Maury*:

> "Our echo sounders *did* pick up a strange echo, when we were about three-quarters of a mile off the reported location of the 'reef'. It seemed that the sounders had got an echo from a mass about 1,600 yards away. We changed course, and started right towards it. Four hundred yards away from it, we found it had vanished, and we got no other echo. We tracked and re-tracked the area, using fathometers and echo-sounders. We covered five square miles very carefully, and another five miles round the outside of that area."

Of course, the mystery is baffling; but it does recall the various reports, made in the 19th century by captains of steamers, or windjammers in the Arabian Sea, the China Sea, and the Indian Ocean, of strange spheres rising from the sea and soaring into the air! Some have supposed—fantastic as it sounds!—that cosmic aircraft have had some reason to descend from the upper reaches of our atmosphere, either to cool off too radiant a heat generated by their machines, or to dump slag and metal on the ocean floors! Who can say? The late Charles Fort, the remarkable New York writer, came across many such reports when he was researching at the British

79

Museum, in the early 1920's and, before that time. I may say that I have worked such 'mines' of curious and inexplicable phenomena, but ranging far back from the beginning of the 19th century, which was Fort's chronological limit.

Towards the end of 1947, radar, in the U.S., was applied to the detection of mysterious objects far aloft. Nothing of this sort was done in Britain, though that did not stop the Lord President of the Council, the Right Hon. Herbert Morrison, M.P., from stating, in the House of Commons, on November 16th, 1947, that "Britain now leads the world in radar". To say the least, that is a very questionable assertion and ignored what was being done both in Australia and the U.S. at that time. It was now found by U.S. experts that mysterious objects were flying aloft, and were *invisible*! An American aircraft carrier reported a radar observation of a mysterious object travelling at a speed of 1,000 miles an hour, and *very high* in the sky.

Now, it may be noted that radar echoes, called 'angels', return at an interval of some ten seconds, and seem most numerous in the first half mile above the ground. But, sometimes, they return from ten miles up. We know that both U.S. and Australian scientific experts have had radar echoes bounced off the moon, and the U.S. Navy laboratory has even reported strange echoes from the Crab nebula in the Milky Way! But, of course, the 'angels' from our own terrestrial regions often come from *unidentified objects*. The U.S. Army Signals Laboratory at Belmar, New Jersey, which, some time back, received radar echoes from the moon, states that the radar 'angels' are unidentified echoes observed to a maximum range of 3,000 yards above the surface of the earth.

It is pointed out that these mysterious echoes, dubbed 'angels', are different from those obtained from radar echoes, or signals, reflected from dust particles, or turbulent atmospheric phenomena.

"Angels?"

If so, then it seems that the angels have taken to coursing through the voids of space in flying saucers!

All I can say is that Mr. Wesley Price, a U.S. radar expert, stated, in 1948, that these mysterious invisible objects—whatever they are, and whencesoever they come—appear on the radarscope only in the form of little spots of light, and that the images they project have very much the *characteristics of an airliner*!

He says that, at an experimental station near Arcata, California, he saw, not long ago, three 'discontinuities' that appeared on the screen of a radarscope. Usually these signals are from tangible objects, like 'planes, clouds, or patches of ionised air; *but,* the 'discontinuities' he saw were sharply defined and denoted that *invisible aircraft were proceeding over this Californian airfield*! On his radarscope, he saw three spots of light, indicating three mysterious aircraft flying at a height of some 850 feet in the sky, but at the low speed, for a 'plane, of under 35 miles an hour. He went outside the station and looked up into the sky. *He saw nothing of any aircraft in the sky!*

Another expert at the same station, whose name is Ehlers, says the radarscope has frequently recorded signals of this kind. They come from objects invisible to the human naked eye, and they seem to be flying singly, or in groups up to five, at about the speed of 35 miles an hour, and by night or day! Their altitude varies from less than 900 feet to sub-stratospheric height. They are not patches of ionised air, because they fly with the wind across it, or against it. (*Vide* page 217 on the strange half-moon object with curious tail, seen settling into the wind's eye, or flying against it, by Capt. Banner of the British ship, *Lady of the Lake,* in mid-Atlantic, on March 22, 1870.)

He further says:

> " I radioed the pilot of a 'plane, then in the sky, to go to the spot indicated on the radarscope and look for the mysterious objects. He went there, but saw nothing, nor did his instruments record anything of an electrical nature."

Yet, Mr. Price and Mr. Ehlers are by no means the only people who have seen these mysterious objects on the radar-

scope. It has been stated in the U.S. press that Dr. F. W. van
Straten, the U.S. Navy's weather man, has seen these mysterious spots on the radarscope, and, also, they have been seen by
Dr. L. Alvarez, a radar expert. Both men are baffled and offer
no explanation. All they are inclined to say is that the spots
seen on the radarscope, *in this case,* are not signals from meteor
trains, or ionised air. They are too much like the signals on the
radarscope that indicate aircraft in the sky!

A very singular thing has been observed about these 'angels',
which, after four and five years of research and study, scientists
can neither explain nor identify. On the radar screen, they
have been seen to come to a sudden stop, when an individual
'angel' has split into two, each part one-half the brightness, or
intensity of the original undivided 'angel'. The parts then
travel in opposite directions, for from two to seven miles, and
either continue on these courses, or merge back into one invisible object.

A radar technician, Mr. D. W. Chase of Phoenix, Oregon,
who, himself, has twice seen flying saucers, theorises that there
is a type of saucer which is of extra-terrestrial origin—no
theory can be yet advanced as to whence it comes—which is
multi-cellular, and can be quickly disassembled as it travels
through space. Then, in our atmosphere, the separate cells
can be sent out on exploratory expeditions, can return, and
then be re-assembled in the larger unit of the space ship, and
its own individual power be used to combine with the other
cells to drive the large ships at a terrific speed. But he advances
a strange, not to say fantastic, hypothesis: That these cells, or
small saucers, are the beings themselves, probably without any
mechanical covering around them! (I return to Mr. Chase's
very interesting theories, a few pages on in this chapter).

Who can say? But are these mysterious 'angels' cells of *such*
an invisible type of 'etherian' flying saucer?

I stated, earlier in this book, that experiments in London
and New York, back in the late 1920's and early 1930's, rendered a man on a stage invisible. This was done by warping
light rays in a rotating electro-magnetic field. But nothing on
the scale of these mysterious objects has been achieved. If 'they'

use some form of radio-magnetic radiation to produce the effect of invisibility, 'they' seem able to achieve it when an object is going at a very high speed.

What is so strange is that these weird visible, and then alternately invisible machines seem to be linked with mysterious bodies that are both vertiginously fast, and then remarkably slow bodies, shaped like cones, cigars, sausages, torpedoes, of blue, green, red, yellow and blazing, which can roar, flash, or explode in the air, and have been called 'flying saucers'. They may, or may not be, satellite objects under the control of some unseen mother-ship of fantastic size. Or, again, as seems likely, more than one entity is, or may be, involved, and more than one extra-terrestrial world may be visiting our skies!

We cannot yet say! All we can say is that these weird things are not meteors or comets. They range from the fantastic size of *half a mile, or even more,* to that of a 55-feet long airliner, and much smaller discs. There are even vast golden-hued spheres, *a mile in diameter,* tracked by radar, as flying in the stratosphere! It has to be believed, or not. It would also *seem* that these bodies emanate from vastly different worlds than ours, *some* of them apparently of a very different order of wave length, whose analogy is that of the invisible rays in the solar spectrum contrasted with the visible octaves at the red or blue end, or sound waves, perceptible to normal human hearing, as compared with ultra-sonic waves perceptible by some animals or birds, but not by human beings. I recall to the reader how pigeons on the ground detected the presence of flying discs far aloft over Portland, Oregon, an appreciable time before the policeman did. And yet the weird discs appeared to people—human beings—to be soundless! On the other hand, it would appear that some of these mysterious bodies may come from worlds as tangible and material as our own, and likely to be populated with beings like ourselves—that is, visible in what we may call 'normal' conditions!

Project Saucer's experts who, in December 1949, styled believers, or observers in, or of, flying saucers as misinterpreters of natural phenomena, toyed with the idea of the existence of 'space animals'.

They say:

> "The possible existence of some sort of strange, extra-terrestrial animals has also been remotely considered. Many of these objects described acted more like animals than anything else. However, there are few reliable reports on 'extra-terrestrial animals'."

No doubt, this was written with a desire to ridicule the hardened believer in the flying saucers; but, can these Project Saucer experts—high and dry scientists of Professor-astronomer Howard Shapley's type—be given, in their off-times, to the reading of 'sci-fantasy' fiction, or have heard of the late Sir Arthur Conan Doyle's very fetching and 'creepy' story of the balloonist, or airman, who was carried aloft into a very aery region tenanted by monstrous flying reptiles?

Come, come, gentlemen of the secret files of Project Saucer, who would have thought you were so human?

Note. I must emphatically say, that, in my eight years' study of the phenomena of the flying saucers, all over the world, I have *not* yet come across any reports of a sighting, anywhere in the world, that even remotely conveys the impression that those who saw it believed that strange extra-terrestrial animals were ranging the upper and lower reaches of our earth's atmosphere! This humorous remark of the Project Saucer may, however, have been aimed at the late Charles Fort and the Fortean Society of America.

By the end of 1947, a pilot flying over Walla Walla, Washington—a curiously Australian 'abo' place-name!—got what he described as a mighty shock. He was at a height of 11,000 feet, when he was startled by a 'terrific light' that seemed to come up from the ground. This light was bluish. It was seen over three states in the west of the U.S. (Idaho, Washington, and Oregon). A pilot of a military air transport 'plane saw the blue light, at 8.23 p.m.

He said:

> "It was like a terrific blue-green ball of fire, and it came across the nose of my 'plane, so close that I thought it would crash into me. Then it went straight up till it vanished."

At 8.43 p.m., over Baker, Idaho, another pilot saw a ball of fire travelling horizontally. He said: "It was certainly not a meteor, and I was badly scared." Two other pilots flying over Idaho also saw a brilliant blue-green light travelling horizontally, but what they saw was trailing an emerald tail four miles long! (Was it neutralizing radioactivity from atomic bomb explosions? Who knows?)

Summing up what has gone before, it will be seen that 1947 was a hectic year, as regards these phenomena. A bridge was mysteriously burnt as if some Martian sort of ray had been directed on to it; naval men were startled by the sudden appearance of a mysterious 'reef' under water in a busy sea lane off San Francisco harbour; a truck driver was frightened by a blazing ball that 'welded' part of its abraded surface into the top of his cab; other airplane pilots tried to chase mysterious objects. flying at terrific speed high in the sky; while sober U.S. Coast Guard men—*if* we may believe Project Saucer's experts, and the author of this book scouts this allegation—had their wits so deranged by the strange machines that dropped white hot metal by the ton on an uninhabited island, that they even tried their hands at what Americans call the composition of 'sci-fantasy fiction'! But—and certainly no irony is intended!—1948 was to witness a real tragedy of lost life, when a first-class pilot, acting under superior orders, tried to close in with a tremendous machine of origin unknown, flying high in the sky over Fort Knox airfield, Kentucky.

A queer peculiarity about the flight of these saucers has been noted by people in the Middle West and Western states. For example, Mrs. C. W. Vallette, who tells me that her ancestors came over in the ship of the Pilgrim Fathers from 17th century England, wrote to me from the township of Declo, Idaho:

"Dear Mr. Wilkins,
We round here have lots of flying saucer stories. We aren't too far from where they were first reported. The 'Twin Falls' paper has frequent reports of them. Only a few months ago—in 1950—one saucer seemed to be looking over three men, and hovered near them for more than an hour. One of the men was a student-meteorologist,

85

and he said that the strange object was definitely not any test or weather balloon. *I've never seen a saucer myself*, but one night in 1947, I did see some mysterious lights. *This one was flying along, dipping up and down, in undulatory fashion, or zigzagging.* It was a lot like a firefly. At first, I thought it was one, till I recalled that we, here, don't have fireflies. I watched it for several minutes. It was going quite slowly, how far away or high it was I could not determine. All I saw was the light just moving along. After a few minutes, it paused in a direction slightly E. of N.E., and for about a minute, it hovered, while a flood of blinding light poured from it, in the form of a cone. Suddenly, the light was extinguished. It was about 10.10 p.m. in the middle of June. I tried to get my husband up to look at it, but he was too sleepy, and said he had seen plenty of lights before, without getting up specially to look at one. The light wavered along, in an apparently aimless hover. Then it darted away at great speed. There is desert in the direction where it was going, and the place where it was hovering must have been over the lava desert, north of the Snake River, where no one lives, and there are no towns near."

I have italicised the statement above that Mrs. Vallette had never seen a saucer.

Now, compare with her story the following report made by Mr. D. W. Chase, radar technician, of Phoenix, Oregon, to the well known U.S. magazine, *True*:

"My first view of a saucer was on July 7, 1947, five miles south of Medford, Oregon. It was 5.20 p.m., and the sun was still in the sky. It passed east of me, about 10,000 feet up, at a speed of about 700 miles an hour. I saw it for 70 seconds till it vanished over the horizon. The air was clear and the saucer edge-wise; the large surface area was either reflecting, or giving off a tremendous amount of light . . . the colour of an arc welder's bright blue light . . . reminding me of the reflections from the facets of a diamond under a brilliant light.

"The course that the saucer took was over a terrain that has small hills, and mountains, from 500 to 1,000 feet high. In watching the saucer, *I had the impression that it was flying the contour of the terrain . . . and bobbing up and down*, not in a steady rhythm, but with variations, as if it were repelled away from the earth, and that the difference in the height of the terrain made a difference in the altitude of the saucer."

Mr. Chase deduces that the saucer was flying on some system of gravity propulsion, and that the saucers have instruments that detect radiation given off by atomic plants, and piles. He plotted the direction of their flights, which was to and from the direction of an atomic pile plant at Handford, Washington, one of the largest in the world. 'They' know that such energy is not natural, and, therefore, are moved by curiosity to investigate. (*Vide* my own story of my observations at Bexleyheath, Kent, England, p.p. 11-12).

A Chilean Navy commander reported, in spring 1950, that he and his men saw and photographed flying saucers in the Antarctic. They were one above the other and turning at tremendous speeds. Mr. Chase's hypothesis is that:

> "'The saucers are powered by some type of force field that has a direct effect on gravity, so that the force of gravity can be used to draw the saucer to or repel it from the earth. They get the power that keeps this field of force in action by setting themselves up as a sort of rotor ... in the earth's magnetic field. This explains why the stricken craft (at Maury Island) did not fall, once the others had set up a field of force round it ... The saucers seen by the Chilean naval man were, so to speak, charging their batteries by circling each other near the south magnetic pole."

Mr. Chase seems to soar into the field of fantasy when he theorises that the smaller saucers may form the parts of a large ship that could be assembled and disassembled easily in space. Any large space ship, he thinks, big enough to carry the power plant and equipment necessary for space travel, would have to be built on the multi-cellular system, "—as it would otherwise be too big for such travel ... I saw a saucer on July 7, 1947, that was 200 feet in diameter," he adds. Mr. Chase seems to suggest that these units are reassembled on the "plane of the obliquity of the ecliptic, as that would be the hardest place to view the process." Where Mr. Chase appears to soar

87

into aery fantasy is where he theorises that the unknown beings in the saucers may themselves be saucer-shaped and flying
a profile of themselves! Their robot space machines, he supposes, may be in their own image! One may, or may not,
choose to accept Mr. Chases' fantasy about the shape of these
unknown entities; but his *facts* are certainly remarkable.

CHAPTER VI

COLOSSAL DEATH RAY
AEROFORM

In the previous chapter, I emphasised the folly of theories that *all* the flying saucers are inoffensive. Now, we pass from the stage in which bridges and forests are set on fire by mysterious non-terrestrial entities aloft in our skies—or perhaps even out in space—to a dramatic adventure in which a fine U.S. pilot lost his life. The story has been given in other saucer books; but strange and mysterious phases, here recorded, have *not* been given, and are very little known outside the camaraderie of American Air Force pilots who dare not tell all they know.

It was on January 7, 1948, that Captain Thos. F. Mantell, a Kentucky Air-pilot of the National Guard, with a first-class record in the second World War, was ordered, with two other pilots then in the air, to give chase to a strange, unidentified object, looking like an ice cream cone with a tip of red, which had been seen hovering high in the air over the air base at Godman, near Fort Knox, Kentucky. It may be recalled that, at Fort Knox, is, or was stored the immense hoard of gold accumulated by the U.S.A. from the munition debtors, principally Great Britain in the first world war.

Mantell was in the air, and the orders came from the commandant of the Godman Air Base, Colonel Guy F. Hix, who, in growing excitement, had for some time been watching through binoculars, from the top of the air tower, the curious antics of this mysterious body. As the sun glanced on it, the body gleamed like burnished silver.

Colonel Hix said:

> "It was umbrella-shaped, half the apparent size of the moon, and white in colour, except for a streamer of red which seemed to be rotating."

89

He had been watching the mysterious thing for two hours, so that it is obvious that the region had some strong attraction for the entities, whoever, or whatever they were. It might be that they had instruments which reacted strongly from radiations thrown out by the vast gold vaults below—instruments which, despite yarns to the contrary, no terrestrial treasure hunter possesses at this time! However, that is merely conjecture.

Three of the pilots tried to close in on the thing, and reported on their radio telephone back to the Godman air tower, that the "size of this thing is *tremendous*!" One pilot said it looked like a tear drop, and at times seemed almost fluid! Then the flotilla (flight) leader, Mantell, came in on the air, with his radio report.:

> "The object is travelling at half my speed, and 12 o'clock high." (Overhead—*Author*). "I'm going to close in right now, for a good look. It's directly ahead of me. The thing looks metallic and of *tremendous size*. It's going up now and forward as fast as I am. That's 360 miles an hour. I'm going up to 20,000 feet, and if I'm no closer, I'll abandon chase."

The time was 1515 (3.15 p.m.). It is said to have been the last radio contact made by Mantell, with Godman air base tower; but I have to say that an observer, on that airfield, told me that not *all* the report made by Mantell has been revealed by the Project Saucer.

The two other pilots radioed back that the thing was still far above them, and their 'planes had reached a ceiling of 20,000 feet. They added:

> "This strange object is too high for us to catch. It's going too fast."

At this time, Colonel Hix, his executive officer, Lieut-Col. Garrison Wood, and other officers were watching this flying saucer through 8-power binoculars.

Said Hix:

> "I can't account for the fact that this celestial body—

as I think it is—*did not move as we looked at it.* I don't know what it was."

Now came a radio from the two other pilots that the object had vanished into cloud at a *terrific speed.* They broke off pursuit, but Mantell went on climbing. He must have been well over 20,000 feet, when he radioed back—this does *not* occur in the official report of Project Saucer:

"Am not gaining on it. I shall have to break off the chase soon."

It is believed that Mantell also added some remarkable details about the fantastic speed, the tremendous size, and the appearance of the weird object, and I am told that not even Mantell's widow was given *all* his last message. A few seconds after this last message something happened! His machine was seen to explode in mid-air. A Mr. Glen Moyes, who saw the crash, said that Mantell's 'plane—a first-class machine, P.51 (called F.51 in Project Saucer's report)—went into a dive, at 20,000 feet, and began to disintegrate when about half that height above the ground. But, a woman on whose farm poor Mantell's 'plane crashed, said she had heard it roar over her house and then saw it fall apart at tree top height. All accounts, however, agree that Mantell was instantaneously killed.*

Some may say—and the present author is impenitently among them!—that some lethal ray of immense power and unknown type had been directed at Mantell and his 'plane by the entities in the weird and vast machine, who may have deemed that they were going to be attacked, or wished to demonstrate to terrestrial military power, with its anti-aircraft

---

* I am asked, by a mechanical engineer living at Cuyahoga Falls, Ohio, U.S.A., to note that a P.51, flown by Capt. Mantell, does not crash, when the pilot drops the controls. It glides. He also points out that a crashed 'plane does not spread wreckage over an area of half a mile, as did Mantell's P.51. The inference, therefore, is that Mantell's 'plane met something far more mysterious than a crash, or a glide, resulting from an alleged dropping of controls. Moreover, Mantell, as a pilot in world war II, knew well the signs of oxygen deficiency, resulting in a black-out at a high altitude. Again, something more than a mere black-out occurred.

batteries, the folly of any close approach. It reminds us of the heat ray directed by the Men from Mars in the late H. G.Wells' novel, against the British Army embattled in Surrey, with heavy artillery, and the British battleships in the English Channel and Straits of Dover, when the fantastically stilted walking machines of the Martians advanced from about Margrate across the sea towards the British Navy. In this case, it will be recalled, a monitor-ram fused under the tremendous blast of Martian heat rays and exploded in live steam and flames.

But one thing must be emphasised: Mantell was a man with a fine record, level-headed and certainly not a man to have given chase to the planet Venus—actually at the time invisible in the sky!—or to have rashly persisted until blackout and loss of oxygen, with suffocation.

An amazing circumstance must here be recorded: Colonel Hix and another officer had sighted the strange machine, *for hours*, along an upright staff use as a 'fix', *when, all that time, it remained motionless*, as not even a helicopter would, or could do.

On the day of the crash, about 5 p.m. (1700 hours), came a report from an airfield at Columbus, Ohio, that a glowing disc was seen hurtling across the sky at an estimated speed of 550 miles an hour. It was white, and orange, and emitted an exhaust some five times its own length. This was at Lockbourne air base, and the observers said the disc was followed from the obstervation tower for more than 20 minutes. It glowed from white to amber, appeared round or oval, and travelled in level flight. At one time it seemed to "motion like an elevator", and then appeared "to touch the ground". No sound was heard from it, and it finally faded and lowered towards the horizon. At the Clinton County Army Air Base, at Wilmington, Ohio, observers reported:

> "A flaming red cone trailing a gaseous green mist tore through the sky at 7.55 p.m. (19.55 hours)."

This apparition looks very much like the machine that, over four hours earlier, smashed Mantell and his 'plane, or, if not,

it was one of the same type. At the same control tower, a staff
sergeant and corporal saw the "red cone manoeuvring for 35
minutes, when it seemed to vanish over the horizon".

They added:

> "It seemed to hang suspended in the air at intervals.
> Then it came down. It then ascended at what looked like
> a terrific speed. The intense brightness from this phenom-
> enon in the sky pierced through a heavy cloud layer
> which intermittently passed over the region."

It is to be noted that thousands of people witnessed this
phenomenon. Now came an amazing fact about the appearance of this phenomenal visitant: It was seen at places set
apart by a distance of 180-190 miles, and at an immense height.
Calculations by radar and the theodolite indicated that, in
order to be visible to the eye in such circumstances, such a
stupendous machine—and stupendous *is* the adjective!—must
have been well *over 500 feet in diameter*! The largest airplane on earth at this moment, cannot be seen by the naked
eye if it be 25 to 30 miles distant.

What, then, was its length? (*N.B.*—The height of Mont
Blanc, Europe's loftiest mountain, is 15,782 feet).

The answer is that it has been computed by later theodolite
observations and mathematical calculations that the *length*
of this colossal cosmic machine that smashed up Mantell and
his 'plane was *about* 15,000 *feet*! One might be forgiven for
supposing that it had, by analogy, come from the giant planet,
Jupiter!

The imagination reels under such a Brobdingnagian vision.
Apart from the truly colossal force needed merely to *hold* such
a machine far aloft in the stratosphere, what about the incalculable motive force required to impel this vast machine
at the terrific bursts of speed of which more than one observer
speaks? And at speeds of which no machine on earth is capable? One might be pardoned for theorising that a whole
large Jupiterian city of giants—giants in stature, as well as in
intellect—may have been aboard this colossal interplanetary
machine. It also seems obvious that the acceleration involved

in the speed bursts of this vast thing must involve such immense gravitational pulls and stresses that every cell in the body of a normal human being would have been ruptured, had beings of our terrestrial stature manned it!

I need not say how a vast space ship of this sort, whose origin and manning are shrouded in the deepest mystery, might react if it considered that the amenities, or safety of its own unknown world were menaced by our insane action of tossing around cobalt, or hydrogen bombs, and, so, releasing lethal and tremendous radioactivities of the type, that, as I myself saw, in Scotland, in June 1953, brought a typhoon wind of, 120 miles an hour that, from the region of John o' Groats, down to Braemar and Balmoral, quite 130 miles as the crow flies, and from 80 to 100 miles wide, devastated forests and farms, mile on mile. One might have supposed that every mile of the long trek a vast fleet of bombers had dropped millions of high explosive bombs. I saw that, in many cases, even the wires had not been restored to the many miles of telegraph and telephone lines. No wonder that our British Board of Trade has, in summer 1953, banned the import of timber! There is enough timber to last for years in devastated Scotland, cast down by distant explosions of hydrogen bombs.

Dr. Paul Elliott, an American atomic fission expert, who has issued a warning about the possible dire consequences of the simultaneous explosion of hydrogen bombs, very high up in the air, points out that the solar energy radiated to the earth is equivalent to that derived from the explosion of some $4\frac{1}{2}$lbs. of hydrogen a second. In any event, the explosions of these super-bombs might be catastrophic; since they might smash off from our own globe a fragment the size of a large planetoid. As is known, the many hundreds of planetoids circling round the sun, in an orbit between Mars and Jupiter, are very probably the débris of a world that once spun on an orbit between Mars and Jupiter and which, aeons ago, if Bode's Law be any criterion, was the victim of some dreadful catastrophe. Some might say that it was the victim of a race that had reached a very high degree of scientific culture and sent itself and its planet to chaos and destruction. Who may say?

What we *can* say is that nature has it in her power to create a more dreadful catastrophe than paranoiac man can himself bring about on the earth, and that he might just as well live and behave decently while he can. Anyway, the missing planet was three times farther from our central sun than is the orbit of the earth. Who may say, or gainsay, on our present extremely scanty knowledge, whether the cosmos has a police deputed to watch what sort of insane experimentation is going forward on the earth, in these days of warring ideologies and struggle for global power? We are probably not the only human races even of the solar universe, and certainly have no monopoly in the sun, which, very likely, we share with others. This blasting forth of lethal and uncontrollable radioactivity threatens other planets in the solar system.

Do we, here, wish to bring about a post-catastrophic state of affairs wherein our posterity, thrown back again to the stone age, will be wearing wiring diagrams as amulets, or old electric light bulbs as magic mascots, and the grim shadow of what has been?

But, we may ask again, was the following phenomenon of astronomical origin?

On February 18, 1948, a terrific explosion in the sky over Kansas rocked buildings, broke windows, and did damage over a wide area in Kansas, Nebraska, and Oklahoma. On that day, a ball of fire exploded over Nortons, Kansas, and a blue-white cloud, the result of the explosion, was visible for hours, and was photographed. (I have a copy of the photograph). The explosion was so abnormal that it was seen in six states: Kansas, Texas, New Mexico, Oklahoma, Nebraska, and Colorado. The authorities at Chamberlain Observatory, University of Denver, were positive that it was no meteor, and they knew of no astronomical phenomena that explained it. This strange sphere of fire was seen over two towns in Oklahoma, and its speed was reckoned at 600 miles an hour, too slow for a meteor, which moves in miles a second. There was, first, the terrific blast of an explosion, that shook buildings with the force of an earthquake. The blast was followed by a roar of appalling character, that lasted ten seconds. Then there appeared, at what was calculated to be 35 miles high in the sky, a strange blue cloud that rolled and bellied forth like a monstrous dragon *in extremis*! Two hours later, there appeared a B.29 bomber which circled round the area of the cloud till sunset.

There is, however, no confirmation of the reports of two other B.29 pilots that, before the appalling explosion, they had seen a long, cylindrical, shining metal projectile with a shiny nose, and a terrific burst of flame at its rear end. This amazing 'projectile' was said to have had the prodigious length of *ten miles* and to have travelled at 1,800 miles an hour! Truly, an incredible story! Oddly enough, between the two blasts, very high in the sky, a streak of smoke punctuated by a jelly roll of gases, or steam, which blossomed into another curious roll, suggested *rocket-blasts*, but not from any terrestrial firing range. No; possibly from a *rocket-type* of mysterious space ship of non-terrestrial origin!

Had some mysterious cosmic visitant met with a terrible accident?

Whatever this phenomenon was, there came reports that it travelled *erratically before the explosions*, and in a way no meteor would do. A pilot, flying at 12,500 feet, said that the explosion seemed to come from the ground. Yet no fragments were found on the ground! He was flying over Walla Walla when he saw a blue-green ball come across the nose of his 'plane, so near that he feared a crash. But the strange ball ascended straight on up and vanished. Twenty minutes later, when his 'plane was midway between Baker, Idaho, and La Grande, he saw another ball of blue fire, travelling *horizontally*. He said that in all the war years when he had travelled the Burma road, he had never been so frightened, and he had been used to dangerous missions. At about this time, two other pilots, in the air above Burley, Idaho—this state seems to hold some attraction for these amazing visitants!— saw a brilliant blue-green light travelling horizontally, with a bright sea-green tail. It was some four miles away. It very definitely shot up into space.

Another singular feature about these explosions is that they *seemed* to pilots to start *on the ground below them* as a ball of flame, and that there was smoke on the ground, none in the middle, and then gases or smoke at the height of the column! Yet no fragment was found on the ground, as would be the case of a meteor. Moreover, this was *not* the trajectory of any meteor. The area in which this blue flash was seen covered 280 miles.

Have we, here, yet another type of vast flying saucer—one which flies in rocket-ship manner?

Queer stories were associated with this portentous explosion of the mysterious blue object. A Stockton, Kansas, farmer, said that just before the explosion he saw a strange saucer "wobbling over his home":

> "When it came within six feet of him, it stopped in the air, level with his face, and wobbled round for an instant with fire belching out, and then being sucked back in. It was about four feet long and shaped like a funnel. Sparks suddenly showered from it and the fire increased as if a fuse had been lit. It took off in a north-west direction, very fast, gaining altitude as it went. My wife came out and watched it fly off, leaving a trail of smoke. On a sudden, a great cloud of smoke appeared in the sky and in a few seconds, we heard a terrible explosion. I could feel the heat from where the object came near the ground."

But was this the amazing projectile seen by the pilots on the B.29 'planes? Surely not! They said it was of immense size. It may be that it had a satellite connection with the immense object, or even, as a Texas astronomer averred, was really an achondrite, or peculiar stone meteorite. Anyway, it gave the Project Saucer experts a chance to align this small body with the immense one, and explain both as meteorites—which is an absurdity. In any event, unless the farmer and his wife were born and imaginative liars, even the achondrite showed very peculiar behaviour for a meteorite!

Now the cosmic picture shifts to Europe. A British European Airways 'plane, arriving at Lisbon, from London, on 23 February 1948, reported that a flaming ball had hurtled towards them when the 'pilot was circling over a storm centre. The ball bounced off the nose of the 'plane, shook it violently, and cut a hole in the rudder. The ball was travelling horizontally, and so could not have been a rocket, nor a meteor, whose speed is that of miles a second. It, therefore, looks as if these flaming balls, *if* they are remotely controlled from some unseen cosmic ship, get out of control at times. However, there may be some doubt, in *this* case, of the nature of *this* fire-ball.

Again, on March 23, 1948, strange discs and ball-shaped objects were seen passing in the skies over Florence (Firenze), Italy. They came from the direction of the Adriatic, and in their passing roared like the reverberations of a heavy thunderstorm! They also jetted white gases, or clouds of smoke. Next day, they were seen over Carrara, and in the skies of Surrey and Kent! The queer thing about the apparitions in Surrey and Kent was that the objects were seen to be flying in opposite directions! This was between 5 and 6.30 p.m. At midnight, they were seen in the skies of Birmingham. (It may be said that, sixteen months later—July 1949—similar discs and balls were seen passing over Sweden in the direction of the U.S.S.R.)

In Idaho, a group of surveyors were at work on a power sub-station. One surveyor, E. G. Hall of Boise, Idaho, was standing by a transit-instrument, when, at 1.15 p.m.. on February 20, 1938, a phenomenon occurred. He was startled when a colleague named Evans rushed over to him and pointed to a strange body in the sky. Mr. Hall at once looked through his telescope and saw a heart-shaped object blurred round the rear edges, as though it were rotating swiftly. The blurring effect went right along the disc, but he could see no cockpit, nor engine mountings, nor any vapour or exhaust trail. So rapidly was the object moving that Mr. Hall could hardly turn the screws of his telescope fast enough to keep pace with it. He, however, thought it might be a small, light 'plane. He saw it pass beneath a bank of clouds some 4,000 feet high. No sound came from it.

Still another type of saucer was seen, on April 8, 1948, by eye-witnesses, when it flew in the sky over Delaware, Ohio. It looked like an "oblong silver streak, or a large cylindrical body shining like an opalescent stick of mother of pearl."

Let it be noted this was *not* a sky-hook balloon of the military type! These balloons, when photographed at their altitude of 8,000 feet through a refracting telescope, show a peculiar ribbed effect *not* seen in the flying saucers, and the speed and manner of flight of these latest stratosphere balloons are very different from those of the flying saucer.

I want to draw attention, here, to the mysterious falls of ice, often not ice at all, from the skies of England, over Exmoor, North Devon, Essex, London, and Dumbarton, Scotland; as well as at Kempten, in Bavaria, Germany, in 1950 and 1951. The first falls happened on the night of November 10, 1950, when sheep on Exmoor were found dead, with deep wounds in the neck, and, by them, a block of ice weighing 14 pounds. On lone tracks nearby more ice was found, and yet the weather had been very mild and calm. It is recorded that similar falls of ice over Exmoor occurred forty years before, in 1910, when sheep were also found killed, with ice all round them.

It is not, at the moment, possible to say whether these mysterious falls of ice over Exmoor, had anything to do with the fact that, ten days before (night of 31 October 1950), the same Exmoor farmers were startled by the sudden appearance, in starry skies, of strange discs, spurting blue-white flames. They had come in from over the nearby Atlantic Ocean and Irish Sea.

But I wish to draw particular notice to the fact that, on 28 November, 1950, the British Air Ministry sent an inspector down to the house of a Mr. R. Butcher, of the village of Stebbing, near Dunmow, Essex, to take official possession of a strange block of material, *looking like ice, but not ice,* being, in fact, *some strange, translucent and unknown material.* The day before, Butcher had gone into his garden at Stebbing and found, lying on the path, a piece of a strange substance.

What Butcher said was remarkable:

"I heard no 'plane pass over my house, either in the night before or in the day. On the path of my garden, I picked up a substance, weighing one pound, that was no substance known to me. It was not ice. It was not glass. Yet is was slightly transparent, but not of crystal formation. I put some pices of it into my refrigerator. Other pieces I left out on the path. *After many hours, I found that those pieces on the path had not melted, but remained as they had been when I first saw them."*

Down swooped a police officer, removed the translucent material, and, by orders of higher officials in the Air Ministry, no photographs were taken of the stuff. Said Butcher: "Why the police want to make a mystery of it, beats me."

Had this translucent material fallen from one of the translucent types of flying saucers, like that seen in the sky over Delaware, Ohio?

Who knows?

Twice, too, in December 1950, and again in March 1951, queer objects like cylinders of metal have crashed from the skies into a garden at Mitcham, London, and into an English Midland town's market-place.

The British air authorities have sought to explain away these mysteries as arising from the defective de-icing plant of 'planes; but experienced air pilots with whom I have talked ridicule that theory. They say that ice, falling from de-icing plant carried by 'planes, is dissipated into spray long before it reaches the ground. Another theory advanced by a professor of chemistry and astronomy at the British Air Ministry, is that the ice may come from one of the frozen satellites of Saturn, which, by the way, is distant from the earth by 797,300,000 miles. It is possible, of course; but as the ice, *when it is ice,* bears no trade mark of origin, who is to prove it? We know nothing of the "machinery of the operation of ice meteorites," says Professor F. A. Paneth, of Durham University, England.

One pointer to a *possible* connection with mysterious visitants from outer space is that, when a mass of "ice-coated, meteoric stones", as large as cannon-balls, fell from the sky at Dharmsalla, in Northern India, in July 1860, a British Deputy Commissioner said that, shortly before the fall:

"I saw strange lights, not very high in the sky. They

moved like balloons, but I am sure they were *not*! I believe they were *bona-fide lights in the heavens.*"

He said the lights *seemed to wink in and out,* which is precisely what was reported of the 'foo fighters' met over the Rhine by U.S. pilots, in November and December 1944, and over Japan and the Pacific, in 1945. It may be pointed out, too, that no 'planes were overhead when a forty pound chunk of ice whirled out of a clear sky, one hot summer afternoon, at Tipton Ranch, Stephens County, Texas. As a British astronomer says: "Almost anything may happen out in space!"

I may note, in passing, that one piece of ice that *was* ice, and not an unknown substance, and that fell from the sky over Wandsworth, London, in November 1950, seemed to have been *formed against a flat object.* Was this flat object the underside of a 'plane? Or was it the underside of some flying saucer which passed noiselessly in the air, very far up in the stratosphere? No one can make any positive assertion, one way or the other; but one may again stress the fact that no 'plane was ever in sight or sound when this mysterious ice fell over England, or in the States. And such falls of ice from the skies can be traced farther back to the beginning of the 19th century. I have many records of such phenomena, occurring in England, Belgium, and the U.S.A., between 1811 and 1889.

I may, however, add, before dismissing this mysterious affair of ice falling from the sky, that more of this ice fell from the skies over Devon, and High Wycombe, Bucks, England, and London, in November and December, 1950—twice in the same London area at different times—and an enormous block weighing 112 pounds crashed from a blue sky on to a road at Helensburgh, Dumbarton, Scotland, on 26 December, 1950! Another big block of ice from the sky crashed through the roof of a house at Windsor, England, on January 1, 1951. It made a hole three feet square. On January 10, 1951, a carpenter, at Kempten, Bavaria, Germany, was killed by a six-foot icicle falling from the sky. Again, on 7 April, following, a block of ice weighing more than 28lb. fell into a garden, at Purley, Surrey. It was then stated that "this ice is being analysed". If it were, no official or any sort of statement has been made about what the result was. Again, in the first week of April 1951, a cyclist at Quorn, Leicestershire, narrowly escaped death or serious injury when a block of 'ice', more than ten inches square, crashed from the sky, about twenty yards ahead of his front wheel. As before, no 'planes were in sight or sound. This ice was found to be in layers tapering outwards from the centre to the edge, which was ⅜in. thick.

Naturally, thoughtful people are asking if it is *ice* that, in every case, falls from the sky? Very definitely, it was *not* ice that crashed from the sky in the village of Stebbing, Essex (*Vide* pages 99-100 *supra*). Then why the official secrecy about the result of the analysis of this 'ice' not *ice*? Is there something that is being hidden, something more than a non-confession of scientific ignorance?

There is a curious passage in *Revelations*, c.16, v.21 :

"And there fell upon men a great hail out of heaven, every stone about the weight of a talent." (*N.B.* The Attic talent was about 57½lb.)

Clearly, there is a very long history of these falls of ice, and *not ice*, from the skies.

But what about the 'cylinder' that fell from the sky over Wandsworth, London, in 1950, and the other metallic object that fell in an English Midland town in spring 1951? In neither case was a photograph, or accurate description, published of the mysterious objects. Here, it may be said that such objects have fallen from the sky in days long before the coming of the airplane. For example, on January 31, 1888, an iron object shaped an oblate spheroid fell from the sky into a garden at Brixton, London. It was analysed and found *not* to be a meteorite. Symmetrical objects of metal, or iron fell from the skies, in Orenburg, Russia, in 1824, and in Siberia, in 1825. In 1858, there fell from the skies at Marblehead, Mass., a mass of metal that proved to be *pig* iron, *not* meteoric in origin, and compounded of copper and iron melted. Pig iron suggests a mysterious foundry. But where?

On this mysterious subject of ice, or not ice, falling from

the sky, and other mysteries of nature, one may regret that scientists do not pay more attention to the history of science. In the case of this phenomenon, they would find that it is *not new*! For example, pieces of ice "with a sulphurous odour" fell from the sky over the Orkneys, on July 24, 1818. On two occasions, at Pontiac, Canada, on July 11, 1864, and at Dubuque, Ohio, in June 1882, a farmer, in one case and a foreman of an iron works, in the other case, found small frogs in the middle of the ice! A most bizarre and inexplicable discovery! In England, as the *Annual Register* records, ice fell from the sky over Derbyshire, on May 12, 1811, and at Birmingham, on 7 June 1811; ice "as large as pumpkins" fell at Bangalore, India, on May 21, 1851; pieces of ice so large that they killed thousands of sheep crashed from the sky over Texas, on May 3, 1877. Then the famous French astronomer, Camille Flammarion, cites similar phenomena as happening in Spain, France, and Hungary, between the years 1807 and 1844. In Upper Wasdale, Cumberland, blocks of ice, so large that they looked like a flock of sheep, fell from the sky, on 16 March 1860. They have fallen in Victoria, Australia.

One can cite here only a tithe of such cases, happening all over the world. They form a reminder of our ignorance of nature, nor is the matter helped by the natural tendency of scientists to discard and forget phenomena they cannot explain, and which fit into no theory of the workings of the strange cosmos.

Yes, as the British astronomer said: "Anything may happen out in space."

My reader may recall my suggestion that, when one has a mystery, one should look round and see if something akin to that mystery has happened elsewhere at any time. Sometimes, one may have to wait some years in order to make such a comparison. Maybe—or maybe not—an accident has occurred to some mysterious body in the sky, passing soundlessly overhead, which caused it to jettison part of its structure.

But to return to mysterious non-terrestrial aeroforms engaged in spying on our earth and her ways of life and mechanism:

What was the extraordinary aeroform, shooting out violent red flames, with a blue glow underneath, with rows of square ports on an upper and lower deck, and jetting an exhaust flame roaring for 45 feet, which startled two air line pilots bound from Houston, Texas to Boston, Mass., at 2.45 a.m., on July 22, 1948? Its speed was over 750 miles an hour, and it veered as did the airliner. It had no fins, but a snout in front like a radar pole; and no human, or humanoid, or any sort of entity could be seen within the blinding interior, glowing like a magnesium flare. In front of it were things like louvres. Pulling up abruptly, alongside the startled pilots, the thing jetted a veritable blast of blinding light from its rear, shot up to a height of 50 feet, and then vanished.

Was it identical with the strange thing seen at Las Cruces, New Mexico, in daylight, in summer 1948, by Mr. Clyde Tombaugh, sitting out in his backyard with his wife and mother-in-law:

> "At 11 a.m. we saw something rush noiselessly through the sky, very low in altitude. It was solid, and an aerial ship of no sort ever seen before. It was ovaloid, and from its rear was a formless luminescent train, while all round it was a strange blue glow. We saw on it six ports or windows, clearly visible at the front of the ship, and glowing green-blue, brighter than the rest of the thing."

To this day, no one knows, and the controllers of the U.S. Air Force had and have no clue to this mystery of the night skies. What amazing source of power was represented by this blinding light in the interior? We might suppose that whatever was in it could see, but could not be seen from the outside. All one knows is that at 3 a.m. that morning, two men, out hunting near Covington, in south-east Georgia, saw in the light of the dawn a vivid thing "like a lighted room".

In August 1948, two children, playing in the yard of a house at Hemel, Minnesota, looked up and saw a singular object. It was 12 feet off the ground, and descended between the children. Said they:

> "It hit the ground, spun round, once, made a whistling

sound and then shot straight up about 20 feet, stopped
again, and made more whistling noises. It then shot up
about 10 feet more, manoeuvred round tree branches and
telephone wires, and suddenly sped off to the north-west.
It was dull grey in colour, and about 2 feet wide."

Project Saucer was told about it, and made an analysis of
the recession in the ground where the children said the disc
had landed. "The result was negative."

It was as mysterious as a strange round object, flying aloft,
and about 30 feet wide that startled people at Columbus, Ohio.
It was reported that the mysterious object had a greyish-black
perimeter, with a transparent centre. It moved at a slow, steady
pace over the city, as no meteor or rocket would do, and it
made no noise, although a thin trail of gases issued from it.
Project Saucer suggests it was a 'carnival balloon'.

But *was it?*

The year 1948 in the Flying Saucer drama was not to close
before another remarkable chapter had been written in it by
Lieutenant George Gorman of the North Dakota National
Guard. He had what he described as a "Twenty-five minutes
dog fight with a flying saucer over the town of Fargo". Mr.
Gorman is manager of a construction company in Fargo, N.
Dakota, and one may say that his story 'stumped' the person-
nel of Project Saucer.

This is what he says:

> "On the night of October 1, 1948, at 9 p.m., I was
> about to land at the Fargo airport, after a routine patrol
> flight with an F.51 'plane. I was cleared by the tower to
> land, when I noticed what seemed to be the tail light of
> another 'plane, about 1,000 yards away. I queried the
> tower and they told me that the only other aircraft over
> the field was a Piper Cub. This little 'plane I could see
> plainly outlined below me. It was *not* the one I had
> noticed. I looked again, and queerly, now, I could see
> no outline of anything around the moving light. I de-
> cided to take a close-up look at it. It was about 8 inches
> in diameter, clear white, and completely round, with a
> sort of fuzz at the edges. But as I approached, the light
> suddenly became steady and pulled into a sharp left
> bend! I thought it was making a pass at the tower.

"I dived after it and brought my manifold pressure up to 60 inches, but I couldn't catch up with the thing. It started gaining altitude and again made a left bank, I now put my F.51 into a sharp turn and tried to cut off the light, in my turn. By then, we were at 7,000 feet. Suddenly, the thing made a sharp turn right, and we headed straight for each other! Just when we were about to collide, I guess I got scared. I went into a dive and the light passed over my canopy at about 500 feet. Then the thing made a left circle about 1,000 feet above, and I gave chase again.

"I cut sharply towards the light which once more was coming at me! When collision seemed imminent, the object shot straight up into the air. I climbed after it to a height of about 14,000 feet, when my 'plane went into a power stall. The thing now turned in a northwest-north heading, and vanished."

Mr. Gorman said that, during this weird heading and veering, he saw no deviation in his instruments, heard no sounds, and smelt or saw no odours or exhaust trails from the strange object. Its speed was "excessive". He added:

"At times during the chase, my own 'plane was under full power, with speed from 300 to 400 miles an hour. The strange lit disc was under observation for more than 27 minutes. It seemed to have depth, though it appeared flat."

Mr. Gorman was a pilot instructor for French military students in the second world war; so his opinion carries weight:

"I am convinced there was *thought* behind the thing's manoeuvres. I am also certain that it was governed by the laws of inertia, because its acceleration was rapid, but not immediate, and although it was able to turn fairly tightly, at considerable speed, it still followed a natural curve. It could out-turn and outspeed my 'plane and was able to attain a much steeper climb, and maintain a constant rate of climb far in excess of the Air Force Fighter. When I attempted to turn with the thing, I blacked out temporarily, though I am in fairly good physical condition; and I don't believe there are many, if any, pilots who could withstand the turn and speed effected by the thing with its light, and yet remain conscious."

Now, all this time, down below on the ground of the Fargo airport, the traffic controller, Mr. L. D. Jensen, had with astonishment noticed the strange antics of the light and Mr. Gorman. He watched through binoculars. He said he could not make out any shape or form other than what seemed to be the tail light of a very fast-moving aircraft. At the same time, a pilot named Cannon said that he and a passenger were watching this strange light and and its very high speed manoeuvres. He thought it might be a Canadian jet plane, but the Canadian Air Force said that no Canadian jet 'plane had been in operation near Fargo, on that night.

One question may be asked: Did the U.S. Air Force laboratory physicists test Gorman's 'plane for radioactivity? If so, their Geiger counters may have told a significant tale! Suppose that one of the quests of these weird discs is the detection of terrestrial deposits of uranium, and its isotopes?

We do not know; but let it be pointed out, here, that the U.S. Geological Survey is known to have devised special Geiger counters screened with lead shields—to offset cosmic ray radiation—that, when carried in 'planes, can detect uranium ores in the ground, or in mountains. If, as seems likely, we are here dealing with very advanced cosmic entities they may have aboard these weird machines much more effective means for detecting such ores, and also, it may be, for examining our atomic research stations. Or, more significant: stockpiles of atomic fission bombs, or, later on, hydrogen-tritium bombs! My reader may recall the warning given previously, in this book.

Now, on the Gorman incident, the Project Saucer could neither give an explanation or *explain the incident away*! There were too many eye-witnesses, and observers who could not be reduced to idiocy. But Project Saucer asks a curious question:

> "Is it possible for an object without appreciable shape or known aeronautical configuration to appear to travel at various speeds and manoeuvre intelligently?"

Well, if we accept the story of Gorman, again, a level-headed and expert observer and pilot, one may reply: "Yes, it seems possible that these mysterious entities can do all these things —and more!" But, again, who these mysterious entities are, or whence they come remains a riddle unsolved. So far as Project Saucer's files are concerned, the light that never was on sea or land, but *over* them, remains *unidentified*!

I am informed, by a friend in the U.S. Army Air Force, that it is said, in the messes and officers' common rooms all over U.S.A., that, when Gorman's plane was, later, tested with Geiger counters, it was found that there were reactions denoting that *something associated with atomic propulsion had been in the air over the Fargo field, that night of the chase!* And it was not Gorman's own 'plane! Project Saucer's secret files *must* have recorded this remarkable fact, if it be so; but nothing has ever been said, and nothing ever will be said officially about it, unless events force official hands.

But Gorman's adventure was not the only one of its kind. On November 18, 1948, there occurred another strange encounter in the sky above Andrews Field, in the state of Washington, D.C. Here, Lieutenants Combs and Jackson were flying a T.6 'plane. Combs was preparing to land, when, at 9.40 p.m., on a sudden, there approached his 'plane a mysterious globe, grey in colour, and throwing off a curious blurred light. Like Gorman, six weeks earlier, Combs gave chase to the mystery sphere. He estimated that its speed was 570 miles an hour. He shot his 'plane up at a very steep angle, in order to beam his landing lights onto the sphere. *But it eluded him!* Speeding at a high velocity to the eastwards, it vanished.

There was even a third adventure of this kind! On the night of December 3, 1948, a pilot at the Fairfield-Susan U.S. Air Force Base, reported:

> "Suddenly, a strange blazing ball rose to sight, some 900 feet from the ground. At the time, a regular hurricane was blowing. The ball shot upward, against the force of powerful winds, and, in no time, it had attained an altitude of close on 30,000 feet, when it vanished from sight."

In the case of Lieut. Combs, the Project Saucer of the U.S.

Air Force made the fatuous observation that what he had seen
was just "a cluster of cosmic ray research balloons"! Could
anything be more absurd than to say that he did not recognise,
or distinguish between *one light* and a cluster of three lights,
cosmic ray balloons, which are of large size and gleam brightly?
(These cosmic ray balloons have recently been tested at Bristol
University, England). Whatever else Combs did, he would
not be so foolish as to try to ram cosmic ray balloons.

In order to explain away these sightings of and encounters
with strange visitants, in the skies, Project Saucer's experts are
taking the line of the case-hardened sceptic in relation to, let
us say, the existence of the Loch Ness monster, and the centuries of sightings of and encounters with what are called sea
serpents. That is, they are driven down psychological alleys.
They assert that what is in evidence is not an objective, and
mysterious *fact*, but just psychological aberration.

Of course, it is best not to use the word *hallucination*, because so much ridicule has fallen on the experts of Project
Saucer—some of it started at my own instigation, in an article
I wrote in the July 1950 number of the 'London Contemporary Review'—that it has recoiled like a boomerang on the
press and the service departments.

Over Goose Bay, Labrador, on October 31, 1948, a strange
object was observed on the radarscope. It was of the type
known as an 'angel', or low altitude signal from some invisible
object. "Not astronomical," says Project Saucer's case-sum-
mary. Another mysterious object travelling directly into the
wind, appeared on the radarscope, and still another mysterious
object, moving at high speed and frequently changing its
direction, was signalled on the radarscope. This latter, with a
speed of 500 miles an hour and altitudes varying from 25,000
to 40,000 feet, was in the sky over Fürstenfeldbruck, Germany,
on November 14, 1948.*

* Even in the war year 1944, the British coastal radar warning system
could detect aircraft at 40,000 feet and 200 miles away, as also V.2
rockets at the same height, and indeed, considerably higher still. In
U.S., the microwave radar was equally efficient. It is not so easy to
detect low-flying bodies. *Au.*

A film cameraman was in Alaska, in May 1948, when he was told by Eskimos that strange discs were in the skies. He took kinema-pictures, and the U.S. Government deposited them in a vault at Los Angeles, releasing them later. Over Arnhem, Holland, on July 20, 1948, an object was seen four times. It had no wings, but two decks and a very high speed, as high as that of a V.2 rocket! (*Vide* page 104 *supra*).

In another case at Las Vegas, New Mexico, two agents of the Federal Bureau of Investigation, Washington, D.C., saw and reported a strange green flare travelling at a fantastic speed and very high up. All in all, I have very good reason to assert that well over 250 cases of sightings remain unsolved and unidentified by Project Saucer, though this is something they have most carefully concealed from the U.S. public and press.

At this point, readers may like to have some data about high-flying 'planes and high trajectory rockets and guided missiles, so far as they are not on the various secret files of the world's governments. They are up-to-date: *1950-51*—First, it may be said that neither the U.S.A., Britain, nor the U.S.S.R. has any aerodynamical machine capable of the speed of 1,200 miles an hour, as are some of the flying saucers. The sonic speed of an airplane is, theoretically, about 760 miles per hour at sea level. Moreover, no existing terrestrial power plant can fly any air machine at 1,000 miles an hour. The V.2 rocket, such as the Nazis fired on England in 1944—I saw these explode over Bexleyheath, Kent, less than a fifth of a mile away from me when I was, one dark night, on the way home from a newspaper office in Fleet Street, and the metal casings showered all round me where I stood in the open street—had a speed of 3,000 miles an hour. But this was *not* in level flight, as has been the case of some of the most portentous of the cosmic flying saucers! It is true that, in 1948, the U.S. had an experimental type of 'plane shaped something like a saucer. It was called the Chance-Vought, or V.173, but it was *slow in flight*. It is also true that, in 1928, one Monsieur Georges du Bay invented a saucer-domed machine, of which he made a model, in which the power was transmitted by rubber bands.

He offered the machine to various governments, including the U.S.A., but they showed no interest—but, too, it had not anywhere near the speed of 1,200 miles an hour, as have some of the saucers.

Again, in 1938—and I have photographs of it—Jonathan Caldwell, an American, constructed saucer-shaped machines like an auto-giro, or helicopter. The dome-shaped discs surmounted a central tripod column attached to the fuselage, and rotor blades projected from the top rim of the dome. He had another machine shaped like a tub, with the pilot sitting in the middle, controlling the engines. Propellers with four blades rotated in opposite directions. Caldwell had no official encouragement, and mysteriously disappeared in 1940. His creations were found, in 1949, battered and rusty, in a shed at Maryborough. No one knows where he is, and the U.S. would be glad if someone did! But, again, they are *not* Caldwell's machines that have been seen as saucers all over the world! Obviously not!

Up to November 1953, here are the latest air-speed records:

New British Ministry of Supply guided rocket-missile: 2,000 miles an hour, at altitude of ten miles (August 22, 1953).

Squadron-Leader Neville Duke, at Tangmere (R.A.F.) station, flew a Hawker Jet 'plane at 722 miles an hour (September 1, 1953).

'Lieut.-Cdr. Mitchell Lithgow, over a desert course at Castel Idris, in the Libyan desert, reached at speed of 733.3 miles an hour (25 September, 1953). The temperature in his cockpit of the Vickers Swift Supermarine F.4 jet rose to 180° F !

Up to 1950-51, air-screw, or propeller-driven craft were automatically limited to a speed less than that of the transmission of sound waves. I suggest that my reader refer to these data above, when he or she wants a terrestrial comparison with the amazing flying saucers.

Has Soviet Russia constructed a flying saucer *terrestrial* machine?

In November, 1953, the 'Intelligence Digest' said that its

observer in Berlin had met a man from the Soviet Zone who was wanted by the secret Russian police, the M.V.D. This man told a story of what seems to be one of the Russian secret weapons of which Mr. Vyshinsky hinted to United Nations at Lake Success, N.Y., in November, 1953. While, as he said, the U.S. was encircling the Soviet territory with air bases, there were in Russia "secret weapons that the West may not possess". According to the 'Digest', above, on July 26, 1953, people in towns and villages on the Baltic Coast, along the Polish border, saw in flight extraordinary round objects in formations of six. They flew with many abrupt turns at a very high speed. On July 31, at 7 p.m., a strange object landed on a country road running parallel to a railroad near Wolin. Five Poles and two Germans were working in a field. They noticed that the aeroform made no noise, and descended at a high speed, in helicopter fashion; it was of metal, about 65 feet in diameter, and had a closed spherical centre. On the exterior was a flat circle in which were wide exhaust ports, like jets, that could be seen. But no engine was visible, nor were any human beings aboard, and there was neither sound nor movement. It is also alleged that this object bore Russian inscriptions.

It is impossible to corroborate this story; but one may say that, just as the A. V. Roe company in Canada are known to be constructing a terrestrial saucer aeroform—of which I speak elsewhere in this book—it is not impossible that Russia may have taken a hint from what has been reported of flying saucers. *But*, I again stress, this does not solve the mystery of non-terrestrial aeroforms; and it must be noted that this strange object, said to be bearing Russian inscriptions, landed well inside, and not far outside the Russian zone of influence. If Russia does possess an aeroform of this type, she is unlikely to risk the consequences of testing or flying it over countries of the Western world, in all the skies of which flying saucers have been reported to be seen, long before 1953.

At the end of 1948, Mr. James Forrestal, Secretary of the U.S. Defence Department, at Washington, D.C., announced that the Earth Satellite Vehicle Programme, which includes rocket-propelled vehicles with an alleged speed of 2,300 miles an hour, is being carried out under research by each military service of the U.S. Government. The research is to be co-ordinated by the Guided Missiles Committee. The U.S. Congress has voted grants for space ships and space exploration plans, space bases, and studies and designs allotted to each of the three military departments. But, it must be noted that only the stages of initial research have been entered upon, and details are not likely to be given as to progress.

There are quarters that allege that the Nazis had, in 1944, plans for a space satellite vehicle to circle the earth some 500 miles out, and—so it is said—radiate on it solar beams focused in very powerful lenses. It is also alleged that the Nazis had observed flying saucers, before 1940! I have no information of any similar projects by the British or Commonwealth Governments, or of any plans to have an inner space satellite vehicle which will circle 500 miles from the earth, and an outer vehicle which may, or may not be fixed on the moon.

But, assuming what was hinted at in Chapter IV of this book (that some of these elusive flying saucers possibly have spies, whether their own landed men going round unsuspected in our streets or countryside, or terrestrial agents), is not a mere fantasy, then it may very well be that rumours of our own plans to land on the moon at some time before this tumultuous century closes, may already have reached these mysterious entities! (*Vide*, Appendix, *infra*).

If so, what may follow at some later time?

CHAPTER VII

BRITAIN'S NAVY AND AIR FORCE AWAKENED

In the last three or four years, right up to March 1954, the strange behaviours of these elusive fleets of the cosmos have been such that one might fairly ask the question: Have some of them a General Staff, stationed on board carriers, or cosmic "battleships" of tremendous size, out in space, which now maintains an amazing intelligence and espionage section whose duties are to descend on to our own planet and spy upon atomic pile stations, secret long-range missile depôts, naval and military centres, airways, railways, docks, airports, even upon Washington and the White House, and to rove widely over the earth, using wonderful devices for discovering deposits of uranium, and other scarce metals? Is their far-ranging exploration of the earth not only, in a sense, military, but economic?

To say that *none* of these things have occupied the attentions of the War and Defence departments and Ministries of the great powers of the world, from the aspect of security alone, would be nonsense. For example, it became known in November, 1953, that the British Air Ministry officials have handed this mystery over to Intelligence sections, and that the senior service, the British Admiralty, has for a long time been collating data received from the Fleet Air Arm on reports made about the flying saucers. Of course, little or nothing will be said, and it is known that several incidents have been withheld from the public, and reports are now classified as 'highly secret'.

There has, for a long time, been an interchange of information about saucers between the British and the U.S. Air Forces, and there is reason to think that, just as in the U.S., British aircrews are now supplied with confidential questionnaires on which they are required to note details of "unidentified aerial objects', to make sketches, and to record on special sheets electronic data that may be of use to radar staffs, at ground stations who, too, are directed to keep careful watch on the screens of radarscopes. In December 1953, it became known that one high official of the British Air Ministry had admitted that at least ten, later qualified to five, per cent of the sightings of mysterious aeroforms cannot be explained. (*Vide* Author's note, at the end of this chapter).

I am being constantly told by friends in the U.S.A., that it is believed that, behind all this screen of official secrecy, there exists, in America, some plan to make a revelation to the public, "at some time". It is being hinted that both the press and public are being "prepared for something'. But *what*, is, at this time, anyone's guess. I could name at least one distinguished British Air Marshal, who, for six years past, has told close friends that he believes the phenomena, when they cannot be otherwise explained, are of cosmic and interplanetary origin. In other words, that flying saucers come from other worlds in space.

I do not wish to be guilty of egotism if I say that I am pretty sure that a series of curious incidents I, myself, investigated in England, in summer 1953, came against a dead wall of 'no information', because of the imposition of a secret ban by the Air Ministry, or the Royal Air Force. In this case, the strange phenomenon, as I shall relate, occurred, also, as far back as 1763!

The above may be deemed the curtain-raiser to the demonstrations of the astounding 'five-mile-a-minute' flying saucers, over United States territory. One may add that, while certain members of the British House of Commons make a joke of these phenomena, high military and security departments have been forced to conclude that there is nothing for laughter in this revolution of the Time Machine. It will compel a violent re-orientation of our science, our philosophies, our knowledge, and our realisation of our place in the vast cosmos.

In the sands of New Mexico lies the region where the first atomic bomb was exploded, before these bombs were dropped on Hiroshima, and Nagasaki, in 1945. At White Sands, New

Mexico, there is a very important and secret military centre, called the Upper Air Research Centre, or Dépôt, where the latest high trajectory flying bombs and guided missiles are tried out. It seems significant of some intelligent cosmic concern that, in 1949, this 'hush-hush' location was visited by the mysterious flying saucers.

Officers at White Sands reported that they had seen them flying a heights computed to be 35 miles high in the sky, at the time when preparations were being made for high altitude missile flight. One officer said that ballistic calculations, applied to one strange object in the sky, seen through a photo-theodolite, showed that it was egg-shaped, and travelling at the fantastic speed of 3-4 *miles a second!* Astronomical experts, then on the range, had used a very powerful elevation telescope to trace the flight of two flying discs which were clearly following the trial of a V.2 rocket, some 100 miles above the ground! It is the fact that these flying discs had been photographed by the Research Centre at White Sands. Some of the officers thought they might be space ships, while others thought they were merely dual images and optical illusions.

Early on New Year's Day, 1949, a cigar-shaped aerial object, said to be wingless, 60 feet long, and 10 feet wide, with one edge tapering to a four-foot trailing rim, actually crossed some 500 feet in front of a private 'plane piloted by Mr. and Mrs. Tom Rush, of Jackson, Mississippi. The Rushes were about to land at Dixie Airport. They said that the object accelerated from 200 to 500 miles an hour and flew out of sight.

In April 1949, these aerial phenomena reached a crescendo of strangeness. On the 7th of that month, at 4.30 a.m., a Mr. Ahern of Des Moines, Iowa, was awakened by a dazzling light that came under a curtain in his bedroom. He got up, went to the curtain, raised it, and looked out at a very queer object in the sky. Then he went back to bed in order to determine whether the shadow cast by the queer thing, under his blinds, moved or not. He found that it did: it moved southward. Going to the window again, he watched it slowly disappear. He then sat down and wrote an impression of the object:

117

"It was like the letter B, with a thick iron, or aluminium column on the left side. Halfway down the vertical column, a bar at right angles divided it into two compartments. The upper part was transparent and full of fire. The lower part emitted blue, black, yellow and bright purple lights. I have never seen so sinister a thing. It travelled slowly north. Now, in these regions there are sink holes in river-bottoms, and wooded hills. It is strange that phenomena like this one have been seen over regions of this wooded and desolate and hilly type. Was this queer object travelling slowly, and looking for something?"

Mr. Ahern will not know that an object, like this, but shaped more like a large tennis racket, was seen by a Fellow of the English Royal Society, when he was going home across St. James's Park, London, at about 8 p.m., on December 16, 1742. (*Vide* my chapter on 'Flying Saucers of Other Days').

A query arises here: Was this weird object looking for metallic deposits, such as uranium ores? Who can say?

It is known that, two days before the Des Moines apparition was in that sky, a similar strange object was seen over Salt Lake City, and farther north. Another Des Moines resident—a woman, named Mrs. B. Bubany—was similarly startled, that morning, by a dazzling light in the sky, very high in the south-west. She said: "Fire trailed from it like a Roman candle." In California and Utah, it was reported that these flares, or dazzling lights in the sky, preceded explosions, and the epicentre always seemed to be from some object in the sky, travelling northwards.

The saucer scene now shifted from Iowa and the Mississipi, some 650 miles south-westward, as the crow flies, to New Mexico, where Commander Robert McLaughlin, U.S.N., then stationed at the Holloman Air Base, had a most remarkable experience that Project Saucer has not been able to explain, or explain away. It happened about the time that this queer object appeared over Des Moines. In the case-summaries of Project Saucer, of which I was unable to obtain a copy in July 1950, but of which I have been sent a few extracts, from a friend in the States, these experts were forced to admit: "There is no logical explanation of this case (at Holloman Air base)".

118

Let us see what it was.

The day was Sunday, April 6, 1949, the sky bright and sunny, and as this is an arid region where rain may not fall even once a year, the air was crystalline. Scientists and U.S. Navy officers had sent up a weather-balloon, north-west of the White Sands Proving Ground. Its upward flight was tracked by theodolites and a stop-watch. Of the five observers, one held the watch, and another the telescope. The balloon was well aloft when the man with the telescope was startled. Swivelling his telescope round to the east, he watched a singular disc approaching the upward path of the balloon. As he did so, a scientist tracked the disc through a theodolite. The strange object appeared to be an ellipsoid, about 100 feet wide, and some 56 miles high. Seen from the rear end, its shape might have suggested a pointed cigar, with a saucer-shaped or convex surface.

Now, a ballistics expert calculated the speed of the disc. *It was five miles a second!* He must have gasped with astonishment. There has yet been devised no motor on earth that will power a machine to travel at this fantastic speed! That is, a speed of flight of *18,000 miles an hour*. And it must be realised that this mysterious discoidal machine, seen 56 miles high in the sky, was *not* a high trajectory rocket missile.

Then came another amazing incident.

The thing suddenly swerved upwards, *and in ten seconds* had increased its altitude above the earth *by 25 miles*. Again, mathematicians, astro-physicists, and ballistics experts calculated that the tremendous force exerted in this prodigious acceleration was equivalent to *twenty times the pull of the terrestrial gravity field*. No human being of our earth could endure such a terrific pull without having every cell in his body ruptured. The strange disc was in sight for about a minute.

The experts of the U.S. Air Force Project Saucer, at the Wright-Patterson airfield at Dayton, Ohio, investigated this amazing affair, and were told by responsible eye-witnesses that this ellipsoidal disc was white, emitted no stream of light, and jetted out no exhaust or trail of vapour. But this was not the last amazing experience.

These strange machines put in another sensational appearance at the White Sands Proving Ground, New Mexico, on June 10, 1949. On that day, a high trajectory, stratospheric guided missile was being fired. As the missile roared upwards into the sunlit sky, observers were astonished. Two white balls suddenly appeared, and lit out in pursuit of the missile whose speed was then about 2097.3 feet a second, or approximately 1,430 miles an hour. Both balls shot through the exhaust trails of the rocket-missile, got ahead of it, and then joined each other well in front of the roaring rocket! They then ascended and vanished from sight. One of these balls was tracked by a Navy observation post, located on the Organ Mountains, and seen to be speeding to the west. The observer at the time did not know what it was; but seems to have supposed that it was a high trajectory rocket that had got out of control and might crash on some city, with catastrophic effect.

It may also be noted that, on the day these vertiginous white balls were seen, high in the skies of New Mexico, the wind at an altitude of 20 miles in the sky was moving in a direction opposite to that taken by the ball seen from Organ Mountains' observation post; so that the ball was moving at great speed *against a very strong wind.*

None can say whence these amazing balls come. To say Mars or Venus is to beg a very big question that cannot now be answered, in the present state of our astronomical knowledge.

It is true that, when the first atomic bomb was exploded in the deserts of New Mexico, at 5.30 a.m., on July 16, 1945—on the *same* range as that from which the vertiginous discs were seen in 1949—Mars may have observed the flash. But we have *no evidence* that this red star possesses electrical, or optical devices capable of noting a flash in so small a part of the earth. Its redness probably denotes a very far advanced state of cosmic evolution, but we *know* nothing about what sentient or intelligent life may exist in Mars. It may be recalled that dense billowing clouds, seen on the surface of Mars, on January 6, 1950, and, again, on six days on April 1-6, 1950, by an astronomer at Osaka, Japan, were said by him to be gases of an explosion covering an area of some 700 miles in diameter. He thought they might be volcanic in origin. Mars has a volume one-seventh that of the earth; but we have no proof that the red planet is populated by men of midget, or, indeed, *any* size such as might have been able to stand the terrific pulls of twenty times the earth's gravitational pull, which were involved in the amazing acceleration of the discs, or white balls seen chasing the rocket over New Mexico.

If they *were* midget-sized beings, who have devised space ships driven by atomic energy, they would need shields to protect themselves from the lethal and extremely powerful radioactivity which would be radiated and be absorbed by any water or fluid they might carry. And the problem of devising tubes, used in these radiation motors, which would not disintegrate under the terrific blasting forth of energy of atomic fission and chain reactions, is not one that we, here, in our atomic experimental stations, appear as yet to have solved. They would also need some means of averting collisions with meteors out in space!

It looks as if some of these fantastic theories about midget men from Mars, or some other world, controlling these discs, spheres, or space ships are based, by analogy, on the relative volumes of the planets compared with that of the earth, and, therefore, on these theories, may have beings about one-fifth the average stature of terrestrial human beings (say 5 feet 6 inches). That is, a Martian has a height of about 14 inches, on this theory! This *may* be; but we do *not* yet know.

If a species of small-sized beings—of course, mere size has little relation to brain power or intellect—are actually manning *some* of these saucers, they may come from some other planet in the solar system, which has not been detected by our most powerful telescopes. They might even come from the moon which may not be the entirely airless, waterless waste that is generally supposed! Those who fancy such an unproved theory—and, after all, life seems to be more a matter of air and water, than gravitational pressures—might point to the mysterious lights and vast shadows seen in dark regions of the moon, and usually in the same quadrant of craters, in the 18th century and many times in the 19th century.

An extraordinary variety of unknown aeroforms were seen between April 24 and September 10, in the skies of the U.S.A., and in Europe, in 1949. They included:

A white oval thing, 150 feet long, sixty miles high, with a speed of 7 *miles a second* (calculated by the instruments of technicians of the U.S. Office of Naval Research); a luminous object discharging a 'white gas' (Florida); strange luminous object moving like a pendulum, with streamers above and below (Spokane, Wash.); something that caused a freak tornado, and hurled a 460lb. boat high into the air (Seattle, Wash.); bright cigar-shaped object in horizontal flight (Milford, Mich.); strange formation of V-shaped discs, *again* seen over Boise, Idaho, speed tremendous, no exhaust or visible signs of propulsion-mechanism. Over Wisconsin, they flew at all speeds, under intelligent control, and some exploded, leaving on the ground an unknown substance, the colour of gypsum. A man was hurt when one disc hit the ground; a round transparent disc emitting a sound like a saw flew over Snoqualmie Pass, Washington, too fast for any camera; remarkable acrobatics of saucers, stopping dead at high speed, then turning at abrupt angle (Salem, Oregon); object, black and spherical, darted from cloud, 14,000 feet up, jerked, turned edge-wise, and vanished at terrific speed (Boise, Idaho); discs in formation caught in radar-scope; saucers over Graz, Austria; a mysterious stream of fire raced across sky, then looped the loop, at Temagan, Ontario, also, a tremendous, jagged flash of light lit up the sky, *for eight minutes*; at Port Hope, Ontario, a star-like object moved across the sky, and, seen through tele-scope, appeared spherical, with bright centre. The sun's rays reflected long streaming threads coming from it.

Now, a word about these cigar-shaped flying saucers, which, as I have noted in this book, are probably hostile, and, in 1947, in Oregon, and in 1953, *in England*, have caused fires and are suspected of incendiarism, in forests, and on farms.

"Cigar-shaped" and unknown objects have been seen before in America's skies. Take this story from the 'New York Herald', of April 11, 1897, and the 'New York Sun' of April 2-18,

1897, at a time when the planet Venus was in inferior conjunction. Collating both newspapers' reports, we see that people had written to 'Popular Astronomy', reporting objects "like airships in the sky":

> "Something like a powerful searchlight in sky over Kansas City ... directed towards the earth, travelling east at around 60 miles an hour. Same thing seen over Chicago. At Evanston, Ill., students saw swaying red and green lights in sky ... on April 9 crowd, on skyscraper in Chicago, saw strange lights high in sky ... April 16, 1897, at Benton, Texas, a dark object was seen to pass across the moon. Four towns in Texas say it was shaped like a Mexican cigar, large in the middle, small at both ends, with great wings, like those of an enormous butterfly. It was brilliantly lit by the rays of two great searchlights, and was sailing south-east, with the velocity of the wind, presenting a magnificent appearance. At Chicago, night of April 9-10, 1897, until 2 a.m., thousands of amazed spectators saw ... miles above the earth, two cigar-shaped objects and great wings ... white, red, and green lights had also been seen ... On April 11, 1897, the 'N.Y. Herald' said that 'a cigar-shaped object had been photographed at Chicago, seen in the sky'. On March 29, 1897, Omaha saw the object, and next night, Denver saw it, and it was also seen over Wisconsin, Missouri, Indiana and Iowa ... On 19 April, 1897, in the sky over Sistersville, W. Va., there approached, from the north-west quadrant of the sky, a luminous object flashing brilliant red, white and green lights. A man, who examined it through powerful binoculars, said it looked like a huge, cone-shaped thing, some 180 feet long, with large fins on either side."

This curious description of "fins and large wings" should be compared with that of the strange thing called the 'Kareeta', which startled people in San Diego, California, in 1949 (*Vide* pages 41-5).

A resident in a township in North Carolina, was looking at the moon, through a telescope, when he saw a phenomenon which has been seen many times before his day, in autumn 1950:

> "A dark body moved across the lunar disc, from east

to west. It took $1\frac{1}{2}$ seconds to make the traverse. It looked oval, and was in sharp focus, for it cut a clearly defined path. The naked eye could not have seen it. It was no bird, nor airplane. I think it was moving in space between the earth and the moon. Its velocity was high. If it were some 4,000 miles from the earth, its speed would have been 12 miles a second, and it would be some 500 feet in diameter." (*John J. O'Neill*).

A flying saucer was even *trapped in the beams of a searchlight*, at Milford, Ohio!

Listen to the report of the searchlight operator, on this remarkable incident. He was Sgt. Berger, and was working a searchlight belonging to a church which was holding a festival at Milford, Ohio:

"The thing was some 7,000 feet up, when it began to climb out of sight. I moved the beam and caught it again, two hours later. This time, it did not try to escape the beam as before. I watched it continuously for nearly three hours. I think it was then eight miles up. Its diameter may have been 160 feet, and it seemed to be constructed of some gleaming metal like aluminium. I saw that the longer the beams of my searchlight remained on this saucer-disc, the greater it glowed. I then experimented by moving the beam. The disc glowed brightly as ever. Then it moved back into the path of the beam, of its own accord. Some people here who saw this disc told me that, to them, it seemed like two globes, one on top of the other. When I looked straight up at it, it was like looking at the bottom of a plate."

It has already been noted, as at Portland, Oregon, that birds, like pigeons, can sense these mysterious discs in the air, when people, on the ground, do not see them. This was again borne out at Osborne, a township in Kansas, when geese, honking loudly, caused a man to look up into the air. He saw a saucer, about two miles up, going northwards. He said its speed was "terrific", and it remained in sight for eight seconds. About its motion, he observed a queer little dip, every second.

A mysterious sensitivity in relation to some unknown radiation may enable the pedigree homer pigeon—and other birds

—to find their way over long distances to their home-lofts. This 'sixth sense' can be so atrophied by radioactivity that it becomes lost. For example, on November 21, 1953, *only three* out of 350 pigeons—homer, pedigree birds—returned to lofts, after being sent out from Bookaloo, South Australia. Mr. H. Parkinson, of the Victorian Racing Pigeon Union, believes they were disorientated by the radioactivity liberated after the British Ministry of Supply exploded a new atomic bomb, at Woomera, in the Central Australian Desert. He is right!

In some quarters, both in Britain and U.S.A., it has been theorised that the atomic bomb explosions, as at Bikini, and in Usbekistan of the U.S.S.R., had sent forth clouds of radio-active particles so powerful that the incandescent envelope, or photosphere of the sun had been disturbed. It was supposed that the protective layer of ozone in the upper stratosphere of the earth had been perforated, so as to let in extremes of heat and cold. But, however this may be, it is pertinent again to ask our astro-physicists and chemists one question, which is this: How do you reconcile the theoretical absolute zero of outer space, where molecular movement of particles is not possible, with the co-existence of the direct transmission of heat rays from the sun? If outer space be the vacuum contended for by scientists, how can *heat* be transmitted through a vacuum? It is assumed that outer space, beyond the earth, or the atmospheric envelope of any planet, *is* a vacuum. I have yet to see any text book on physics, or astro-physics, which seriously attempts to resolve this enigma.

Now let us consider—explanation, we know not!—the very remarkable phenomenon that happened in Portugal, in July 1949. The news of it did not appear in the British press, which might plead short supply of paper and paucity of space; though it may also be said that, on the whole, British news-papers by no means pay the same attention, even in normal times, to non-political foreign affairs as do their contemporaries in other parts of the British Commonwealth, or in Canada and the U.S.A. Be it noted that I happen to be an ex-Fleet Street newspaper man:

I take this item from the 'Montreal Daily Star', of July 7, 1949:

"*Lisbon, Portugal.* July 6, 1949: A freak blast of heat, lasting two minutes, shot thermometers up to an unofficial reading of 158 degrees along the central Portuguese coast yesterday. Hundreds of persons were left prostrate in the streets, and thousands of fish and fowl were killed by the scorching wave of hot air. The phenomena swept over a large coastal area, following on a hurricane that rolled through northern Portugal. In New York, a weather expert said that such a reading was 'unlikely', though he admitted that heat blasts often follow hurricanes in tropical countries. (*Note*: Portugal is hardly a tropical country! *Author*). He said that the highest temperature ever officially recorded in the U.S.A. was at Death Valley, Arizona, which was 130 degrees. The National Geographic Society, of Washington, D.C., say that the highest officially recorded temperature, anywhere, was at Arizia, in south Tripoli, which was 131.4 degrees, and the highest unofficial reading was 189 degrees, at Abadan Island, in the Persian Gulf.

"The Portuguese heat blast first struck at the town of Figueira, just as thousands (*sic*) of women jammed the market-place in their morning shopping. Many fell prostrate in the streets, others knelt and prayed. Reports said that the blast felt like 'tongues of fire'. It killed thousands of barnyard fowls. The Mondego river, which empties into the Atlantic, at Figueira, dried up at several points, and at one village millions of fish died in the mud that was rapidly becoming a dessicated bed of sand, under the heat-blast. A naval spokesman at Figueira, said that 158 degrees were recorded that morning, and that the heat-blast passed after two minutes; but the sun was still broiling hot, and the temperature, generally, throughout the region, was more than 100 degrees. The hot air swept on to Coimbra, 30 miles inland, where similar scenes were recorded."

What was the cause of this phenomenon in a land which is in the southern temperate zone?

Had it anything to do with the cloud of radioactive gases reported to have been detected, in this year 1949, over the Pyrenees, north of Portugal, and which arrived some time after the atomic bomb explosions at Bikini?

Wherever these cosmic visitants, with their strange machines of so many types, may come from—these aeroforms of discs, saucers, cones, ellipsoids, balls, and so forth—it may be supposed that their visits may not be altogether unconnected with the blasting forth into space from the earth of dangerous radio-activity which is likely to disturb them seriously, the sun, and the space which they seem to traverse in their amazing machines. They may want to see for themselves what is going on in this planet, called by Mark Twain's Jupiterians, *The Wart*.

The periodicity of sightings in March and April 1950, was remarkable, and if we had a clue to their cosmic cause, we might be able to solve the mystery of whence and why these saucers originate. Whether or not it may be connected with the oppositions or conjunctions of some planets in relation to the earth, rendering them far or near from us, is a problem that might be solved only after prolonged observation and collation of data. There may also be some other factor—say, connected with radiations from the earth, or magnetic or electro-magnetic phenomena associated with the earth's rotation in space. We do *not* know. Reports came from all over the world. In the skies of New Zealand, they were seen, and over the Balearic Islands, Spain, a rotating globe, exactly like a fiery Catherine Wheel, was seen, and it emitted a loud drone. This 'platillo volante' was photographed at 3 a.m., on March 25, by a news cameraman, *Señor* Enrique Miller.

These sightings in 1950, from March 10 to 30, included:

> A mysterious space ship (N. Carolina), "larger than an air-liner"; faintly droning, and over St. Matthew, something "like a half-moon with a tail in it" (*N.B.*—An object exactly like this was seen in the S. Atlantic, miles west of Liberia, W. Africa, on March 22, 1870, by the British barque, "Lady of the Lake", and going against the wind. Remark *the singular periodicity in the month!*); a "flying dish", yellow in centre, red at sides, over Miraflores Beach, Peru; three saucers in perfect formation, "speed staggering", seen by pilot of Egyptian Misr Line (off Haifa, Mediterranean); weird object with winking lights, approached,

127

at night, air-liner of U.S. airline, over Arkansas, was like "a Chinese coolie's hat", and had ports spaced round rim: moon-like discs, speed immense, flew over Jordan, Israel, Italy, Caribbean, Cyprus, Rio de Janeiro, Abyssinia, Chile, Colombia (S.A.), and Las Vegas, U.S.; five saucers like full moons, with wakes of fire, pass over Italy, at immense speed; a saucer over Heidelberg, Germany.

An astounding demonstration, like a mimic battle of aerial fleets, was 'arranged' by fleets of saucers, in March 1950!

At Farmington, in New Mexico, is a population of some 5,500 people who get their living out of oil. On March 18, 1950, more than half the population were looking up to the skies in amazement, and some fright. All the staff of reporters of the town's newspaper turned out with the editor, and a number of pilots, waiting to take off on passenger flights. They saw "hundreds of strange objects" flying around like English rooks in autumn in a congress dance. Some of the objects flashed away at a speed which a man with a theodolite calculated to be more than 1,000 miles an hour. The things seemed to be gleaming silver in colour. They were high up in the skies for more than one hour. Then, about 11.30 a.m., they vanished, only to reappear in the afternoon. It seemed as if the strange machines were looking for something, which they could not find! No sounds came from them, and no exhaust gases were seen jetting from them. They seemed about 15 miles up in the skies. Everybody, including local newspapers, thought they were 'space ships'. Observers, who reported that the day was calm and sunny, said that these objects seemed to be flying in group formations.

April 2-28, 1950 sightings were world-wide (early in the month, Boulder, Calif., Observatory saw 32 gigantic eruptions of hydrogen gas, in the sun):

"Flying banana groups" photographed over Texas; three women at Whitby. Yorks, see two pure white, revolving hoops, one inside the other, with two rods emitting a dazzling light, very high in the sky; crowds block streets in Buenos Aires, watching, at noon, antics of a stationary white 'plativolo' (saucer), with white film on rim; shepherds in Hautes Pyrenées, France, watch red

saucers flash over sky; at Preston, Lancs., a thing like a
swinging pendulum, noiseless, very bright, moved slowly
east against the wind; black marketeers, in Munich, start
off for Bavarian mountains, with loaded cars, saying they
were terrified by flying saucers!; 12 saucers seen by crowds
at Palermo, Sicily, and in formations of threes; New Zealand sees a "200-foot long saucer with lights from ports";
a 200-foot "ice-cream cone" object flies over Vancouver,
B.C., airport. (In June 1950, three U.S. Air pilots saw similar object, speed 1,500 miles an hour, over Hamilton airfield); at midnight, a queer object, "like a house on fire",
flew low over freight yards of Alaska Railroads. It had
come all down the coast and was noiseless, speed terrific;
a strange glowing disc coquetted with air-liner bound for
Washington. It whizzed under the 'plane and vanished at
high speed. At Sydney, New South Wales, in daytime, a
saucer flew over at incalculable speed, while, at the same
time, crowds on beach saw a three-humped sea saurian,
50 feet long, break the surface, about 200 yards off!

What an air liner pilot called "a round glowing mass, which
seemed to be equipped with repulse-radar mechanism", was
encountered by him on a night flight to Chicago, on April 27,
1950. This pilot, Captain Robert Adickes, says he had always
been derisive of the existence of flying saucers.

He said:

"We were 2,000 feet up, when the thing flew alongside.
It was round, and thick, smooth and streamlined, and
glowed evenly with a bright red colour. But it emitted
no gases or vapour, and seemed to fly edgewise, like a
wheel. The passengers saw it, too. I called up South Bend
air port, but the controller said they had no message of
any unusual machines being in the sky. I banked to get
closer to it; but, as soon as I turned towards it, it veered
away, as if it had some sort of radar-repulse mechanism.
I judge its speed as 450 miles an hour. It went down to
1,500 feet from the ground, and then shot off into the
night. None of the passengers saw any details of it."

At the end of this rather hectic month in the flying saucer
drama—a drama, as we see, by no means conducted, by the
cosmic playwright, according to the famous Aristotelian
unities!—Dr. Irving Langmuir, Nobel prizewinner, and direc-

E

tor of the U.S. Air Force Scientific Advisory Board, advised people to "forget the saucer". The onus of proof was on the true believer, he said. Well, some of us have accepted Dr. Langmuir's challenge, but with no illusions that he, or other hardened sceptics, will agree that we have made out a case. If one has not the will to believe, then vain is—for man or woman—any labour in the direction of accumulating a corpus of evidence.

Another air liner pilot, Captain Willis Sperry (of American Airlines), had an adventure on the night airways, on May 29, 1950. He, too, said he had always been a sceptic about saucers. Here is what he, later, wrote to the U.S. journal, 'Flying':

> "We left Washington at 9.15 that night, bound for Tulsa, Oklahoma. About 30 miles out from Washington, when we were going up to 18,000 feet, my first officer, Gates shouted and pointed: 'Say, look, what's this?' I turned my head and saw coming towards us a brilliant bluish light of fluorescent type. It seemed to me about 25 times as bright as the brightest star. It stopped for about five seconds, and then changed course, passing between us and the full moon, against which it stood out in silhouette, like a torpedo, or submarine, but with no fins or external structure. It seemed streamlined and metallic. I'd say there is no doubt that its spread was far beyond that of a jet 'plane. In fact, the speed was fantastic. We saw it only for a minute. I tried to follow its path by veering my 'plane round. It reversed its direction, and passed out of sight. I called the Washington control tower, but they said they were unable to pick it up on their radarscope. I expected a 'ribbing' from other pilots; but, instead, there have been serious discussions."

Captain Sperry is clearly one who will find it hard to take Langmuir's advice.

There were two thrilling sightings in England, in May 1950:

> A silent thing, like Saturn in his rings, seen at 9.45 a.m., May 7, over Llantarnam, Monmouthshire; pilot of British European Airways saw, high over English Channel, a large silver disc, 20,000 feet up.

In Oregon, U.S.A., a farmer also forgot to take Dr. Langmuir's advice, when he took photographs of an object that flew noiselessly over his farm, and looked like an inverted soup plate. That was on June 12, 1950. On June 21, 1950, several mysterious and unexplained things were reported—one in the Pacific. The latter was a vast cloud of unidentified nature and origin, which meteorologists estimated covered an area of 1,200,000 square miles, and at Wake Island, in mid-Pacific, reached a height of more than 16,000 feet. Geiger counters, used in the Hawaiian Islands, which are more than 2,000 miles south-east of Wake Island, registered no radioactivity, and the scientists were driven back on the hypothesis of a volcanic eruption somewhere, "perhaps at Maunu Loa, in Hawaii".

The second mystery was a disc shooting out blue flames, and roaring over an air base at Oakland, California. Its speed was estimated to be *1,500 miles an hour*! Three U.S. airmen saw it, and said it reverberated like thunder, was circular, and thick in the centre, and tapered at the sides. The same, or a similar object, was sighted *five times* over the U.S. Air Force base at Hamilton, California.

Said a man on the control tower of the air base:

"If it were a shooting star, why did it keep on going, and not fall?"

Yes, why? The answer is that it was very clearly *not* a meteor, or shooting star! Nor even a rocket, or long-range missile.

Now comes what is probably the most remarkable sighting in the year 1950. This weird machine was photographed by the Oregon farmer who saw it, and I draw special notice to the singular protuberance, like a miniature lighthouse with a cross for finial, that is on top of the disc.

Here is the story as I had it from a friend in Oregon:

"Paul Trent is a farmer of the township of Minneville, Oregon. On May 11, 1950, he was out on his farm when he saw, flying in the sky, a strange thing like a very large lid of a dustbin, with a sort of spur on the top of the curved rim over it. He says the thing was shining like burnished silver, was noiseless, and gave off no smoke or vapour. After a few minutes, it went off to the north-

131

west and vanished over the skyline. He saw it late in the evening. At first, it did not move very swiftly. He thought it might be around 30 feet in diameter. It did not rotate."

Now, when the photograph Mr. Trent took is enlarged, one notices on the very tip of the cambered upper rim a singular appendage like a lighthouse, with a lantern gallery. This is probably the nerve centre of the strange machine, and may be used for some sort of purpose like radar-television, or for the transmission and reception of teleaugmentative beams. We can only surmise, of course. That broadminded man, Sir Philip Joubert, Marshal of the British Royal Air Force, was shown this photo, and says that, whatever it is, it is not a picture of a meteor. It is very odd, and he does not care to hazard an opinion as to what the thing may be. To him, it seems machined and a cast structure. He comments, as we all do, on the singular "little stump" on the top of it. "Whatever it is, and wherever it comes from, this disc and the others return somewhere out of the sight of man. I cannot say what its propulsive power may be."

It also seems that a British Overseas Airways pilot saw a strange machine of this type over the Bay of Biscay. He thought it might be a meteorological phenomenon; but, as says Rear Admiral C. P. Thomson, well known in the British Ministry of Information of world war two, flying saucers seen in the U.S.A. cannot so easily be dismissed. It clearly is not a guided missile. *The London Sunday Dispatch* drew to this weird disc the attention of Professor A. M. Low and Mr. A. C. Clarke B.Sc., who is on the council of the British Astronomical Association, and assistant secretary of the British Interplanetary Society.

Professor Low says:

"If beings on another planet are 500 years ahead of us, why should not they already visit us?"

Mr. Clarke wondered if this weird machine, seen and photographed by Paul Trent, the Oregon farmer, came from some extra-terrestrial world.

The flying saucer drama continued in June and August, 1950. We may summarise reports, from June 26 to August 20:

Object with blue centre and red glow, flew very fast and horizontally, 14,000 feet above U.S. air-liner; thirteen globes like soap bubbles seen travelling in opalescent line, with three on flank, and playing in circle, with shrill sound (time 8.45 a.m., at Ocala, Florida); unknown green light passed under 'plane at Oonta, Australia; bright light roused farmer from bed at Geelong, Australia, and he saw seven shining discs rise from horizon and streak at terrific speed, one returning whence it came; unknown object, with hard, brilliant light, seen by airman over Cowes, Isle of Wight; ten-foot long aeroform drove straight at 'plane's propeller, over Springfield, Ohio, was shaped like a sausage, and exploded with "popping sound". This object, trailing yellow light, had been seen earlier that day. The 'plane was not damaged, and did not even feel rocked (time midnight); unknown flares seen two nights off east Australian coast, flashing on and off from 8.30 p.m. until midnight. Ships could not solve the mystery, which was not auroral; 100 strange discs with bright wake, and emitting an organ note, flew over Alpine village, near Lugano, Switzerland; crowds at Portland, Oregon, see 100 flaming objects like cubes and saucers tear across the day sky; vivid ball of light travels horizontally, and explodes after an interval over Miramichi, New Brunswick. (Not a meteorite). (N.B. Several of these phenomena were seen on other August nights, over Miramichi, and one exploded with shattering roar, and then each section exploded in turn! Altitude: 150 to 950 feet); thing like ice-cream cone, speed 1,500 miles an hour, emitting intense blue light, flew thrice over Hamilton Airfield.

The finger of mystery again touched Australia, on 3rd September, 1950.

"Brisbane, Queensland, September 3, 50—There was a clear sky and no wind in western Queensland, when 'things' began to fall. Down floated thousands of them—2 ft. strands of a white sticky substance. each with a white, thumb-sized ball—like sticky cotton wool—on the end. Guesses vary from a new secret weapon to the work of an unknown type of spider."

Mr. H. K. Hotham, of Melbourne, Australia, and gold-prospector of Barry's Reef, Victoria—he is an old friend of mine—sent me a clipping from the *Sun* newspaper, on 16 September 1950. "Can you comment on this?" he asks.

"This", is the paragraph following:

"Lightning killed a record total of 130 Spaniards, in 1949, according to recent statistics. This total brought the number of Spanish deaths from lightning, since 1941, up to 541."

"No," I wrote. "I leave it to the meteorologists, or the astronomers. I've quite enough to worry about over these flying saucers, seen all over the world, from China to Peru, and from the Bering Straits and Alaska to Australia and the Bight of Benin."

The phenomenon is as mysterious as the mysterious fires that broke out in the Spanish mountain town of Laroya, in July 1950, and badly frightened the local people. These fires sprang up without warning, burned bed clothes, grain, straw, and even clothes on women's, children's and men's backs! Scientists investigated, and now believe "that the mystery fires are caused by special magnetic conditions in the ground". This means, of course, that the scientists have no idea what causes these mysterious fires. Similar and even identical phenomena have happened in Paris, France, August 1869; Hudson, Ottawa River, Canada, October 1880; Findlay, Ohio, October 1889; Ayer, New Orleans, May 1890; Rosehall, Falkirk, Scotland. Binbrook Farm, Grimsby, Whitley Bay, Blyth, Butlock Heath, near Southampton, in 1904 and 1905; Manner, Dinapore, India, May 1907; Derby, England, March 1907; Lake Denmark, Dover, N.Y., October 1916; Bladenborough, North Carolina, February 1932.

It may be observed that, in times of turmoil, commotion, and recurrent world crises, inexplicable phenomena, as in our times, may and do occur. They remind *some* of us that scientists do not know and cannot explain *all*, and that this planet of ours is a more mysterious place than many of them are disposed to recognise.

There was no cessation in mysteries in the skies, in September to December 1950 (September 19 to December 12):

Solid object, like a silvery ball, high in the sky for three minutes, over Blackheath, south-east London. It vanished and was followed by another ball, then eighteen more came, all flying north-east, silent, and at great altitude; near Paignton, Devon, flaming object with funnel of fire, high up, flame lessened, and, then, ahead, were seen, one above the other, two blue discs, apparently controlled from the first object; cigar-shaped object, of fantastic speed, and silent, was seen over Ramsey, Isle of Man, while, at Peterhead, Aberdeenshire, an oval disc flashed at terrific speed; poised, stationary, over Bridlington, Yorks, three saucers, which went north-west; over London Airport tarmac, mysterious object of white flame, trailing blue light and emitting high-pitched whine, flew in straight line. High speed and cigarette-shaped; all over south-eastern skies in U.S., a thing like a washing-tub startled people. Airmen chased it over the Mississippi, stating that it looked like two linked globes, one under the other, "and most strange". National Guard pilot went up to 35,000 feet, but had to break off. He said the thing moved erratically, hovered, and flashed off under unseen and intelligent control; sausage-like saucer, with discoidal terminations, something between a barrage-balloon and a submarine, seen gleaming over Barrow-in-Furness. One man said it was 200 feet long and fusiform; unknown circular body, whose underside carried a white light, over Didsbury, Lancs, while Exmoor, Somerset, farmers saw numbers of blue-green saucers jetting flames; two blazing objects sped at amazing speed, at night, from north to south Devon, and at Exmouth, one was seen in two parts with luminous tail. Movement silent and rotary, and came in from Irish Sea; in sunshine, a thing like a dull disc shot from a cloud-belt, 50,000 feet high, and at an amazing speed, over Moorabbin, Australia. Visible 30 seconds; green, large and transparent 'platovolador' circled Carauri, Argentina; blue-silver disc, large as a gasometer, over Selsea Bill, Sussex, at 4.10 p.m.; a fireman on the footplate of a London-Midland express, near Coventry, drew the driver's attention to a terrifically fast brilliant oval object in the sky; bright blue globe shot across sky at Carlisle, at 4 p.m., ascended and vanished. At dusk at Ruspidge, Forest of Dean, things seen flashing on and off lights in the sky; noiseless globes, sparking, long black thing with flaming tail, "four miles long", a sausage with mass of blue light round it, and what looked like "an archery target in sky, throwing off arrow of light", seen in Cornwall, Devon, and Wales. In Tennessee and Arkansas, saucer tracked by radarscope, "helmet-shaped, with glare in centre, about 45 feet in diameter, like a gleaming bowl, upside-down". Speed: 250 miles an hour.

So far, it has been found that earth has one weapon which may be, and actually has been—though the facts have been hushed up by the U.S. Air Force—used to cause one type of flying saucer to crash on the ground! *It is radar, which interrupts their drive.* I have seen a letter from an American flier who wrote:

"Several crashes have been reported after a radar beam has been put on the flying saucers. But if you suppose that any man in our armed services is going to talk about these things, and to tell you what was found when these crashed saucers were examined, you must expect that such a talkative guy is anxious for a court-martial, which he would certainly get, by order of the Pentagon, the headquarters of the U.S. Air Force, in Washington, D.C."

There have been rumours, which no one can confirm, that some of these discs, crashed by radar, were manless, while one was found to have beings inside it. *If so*, it is a secret of the Pentagon, the U.S. Air Force G.H.Q., at Washington, D.C.

On October 17, 1950, came reports of 'blue moons', blue saucers, and violet glows in the skies, which caused many people to worry out the lives of British Air Ministry officials, as to what these mysterious phenomena and apparitions were.

A word or two about this curious phenomenon may be of interest.

These 'blue moons', and even 'blue suns', in some regions, were also seen in Eastern Canada, north-eastern U.S.A., and over the North Atlantic, on Sunday, September 24, 1950, and over four Western European countries, including Great Britain, on September 27th, 1950. Over Ohio, the sky was blood-red, and people were terrified, since such a phenomenon often precedes a hurricane. The theory that the blue moons and suns were caused by particles of atmospheric dust has been ridiculed by scientists. At this time, there also appeared over vast areas of the North Pacific a mysterious cloud. Had these phenomena any connection with gigantic explosions reported on the planet Mars? These explosions, whose origin has never been cleared up—readers will remember their cause and consequences, in the late H. G. Wells's fantasy fiction, 'War of the Worlds'!—happened on January 16, and for five successive nights, on April 1—5, 1950. No one, not even the British Astronomer Royal, or Howard Shapley of Harvard Observatory, has the knowledge that can either prove or disprove such a theory of causation. But it may be noted that the 'blue moons' were seen *eight months after the Martian phenomena.*

I now come to the mystery of the roaring explosions off the coast of Norfolk, on November 19th, 1950, which baffled the Royal Air Force and British Air Ministry. They had no solution to offer. Out at sea, off the quiet family bathing-beaches at Hunstanton, Norfolk, which I strolled round, earlier in September 1950, looking for jet, amber and rocks of a sort seen nowhere else in England, there came, on November 19, 1950, roaring explosions that shook windows and broke ceilings in the town, which stands on cliffs. A municipal official was so startled that he rang up all the local Royal Air Force stations; but they said no 'planes were out, and no practice bombs being dropped in the sea. As the official put down the receiver, more roaring explosions came from out at sea, so he telephoned the Air Ministry, in London, that he was "fed up with the mysterious explosions". They advised him to put it in writing.

May one ask if these mysterious explosions had anything to do with flying saucers exploding and falling into the North Sea? It is not known; but minefields and other submarine explosives of war-time are ruled out. In past years, in the last five decades, as I again remind the reader, there have been reports, from steamers all over the seven seas, that mysterious discs have been seen rising from the sea and ascending in the air! If this is so, do some of these elusive visitants seek the sea-bed for some cooling and jettisoning process?

The question may be asked: "Do professional astronomers ever see flying saucers, or space ships, in the skies, or in space, when they survey the starry heavens with their powerful refracting telescopes?"

As to British professional astronomers, I have no information, nor can I say whether their attitude may be like that of the British naval officer who refrains from logging any encounter with a sea serpent. But, I have one account of two American astronomers, who albeit with caution, reported what they had seen, and, in one case, photographed on eight plates. Mr. Seymour Hess, astronomer at the Lowell Observatory, at Flagstaff, Arizona, says he saw in the sky a bright object, visible to the naked eye, as a disc. It seemed to be powered by some means, and was moving fast against the wind. On February 16, 1950, Dr. C. D. Shane, of the Lick Observatory, Mount Hamilton, Santa Clara County, California, took eight photographic plates of a queer object, that, while it may have been an asteroid, was yet "moving unusually swiftly. I call this celestial phenomenon one of the most unusual objects sighted in the sky for a long time. It happens that I saw it by chance."

One risks the charge that one is a *fantaisiste* when one asks if there are attempts of other planets, unknown, to communicate with the earth; but since the communications cannot possibly be understood, by earth-people, whether they may be, in fact, trying to send messages to entities who are thought by them to have effected landings on the earth?

Who can say?

But consider the singular facts that follow:

From time to time, strange words in unknown tongues, or messages come through the ether, and are received on radio instruments. In the early days of wireless telegraphy, the late Senator Marconi believed that he received, in the course of wireless experiments at Newfoundland, words in some unknown tongue, which, he theorised, might be from Mars. Anyway, whatever these sounds may have been, they had penetrated the Heaviside-Kenealy layer in the stratosphere, but for whose presence, long wave radio would be impossible; since the electro-magnetic impulses would shoot out into space, and not be reflected back towards the earth. Now, according to *El Diario de Nueva York* (a Spanish newspaper published in New York), on January 31, 1950, something peculiar happened in the midnight skies over Madrid, Spain:

"In the last two days, near midnight, intense phosphorescence and the forms of strange lights have been observed at the same time. They have passed through the sky from north to south, and radio receivers have heard, during the occurrence of this phenomenon, words pronounced in an incomprehensible tongue. Popular fancy supposes that these luminous signals may come from the planet, Mars."

I have stated, elsewhere in this book, that, when one is faced with a mystery, it is useful to look round and see if something similar has happened before. Perhaps it has.

On August 2, 1947, the British South American Airways 'plane, 'Lancastrian Star Dust', mysteriously vanished on a flight over the Andes. She was due to land at the airport at Santiago, Chile, at 5.45 p.m. At 5.41 p.m., she sent out a signal stating her time of arrival. But at the end of the message came the word "Stendec," loud and clear, and given out very fast.

The Chilean Air Force operator, at Santiago, queried the word, which he did not understand. He heard it twice repeated by the 'plane. No explanation of this word has ever been found. Nothing further was heard from the 'plane, although calls were sent out. The 'plane never arrived, and, from that day to this, the mystery has never been solved. Searches by ski troops and 'planes were started, and skilled mountaineers and motor cars hunted all over an area of 250 square miles; but in vain. 'Star Dust' carried a crew of five men, and there were six passengers. The pilot, Captain R. J. Cook, had crossed the Andes eight times as second pilot, but this was his first flight as captain. He had been warned at Buenos Aires, and also from London, to take a different route, if bad weather were experienced over the Andes. On the afternoon, when this 'plane vanished, as it seems, in the period of four minutes, a gale of 45 knots was blowing over the Andes, and the El Cristo pass over which he flew was veiled in snow and cloud. At 5 p.m., 41 minutes before the last message sent was received, Cook radioed the Santiago airport stating he was climbing to 24,000 feet. There is no evidence that his 'plane overshot Santiago, and fell into the Pacific. Indeed, as, by that time, the 'plane would have passed from the bad weather zone on the Andes, that possibility seems unlikely.

Aboard the 'Star Dust' airliner, when it mysteriously vanished, was a British King's Messenger on a journey for the British Foreign Office. He had had a hectic career in World War two, and had spent some time in South America. Ex-police superintendent Askew, who was senior security officer at the Foreign Office, and among whose staff was this messenger, says: "There were whispers of sabotage, but nothing was ever found to explain the mystery of the airliner Star Dust which vanished over South America."

Sabotage has become an overworked explanation. It does *not* explain this cryptic radio signal : "Stendec"!

Who twice sent out that mysterious word "Stendec", which the Chilian operator said was so loud and clear and fast? It came right at the end of the message announcing arrival time which, as one sees, was four minutes later. Did 'something' intercept the 'plane? If so, what was it?

Why, too, have there been, in 1947 and 1948, and again in 1949, in the *same* region of the Atlantic, *100 to 500 miles from Bermuda*, mysterious disappearances of one U.S. 'plane, and two British airliners?

In 1947, an American Super Fortress bomber strangely vanished when *100 miles off Bermuda*. Searches by many 'planes and ships did not solve the mystery, which U.S. Air Force officers blamed onto a tremendous current of rising air in a cumulo-nimbus cloud, which, they theorised "disintegrated the great bomber". Something of the same has been theorised about the unsolved disappearance, in March 1950, of the U.S. 'Globemaster' flying the Atlantic to Ireland.

On January 30, 1948, a Tudor airliner, the 'Star Tiger' of the British South American Airways, mysteriously vanished

while flying some *400 miles off Bermuda*. That mystery was
never solved, and no wreckage found. She carried 25 passengers and a crew of six. The court of investigation were baffled
and could hint only at "some external cause". Again, on 18
January 1949, a second Tudor airliner of the same company,
the 'Star Ariel', with 13 passengers and a crew of seven, vanished *200 miles from Bermuda*, on a thousand-mile flight to
Kingston, Jamaica. Many 'planes, naval vessels and merchant
ships fanned all over the area, but failed to solve the mystery.
No wreckage was ever found; but a singular thing happened.

On the first night of the search for the missing British Tudor
IV, 'Star Ariel' liner, two 'planes—one of them a U.S. bomber,
and the other a British airliner of the B.O.A.C. line—independently reported seeing *a strange light on the ocean* in the
area where the 'Star Ariel' vanished.

No raft was found. No float with any light attached and
which might have been launched from the lost airliner. No
wreckage of any sort has ever been reported, as the remains
of the lost airliners, or U.S. bomber.

What was that light? What is the hoodoo in the Bermuda
skies? Has it been recollected that, in 1877, the British Association's Report tells of a mysterious group of lights in the English sky, that travelled slowly, left no train, were visible for
three minutes—as no meteor would be—and "seemed huddled
together like a flock of wild geese, with grace of regularity, and
moving with the same velocity"?

These strange lights, in procession, reappeared on the night
of February 9, 1913, *over Canada*, when Professor Chant, of
Toronto, made many observations of them. Here is a brief
summary of his report in the Journal of the Royal Astronomical Society of Canada (November and December, 1913):

> "A strange spectacle was seen in Canada (Saskatchewan
> and Ontario), the U.S.A. (New York), *at sea, and in Ber-
> muda* ... A luminous body was seen, with a long tail at-
> tached to it. The body grew rapidly larger. Observers dif-
> fer whether this body was single, or in three or four parts,
> with a tail to each. The group, or complex structure,
> moved with a peculiar, majestic deliberation. It disap-
> peared in the distance, and another group emerged from

its place of origin. Onward they moved, at the same deliberate pace, in twos, threes, or fours. A third group, or structure, followed."

Some people, who observed these weird bodies, compared the singular spectacle to a fleet of airships—shall we say *space ships?*—others to battleships, attended by cruisers and destroyers.

One observer, cited in this scientific journal, said:

"There were probably 30 or 32 bodies, and the peculiar thing...was their moving in threes or fours, abreast of each other, and so perfect was their lining up that you would have thought it was an aerial fleet manoeuvring after rigid drilling." (*Note that this was in 1913*).

On that night, in 1913, a procession of unknown objects carrying lights passed in the sky over Toronto, and *were seen in Bermuda,* and also in New York state. They took from three to five minutes to pass, and W. F. Denning, who said he had observed the skies since 1865, and had never seen anything like this phenomenon, gave his impression that: "It looked like an express train lighted at night...lights at the tail, one in front, one in the rear, then a succession of lights at the tail." Sounds were heard from them, and they followed the curvature of the earth, at a relatively low velocity, as no meteorite would do.

Chant said that unknown, but dark objects were seen over Toronto on the afternoon of the day following, but not clearly enough to make out their nature:

"People even said they were airships cruising over the city. They passed from west to east in three groups, and then returned west in more scattered formation, about seven or eight in all."

Strange tongues heard on the radio, when lights are in the sky over Spain. Strange signals when an airliner vanishes, crossing the Andes, a strange light on the sea, in 1949, in the region of the ocean where three 'planes have vanished. Then we have this strange procession of what look like space ships, seen, among other parts of North America, *over the Bermudas and adjacent ocean, in 1913.* What would happen were these mysterious cosmic fleets, exploring our atmosphere, met by an airliner, or modern bomber flying at a great altitude?

Would the encounter be as harmless as, in many cases, in U.S. skies, when strange aerial machines, or discs, were met by airliners, or fighter 'planes, as in 1948-1950? Or would the encounter result in a tragedy, as in the case of Mantell, over Fort Knox airfield, in 1948 when he tried to close with a *"tremendous* flying saucer"?

Again, highly fantastic as it sounds: Did the mysterious word 'Stendec' denote that the lost British airliner, 'Lancastrian Star Dust', was, in that four minutes, while flying very high, caught and gripped by some mysterious anti-gravity force, and her crew and passengers removed, and even her structure and contents? Removed by some space ship of a fleet like that seen over Toronto, New York State, and Bermuda, in the night and day of February 9 and 10, 1913?

Removed bodily by a vast ark-ship—"*a mile long*"—like that seen through a theodolite by a U.S. naval observer in 1949? A new terror of the skies, undreamt of by the late H. G. Wells, and Sir Arthur Conan Doyle!

Who knows? Was the word "Stendec" a code message from some cosmic 'interceptor', announcing his capture to another world than ours?

Who knows, too, whether the secret Intelligences of both the U.S.A. and Great Britain know far more than they will ever admit about interplanetary visits of the recent past?

The Pan-American air liner, 'Constellation', with forty people aboard, was on her way from South Africa to New York, and had left Accra, West Africa, for Monrovia, Liberia, on June 20, 1951. She sent out a signal, at 3 a.m., that she was due at Roberts Field air port, at Monrovia, at 3.15 a.m. She was never again heard of, though French and British 'planes searched the sea. The mystery was never cleared up.

Is there any 'fantastic connection' between these mysterious disappearances of airliners and the following phenomena:

La Nature (Paris, France): M. Adrien Arcelin says he

143

was excavating near the Paleolithic cavern at Solutré, in August 1878, on a clear day, with superb sky, when, suddenly, about three dozen sheets of wrapping paper rose from the ground into the air. A dozen men were nearby, but no one felt any wind. It is singular that the dust on the ground, under and around, was undisturbed. The sheets of paper went on into the sky, up and up.

London Times newspaper: "On September 23, 1875, a fishing vessel was caught by some mysterious force, raised into the air, so far, that, when it fell back, it sank. There was no wind, and other vessels a quarter of a mile away, sent rescuers to the sailors thrown overboard into the sea. There was no wind to move the rescuing ships."

Le Courrier des Ardennes (Belgium) reported that, in 1879, on Easter Sunday, in the Commune Signy-le-Petit, when there was not any trace of wind, from an isolated house the slate roof suddenly shot up into the air, then fell to the ground. The mysterious force disturbed nothing else round the house for 30 feet.

Scientific American: On July 10, 1880, two men of East Kent, Ontario, Canada, were in a field, when they heard a loud report and saw stones shooting upward in the field; yet, at the spot, 16 feet wide, nothing was found to account for it.

There is a singular selectivity about these phenomena, above, that suggests some unseen ray, or controlling force, operating from something very high in the sky.

Now take this:

On December 10, 1881, Walter Powell and two men ascended from Bath, Somerset, England, in the Government balloon, 'Saladin'. The balloon came down at Bridport, Dorset, on the shores of the English Channel. Two got out, but before Powell could do so, the balloon suddenly shot upwards. Neither the balloon nor Powell was seen again; but there came reports that, *before and after the balloon vanished, a strange luminous object had been seen moving in various directions over the other side of the Channel, near Cherbourg, France.* Three days later, three Customs guards, at Laredo, Spain, saw a queer object in the sky, and climbed a mountain to investigate

144

it. They said it shot out sparks and vanished, and was later seen over Bilbao, North Spain. On December 15, 1881, the steamship 'Countess of Aberdeen', was 25 miles off Montrose, when, through binoculars, the captain saw a large lighted object high in the sky, that seemed to increase, then diminish in size. It moved against the wind and was seen for 35 minutes. Walter Powell was a British M.P., and his friends had a steamer sweep the Channel, while a big force of coastguards searched the southern shores of England for wreckage. But all that was found was a thermometer in a bag.

In 1951, although many British newspapers ridiculed observers of flying saucers, and propagated the comfortable illusion that they were just figments and American hallucinations, yet I feel sure that the British Air Ministry and the Royal Air Force secretly built up a secret file on these phenomena, and were far, indeed, from deeming that flying saucers had no reality or material existence.

Here follow some sighting reports (January 11 to March 16):

Yellow star with smoke trail over west and north-west London, and Hertford, where it 'buzzed'; two silvery objects following each other high over Ispwich, Suffolk; railroad signalman at Lodi, Ohio, saw in the sky a thing like a barrel, very high, and making a ninety degrees turn; thing like 300-feet long telephone pole, with brilliant light, appeared in the sky of Wisconsin, with a blue flash, gliding silently, not fast; watching motorists crashed. (*N.B.* This phenomenon was also seen 300 miles from Toronto, and frightened people, who said it was "huge"— 5 a.m., 14 November 1949). Strange thing like a "flat dime", milky-white, hovered over and scanned a U.S. naval weather balloon. It gave three blazing flashes and vanished in sight of aerial photo pilots (Ohio); Swedish jet squadron chased luminous object, noiseless, and hovering at 40,000 feet (Swedish Air Ministry did not release the photos of it); British airliner 'Lodestar' sees for seventeen minutes strange space ship, motionless above 19,710 feet Mt. Kilimanjaro. It was bullet-shaped, metallic, and vertically marked on sides. Watched through binoculars, it ascended to height of 40,000 feet, again rose vertically, and with no sound. Large 'fin' at rear, radiant in colour, and whirled at speeds so immense that no clear motion picture was possible. Flying ball, 4 feet wide, *landed* and took off at Hogansburg, N.Y.; cigar-shaped, bullet-nosed object, type unknown, spurting flames from rear, hung over Delhi, for 25 minutes. Jets could not get near it, its speed being immense, and something thick and white coming from it; speed, 2,000 miles an hour. It vanished in seconds. Same aeroform seen at Allahabad, and again over Delhi. Climbed at tremendous speed, left wake of swirling clouds, visible for 90 minutes. Tail fluorescent in darkness. It came from north and vanished east.

A weird occurrence happened on April 17, 1951, which puzzled the U.S. press and U.S. Air Force, and for which I suggest a solution of a fantastic mystery. Opposite to a farmhouse near Georgetown, S.C., is an untenanted house. At 2 p.m., Mrs. E. Harrelson, at work in her kitchen in the farmhouse, heard, overhead, a noice like a 'plane. Then came a terrific crash. She rushed out to see what had happened. The house over the way had been almost unroofed, and timbers, shingles and bricks were scattered widely around. Yet, there was no 'plane in the sky! So loud was the sound of the crash that it was heard half a mile away. It is improbable that any terrestrial 'plane could have crashed into the house without itself being wrecked. U.S. Officers at the local (Shaw) air force base called the story "fantastic". Yes, so are the types of *invisible* flying saucers. Anyway, the house is minus most of its roof, whatever was the nature of the force applied by the unseen visitant!

I hope my reader may forgive me if, once more, I stress the sentimental foolishness of certain mystics who are sure that flying saucers are *always* inoffensive in relation to our own planet. And I suggest that with this mysterious incident that happened close to the South Carolina farmhouse, in April 1951, one compares what happened, only a few miles from where I am now writing, on November 27, 1953:

"From the sky over Shorne, near Gravesend, Kent, there came a sudden blinding light, at a time when some mysterious aeroform was overhead. Two explosions followed, causing a 12-feet trench to cave in and suffocate a labourer, John J. Sullivan; while, at Idleigh, not far away,

146

coals were blown from a grate, and at Meopham, doors of a farmhouse were blown open and a ceiling collapsed."

I am far, indeed, from supposing that the Air Ministry takes the facile view that this was just caused by a jet 'plane passing the sonic barrier. They need only refer to similar incidents in their secret files, and they may align this incident with that of the mysterious fires on farms on the Cotswold Hills, and in Essex, in August and November 1953.

Let us proceed with the 1951 sightings (May 22 to August 25):

> Adventure of pilot on airway to Chicago, from Phoe-nix: South-west of Dodge City, Kansas, strange blue star-like thing dashed around his 'plane, at 500 miles an hour, reaching 2,000 miles an hour (!), moved up and down, to and fro, but did not halt. Repeated the antics over and over for 20 minutes, vanishing south-west at 3.15 a.m. On that day, fifty people at Rainy Lake, Minn., saw a crystal ball in sky dart like a humming-bird, hover like a helicopter over the lake, shoot up into a cloud, where it was joined by a similar aeroform, remaining motionless for 15 minutes; thirty glowing objects fanned out in east-ern quadrant of sky, over aviation plant at Downey, Calif., did sharp 90 degrees turn in vertical and undulating for-mation, like tuning-fork on edge. Each object took 25 seconds to cross horizon in arc of 90 degrees, then did another turn and vanished west. Pilot estimated their speed at 1,700 miles an hour, and each emitted an intense electric blue light. Moving light over Maquota, Iowa, 10.20 p.m., turned red, and was joined by another object with white light, and abruptly vanished. Two saucers took off in blinding flash of light, in broad day, over Coggan, near Cedar Rapids. U.S. Commercial Line pilots reported that discs follow their liners. An American (U.S. Air Force) pilot says that a strange oval disc suddenly closed in from ahead on his F.51 fighter 'plane, narrowly missed his propeller, shot right under his fuselage, and was joined 15 seconds later by another disc, which also followed his 'plane, for 15 minutes. Crystal balls appear, again, like humming-birds, at International Falls, Minn., shoot up at immense speed, and are joined in a cloud by another ball. Computed that no human being could sur-vive the terrific gravity forces involved in the tremendous

147

acceleration of these marvellous aeroforms. Crescent formation of lights cross sky, at 9.10 p.m., in Texas, and
are joined by a similar formation. The cosmic fleet were
a mile high, had speeds of 18,000 miles an hour (*five
miles a second!*), and their diameters were *two miles*. No
shock waves reached the ground.

Formations of unknown bodies in the sky have been seen
before the appearance of these "Lubbock crescentiform squadrons". For example, in 1877, the British Association for the
Advancement of science reported:

"What seemed like a group of meteors travelled with
remarkable slowness" (not the characteristic of meteors),
"and were in sight for about three minutes. They left no
train, and seemed huddled together like a flock of wild
geese, moving with the same velocity and grace of regularity."

Common observation is that wild geese and ducks fly in V
formation.

In the evening of July 30, 1880, a large spherical light and
two smaller ones moved along a ravine near St. Petersburg
(now Leningrad, U.S.S.R), were seen for three minutes, and
vanished without noise. Says the British scientific journal,
'Nature':

"In 1893, during the recent winter cruise of 'H.M.S.
Caroline', a curious phenomenon was seen. The officer of
the watch reported seeing unusual lights, sometimes in a
mass, at others, spread out in an irregular line. They
bore north, until he lost sight of them at midnight....
These globes of fire altered their formation... now in a
massed group with an outlying light, then the isolated
one would disappear, and the others would take the form
of a *crescent of diamonds*."

Charles Fort adds ("Book of the Damned"), that Capt. Nor-
cock of 'H.M.S. Caroline' said the ship was between Shanghai
and Japan, at 10 p.m., on 24 February 1893, and that the
strange lights seemed to be between his ship and a mountain,
which was 6,000 feet high. The lights were globular and visible

for two hours. He saw them again next night:

> "They were lights that cast a reflection. There was a glare upon the horizon under them. A telescope brought out a few details, but they were reddish, and seemed to emit a faint smoke. This time, they were visible for 7½ hours. In the same locality, at this time, Capt. Castle of 'H.M.S. Leander' saw these strange lights. He altered course to come towards them, and the lights fled before him. They moved higher in the sky."

Considering all these strange spectacles in the sky, one might wonder if our 'influence benign on planets pale' is appreciated by these mysterious squadrons of the cosmos? Do 'they' esteem us as good neighbours with whom they might wish to have a pow-wow? My reader, with his and her memories of two world wars, with a third one looming in the offing—let us hope this *is* one of Dr. Menzel's 'looming mirages'!—may answer the question in his or her own fashion.

What caused eight U.S. jet fighters to crash within minutes of each other over Dayton, Ohio, in June 1951? It will be recalled by my readers that Dayton is the location of the U.S. Air Force Project Saucer inquiry of 1948-1950.

> "Senior Officers of the U.S. Air Force, led by Lieut-Gen. Le May, Chief of the Strategic Air Command, face a riddle in trying to find why eight jet fighters crashed within minutes of each other over Dayton, Ohio. Sabotage is thought possible. Three pilots were killed. Others saved themselves by crash-landing their 'planes, or using parachutes. The 'planes were part of a formation of seventy-one, on manoeuvres. The crashes happened 10 minutes after take-off. A surviving pilot said: 'My engine exploded after I had gone through a thunder-cloud. I do *not* think the crashes were caused by the weather.'"

Then what was the cause? Did any of the court of inquiry recall the crash which killed Pilot Mantell, in 1948? In another chapter of this book I have noted how, in the 18th century, strange things like balls of light, and *not* meteors, were seen zooming in and out of thunderclouds, and under some mysterious control.

149

An American airwoman, reading an article by the author of this book, in the 'U.S. magazine, 'Fate', wrote to me that she was attached to the Hamilton Air Force Base, Calif., (which, as she did not say, happens to be associated with a mysterious air crash when saucers were seen around there). She told me:

> "On Sunday, January 7, 1951, I saw something that I had never understood till I saw your article in 'Fate'. I was flying in a C.46, somewhere over a central mid-western state, when one of the officers drew my attention to a weird thing in the sky. I looked, and saw a reddish light off in the distance. It wasn't another 'plane, for there was only one light, and it didn't blink as a 'plane's will. Clouds beneath us blanked out any sight of the earth; so it didn't come from the ground. Our altitude was 4,000 feet at the time. I have been curious over that happening for months, now. On reading your article, I am inclined to think that what I saw and what you wrote about, are one and the same."

On 21 November 1951, saucers again appeared when guided missiles were being flown:

> Two engineers, watching test flights, in the Nevada desert, were startled by the sudden appearance of 'two-day stars', spiralling round a guided missile. They appeared to examine it, and then vanish. About this time, far across the Rockies, one Guy Marquand with two friends, was in a car on a road in the hills near Riverside, Calif., where, close by, mysterious explosions have occurred in orange groves. On a sudden, a thing like 'flying cap' flew overhead, veered round, and flew back. Marquand photographed the aeroform. I have seen the picture, which is blurred, but suggests a very large bird, like the roc in the 'Arabian Night'. On the same day, an unidentified burning object fell into the Pacific, off the coast of California.

In 1952, there was a veritable rash of saucers in the skies all over the world, including the war front in Korea. Over Washington, D.C., and the Capitol, in July, they came in squadrons, bouncing and vanishing and reappearing for five hours in one night. They did violent turns of 90 degrees, far beyond the powers of any terrestrial 'plane, in the conditions. It is amazing that they seemed to have knowledge of the approach of interceptor jet 'planes long before the jets were in sight of them. Radar beams they invariably evaded, as if fearing a crash. The images on the radarscope in the C.A.A. traffic control centre proved them to be material objects with solidity, and their speed was on occasions computed at *four miles a second!*

I summarise some of the sightings and allied phenomena, and may note that the peak was in September 1952.

A noiseless, vapourless object (May 7) flew in a semi-circle over Brazilian woods and headed out over the S. Atlantic from Ilha das Amores, where two startled news-paper cameramen photographed it; from which it appears that the mysterious object had discoidal surfaces and a domed cupola (also seen over the U.S.A.), and probably the brain of the aeroform. Colour blue, flight sideways and endwise at amazing speed. A strange aeroform over Denham, Bucks, close to U.S. and British airdromes, was seen in September to eject discs which flew off in opposite directions. On the same day (September 20), a Swedish ex-air pilot saw something like a "weird snow-plough, very high in sky, smoke bubbling from its rear, drop what looked like a blue-green shimmering plate, which changed course and vanished as fast as the *mother-ship*, in opposite direction". A thing like a "swinging pendulum" chased a British Meteor jet, about to land at Top-cliffe R.A.F. base, Yorks; it shot off at amazing speed. Wardens and prisoners at Osborne prison colony, Conn., U.S., saw, high in sky, a "top" fall with a roar, black smoke jetting from it, twice a 'plane's size. It righted itself and whizzed at vertiginous speed. Texas State Fair offers £18,000 to anyone who will deliver to it a flying saucer from space. The Norwegian Air Force reported that a saucer had been seen landing in Spitzbergen. Los Angeles Home Show offers one million dollars for a genuine space-man. Shining oval disc seen travelling at "incredible speed" over Newlyn, Cornwall. Kikuyu cattle-thieves and Mau Mau men see saucers, and South Africans see strange discs over their veldts. A brilliant spot of light dropped vertically, then stopped high over Centerville, Va., and, after, ascended in a blue flame; was noiseless. A veteran U.S. Air Force pilot complains that his F.51 fighter 'plane was repeatedly attacked by a saucer, near Cleveland, Ohio. Culver City, Calif., sees a saucer split in two, each section flying independently.

It has also been several times remarked by observers in the U.S.A., in 1952 and 1953, that some types of the flying saucers follow a curious pattern in flight. These objects rise slowly and vertically from the surface of the earth, then move for a short way in a horizontal line, again rise vertically, follow the same horizontal path, and, in a series of steps, reach a desired altitude, and finally accelerate in a tremendous burst of speed. They can also change course at very sharp angles, at immense speeds.

In another case, they may dive at great speed from a great altitude, as witnessed in the last week of July 1953, in Tasmania, by the wife of a civilian airplane pilot, and her three children, who saw a strange grey object dive from a great altitude at very great speed. It then slowly drifted over Burnie, "and, at 800 feet high, was spinning slowly, when it opened out like a big parachute".

More than once in the war theatre over Korea, mysterious aeroforms have been seen that even the field Intelligence sections felt sure were not Russian or Chinese. In one case in the night of January 29, 1952, the crew of a Superfortress bomber on night patrol were frightened:

"A strange disc kept pace with us, when we were flying at 150 miles per hour; rotating, orange colour, kept far aloft on a parallel course with us. It had a rotating rim." ...*Another report*: "Over Sunchon, a revolving globe tagged us for half-a-mile. It vanished aloft." *Gardiner's Bay* saw two objects strike the water with tremendous force, off the ship's port bow, while she was then steaming up the channel from Inchon. Two huge columns of water rose to about 100 feet high at the point of contact. No aircraft could be sighted by radar, or visually overhead, although the ceiling was unlimited. Identification remains a great mystery.

In 1953, strange arrow-head objects have been seen in the

skies in Oklahoma and Texas, and one of these objects was
so brilliant that it lit up a fog at Aston Ingham, in Hereford-
shire, England. Over Brunei oil field in Borneo, a rotating
object, like a pendulum, hovered and then flew off at an
amazing speed; cigar-shaped objects of unknown type have
been repeatedly seen over towns in Ontario; while mysterious
clusters of rotating green, red and white lights hung motionless over N. Japan and the Kurile Islands, and vanished at an
immense speed when U.S. air pilots tried to intercept them.

What looks like a *new type* of saucer twice crossed the path
of Captain B. L. Jones, pilot of a machine of the Australian
Northern Airways line, at 6.8 p.m. on May 17, 1953. He was
flying over Queensland. He said:

> "It appeared to have a glass dome brightly illuminated,
> and beamed a dazzling light on to the aerodrome below.
> It was noiseless, manoeuvred round my 'plane, and twice
> crossed my path. Speed very high. An aircraft control
> tower check-up showed no other 'plane near. Nine hours
> later, a radio operator saw it over the Pacific, ascending
> at great velocity." At Brisbane, observers said the object
> was crescentiform and shone brilliantly.

In November and December 1953, mysterious events in the
air strongly suggest a mystery and that England is being given
a very wide survey by our unseen and seen visitants!

I summarise, as before, incidents occurring between June 1,
1953 and December, all over the world, including the British
Isles:

> The Australian Flying Saucer Investigation Committee
> had so many reports that it inquired into eighteen sight-
> ings of unknown luminous discs. Pan-American airliner,
> over Chesapeake Bay, was startled when eight strange
> discs, luminous, in echelon formation, flew under its keel,
> and shot up to 8,000 feet in seconds. Dimensions: 15 feet
> thick and 100 feet in diameter, solid bodies with intense
> amber light, under intelligent control, and flashed lights
> on and off, possibly related to speed-variability. Speed:
> *five miles a second*. No terrestrial metal or man could en-
> dure the terrific stresses. Dr. F. Zwicky, astro-physicist,
> of Californian Institute of Technology, wants someone to

put up $10,000, in order to fire projectiles, of revolver-bullet size, at the moon, from the Sahara Desert. Things like vast tadpoles dive at each other, then vanish north, over Shiloh, Ohio. Small cloud-like objects go round in a circle in sky over Pittsburg, Penn. A French general startled by a turret-shaped object, flying at immense speed, past his 'plane, over a military airfield near Paris. Black-grey, and barely missed his wing-tips. B.E.A. pilot sees strange oval object, motionless, high over London, when he was *en route* for Paris. Saucer, seen over Norwich, starts the B.B.C. T.V. into activity; was shaped like a dome, and emitting light at the top. This incident rouses hilarity in the House of Commons, and something like a sneer from the Parliamentary Secretary for Air, who alleges that two balloons had escaped. Radioactive clouds detected over Paris. Radar team track saucer over Cape Town Peninsula, say it flew at 1,278 miles an hour and made runs from 5,000 to 15,000 feet up but was not visually to be seen. British War Office have report that radar teams detect saucer over London, size of very large bomber, 70,000 feet up. Over Lee Green, S.E., military radar detects saucer, which through sighting telescope is seen to be circular, white object, visible ten minutes, and moving slowly away. R.A.F. pilots over Kent see strange bright light, speed fantastic, object called "very strange", height 20,000 feet. British Air Ministry admits that five per cent of sightings have beaten experts. Ottawa sets up laboratory to investigate saucer phenomena. Professor F. Zwicky, of Los Angeles, designs a mortar to bombard the moon. Large metallic spherical object seen in blue sky at Newton-le-Willows, Lancs. Twice, a luminous disc radiating light is seen over and near Canvey Island, Essex—"Only radio-sonde balloons" (Air Ministry). U.S. Air Force again says it has flying saucer cameras. Fiery objects in sky over Southend, Essex, frighten people. On horizontal course, and unlike meteorites; while 'planes sent up, say object was brilliant blue-red, with large round end, and *hovered*. One end, like two fluorescent tubes broke away from circular part.

AUTHOR'S NOTE: In November, 1950, the month when I had seen a mysterious aeroform over my house at Bexleyheath, Kent, I ran into Mr. Clement Attlee, then Prime Minister. Along with my boy, Martin, I was, on a snowy day, seeking a footpath from Chequers, the Buckinghamshire manor given to the nation by the late Lord Lee of Fareham, across to Wendover. Attlee reminded me that I was on 'private ground'. Next day, I wrote to him at Chequers and inquired why his colleague at the Air Ministry had ignored my request for some information on whether it was true, as I had been told, that, in 1944, British R.A.F. pilots, on war missions in the Rhine Area, had seen mysterious aeroforms of the type called by the Americans 'foo fighters'. Attlee did not even trouble to acknowledge my letter. Now, exactly three years later, we are told that the Air Ministry and the Royal Air Force have had, in secret existence for at least four years past, files relating to the mystery of many R.A.F. reports on flying saucers seen in England. One well known London newspaper has even quoted a high official in the Air Ministry as saying that it is believed, by *some* in the Air Ministry, that unidentified aeroforms may be of interplanetary origin!

CHAPTER VIII.

FLYING SAUCERS OF
OTHER DAYS

Behind the singular phenomena, crudely called the 'flying saucers', stands a still unresolved problem: Is our earth the only planet in the solar system that is inhabited by sentient beings?

The thoughts of the ordinary man and woman, if not those of the astro-physicist and the professional astronomer, at once go out to the old red star, the planet Mars, whose redness probably indicates an age in evolution much ahead of that of the earth.

There are curious passages in old English chronicles, written in mediaeval Latin, and in Latin incunabula, or books printed before the year 1500 A.D., which suggest that *our earth may have been under observation by extra-terrestrial visitants for some 1250 years past*. And reports and records as well as astronomical ephemerides of the days of the old astronomers and mathematicians, such as Herschel, Kepler and Edmund Halley, and reports made to learned journals of the 17th and 18th centuries, by scientists of those days, living in the British Isles, or France, Germany, or Holland and Italy may also purport *that other planets than Mars* may, also, long ago have *solved the problem of interplanetary travel*.

At the moment, we cannot prove or disprove such theories, or assert that cosmic visitants from planets belonging to systems outside that of our own sun, and far away in space, have, or have not visited our own planet. Short of an actual interplanetary trip made from this earth, or an actual terrestrial landing on the moon, it is not easy to see how such a tremendous riddle can be solved.

The other possible solution would be contact with, or capture of a machine with extra-terrestrial visitants aboard, which has ventured into our own atmosphere. Such a possibility seems very unlikely, having regard to differential gravitational forces, and the elusiveness of flying saucers.

Stories of entities from other planets landing in America and Western Europe, in the years 1949 to 1952, are still in the category of 'believe it or not'. One, at least, is an admitted hoax.

Those who believed that President Truman and the chiefs of the U.S. Navy and War and Defence departments were merely concealing the truth—the author of this book believes they spoke the truth—when they emphatically disowned any connection of the flying saucers with secret experimental devices for offensive or defensive war, may care to glance at the curious historical data, set out below in this chapter. These data considerably broaden the perspective and take it right out of the light of our own day into the far past. It will be seen, indeed, that these weird phenomena range far down the vistas of time into the illimitable past of our earth. They raise the question again: *Is* there life on other planets, or on planets outside our solar system; for after all, is not our system but one of millions of others in an illimitable universe, literally worlds without end?

In the last resort, the riddle may be reduced not so much to a question of pressures and relative gravitational forces as to the existence of air or water. It is difficult, or impossible, to see how beings with the brain and intellect of men, if not the form of human beings, as we know them in our own planet, could exist without these two essentials for chemico-physical and biotic existence (But see Chapter 10, pp. 228-9). *A priori*, it would seem that, unless the accident of life on *one* cooling star—that of our own earth—is unique, and has never been and never will be repeated in the comparatively infinite universe, it may not be unreasonable to suppose that, where air and water exist, or where water can be synthetised, and the conditions are not too hot, or too cold, life and intelligence may have arisen on, say, Mars or Venus. The fashionable theory is that our own solar system originated in the million to one cosmic chance of a collision of our proto-sun with some other vast wandering star, torn from its cosmic moorings, or

158

orbital path in space. Either that, or its grazing with the gaseous, incandescent, chemi-metallic envelope of our sun, caused a titanic splitting and centrifugal dispersion, resulting in a sort of vast Catherine Wheel explosion, that threw off the planets circling our sun and born of its gaseous body.

May be, there *is* life on some other planet; for, how otherwise, shall we explain, what may not necessarily be total legend and myth in the strange stories, of ancient South American prehistory, about fire falling from the sky, seemingly by design and not accident, and not as the incalculable explosions of great meteorites, aerolites, comets, or planetoids, upon ancient South American cities?

There is the very ancient Peruvian tradition of giants who landed near what is now Puerto Viejo. "From the knee down they were as tall as a tall man". Inland, they built great stone houses, and sank splendid stone-lined wells that yielded pure, ice-cold water thousands of years later, in the days of the Spanish conquest, in A.D. 1545. One day, when they were engaged in unnatural amours—for they had no women with them, and the native women of old Perú were too small for their lusts—fire from the skies suddenly fell on them in the market place. Was this falling of fire merely the cosmic accident of the fall of great aerolites, fireballs, or meteorites, which the naïve myths have garbled, or was it from a space ship which had hove in sight?

Perhaps, what is more to the point is the remarkable discovery made in 1941, and investigated up to 1946. It was made in the dunes and sandy deserts along the Rio Grande, in South Perú. Here, in an area of forty-two miles long and nine miles wide have been found what looks like a vast aerodrome, astronomical observatory and centre of some solar or planetary cultus combined. On the desert floor are dead straight lines ranging for many miles in parallels, made by removing the pebbles and piling them up in ridges. Some of them seem to be solstitial lines, and there are remarkable figures of a bird, 400 feet long, a spider, or it might be an octopus (for it has eight arms), plants, serpents, animal heads, spirals and geometrical figures. They are thousands of years old. Close by, runs the Pan Pacific highway, and it was the intention of the Government of Perú to build irrigation works which would wholly or partially obliterate these very ancient remains. The place is called the mesa de Nasca.

There are remains of ancient stone buildings that may have been observatories, and there are long processional roads and avenues. It has been theorised that these amazing monuments may be associated with lunar and solar cults, or with the periodicity of Venus, Jupiter, Mercury and the Pleiades.

But one enigmatic glyph is particularly striking. It is half a mile long, points about due geographical north, and resembles a long, straight rod round which are wound spirals, whose amplitude rises to a peak and then symmetrically decreases, much like a graph on a clock-work, or electrical recording instrument. It ends in a series of concentric circles of the whorled type, very like the winder on a fisherman's rod. One suggestive feature characterises the roads, lines and glyphs in this vast enclosure: they are or were *visible only from the air*, and, indeed, are not visible in all lights. They were found by a pilot of a 'plane passing over the mesa in a run to the north. They raise a startling and sensational query: were they not merely signals to the planets, or the sun, but *indications to an interplanetary space ship where to land*?

The old Irish manuscripts have some very singular and quite unexplained references to 'ships seen in the air', and called 'demon ships'.

The *Speculum Regali in Konungs-Skuggsja*, as also the *Reliquae Antiquae* tell queer stories of the visit of 'demon ships' over the skies of old Ireland. In the *Speculum Regali*, the story, related to the dim and shadowy past of old Eire's heroes and fighting kings, is as follows:

"There happened in the borough of Cloera, one Sunday, while the people were at Mass, a marvel. In this town is a church to the memory of St. Kinarus (Ciaran?). It befell that an anchor was dropped from the sky, with a rope attached to it, and one of the flukes caught in the arch above the church door. The people rushed out of the church and saw in the sky a ship with men on board, floating before the anchor-cable, and they saw a man leap overboard and jump down to the anchor, as if to release it. He looked as if he were swimming in water. The folk rushed up and tried to seize him; but the bishop forbade the people to hold the man, for it might kill him, he said. The man was freed, and hurried up to the ship, where the crew cut the rope and the ship sailed away out of sight. But the anchor is in the church, and has been ever since, as a testimony."

This 'demon ship' is also mentioned in Nennius, an Irish chronologist, who lived around 212 or 213 A.D. He says it happened when Congolash was at the fair of Teltown (Tailtin), in Co. Meath.

This version is told in the Irish *Mirabilia* (Wonders), cited by the well known Celtic scholar, the late Kuno Meyer (in his *Eriu*); but he dates Congalach, "son of Maelmithig", as living around A.D. 956. From the "ship, sailing in the air", one of the crew "cast down a dart at a salmon; but the dart fell down in the presence of the gathering, and a man came out of the ship to seize the end of the dart from above, which a man on the ground caught from below. The man above said: 'I am being drowned!' 'Let him go,' said Congalach, and he is let go up and goes from them swimming."

In the 'Book of Leinster', there are said to have been *three ships in the air*, seen from the fair at Teltown, when King Domnall mac Murchada was at the fair. (This would be around A.D. 763). In the 'Annals', one reads:

"*Navies in aerae uisse sunt* (ships in the air are seen)".

In a Paris MS. in mediaeval Latin, we read the following story of the 'Irish demon ships', which ends in the middle of a line:

"The King was at the spectacle (*fuit in theatro*) of the Scots (or Irish: *Scotorum*) at a certain time, in a crowd of many sorts of men, with soldiers in beautiful array, when, behold, he suddenly saw sailing in the air a ship from which one cast down a spear at a fish. It fell in the earth, and the same one, swimming, drew it back. The

F

161

same about to hear..." *(Here the manuscript suddenly stops short).*

These discrepancies, or uncertainties, about the date of the alleged spectacle of 'demon ships in the air' are almost as curious at the story.

Another variant of the Irish legend of sky ships—and the old Irish are the nearest to the root stock of the Celts—is that of the 'Roth Ramrach', or 'Rowing Wheel'. It is said to have 1,000 'beds' and 1,000 men in each 'bed'. It made sail over land and sea, till it was wrecked by the magic pillar stone of Cnamchoill, an ancient wood near Tipperary. The 'Rowing Wheel' is said to have been made by Simon Magus. Simon Magus was the magician who had the misfortune to be double-crossed by St. Peter, in a contest of levitatory flight in the air through a window, and he made the 'wheel' with the help of two Irish students of Druidism, Mogh Ruith, the arch-duke of Erinn, and Ruith's daughter. The 'wheel' could sail in the air—and it is certainly strange that some of the strange forms of flying saucers, seen by seamen in the 19th century, in the Arabian Sea and Indian Ocean, have been in the form of a rolling wheel. The Druid and his daughter, named Tlachtga, carried the remains of the 'Rowing Wheel' from the continent of Europe to Ireland. It was in two sections, made of rock (*sic*), and one piece she set up near Rathcoole, or Raith Chumhaill, Co. Dublin. These rocks, or pillars, were said to have the power of striking with blindness all who looked at them, and with death any who touched them. It was said by the old Irish saint Colum of Cille that the 'Rowing Wheel' would pass with destructive power all over Europe, because a "student of every nation was at Simon Magus's school".

Just what is at the source of this curious legend—a memory of some sort of space ship, or saucer of other days—no one can say.

Another story is that, in A.D. 1211, "a ship in the clouds" was seen to drop an anchor whose flukes caught in a churchyard at Gravesend, Kent. The cable was, it is said, seen to rise into the clouds. Seamen's voices were heard, and a man slid down the cable and tried to free the anchor, but he could not breathe. The cable was cut, and the ship sailed away, leaving behind the anchor, from which a blacksmith beat out ornaments for a lectern. Bristol also has a legend of a sky ship and sailor who dropped his knife from it on to the roof of a house. (*Vide* Gervase of Tilbury. *Chron.*)

In 1865, the Proceedings of the Royal Irish Academy record, of August 21:

> "This year, on August 21, there fell at Cashel, Tipperary, South Ireland, a disc of marked stone. It came from the sky, and was formed as a wedge. On the black crust of the meteorite were marked lines, as perfectly formed as if they had been made by a rule(r)."

A similar phenomenon happened in France:

> *Comptes Rendus:* "On June 20, 1887, a small stone vessel fell from the sky at Tarbes, France. The stone was 5 mm. thick. It had been cut and shaped by means similar to human hands."

My extensive researches of the historical end of this tremendous problem of the second decade of our 20th century have revealed singular data, which may be held to give something more than slender support to the apparently fantastic theory that, as far back as B.C. 214, mysterious cosmic visitants were even then watching our earth, *and entered its atmosphere!*

This evidence is derived from various sources, both ancient and modern. They include Greek and Latin poets and historians; the old monks who chronicled the events of their own and other days on parchment rolls in the scriptoriums of English abbeys; the annalists and encyclopaedists of the Renaissance; the archivists of the British Royal Society, founded in 1662; the magazines and newspapers of the English 18th century; antiquarians and period historians of England, France and Germany; and modern scientists and meteorologists of the 19th and 20th centuries.

I have carefully sifted a vast amount of evidence and data, and have made due allowance for any phenomena that may be deemed lunar and solar eclipses, comets, meteorites, bolides, mock suns (*parhelia*) and mock moons (*paraselenae*), or auroral displays, and may have been confused with other and different things by mediaeval historians, or classic Greek and Roman writers; because the correct understanding of the nature of such astronomical phenomena was not to be expected in their faraway times. Prodigies and 'miraculous' appearances of all sorts attracted the attention of the learned Latinists and Hellenists of the Renaissance; but, as one might expect, their interpretations were usually coloured and biased by their religious opinions and their notions of the origin of the cosmos.

It must not be assumed, however, that the ancient Greeks and Romans were destitute of the spirit of scientific curiosity, or lacked powers of observation. True, experimental science with its combination of induction and deduction, and the use of apparatus does not go much farther back than the 17th century; but modern scientists and laboratory workers are little given to exploring, except with some contempt and derision, the history of science in the days of old Greece and Rome. Often, the field is left to the compiler of meteorological annals; but even he stops short at the middle ages, or, if he does not, he glances in a very conservative spirit at what is recorded, and brushes off as "probably mythical" what he cannot interpret as misinterpretation of natural phenomena.

Another thing is that very few scientific specialists have any knowledge of Greek or Latin. If, however, there happens to be a modern translation of some Latin or Greek classic work in old black-letter, or in incunabula hard on the eyes, it is human to suppose that he will leave it severely alone.

The earliest Roman annalist who recorded strange facts of often startling nature, which frequently bear on the mystery of the 'flying saucers', or probable interplanetary visitants, was one, Julius Obsequens. He is believed to have lived in the fourth century A.D., before the reign of the Roman emperor, Honorius. Neither his native country, nor the precise date when he was born and died is known, but, as he drew on certain lost books and annals of Roman historians, and especially of Titus Livius, it has been supposed that Julius

Obsequens was not a Christianised, but a pagan, late Roman writer. He wrote the *Prodigia*.

It is amazing to note, that, among the strange natural occurrences and phenomena of all sorts which he records—some of them of paranormal and parapsychological character—is the appearance of what is highly suggestive of a spherical type of flying saucer in *B.C. 90*, over the Roman township of Spoletum, or Spoletium, in Umbria, some 65 miles north of Rome.

He records:

> "Whilst Libius Troso (Livius Drusus?) promulgated the laws at the beginning of the Italian wars, a globe of fire, at sunrise, appeared in the sky with terrific noise, and burning in the north ... In the territory of Spoletum, a globe of fire, golden in colour, fell to the earth from the sky, and was seen to gyrate ... It became greater in size, was seen to rise from the earth, was borne east, and obscured the disc of the sun with its magnitude (*aurea globis ad terram devolutus, e terra ad orientem ferri visus, magnitudinem solis obtexit*)

Let us glance at other strange phenomena, in the skies, recorded by this old Roman:

> *B.C. 222:* "When C. Quintius Flaminius and P. Furius Philon were consuls ... at Ariminum (Rimini, on the Adriatic), there shone a great light, like day, at midnight, when three moons appeared in quarters of the sky distant from each other." (May, or may not have been aurorae and paraselenae. *Au.*)

> *B.C. 216:* "Things like ships were seen in the sky, over Italy ... In Sardinia, a knight was making his rounds, inspecting the posts guarding the rampart, when a stick in his hands burst into flames. The same thing happened to Roman soldiers in Sicily who saw their javelins flame and burn in their hands. River banks and shores shone with many flames ... the circumference of the sun seemed diminished ... At Arpi (180 Roman miles, east of Rome, in Apulia), a *round shield* was seen in the sky. The moon fought with the sun." (Phenomena like St. Elmo's lights; but the apparent

diminution of the sun's disc is recorded several times, at intervals of years B.C. The *round shield* may well have been a flying saucer). "At Antium," (a very old city on the coast, some 45 miles from Ostium) "stalks, coloured like blood, fell into a harvester's basket.. At Faleris, in Etruria, the sky split into two parts... At Capua, the sky was all on fire, and one saw figures like ships. (Cn. Servilius Geminus and C. Quintius Flaminius II were consuls)."

B.C. *214:* "The sea threw out flames near Sinuessam". (A maritime town, south of Rome, in Campania. As the old Romans were well acquainted with vulcanism, was this phenomenon caused by *something* that had fallen from the sky into the sea?)

B.C. *213:* "At Hadria," (Gulf of Venice), "the strange spectacle of men with white clothing was seen in the sky. They seemed to stand round an altar, and were robed in white."

B.C. *209:* "When M. Valerius Levinus II, and M. Claudius Marcellus IV, were consuls, there fell, several days' journey from Tusculum, and before the gate of Anagnia" (a town 40 Roman miles east of Rome), "a thunderbolt; and flames came out of the ground for a day and a night, and none could see what fuel fed them."

B.C. *205:* "At Fregellae," (70 Roman miles east of Rome), "night became bright as day, and at Setie" (about 51 miles from Rome), "a dazzling light like a torch (*fax*) was seen, going east to west in the sky." (Was this a meteor, or a flying saucer? The phenomena at Setie, accompanied by an object speeding in the sky, were seen in B.C. *203.*

B.C. *173:* "Sp. Posthumius Paulus and P. Mutius Scaevola were consuls, when, in broad sky, *in serene weather and clear sky,* there was seen in the sky, over the forum of Rome, a thing like a bow, stretched over the Temple of Saturn" (*arcus super aldem Saturni*).

B.C. *168:* "At Lanuvium" (16 Roman miles from Rome), "a thing like a torch burned in the sky ... and at Anagnia" (40 Roman miles east of Rome), "the year before, a similar thing was seen in the sky, burning ... at Fregellae, in the house of I. Atreus, a lance he had bought for his son, then in the army, burst into flames in full daylight, for several hours; yet it was not damaged by the flames."

B.C. *166:* "At Cassinum" (S. Germany?), "the sun shone at night for several hours."

B.C. *163:* "When T. Gracchus and M. Juventus were consuls, the sun shone at night at Capua" (120 Roman miles, south-east of Rome, as the crow flies). "At Concius, a man was burnt by a ray that came out of a mirror (*ex speculo*). (*N.B.* Lenses were not known to the old Romans. What supernormal affair was this?) "In the island of Cephalonia, in the Ionian Sea, there was seen in the sky a band who sang in a choir (*turba in coelo cantare visa*)." (*N.B.* Inexplicable phenomena, said to be men, or angels, or other entities in the skies, were also recorded by monastic chroniclers in the English middle ages. It is difficult to know what these phenomena were).

B.C. *147:* "The sky and earth were on fire at night, at Caere, (Etruria)." (*If* this were an aurora display, it was certainly a very unusual one!)

B.C. *137:* "A thing like a burning torch (*fax*) was seen in the sky over Praeneste" (a city 21 miles from Rome).

B.C. *133:* "When P. Africanus and C. Fabius were consuls, the sun shone at midnight at Amiterno" (70 Roman miles north-east of Rome), "and lasted so for some time...At Anagnia, a slave's tunic suddenly flamed, and after the fire was put out, one saw no trace of combustion by the flame."

B.C. *129:* "At Terracina" (a place between Rome and Naples), "in *serene weather*, a fire from the sky (*fulmine*) reached down to the sail of a ship, capsized the vessel, and burnt all in the ship."

B.C. *105:* "A Thunderbolt (*fulmine*) carried away the four fingers of a man, as if neatly severed with a knife. The exhalation, alone, of the bolt melted silver money ... A great noise was heard in the air, and a large globe of fire fell from the sky, and it rained blood. At Rome,

167

in daytime, a thing like a burning torch flew in the sky. It was very large and flew high."

B.C. *103:* "In the territory of Vulsinienis" (a lake 60 Roman miles north-west of Rome), "a flame came out of the earth, and, afterwards reached into the sky... and in a place in a forum, where popular assemblies are held to repeal or decree edicts, there came a rain of milk."*

B.C. *99:* "When C. Murius and L. Valerius were consuls, in Tarquinia, there fell in different places" (about 52 Roman miles, north-west of Rome, Etruria), "a thing like a flaming torch, and it came suddenly from the sky. Towards sunset, a round object like a globe, or round or circular shield (*orbis clypei*), took its path in the sky, from west to east." (This may have been a flying 'saucer).

B.C. *93:* "At Vulsiniensis, the new (crescent) moon disappeared, and not till next day at the third hour, (8-9 a.m.) did it reappear. A thing burning like a torch apapeared in the sky, which was all in flames."

B.C. *92:* "When M. Valerius and M. Herennius were consuls, in Lucania" (about 80 Roman miles, south-east of Naples), "a flock of sheep were seen in a meadow, enveloped in flames, which accompanied them to the sheepfold, where it lasted all night, without doing them the least harm. At Vulsiniensis, about break of day, a strange flame was seen to burn in the sky, which, after it concentrated in a single mass, projected a mouth of fire of a blue colour. The sky was seen to descend, and from its opening came vortices of flame." (What on earth, or in the sky, was this phenomenon?)

B.C. *91:* "When Claudius and M. Perpenna were consuls, a thing like a burning torch was seen in the sky" (near Rome?)

B.C. *90:* "At Aenarie" (an island in the Bay of Naples, now called Ischia), "whilst Livius Troso (Drusus?) was

---

* There was what looks like a strange aberration of the moon, in B.C. 103, when, in the skies of Italy, "the moon with a star appeared in the full light of day, from the 3rd to the 7th hour (9 a.m. to 1 p.m.)"

promulgating the laws at the beginning of the Italian war ... at sunrise, there came a terrific noise in the sky, and a globe of fire appeared burning in the north ... Later, at Aenarie, the earth yawned open and a flame issued, which lit up all the country to the horizon. In the territory of Spoletum" (65 Roman miles north of Rome, in Umbria), " a globe of fire, of golden colour, fell to the earth, gyrating. It then seemed to increase in size, rose from the earth, and ascended into the sky, where it obscured the disc of the sun, with its brilliance. It revolved towards the eastern quadrant of the sky." (That day, in B.C.90, the folk in the region of Umbria, saw what was almost certainly a golden flying saucer!)

B.C. 75: "A large natural stone, (when the consuls were L. Martius and Sextus Julius), which rolled forward from a steep rock, suddenly stopped itself in the air, in the middle of its fall. It remained motionless." (Here was a suspension of gravitation, whatever the cause and however modern science professors may laugh at such an absurd notion! It may be noted that an old Roman annalist also records, that, in B.C. 291, a big stone *(saxum ingens)* was seen flying in the air at Reate, (45 Roman miles north-east of Rome). He calls it *saxum ingens,* immense in size. (There is nothing to indicate that it was a bolide, aerolite, or meteorite, but he adds that the sun "was blood-red").

B.C. 42: "Something like a sort of weapon, or missile, rose with a great noise from the earth and soared into the sky" (in Italy). (*N.B.* No "great noise" is known to accompany auroral discharges. The word used is *frag-ore:* with a crashing, cracking, rattling sound.)

B.C. 41: "M. Lepidus and Munatius Plancus were consuls in Rome, when, at Rome, there shone a light like that of the sun, so brilliant in the night, that all people rose, thinking day had come and that it was time to go to work." (Besides Titus Livius, Dion Cassius, who wrote a history of Rome in 80 books, of which little but frag- ments survive—he flourished in A.D. 230—emphasises the brilliance of this phenomenal light. It may be noted that some of the flying saucers, reported in the U.S.A. between 1948-51, have been remarkable for the emis- sion, or projection of brilliant lights.)

> *B.C.16:* "Caius Furnio and Caio Syllano were consuls
> when a flaming light traversed the sky from south to
> north, in the night, throwing out so brilliant a light
> that night was like day. At the foot of the Apennines"
> (the range which runs from the Ligurian coast into
> Umbria), "a light like a flaming torch extended from
> the south to the north." (May have been an aurora, in
> the latter case; but *not* in the first).

One may, perhaps, be forgiven for making special mention
of an amazing and fatal adventure that befell the daughter
of a Roman knight, Pompeius Elmius, who, in B.C. 113, was
returning home from the games in the circus of Rome. His
daughter rode behind him on a horse. In the territory of
Stellate, on the road to Naples, the girl was struck by a
thunderbolt, whose action was almost controlled, or conscious!
It stripped the clothes from her body—as did the *onde de choc*
of shells, exploding close to soldiers in the First World War—
passed into her mouth, cut off her tongue, traversed her
whole body to the region of the pudenda, and deposited the
severed tongue on one of the labia of the vaginal orifice, by
which it issued from the girl's body!

The writers of the Renaissance owe much to learned Jews,
who, in what remained of the old Byzantine empire over-
whelmed by the barbarous Seljuk Turks, gathered and sent
to Italy and Western Europe valuable Greek and Roman
classic literature, sometimes only in fragments. And the dawn-
ing spirit of modern science, after some 900 years of the dark
ages, set scholars, in old Germany and the Low Countries, on
the compilation of what, in some sort, may be called encyclo-
paedic annals, derived from fragments, or mutilated manuscripts of Greek and Roman classic writers.

Two old German writers stand out, in this connection. One
was Conrad Wolffhart, a professor of grammar and dialectics,
who was also a deacon at Basel, in Switzerland. Born at Ruf-
fach, in Upper Elsass (Alsace-Lorraine), on 8 August 1518, he
became a professor at Basel University, in 1539, and, after
a blow that paralysed his right hand, he entered the Convent
of Theologians at Regensburg, Germany, in 1541, where he
wrote with his left hand the learned and curious black letter

compendium: *Prodigiorum ac Ostentorum Chronicon* (Basel, published by Henri cum Petri, 1567). In accord with the custom of his age, he adopted the name of Lycosthenes. Many pages of this curious work, quaintly illustrated with naïve woodcuts and engravings, tell of the falls of large pieces of ice from clear skies, of rains of milk, honey, wood, blood and flesh from the skies, of monstrous births of men and animals, or portents in the heavens, and of all sorts of teratological matters. But Lycosthenes pillaged the pastures of the much older and very obscure writer, Julius Obsequens, of the 4th century A.D., who compiled the strange book of prodigies quoted above. Lycosthenes Wolffhart was a contemporary of another queer old German writer, Jobus Fincelius, who, at 'Jhena', Germany, published his *Wunderzeichen ... vom dem Jar,* 1517 *zu* 1556 (Miraculous Portents of the years 1517-1556). It is a black letter volume and hard on the eyes, and as full of quaintnesses and superstition and credulity as it is replete with erudition of the Renaissance type.

I do not propose tiring the reader with a list of *all* my sources and authorities. He and she may be referred to the short Bibliography at the end of my book. The appearances of strange things in the skies naturally suggested to these old writers, not flying saucers, but flying angels or demons from Heaven or the other place.

Charles Fort would have been amused with the following story of an event said by the Roman poet Livius to have happened in B.C. 461:

> "In the skies of Italy, there was a rain of flesh, and numerous birds flying about in the air are said to have seized the flesh as it lay in rain water. And it happened that, as this flesh from the skies was thrown down and scattered about the fields and streets for several days, no odour changed it, nor was any bad smell emitted from it."

The learned German meteorologist, Dr. R. Hennig (of the Imperial Prussian Institute of Meteorology) was sorely puzzled by this story. He said, in 1904: "It is uncertain what we may understand by it." But a precisely similar phenomenon hap-

171

pened near old Rome, in B.C. 58, when, says Lycosthenes:

> *"Lights were seen in the sky,* and strange noises heard.
> Flesh rained like snow from heaven, which in great gob-
> bets were caught by all kinds of birds flying to and fro,
> and they caught it in their beaks and talons in the air,
> before it reached the ground. The residue, which fell
> down and lay a long time abroad in the city and fields,
> was found to have neither its colour nor odour changed,
> which is contrary to the wont of stale flesh or meat."

I have italicised the words *lights seen in the sky,* and may
note that these same mysterious phenomena are recorded to
have happened in the U.S.A., on several occasions in the 19th
century. For example, a thing like flesh fell from the sky,
accompanied by a brilliant flash of light, at Amherst, Mass.,
in 1819. There were three other occasions when flesh fell from
the skies in the U.S.A.: In 1869, over a farm at Los Nietos,
a Californian township; in 1876, in Bath county, Kentucky;
and, in 1880, in Wilson county, Tenn.

Who knows if these strange lights, that accompanied this
weird phenomenon, were associated with flying saucers, or
space ships? Some gleaming disc in the sky?

Now look at the events following, recorded—unless otherwise stated—by Lycosthenes:

B.C. 220: "A clear light shone at night in the sky over
Areminium (Rimini, Italy).

B.C. 214: "The forms of ships were seen in the sky at
Rome." (As this book shows, these forms have been seen,
long after, in the skies of old Ireland; and we cannot
align them, in every case, with auroral displays, or mock
moons or suns. *Au.*).

B.C. 216: "At Praeneste (65 Roman miles from Rome),
burning lamps fell from the sky, and at Arpinium (42
Roman miles east of Praeneste), a thing *like a round
shield* was seen in the sky." (The *burning lamps* may have
been meteors; but what about the *shield* (*parma,* in
Latin)? Does this not recall the gleaming discs we know
as flying saucers? *Au.*)

B.C. 170: "At Lanupium (on the Appian Way, 16 miles from Rome), a remarkable spectacle of a fleet of ships was seen in the air *(classis magna species in coelo visae).*

B.C. 106: "A bird that flew in the sky, and set houses on fire, was seen over Rome *(avis incendiaria)."* (Was this 'bird' a fire ball, or meteorite—or was it some cosmic incendiarist of the type that set fire to a cycle shed and farms in England, in summer 1953, and to forests, bridges and orchards in the U.S., in the years 1947 to 1953? *Au.*)

B.C. 104: "A rumbling sound was heard in the sky over Italy. A pillar was seen to fall to earth, and it rained blood. In *day time* over Rome, a burning torch was seen in the air.

B.C. 58: "The earth shook ... the air was again seen on fire, which thing was not believed by many. The year before, strange lights were seen in the air ... flesh rained from the sky as it were snow. It fell in small pieces which were caught by all the birds in the air, before the pieces of flesh touched the ground. Yet the residue on the ground had neither colour nor smell, and it remained in the streets of Rome and the country around, and did not decay or stink, as is the wont of stale flesh."

.   .   .   .

A.D. 16: "Beams of fire fell from the skies in the times of the Roman consuls, Sextus Pompeius and Lucius Apuleius.

A.D. 80: "When the Roman Emperor, Agricola was in Scotland (Caledonia), wondrous flames were seen in the skies over Caledon wood, all one winter night. Everywhere the air burned, and on many nights, when the weather was serene, a ship was seen in the air, moving fast. In Athol, a shower of stones fell from the sky into one place, and a shower of paddocks (frogs) fell on one day from the sky. And high in the air, at night, there raged a burning fire, as if knights in armour and on foot or horse fought with great force *(Hector Boece's (Boethius) Boke of the Chroniclis of Scoteland.* From a 16th century MS. in Cambridge University Library, England).

A.D. 98: "At Tarquinia, an old town in Campania, Italy,

a burning torch was seen (*fax ardens*), all about the sky.
It suddenly fell down." (May have been a meteorite. *Au.*)
"At sunset, a burning shield (*clypeus ardens*) passed over
the sky at Rome. It came sparkling from the west and
passed to the east.

A.D. 230: "Armies of footmen and horse were seen in the
the air over London and other places in England. They
were fighting. This was in the time of the Roman Emperor, Alexander Severus." (*John Seller: History of England. London,* 1696).

A.D. 249: "When Decius ascended the throne of the
Roman Empire, it rained blood in Britain, and a terrible
bloody sword was seen in the air for three nights, soon
after sunset" (*Seller*). (Hard to say if this were a *comet.
Au.*)

A.D. 384: "A terrible sign appeared in the sky, shaped
like a pillar (*columna*). It was in the time of the Roman
Emperor, Theodosius."

A.D. 393: "Strange lights were seen in the sky in the days
of the Emperor Theodosius. On a sudden, a bright globe
appeared at midnight. It shone brilliantly near the day
star (planet, Venus), about the circle of the zodiac. This
globe shone little less brilliantly than the planet, and,
little by little, a great number of other glowing orbs drew
near the first globe. The spectacle was like a swarm of
bees flying round the bee-keeper, and the light of these
orbs was as if they were dashing violently against each
other. Soon, they blended together into one awful flame,
and bodied forth to the eye as a horrible two-edged sword.
The strange globe which was first seen now appeared like
the pommel to a handle, and all the little orbs, fused with
the first, shone as brilliantly as the first globe. This sword
burned for forty days, and then vanished." (What was
this weird cosmic phenomenon? It recalls flying saucer
phenomena in U.S.A. *Au*).

A.D. 393: "In the time of Theodosius, a sign like a hanging dove (*columba pendens*) appeared in the sky. It burnt
for thirty days."

A.D. 394: "At night, there appeared in the sky over the
streets of Antioch (Asia Minor), a thing like a woman

clothed and wandering high in the sky. It was of immense size, and of aspect so grim as to appal the many who beheld it. It moved to and fro and up and down (*currens*) in the sky over the streets of the city, and, as it did so, it seemed as if unceasingly lashing a whip that made the air resound. The noise thereof was such as is customarily made when an animal-tamer in the amphitheatre rouses to fury the wild beasts he shows to the spectators. And soon, in that same month, a great and bloody insurrection burst forth in Antioch, by reason of the extraordinary taxes levied on the citizens by order of Theodosius." (Was this a space ship? It was certainly no aurora, comet, or meteor! *Au.*)

A.D. 398: "A thing like a burning globe, presenting a sword, shone brilliantly in the sky over the city of Byzantium (modern Istanbul or Constantinople, Turkey). It seemed almost to touch the earth from the zenith. Such a thing was never recorded to have been seen before by men." (Suggests some type of flying saucer projecting a powerful searchlight over the city. *Au*).

A.D. 457: "Over Brittany, France, a blazing thing like a globe was seen in the sky. Its size was immense, and on its beams hung a ball of fire like a dragon out of whose mouth proceeded two beams, one of which stretched beyond France, and the other reached towards Ireland, and ended in fire, like rays."

A.D. 541: "In this year of Grace, a comet appeared in Gaul, so vast that the whole sky seemed on fire ... Later, blood dropped from the clouds, and dreadful mortality ensued." (*Tighernac's* (O'Braaian) *Annales*, and *Roger of Wendover's Chronicon*).

A.D. 577: "A thing like a lance passed across the sky, from north to west, over France."

A.D. 586: "Hailstones falling from the sky killed men in Constantinople."

A.D. 596: "Armies in rout, and with a great noise like thunder with flashes of lightning were seen in the skies over Surrey, England. Many drops the colour of blood fell from the sky." (*Seller*).

175

A.D. 655: "Fire fell from the skies on England, and great fear came on men" (*Waverley Annales Monasterii*).

A.D. 715: "On midsummer day, a dark cloud spread over the sky, and then withdrew, and all the air seemed on fire, while armies of monstrous creatures appeared in the air. A great storm followed that broke to pieces many ships in English havens, overturned many high towers, and rent up great oaks." (*Seller*).

A.D. 729: "In the third year of King Adelhard, two comets (*cometae*) appeared terribly round the sun. One went before the sun ... east ... the other followed, after the sun, to the west, as if presaging misfortunes dire to come from east and west. And certainly, the one by day, the other by night, preceded the setting and rising of the sun ... Against the north, they bore a face of fire, portending destruction. And they appeared in January, and both remained for nearly a week ..." (*Henry of Huntingdon: Historiae Anglorum*). (I insert this item to show that the old monks of the middle ages knew of comets. *Au.*)

A.D. 746 and 748: "Dragons were seen in the sky ... and ships in which were men were seen in the air." (*Tigernach's* (O'Braaian. Abbot of Cluan). *Annales*).

A.D. 773: "A red cross appeared after sunset, in the sky over England." (*Fabius Ethelwerd's Latin Chronicle* and *Henry, Archdeacon of Huntingdon's Historia Anglorum*). Fabius adds: "Seventeen years passed by, during which King Cynulf seized the kingdom from Sijebyrhte (Sigebert), and in the sky appeared the Lord's Cross, after sunset ... In those days, monstrous serpents were seen among the Southern English, called South Saxons." Huntingdon says: "In 774 ... red signs (*rubea signa*) appeared in the sky after sunset, and horrid serpents were seen in Sudsexe, with great amazement." (The item about the red cross in the sky is said to have come from a lost Chronicle at St. Alban's monastery, or from a version of the Anglo-Saxon Chronicle not now extant).

A.D. 793: "Fiery dragons in the sky alarmed the wretched nation of the English." (*Roger of Wendover's Chronica*). (Brushed off as just aurorae or parhelia—mock suns— but may not have been. *Au.*)

A.D. 796: "Small globes were seen circling round the sun." (*Roger of Wendover*). (These may *not* have been mock suns. Au.)

A.D. 823: "In summer, a piece of ice fell from the sky over Burgundy, France. It was 16 feet long, 7 feet broad, and 2 feet thick."

A.D. 919: "A thing like a burning torch (*fax ardens*) was seen in the sky, and glistening balls like stars moved to and fro in the air over Hungary." (Probably flying saucers. *Au*).

A.D. 936: "In a clear sky, the sun was suddenly darkened red like blood." (*Johann Funck: Chronologie ab orbis condite. Nürnberg*, 1545). (No vulcanism reported in this year. *Au*.)

A.D. 941: "The sun has a terrible appearance for some time, and a stream like blood issued from it." (*Th. Fassband's Geschichte des Kantons Schwyz*).

　　　·　　　·　　　·　　　·　　　·　　　·　　　·

A.D. 1011: "A burning torch like a tower (*fax ardens instar turris*) was seen to flame in the sky with a great noise. This was in the year of the Emperor Henry II, and happened in Lorraine, at the Hill Castrilocum."

Here comes a mystery that has baffled every historian, or scientist, who has heard or read of it: The "Coming of the Wild Fire from the skies"! No one has ever been able to explain it, or explain it away: This phenomenon happened again in England, *in 1953.* I suggest in this book, a startling solution (*Vide*, also, *Chap. XII, pp. 279-283*).

A.D. 1032: The Anglo-Saxon Chronicle records: "In 1032, there appeared in England *wild fire* such as no man before remembered, and it did harm in many places." The *Irish Annals*: "The strange fire did damage at York." *The Chronicon Scotorum*: "There was *Tene Gelain*, or wild fire in Saxon Land, and it burned many men at *Caer Abroc* (?)" *A.D. 1048:* "The *wyld fire*, which none did understand, killed many men and animals all over

England in this year. There came fires in the air, commonly called 'woodland fires' which destroyed towns, standing corn in the field in Derby, and other counties." (*Simeon of Durham's Historia Ecclesiae Dunelmensis*) ... Robert Fabyan's *New Chronicles of England and France* adds: "And by lightning, the corne upon the grounde, was in 1048, wonderfully brent and wasted." *A.D. 1078: Anglo-Saxon Chronicle*: "And this year, the wyld fire came in many shires, in dry summer, and burnt many towns and also many burghs." (It seems too widely spread to have been electrical phenomena, such as lightning, Also, the intervals of 16 and 30 years are curious. *Au.*)

A.D. 1039: "On 6 April there was seen in the sky between the south and the east a wonderful beam of light. It rapidly passed the sun now beginning to set, and appeared to fall on the earth. It left behind a track of light (*vestigia*) which people saw for a long time. This was in the year 15 of the Emperor Conrad."

A.D. 1067: "In this year, people saw a fire that flamed and burned fiercely in the sky. It came near the earth, and for a little time brilliantly lit it up. After, *it revolved, ascended on high, then descended into the bottom of the sea.* In several places it burned woods and plains. In the county of Northumberland, this fire showed itself in two seasons of the year." (*Geoffrey Gaimar's Lestorie des Englis solum Maistre Geffrei*). (The reference to the *revolving* fire strangely recalls the rotating spheres seen at sea in the 19th century, and referred to, later in this chapter. Have we, here, a clue to the startling origin of this mysterious "wyld fire"? *Au.*)

A.D. 1074: "On 1 February, two pillars of golden light were seen on the right and left of the sun, and there was a rainbow the night before, about cockcrow." (*Were* these pillars merely mock suns, or parhelia? *Au.*)

A.D. 1077: "A blazing star was seen near the sun on Palm Sunday, in England."

A.D. 1093: "In this year, a fiery stick (*baculus ignitus*), (or, as the Sijebert MS. has it, *jaculum ignitum*, a burning net), was reported seen at noon in the northern sky on

1 August. A great famine followed, and so great was the mortality among men that there hardly remained alive sufficient men to bury the corpses." (*Matthew of Paris's Chronica Majora*).

A.D. 1094: "In England, a fiery dart was seen flying in the sky from south to west, at the fifth hour of the night (7 p.m.) on Aug. 1." (This seems to refer to the strange event above, 1093). (*Lycosthenes.*)

A.D. 1097: "On 3 Kalends of October (Oct. 5), a comet appeared for 15 days. Several say this wonderful sign burnt almost like a cross in the sky." (*Was* it a comet? *Au.*)

A.D. 1104: "Burning torches, fiery darts, flying fire were often seen in the air in this year. And, there were, near stars, what looked like swarms of butterflies, and little fiery worms of strange kind. They flew in the air and took away the light of the sun as if they had been clouds." (Some of these phenomena may have been auroral displays, but *not all!* Moreover, aurorae are not seen in the day. *Au.*)

A.D. 1115: "On Easter Day, a great gap was torn asunder in the sky (*coelum vasto hiatus*), and a shining light was emitted, which lasted a whole hour. There appeared in the middle, a cross of golden colour. This was in the time of Henry, the first emperor of Germany." (Probably a parhelion, or mock sun. *Au.*)

A.D. 1118: "A cross and a moon shining white appeared in the sky, and it was believed that the end of the world was at hand.' (This was apparently in France. It is hard to say if the cross were a mock moon, or paraselena. *Au.*)

A.D. 1150: "A cross appeared in the sky at noon, in England, when King Richard Coeur de Lion and Philip of France prepared to make war on Saladin, Emperor of the Saracens." (Crosses were seen in the moon in England and France in the years of 1156 and 1161. May have been mock moons, or paraselenae, though the *noon-tide* "cross" may have been something else! *Au.*)

A.D. 1165: "Many people in this year saw a black horse of large size in the province of York, Eng. It always kept hurrying towards the sea, while it was followed by thunder and lightning and fearful noises, with destructive hail. The footprints of this accursèd horse were of enormous size, especially as found on the cliffs and the hill near the town of Scardeburh (modern Scarborough, Yorkshire). From these cliffs, the mysterious horse gave a great leap into the North Sea. For a whole year, the impressions of each of this horse's hoofs were plainly visible; for each hoof was deeply engraved in the soil." (*The Chronica de Mailros* (Chronicle of Melrose Abbey, Scotland), which records this mysterious apparition of a great black horse, adds that, in this year, two comets appeared before sunrise in August, one in the south, the other in the north. It adds that comets always appear before the death of kings, or, if shining like gold, presage the ruins of kingdoms. Was this "horse" a sea saurian (serpent)? *Au.*)

The British magazine, *Notes and Queries*—and this bears out the wisdom of Fort that, if you find an insoluble mystery of nature or man, you should look round to see if something like it has occurred before or after—records that an ancient Chinese book says that a Chinese Emperor woke, one morning, to find that, in the night, there had been left, in the high-walled courtyard of his green-tiled palace, strange footprints like those of a large ox; though no such beasts were to be found anywhere in miles.

In the sandstone of a *cañon* near Carson, Nevada, are footprints of 10 to 20 inches long (but these may be of a mastodon, or mammoth). In England, in February 1855, mysterious tracks, showing clawed feet or hoof-marks of a *biped,* not a quadruped, were found at huge intervals in a garden of a cottage on a moor, *on house tops,* on vertical walls, and in open fields, when snow was on the ground, and on *both sides* of the wide estuary of the river Exe, in a wide area of South Devon. The sight caused great commotion and even terror. Horsemen with hounds followed them to a wood, but the dogs refused to enter the trees. Something unknown and unseen frightened them badly. *The Illustrated London News,* of February 24, 1855, reproduced prints which look like horses' hoofs, sketched on the site in this Devon countryside. Similar mysterious prints, like those of a *great horse,* were found in wild Scottish glens, and high mountains, in March 1840, and on a hill in Galician Poland, marks like these were seen in the snow every year, and sometimes in the sand on the hill, before 1855, and the local folk thought they were supernatural. In October 1866, Maoris in New Zealand were excited by the sudden appearance in a desert of mud, of a huge and hairy animal with antlers. It was an animal unknown to them; for they had no deer in New Zealand. True, this was not a flying saucer mystery; but had the Devon mystery occurred today, someone would have speculated that 'space men', with metal shoes, had been there in the night!

Some time in the 12th century Geoffrey of Monmouth, (Galfredi Monumetensis, as the old chroniclers call him), got hold of a very ancient Brezonec manuscript—one written in the Breton Celtic tongue. This manuscript, long since vanished into the graveyard of time, had been found by an old archdeacon of Oxford, one Walter Mapes, who had been wandering in the byways of Brittany, in the reign of King Henry I, of England. This curious manuscript seems to have been a very old Celtic history of the British Isles. A strange passage in it tells of how a singular apparition suddenly entered the skies over Wales and the Irish Sea while a certain tribal ruler, Guintmias, was defending himself against a misty king of Old Wales, known as Utherpendragon.

Here is this very singular story:

> "A 'star' of wonderful magnitude and brightness suddenly appeared in the skies over Wales, while Aurelius (or Guintmias) was defending himself. It contained a beam (or ray). Towards the ray (*ad radium*), a fiery globe in the likeness of a dragon was stretched out. Out of the mouth of it proceeded two rays (or beams), and the length of one beam was seen to stretch out beyond the region of Wales. The other, in truth, was seen to lie towards the Irish Sea, and it ended in seven lesser rays".

Have we, here, something more portentous than a comet, aerolite, or extraordinary meteor?

> *A.D. 1167:* "At the watch night (*vigilia*) of the Lord's Nativity, 2 stars of the hue of fire appeared in the western sky. One was large, the other small. At first, they appeared

joined together. Afterwards, they were for a long time separated, distinctly." (*Nicholas Trivetus: Annales*). (These "stars" may have been flying saucers. *Au.*)

A.D. 1168: "A globe of fire was seen moving to and fro in the air on 20 March (*globeus igneus per aire discurrere*). This was on 20 March." (*Trivetus*). (Was this a bolide, or aerolite—or something else? *Au.*)

A.D. 1186: "About the ninth hour of the day (2-3 p.m.), on August 9, at the village of Dunstable, Eng., the sky suddenly opened, and the laity and clergy of the abbey saw a cross, very long and of marvellous size. And there appeared on it Jesus Christ fastened on with nails. . . Blood flowed but not to earth. The vision lasted from the ninth hour of the day (2 p.m.) till midnight." (*Benedict of Peterborough: Gesta Regis Henrici Secundum*). (Britton, the British meteorologist, rightly says it is difficult to rationalise this unusual optical phenomenon. *Au.*)

A.D. 1189: "Nor should be passed over in silence a wonderful prodigy that at this time was seen by many in English cities. There is upon the public road that leads to London, a not ignoble village called Dunstable. Here, at about noon, men were looking up into the sky when they saw in the serene and cloudless dome the image of the banner of the Lord, shining and white as silk. Joined to it was the form of a crucified man, which, in Church, is depicted in memory of the Lord of the Passion, for the devotion of the faithful. When, therefore, this awful spectacle was carefully observed for a while, there was seen behind the face the form of a cross. Thus, in mid-air, the space between both was plainly seen. Soon after, the awful thing vanished. Each may interpret it as he wishes. I am merely a narrator. I know not if it be a presage, or a sign of divinity." (*Walter de Hemingford, Canon of Gisseburne: Chronica*). (This seems to refer to the event of 1186, above).

A.D. 1194: "In the lordship of Beauvais, France, four meteorites as large as eggs fell from the sky, and ravens of huge size flew in the air and were seen to carry in their bills quick and burning coals with which they set houses on fire." (Compare this queer affair with the *avis incendiara* of Rome, in B.C. 106, recorded earlier in this chapter. *Au.*)

A.D. 1217: "On the vigil of S. Simon and S. Jude, a certain canon of Dunstable Abbey, Eng., saw high in the sky an immense cross that passed in great glory from the eastern quadrant of sky to the west." (*Annales Prioratus de Dunstaplia*). (Have we, here, a flying saucer? *Au.*)

A.D. 1218: "At Köln (on the Rhine in Germany), and , Munster (in German Westfalen), at Leyden, in Holland, in May, three crosses appeared in the air, white in the north, white towards the south, and the third of a middle colour. The last is said to have had hanging on it the figure of a man with uplifted arms, and nailed at the hands and feet, with his head hanging to one side. This cross was in the middle of the others. And, at the same time, in Friesland, Holland, a cross of blue appeared in the sun. Likewise, there was seen one quite like this, soon after, in the diocese of Trajectum." (Either in Limburg, Holland, or Frankfurt-am-Oder, in Germany, or, perhaps, in Brandenburg, Prussia. What really *was* seen, who can say, at this date, in 1954? *Au.*)

The next report of a strange spectacle in the skies over England occurs in A.D. 1239 (reign of Henry III).
Says the Latin chronicler (Matthew of Paris):

"On July 24, 1239, at the vigil of St. James, in the dusk, but not when the stars came out, but while the air was clear, serene and shining, a great star appeared. It was like a torch, rising from the south, and flying on both sides of it, there was emitted in the height of the sky a very great light. It turned towards the north in the aery region, *not quickly, nor, indeed, with speed,* but exactly as if it wished to ascend to a place in the air. But when it arrived at the apparent middle of the firmament, in our northern hemisphere, it left behind it smoke with sparks."

The old writer supposed that the strange "star, or comet, or dragon" might have been the planet Lucifer (Venus). "It had," he says, "the form of a large head, the front part shining or very bright, the near part smoking and sparking, as here shown." (*Note:* no such picture was given in the ancient manuscript). "All seeing its prodigies, and immense size, wondered what it portended, but knew not; save, that, in the same hour,

the weather suddenly changed from pleasant clearness to a
long lasting rain that suffocated nearly all the crops, and
only a little corn could be gathered with the sickle."

Two comments may be made on the above story of 1239:
First: The strange apparition moved slowly—as meteors do
not do—and it seemed to have been steered or manoeuvred
for an ascending flight. *Second*: When the U.S. pilot, Mantell,
was killed, on the afternoon of January 7, 1948, over Fort
Knox airfield, he radioed back to his base a report on the
immense width of the object his 'plane was trying to close,
and its fantastic length.

It is a good policy in regard to all such fantastic happenings
and phenomena for the scientific historian, as I have said
before, to look round and try to find whether similar events
have taken place in the past. Here, it may be recalled that
some astronomer in the U.S. made the foolish suggestion that,
at the time when Mantell was killed and his 'plane disintegrated, he had been chasing the planet *Venus*! Later evidence
caused the team of investigators of Project Saucer to jettison
this foolish, and, in relation to poor Mantell, insulting theory.
I commend a study of the story of 1239 to the sceptic of today;
though I am under no illusion that he is likely to modify his
opinion about what are called flying saucers.

I may add that the phenomenon of July 24, 1239, was seen
by many folk living on the borders of Hereford and Worcestershire, in that year.

A.D. 1252: "There occurred a change of the moon four
days before its time." (*Matthew of Paris's Chronica*). (A
lunar aberration? A wild-eyed, mystic American correspondent of mine would say that the "Master of the
Moon" had ordered a change and moved the moon (*sic*)
to accommodate a huge space ship desiring to land! I
pass no opinion, myself, on this fantasy. *Au.*)

A.D. 1254: "On the night of the Lord's Circumcision
(Jan. 1), at midnight, in serene sky and clear air, with
stars shining and the moon eight days old, there suddenly
appeared in the sky a kind of large ship elegantly shaped,
and well equipped and of marvellous colour. Certain

monks at St. Albans saw it. . .for a long time, as if it were
painted, and a ship made of planks; but, finally, it began
to disappear." (*Matthew of Paris: Historia Anglorum*).
(Was this a singular cloud—or was it some kind of flying
saucer? *Au.*)

A.D. 1258: "A flaming globe crossed a neighbouring river
(in Scotland), and two villas, at a league apart, were
reduced to ashes." (*Chronicon de Lanercost*). (Was this a
huge fire ball? *Au.*)

A.D. 1269: "On 6 Decr, at twilight, a strange brightness,
shaped like a cross gave light from high in the air and
shone down on the city of Cracow, Poland, and on all
the country." (*Martin Cromer: History of Poland*). (This
may well have been a flying saucer; for similar phenomena
have been recorded in parts of the U.S.A., between 1947
and 1949. *Au.*)

A.D. 1284: "On the 5th of the Kalends of Decr. (Dec. 28),
from the 3rd to the 6th hour of the day (8 a.m. to noon)
the sea appeared on fire, with no very great brightness,
but with a yellow flame." (*Florence de Wigornia (Worcester): Chronicon*). (Compare this mystery with the stories
of flying wheels in the China and other seas, in 19th century. *Vide pp.* 137, 138, 220-1 in this book. *Au*).

A.D. 1290: At Byland, or Begeland Abbey (the largest Cis-
tercian abbey in England), in the North Yorkshire Riding, while the abbot and monks were in the refectorium,
a flat, round, shining, silvery object—*discus*, in the record
—flew over the abbey, and caused the utmost terror
(*maximum terrorem*). (*William of Newburgh's Chronicle*).

A.D. 1298: "In this year, the sun appeared as red as blood
in Ireland (during the battle of the English and Scots at
Falkirk, July 22, 1298). . .also, the morrow after the Feast
of the Seven Sleepers, the sun's beams were changed to
blood colour, all that morning to the great wonder of all."
(*Christopher Pembridge's Annals of Ireland, and Camden's
Britannia (English version)*). (No solar eclipse, at this date,
and no record of volcanic eruptions. *Au.*)

A.D. 1320: "The Abbot (of the Abbey of Durham) died
on the feast of St. Gregory. . .and was buried in the choir
of St. Leonard, before the great altar, and after his death,

> there appeared in the sky a light like the rays of the sun.
> It seemed to shine over the burial-place. Anon, it
> descended in the night and moved from that place to
> another, as if passing quickly from place to place. . . .
> Many saw this, and it was harmless; but they fell on the
> ground in terror." (*Roberti de Greystanes: Historia de
> Statu Ecclesiae Dunelmensis*). (Here, I think, we have
> undoubted evidence of a flying saucer casting a search-
> light onto an ancient abbey at Durham, Eng. Naturally,
> the old monk, who recorded it, ascribed the phenomenon
> to hagiological manifestations of St. Leonard, in the case
> of an abbot who was his disciple. *Au.*)

Phenomena of the sort that happened over Durham Abbey,
in March 1320, have occurred much nearer our own day. For
example, on December 23, 1905, people of Worcester, Mass.,
U.S.A., were startled when, in the early hours of the night, a
strange object appeared in the sky in the south-east, travelled
north-west, hovered over the city, watched by thousands of
people, disappeared in the direction of Marlborough, two
hours later returned, swept the sky with a searchlight of tremendous power, hovered and then headed south and then
east. Next night, the same, or another mysterious object appeared in the sky over Boston, Mass., shot out searchlight
beams, vanished over the horizon, and flew away east. An hour
later, this, or a kindred object appeared hovering with powerful searchlight over Willimantic, Conn., for 15 minutes. At
Boston, Mass., observers said this mysterious cosmic object
had red lights and was long and black. Its speed was variable,
from a hover to "terrific". Marlborough, Mass., saw it nine
times at this date. At Huntingdon, West Va., three huge lights
of about uniform dimensions were projected in the early
morning sky, on January 1, 1909, and on three successive *days*
a mysterious white object flashed high in the sky over Chattanooga, Tenn. On October 31, 1908, at 4 a.m., two men saw
a searchlight in the sky, playing down onto the earth, and
then flashing upward. (*N.B.* in December 1909, a dirigible
in France managed to fly the 25 miles from St. Cyr to the
Eiffel Tower, in Paris, and the German, Graf Zeppelin, at
this date, had no airship capable of anything remotely like

a trans-oceanic flight.) Earlier, on April 19, 1897, at 9 p.m., a huge cone-shaped object appeared in the sky over Sisterville, West Va., was seen through binoculars, and judged to be 180 feet long, seemed to have something like fins on each side, and approached the township from the north-west, flashing brilliant red, white and green lights, Chicago residents say they had seen an object like this at 2 a.m., April 2, 1897, when an amazed crowd gazed at it from the top of a skyscraper. It projected searchlights. At several towns in Texas, on April 15, 1897, people saw a dark object pass apparently across the moon—out in space between the earth and the moon—while from four other towns in Texas, newspaper men wired New York:

> "An object shaped like a big Mexican cigar appeared in the sky last night. It was large in the middle, small at both ends, had great wings like an enormous butterfly, and was brilliantly illuminated, with rays of two great searchlights. It sailed in south-easterly direction with wind-velocity, and presented a magnificent appearance." (*New York Sun*, April 16, which also reported, on 1 April, 1897, that, in the sky over Kansas City, "something like a powerful searchlight was directed towards the earth, and travelled east at a rate of around 60 miles an hour".)

. . . .

We will continue reports of mysteries in the skies of Western Europe, in the 14th, 15th, and 16th centuries:

> *A.D. 1322:* "In the first hour of the night of Novr. 4 (after 7 p.m.), there was seen in the sky over Uxbridge, England, a pile (pillar) of fire the size of a small boat, pallid and livid in colour. It rose from the south, crossed the sky with a *slow and grave motion,* and went north. Out of the front of the pile, a fervent red flame burst forth with great beams of light. Its speed increased, and it flew thro' the air. . .Many beholders saw it in collision, and there came blows as of a fearful combat, and sounds of crashes were heard at a distance." (*Robert of Reading's Continuation of Matthew Paris's Chronicon*). (The variable motion is *not* that of a meteorite. Flying saucer phenomena of this type, where explosions have occurred in the mysterious visitant have been recorded in U.S.A., in 1948-50. *Au.*)

A.D. 1352: "A beam of light was seen to slide along the sky, having the forepart afire, in Decr. . .It was seen in the north." (Country not stated by Lycosthenes, but appears to have been either Scandinavia, or Germany. *Au.*)

A.D. 1355: "In summer, a red and blue banner appeared in the sky, and was seen in many parts of England. They seemed to come together in clashes. Finally, the red defeated the blue banner, and cast it down to the earth below, as people saw." (*Henry Knighton's Chronicon Monachi Leycestrensis*).

A.D. 1360: "In summer time, in flat and deserted places in England and France, in this year, many often saw appear suddenly two towers from which, high in the sky, two large armies went forth, one of which was crowned with a warlike sign, and the other clothed in black. They met, and the soldiers overcame them in black, and a second time, the warriors overcame the black tower, and the whole vanished." (*Chronicon Angliae ab A.D. 1328 usque 1388. . .auctore monacho quodam Sancti Albani*). (Monk does not say if this was at night or day. It may be compared with supernormal phenomena of a fight re-enacted in the sky over a lonely moor, the site of battle between Cromwell's armies and those of Charles I., about 1670. There are curious attestations of local magistrates who witnessed this sky phenomenon, about 1670. *Au.*)

A.D. 1387: "In Novr. and Decr. of this year, a fire in the sky, like a burning and revolving wheel, or round barrel of flame, emitting fire from above, and others in the shape of a long fiery beam, were seen through a great deal of the winter, in the county of Leicester, Eng., and in Northamptonshire." (*Henry Knighton: Continuation of the Chronicle of Leicester, by another hand*). (*Vide* pp. 137, 220-1, of this book. *Au.*)

A.D. 1388: "A flying dragon (*draco volans*) was seen in April in many places." (*Knighton's Continuator*). (Difficult to say if this may have been auroral display, a fireball, a meteorite, or something else—like a flying saucer. *Au.*)

A.D. 1478: "Divers kinds of crosses and fiery bowls fell to the ground from the sky, leaving tokens behind, in

Switzerland." (*Chronicles of Basel*). (May have been types of flying saucers. *Au.*)

A.D. 1479: "In Arabia, a comet was seen like a sharp beam set with points, with the form of a scythe."

The above was certainly an extraordinary comet! It looks, however, more like some sort of space ship.

A.D. 1501-1503: "In the whole of Europe, very numerous *Kreuzregen* (Cross-rains) were seen." (Hennig rightly calls this a "most puzzling phenomenon," and it has never been explained by meteorologists). (*Dortmünder Kronik; Johann Wassenbloch's Duisbürger Kronik; and Lycosthenes*). In Nürnberg, Germany, the phenomena of these "cross rains" appeared for 26 days, in those years. They remind us that scientists adroitly cast into the discard all phenomena like these which they cannot explain, or explain away. *Au.*)

A.D. 1520: "At Wissenburg, in the Rhineland, at noon, a great and horrid clashing and clattering as of arms and armour, was heard to resound from the sky. The citizens of this town, supposing a host had come to blockade their city, caught up arms in fear and astonishment, and sallied forth in a body into the country beyond the walls." (Of course, they found nothing and saw nobody. See below, under date 1642. *Au.*)

A.D. 1520: "At Erdfurt (Erfurt, Prussia), in the time of Emperor Carlos V, two burning suns (parhelia, or mock suns) were seen. . .and a wonderful burning beam of great size, suddenly appeared in the sky, fell upon the ground and destroyed many places. It then revolved, turned round and ascended into the sky, where it put on a circular form (*formum circularem*)." (The "beam" looks like a flying saucer, rather than a fire-ball. *Vide* pp. 169, 174, 178, in this book. *Au.*)

A.D. 1528: "The city of Utrecht, Holland (*Vltrajectua*), was under siege, when a cruel and strange sight was seen in the sky, which terrified the townsmen, and made the enemy think he would get the city. It was the form of a Burgundian cross right over the city, high in the sky, yellow in colour, and fearful to behold." (*N.B.* This

189

phenomenon was also seen in May 1554, over German towns, at 5 p.m. Was this a flying saucer? It seems so! *Au.*)

A.D. 1535: "In the sky over Weimar, Germany (*Vinarium*), three beams of fire suddenly appeared in serene air." (Probably, flying saucers; for Lycosthenes, as seen above, knew what were solar haloes, mock suns, and meteorites. *Au.*)

A.D. 1547: "In Italy, near Rome, on the 1st of the Ides of December (Decr. 13), about 3 p.m., in fair weather and serene sky, a red rod and red cross were seen in the air for nearly three hours, and over the top an eagle soared on her wings." (*Vide* p. 17, in this book, where a similar phenomenon was seen by an American traveller in Central Asia, in 1920. *Au.*)

A.D. 1547: "In the whole of France, and Germany, and England, the sun appeared reddish without lustre, like a ball with spots, so that at noon the stars were visible, especially was this seen in the battle of Mühlberg, on 24 April." (*Thanner Kronik des Klosters in Elsass; Deutsche Kronik bis 1077 zu 1472; Chronica Magdeburg, 1584; Braunschweigische und Lünenburgische Chronica; Paulus Crusius: De Epochis seu aeris temporum, Basel, 1578*).

A.D. 1551: "Red rods were seen in the air over Lisbon, Portugal, on 3 Jan. There were also seen fearful fires in the air, and it rained blood."

A.D. 1554: "Two red crosses were seen in the sky at Nebra (Nebra: Preussen, Saxony), and the same day at Griessesie, a town in Thuringia, amidst the sun, then shining very brightly, appeared a red cross which covered the whole disc of the sun, and on both sides a huge beam with diverse circles, appeared in the elements. (*Jobus Fincelius*) . . .On 6 Ides of March (10 March), there appeared at Schulen(?), in France, between 6 and 8 p.m., about the moon, a burning fire, emitting a great noise, that seemed to be the point of a lance, turning from side to side, from east to west, casting out flames on all sides. . .In July, a haze appeared in Siebenbürgen. Frequently, the bright sun strove with darkness, as if fearing for the destruction of mankind, and a thick, stinking mist rose up, also many fantastic ghosts have risen from graves and in churchyards." (*Mathias Miles: Siebenbürgischer Würgenengel,*

Hermannstadt, 1670). (Among these possible parhelia appears a probable flying saucer—at Schulen, in France. *Au.*)

A.D. 1554: "At Zopeda (Holland?), the sun rose red and over it stood a gorgeous house which burned on both sides of the sun. There stood upright high pillars like those of Hercules, and they were coloured like a rainbow, yet were not arched. The bases seemed to touch the surface of the earth, extending themselves widely. The next day, the sun rose in the morning without changing colours and somewhat pale. The house, as before, stood bright and shining, and the pillars also showed themselves again, embracing the sun in the middle, but not so plainly as on the first day. And they were seen in the air, but no more touched the ground." (*Jobus Fincelius*). (All one can comment is that whatever this remarkable phenomenon was, it was hardly a mock sun! *Au.*)

A.D. 1557: "On 3 March, a thunderbolt pierced the bridal chamber of François Montmorency, and Diane de France, running into every corner of the tent, but nevertheless finally exploding harmlessly." (*Joachimus du Bellay, or Bellaius: Oeuvres, Paris. 1569*).

Surely, few newly married couples can ever have consummated the delights of Venus in such remarkable circumstances!

The 17th and the early years of the 18th century were remarkable for mysterious lights in the sky and strange noises, such as beating of drums, cannonades, and the "music of the orchestral spheres". To this day, they have never been explained. Let us take the mysterious 'heavenly lights', first.

These phenomena often took the form of burning streams of light. Such lights were seen over London in 1560 and 1564, and over Brabant, in what is now Belgium, in 1575, when a professor of medicine, Cornelius Gemma, of the University of Louvain described them. Often, such lights were so powerful that one could see the smallest pin or straw on the ground, in their brilliant illumination. They seemed to be extremely powerful searchlights, projected from the skies to the ground.

Here is the report of a Fellow of the British Royal Society, (founded in 1662 for the discussion of scientific matters):

191

"At 7 p.m., on 20 September, 1676, a strange spectacle
—a meteor?—was seen in Northamptonshire, Gloucestershire, Worcestershire, Somerset, Kent, Hampshire, Essex,
and London, and in many other parts of England at the
same time. It passed very near the earth. It appeared in
the dusk, with a sudden light like that of noonday, so
that the smallest pin or straw could be seen on the ground.
Above in the air was seen, at no great apparent distance,
a long appearance of fiery sort, like a long arm with a
great knob at the end. As it vanished, it seemed to break
into small fires or sparks, like rockets."

Next year, in May, 1677, the famous astronomer, Edmund
Halley, Savilian professor of geometry at Oxford University,
reported observing a "great light in the sky all over southern
England, many miles high". Later, on 31 July, 1708, from 9
to 10 p.m., a similar apparition, thought to be 50 miles high,
passed over Sheerness, and the 'Buoy at the Nore', Suffolk,
and London. It moved "with incredible speed, and was very
bright. It seemed to vanish and left a pale white light behind
it. There were no hissing sounds and no explosion".

Ten years later, in 1686, strange reports came from Gott-
fried Kirch, a German astronomer at Leipzig. I translate from
his Latin:

"On 9 July, 1686, at 1.30 a.m., a burning globe, furnished
with a tail, appeared apparently 8½ degrees from Aquarius,
and remained immovable for one-eighth of an hour. Its
diameter was about half that of the moon. It emitted so
much light that at first one could read without a candle.
Afterwards, it vanished in its place, but very gradually.
This phenomenon was also seen by others at the same
time, and especially by Schlazius, at a city eleven miles
away in Germany, from Leipzig. The time was about midnight, and the altitude about 60 degrees from the southern
horizon. It seemed about 30 miles high in the sky, and
darted obliquely downwards, where it left two globules
to be seen only with an optic tube (telescope).—*Note* that
a similar phenomenon was seen at Leipzig, on 22 March,
1680, and also at Hamburg, at 3 a.m., when it seemed 40
miles high, in the NNE."

Halley had received another report of a similar phenomenon, on 21 March 1676. He said: "I find it one of the hardest things to account for, that I have ever yet met." His report came from the Italian Professor of Mathematics, Signor Montanori. What Montanori said is of remarkable interest to those who have studied flying saucer reports from U.S.A, in 1947-50:

> "It appeared 1½ hours after sunset, coming over the Adriatic from Dalmatia. It crossed over all Italy, at a height of some 40 miles, and hissed as it passed, over Ronzare. It passed over the sea from Leghorn to Corsica, with a sound like the rattling of a great cart over stones. I compute that it travelled 160 miles a minute. It seemed to be a *vast body apparently bigger than the moon!*"

No wonder that Halley was staggered!
In 1716, Halley himself witnessed again the same phenomenon. The time was about 7 p.m., on 6 March:

> "A man could easily read print in the light thrown out by these spears from the same body. It did not change for two hours, and then it seemed as if new fuel had been cast on a fire."

Sir Hans Sloan himself was amazed by the apparition of a "great light that suddenly appeared in the western sky, on March 19, 1718, at 7.45 p.m." Said he:

> "It shone with a brightness much greater than the moon, which was then shining brightly. At first, I thought it was only a rocket, but it *moved more slowly than a falling star in a direct line*. It seemed to descend below the stars in the constellation of Orion. A long stream was branched in the middle, and the meteor (*sic*) turned pear-shape, or tapered upwards. At the lower end, it became spherical, but not so big as the full moon. The colour of it was white and blue, and the lustre was dazzling, like the sun on a clear day. I had to turn my eyes from it, so bright was it. It moved about 30 seconds, and went out about 20 degrees above the horizon, Behind it, it left a track of faint red yellow, like glowing coals. It seemed to sparkle, but *kept place without falling*. I hear it was also seen at Oxford and Worcester."

This slow moving body, so bright and dazzling, had all the

G

appearance of what we should today call a 'space ship'! But one does not dogmatise.

A strange apparition of "an uncommon bright glade of light" was seen from the top of his house in Buckingham street, off the Strand, London, by John Bevis, at 8.5 p.m., on March 17, 1735, when he was observing Mars, in the west. Said he:

> "It was quite unlike the Aurora Borealis, *being steady and not tremulous* in motion. The stars could be seen through it. It was *not* a comet; for I could see no nucleus through my 17-foot optical glass. It grew dim in the middle in half an hour, and then seemed to split into two very luminous parts, which grew dimmer till about 9."

The same thing was seen, three years later in sunshine, at 5 p.m., on August 28, 1738, by Thomas Short, M.D., of Sheffield:

> "The sun was shining when it appeared in the N.E. and ran north like a spear of light. It had a great round head, and seemed to burst like a rocket and spread about in a large fire. It vanished suddenly. I had seen the Aurora Borealis on Sepr. 3, 1737, at 1 a.m., but it was not like that."

The *Gentleman's Magazine* of 1738 adds:

> "It was seen in bright sunshine in Dorset, Berks, Devon and Derby (in south, north and west England), and at Reading, where there came from it a great noise of the sort naturalists call *draco volans* (flying dragon)."

Was this a meteor?

Short said that, on December 5th, 1737, at 5 p.m., he had been startled:

> "by the appearance of a deep red cloud under which a luminous body sent out streamers of very bright light by which I could easily read in a large Church Bible. It differed entirely from the Aurora Borealis; for the streamers of light moved slowly for some time and stood still. It became so hot that I *had to strip to my shirt in the open*

air. This meteor (*sic*) I find was seen at Venice, and over Kilkenny in Ireland, where it was like a great ball of fire. It is said that it shook all the island with an explosion and all the sky seemed on fire."

Did this singular ball in the sky project something like the heat rays of the Men from Mars, in the late H. G. Wells's famous novel? Again, *was* this a meteor?

Says the *Gentleman's Magazine*:

> "In March, 1719, and again on 29 Aug., 1738, there appeared in the sky over England at 3 p.m. in the north-east, in 1738, a glowing ball like a cone, with a jet of flame at the rear. A letter from Cranborne, Dorset, says the exhaust flame soon vanished. The object was also over Somerset, Staffs, and Derby. It was like a cone of fire, ending in a sharp point, with a bright ball at the thicker end. The ball seemed to burst and go away in a jet of flame. . .For 15 miles round Reading, an astonishing noise was heard in the sky, like a violent crack, with a rumble lasting one minute."

Did this flying saucer explode in our atmosphere?

Old London had another of these cosmic visitants in broad light of day with the sun shining brightly, at 9.45 a.m., on December 11, 1741. Lord Beauchamp reported:

> "The sky was serene, the sun shone brightly. I was on the mount in Kensington Gardens, London, when, in the south, I saw a ball of fire, as it seemed, 8 inches in diameter, *but oval in shape.* It grew to the size of a yard and a half in diameter, and seemed to descend from above to about half a mile from the earth. It went east and seemed to drop over Westminster. In its course it assumed a tail 80 yards long, and before disappearing, it divided into two heads. It left a trail of smoke, all the way, and where it dropped, or seemed to drop, smoke ascended for 20 minutes, and at length formed into a cloud which assumed different colours."

Other people reported that they had seen this strange object in the skies over Sussex, between 12 and 1 o'clock on the same afternoon. One man said:

"A most terrible clap of thunder was then heard in the north, like two very large cannons fired a second after each other. But the rolling and echoing were not like cannon shot. All the houses were shaken 20 miles around."

A minor canon of Canterbury Cathedral found his house violently shaken by the same cosmic visitant, at 1 p.m., on 11 December 1741:

"I thought it was an earthquake; but, outside, from the top of my house I saw what looked like a thunder cloud in the sky. This ball of light passed very swiftly over our country from east to west. It began with two great blows like cannon. It looked like a very large shooting star with a *train of light at noon-day*. The explosion shook a ship going from Gravesend to the Nore."

Comment: Shooting stars do not commonly appear in daylight in bright sunshine. But, in the years 1948-49, there have been similar reports of so-called flying saucers coming into the skies, far below the stratosphere, in various states of the U.S.A., and, as if disrupted by gravitational or other internal stresses, exploding and bursting into fragments.

All England again saw these mysterious "spears of light", 23 years later—in March 1764. They first appeared as a dusky cloud in the N.E. It was tinged with yellow as if the moon shone behind it. It passed to the north, emitting rays which seemed to form a corona at the zenith. The sky at the time was "pure and serene". The rays rose perpendicularly from the strange cloud. Some of these rays seemed fixed, others moved fast. After $1\frac{1}{2}$ hours the rays passed into a diffused light and settled down on the horizon. Observers in that year commented that the phenomena had *not the tremulous appearance of an aurora*.

(Royal Society Report). Was the strange dusky cloud some vast body emitting an unknown physical energy, or radiation, like that coming from various mysterious machines encountered, by U.S. air pilots, in the sky, in 1948, and like that which killed Mantell over Fort Knox? Who can say!

It is the fact that, 48 years earlier—in March 1716—the

same phenomenon was seen in the sky over the Atlantic, by a captain of an English ship, which was then sailing off the north-west coast of Spain. When he arrived at Nevis road, in the West Indies, he wrote to one, Alexander Geikie:

> "On 1st March, at 9 in the evening, we being in the Lat. 45° 36', off coast of north-west Spain, a clear cloud appeared east of us, not far distant from our zenith, which afterwards darted itself forth into a number of rays of light, every way like the tail of a comet, of such great length that it reached within a short way of the horizon. There likewise appeared a body of light, NNE. of us, and continued as light almost as day till after 12 a clock. It appeared a good distance from us, and darkened on a sudden. It seemed to arise out of the deep ocean sea, as well as from land."

This same phenomenon was also seen, at night, on March 31, 1716, at London; on April 2, near Oundle, Northampton-shire; at 9.10 p.m. at Dublin and Paris; and on April 2:

> "A man in the open air at London, at 9 p.m., saw a bright ray, of very white light, appear in the east, out of a pure sky, like the tail of a comet. It vanished and another sudden beam appeared. It travelled north in ten minutes."

Was this really two satellite discs, or space ships, rather than a comet? The different observers' reports, taken together, suggest that something stranger than a comet was seen between March 31 and April 2, 1716.

Now we come to the mysterious noises from the skies in Western Europe, ranging in gamut from cannonades to the sounds of carts rattling over stones. Halley and others, had, as we saw, already noted this aural phenomenon.

Here, again, let us note that the great astronomer Kepler had reported, on 17 November 1623—and others were to report in England, several times in the following or 18th century—the appearance of remarkable bodies in the sky, both by day and night, that gave out this same noise of a great cart rattling over stones, and, in some cases, did damage to fields, farms, cattle and houses.

197

Says Kepler:

> "*A burning globe* appeared at sunset—on 17 November, 1623. It was visible in different places all over Germany. In Austria, it is affirmed a sound of cracking or crushing came from it, as if from a thunderbolt, which, however, I take to be groundless."

The repetition of such a phenomenon some dozen times in two succeeding centuries may serve to modify the feeling of 'groundlessness', though, today, in U.S.A., as in England, one feels that the professional astronomer might assert that it was merely a meteor or bolide. *But was it?*

A mysterious series of cannonades in the sky startled a whole countryside, in Berkshire, England, at 5 p.m., on April 9, 1628. This phenomenon also occurred in the mid-18th century, and has never been explained.

Says the *Gentleman's Magazine*:

> "The weather was warm, and on a sudden a hideous rumbling was heard in the air, followed by a strange and fearful peal like thunder. It sounded like a fought battle. A great cannon seemed to roar. Then it came a second time, till 20 cannon shots seemed to have been discharged in the sky. Then was heard a sound like the beat of a drum sounding a retreat. There now came a hissing sound and a stone fell on the ground. Later, it was dug out by Mistress Greene who saw it fall at Bawikin Green. It was three-square, pricked at the end, and weighed 19½ pounds. Another stone weighed 5 pounds."

We are content to leave this mystery unexplained. Leave it to the astronomers who are earnestly begged not to dismiss it as *only* a meteorite, and nothing more. Who ever heard a meteorite sounding a drum retreat, after some strange battle of Unknown Cosmic Giants in the Sky, over old England?

In 1642, more mysterious phenomena of the skies, like that of 1628, in England, startled people in both France and England. I quote from the Journal of Antoine Denesde, a farrier of Poitiers, France, and of Marie, his wife (1628-1687):

"*Wed. 9 Sepr. 1642:* "In the town and citadel of Perpignan

. . .on this day, between 6 and 7 in the morning, all France heard, each believing that it came from over his head, in the clear and serene air, and on as fine a day as could be, a noise (coup) like an artillery discharge. This, after rolling and reverberating for some time, frightened everybody. Some said they saw one thing, some another; others that it came from the ground, or was a thunderbolt. And this was on the day that Perpignan surrendered to Messires de Chambert and la Mailleray, marshals of France."

It is also noted in the Journal de Simon Robert (at Germond), notary public, in Lower Poitou, 1621-1654:

"9 Sepr. 1642: "At the time when a general requiem mass was being celebrated for the deceased Queen Marie de Medici, the King's mother, in the parochial churches, about 7 in the morning, a noise was heard in the air as if it came from Saint Maxant or from Poitiers, to those here at Germond. At the beginning, people said it was four or five cannon shots, one after the other, and, later, that it was thunder lasting a very long time. Yet all the sky was blue and clear, with no wind; for it drew near the time of the cold dry north wind (la bise). No cloud was in any part of the sky, and the brilliant sun showed a clear and beautiful disc. Many people, here, believed it was the feux de pipe coming down from the cueille de Saint James, going from Champdenier to Nyort (glass-blowers' factory exhaust). Nota: Everywhere, for more than 10 to 12 hours, the same noise was heard, and as loudly in one place as another. Before, the weather was rainy, and from then, always fine . . ."

. The same phenomenon was also heard over a wide stretch of England, at that time, from Hafford, about six miles from Oxford, in Berkshire, to Woodbridge, in Suffolk, which, as the crow flies, is 170 miles east, towards the North Sea. At Hafford, on August 4, 1642, people said the weather was warm, when, between 4 and 5 p.m., they heard in the sky a strange noise like drums beaten loudly and hit fiercely. It was followed by a noise like a cannon-shot, which lasted for 1½ hours. At Woodbridge, in Suffolk, the noises—and it will be noted that a similar phenomenon had been heard in Berkshire, fourteen

years earlier, in 1628, on April 9, also at 5 p.m.—were followed
by a violent report, when there was seen to fall from the sky
"a stone about four pounds in weight".

> "Captain Johnson, of Woodbridge, dug it up hot.
> People of Alborow, Suffolk, ran out of their houses sup-
> posing a great battle was being fought in the air, but saw
> nothing; when suddenly was heard a joyful noise, as of
> musick and sounding instruments, all in a melodious
> manner. It lasted for a good space, and ended in a harmon-
> ious ringing of bells. The stone then fell onto a heath.
> It was 8 inches long, 15 inches broad, and 2 inches thick."

How could a falling meteorite be the cause of these strange
orchestral sounds and fierce beating of drums, as if from a
great battle in the skies? Whence came this strange music of
the spheres, heard both in England and France, at intervals
of fourteen years?

Yet a meteorite may have fallen, as in other mysterious
phenomena of this kind; but it would seem this was coinciden-
tal. It certainly does *not* explain the other mysterious phenomena. There is a long list of these explosions in the air, which
have never been explained. I set out only a few of them, which
have occurred both in Great Britain and in the U.S.A., and
all over Europe:

> Mysterious explosions in the sky at East Hadam, U.S.A.,
> on July 1, 1812 and Decr. 28, 1813; over the island of
> Melida, in the Adriatic, it sounded like cannonading, and
> lasted 30 days, with several hundred detonations a day;
> in the sky over Comrie, Scotland, on April 13, 1822; in
> Cardiganshire, Wales, at intervals of weeks, in the fall
> of 1855; *ditto*, in 1858; in New Zealand, in 1848; a lumin-
> ous object exploded in the sky over Kuttenberg, Bohemia
> (now Czecho-Slovakia), on April 10, 1874, when there was
> a glare like sunlight and a detonation lasting one minute;
> a violent detonation in the sky over Rosena, Hungary,
> on April 9, 1876; in Indian Bengal, there are the mys-
> terious "Barisal guns" which detonate in series of three
> explosions, and are heard far inland, like cannonading,
> on clear days, as in April 1888 and March 1889. (No one
> has ever solved the mystery of their origin); in 1894, 1895
> and 1896, unexplained explosions were heard in Belgium,

the English Channel, and at Southampton, Eng.; on Novr. 15, 1895, people in offices, shops and buildings, rushed into the streets of central London, Eng., following violent explosions in the air, and the police were baffled in discovering any explanation; in Novr. 1905, people in English southern and western counties were startled by similar explosions in the sky, occurring in a series of three; a terrific, unexplained sky explosion in Berkshire, England, on Novr. 19, 1912.

In some of these cases, objects like flying saucers exploded in the sky or fell to the ground. In other cases, one is driven back on the fantastic theory that other worlds may have been signalling ours, as in August 1921, when the late Signore Marconi, of wireless fame, picked up electro-magnetic vibrations of the order of 150,000 metres in wave length. They seemed to be in code, were in singular regularity, and Mars was not in opposition, at the time.

On March 12, 1722, between 1 and 2 p.m., what looked like a "red hot millstone" fell from the sky, after an explosion over Halstead, Essex, Eng. The water of a pond foamed for 30 hours after. It happened again on Aug. 15, 1732, also in Essex, at Springfield, when people saw the waters of a canal foam until waves were tossed 6 feet into the air, for 30 seconds. All that was heard was an explosion in the air, but nothing was seen to fall from the sky into the canal.

Jacob Bee's *Diary*—he died at Durham, England, in 1711— records how, on December 20, 1689:

"A comet appeared at 4.45 p.m. . . . first in ye forme of halfe a moone, very firie, and afterwards did change itself to a firye sword, and run westward." (This is more like a flying saucer than a comet. *Au.*)

Here are other records of strange phenomena seen in France, from 1726 to 1848:

1726, May: "Several people in England have been killed by hail stones as big as the fist. On 19 October, in western France, there appeared in the air a phenomenon that

201

lasted from 8 p.m. till after midnight. People came out of their houses and sank on their knees at prayer in the streets, thinking the end of the world had come. The thing was seen as clearly as if the moon shone, though the moon was in the last quarter." (*Veuclin: Petits Documents.*) (What the thing was is not stated. *Au.*)

1732: "On 3 June, in the evening, and the next day, in the morning, one saw, at Lessay, the whole sky on fire, from the horizon to the zenith. In the focus, as if in a pyrotechnic display, there was the play of an infinity of lights like sky-rockets. It fell from all parts, like drops of metal on fire; and the spectacle might have been charming, but for the thunder-claps that terrified the most valorous people. Buildings were shaken, for some time, and some were reduced to ashes. Cattle were killed in the fields. But the rain was not abundant, and on the day following the drought continued as before." (*Dom Halley, prieur of the Benedictins, writing to the academician, Mairan, about phenomena in the department of La Manche, W. France.*) (Auroral displays do *not* explain the above.)

1749, 11 October: "About noon, there was heard all over the countryside, between Cherbourg and Avranches, and even at Bayeux, a hollow sound like the discharge of artillery far off, or, indeed, like the noise of something very considerable falling down. During what seemed a subterranean disturbance, said the Abbé Outhier, several people thought they felt a shock of the earth in movement." (*Vérusmoir: Annuaire de la Manche, 1839*).

Some of the French Catholic clergy saw a good chance to capitalise these strange phenomena, in 1751; for, writes M. Philippe Lesueur, *curé*, in his parochial register:

"God has wished to give to his people the means of gaining indulgences: To the rich, alms to ransom their sins. To the poor, expiation of them by hunger."

Yes, the hunger that, 38 years later, helped precipitate the French Revolution!

Lange records in his *Ephémérides*:

1830, 14 Sepr.: "At night, and principally from 4-5 a.m.,

a veritable rain of fire was observed in several places in the department of Calvados, and, in the Orne, in the suburbs of Argentan, a great fire was inspired by it." (Was it an auroral display? Or a very extraordinary fall of meteorites?)

1848, 10 July: "A meteor ravaged the department of the Orne, particularly the Canton of Ecouché." (Something that ravaged a French department about 37 miles long by 75 miles wide, must have been either a tremendous acrolite—of which there is no record—*or something else! Au.*)

Summer 1883: "All the children and the teacher in the public elementary school at Segeberg, saw in the sky two fiery balls, the size of full moons, travelling side by side, not very swiftly, from north to south, on a clear and sunny day." (West German Magazine, *Der Stern*, letter from Herr Blunk, of Hamburg.)

In the 18th and 19th centuries, so many mysterious objects, like cones, balls, kites, luminous frames, whirling wheels, and other queer shapes appeared in the skies, or over the seas, which aeroforms could not be explained as auroras, or comets, or meteorites—and many of them recorded in the archives of the British Royal Society—that they seem worth a separate chapter. The only difference, apart from the amazing characteristics of these mysterious aeroforms, between the 18th and 19th century observations, is a psychological one. To-day, we have a greater awareness of these strange phenomena, and perhaps less inclination, except among certain members of the British House of Commons, to dismiss them as mere hallucinations or mass hysteria.

Author's Note—Giant footprints, 22 inches long, with five toe-marks, trailed in snow from inland, vanishing over a cliff near the Needles, Isle of Wight. They were seen by coastguards, on 7 February 1954. (*Vide* p.180, *supra*).

CHAPTER IX

WHAT ON EARTH WAS IT?

Our 18th century "of prose and reason", and the roaring century of "progress", the 19th, appear to have been studied by mysterious visitors from outer space; but their irruptions into our stratosphere and atmosphere were sporadic and scattered over the years. We do not note the suddenly quickened tempo that marked the appearance of cosmic signs and wonders during the close of the second world war, and particularly after the explosions of atomic and hydrogen bombs. Shall we say that, in the 18th and to the fourth decade of the present century, these elusive entities of the flying saucers may have been moved by curiosity, and not by *fear* of our use of scientific devices, by international financiers, militarists, and their lackeys, the official scientists of the 1940's and 1950's?

Space will not permit me to cite the full records, many of which are in the Royal Society's archives, or in such well known 18th century journals, as the 'Gentleman's Magazine', or the 'Scottish Magazine', or the 'Annual Register'. I, here, summarise them accurately—all strange unknown things in the skies:

Something "like a boy's kite", but burnished like silver, seen darting in and out of clouds. (*Mr. Cracker of Fleet, Dorset. Time: sunny day, 11.45 a.m., Decr. 8, 1733*). The thing was again seen at 5 p.m., Decr. 11, 1741, from Berkshire to London and Kent, and, this time, preceded by an explosion like thunder.

Object like a slender pyramid, seen by Rev. Wm. Derham, F.R.S., red, visible 15 minutes after sunset, April 3, 1707, at Upminster, Essex.

"Shape of thing like trumpet" seen over Leeds, Yorks., by Ralph Thoresby, F.R.S. (9.45 p.m., May 18, 1710); at 11.11 p.m., on 27 May, 1744, by Henry Baker, F.R.S., over terrace of Somerset House, Gardens, old London, when it emitted a white flame; on July 4, 1745, by Rev. George Costard. (Time: 8 p.m.; place: Stanlake Broad, Norfolk).

Surely, it is singular that, *if* this were a meteor, it should take precisely the same curious shape at three intervals of 34 and 35 years! The data, here given, suggest that we have a curious extra-terrestrial machine—whether manned or remotely controlled—observing old England!

There was the extraordinary experience of a Fellow of the Royal Society, going home from a meeting, on December 16, 1742. As he entered St. James's Park, at 8.40 p.m., he was startled by the sight of a remarkable object that suddenly rose above the tree tops in the park:

> "I was crossing St. James's Park, when a light arose from behind the trees and houses, to the south and west, which at first I thought was a rocket, of large size. But when it rose 20 degrees, it moved parallel to the horizon, but waved like this"—he draws an undulating line—"and went on in the direction of north by east. It seemed very near. *Its motion was very slow.* I had it for about half a mile in view. A light flame was turned backward by the resistance the air made to it. From one end, it emitted a bright glare and fire like that of burning charcoal. That end was a frame like bars of iron, and quite opaque to my sight. At one point, on the longitudinal frame, or cylinder, issued a train in the shape of a tail of light more bright at one point on the rod or cylinder, and growing gradually fainter at the end of rod or cylinder; so that it was transparent for more than half of its length. The head of this strange object seemed about half a degree in diameter, and the tail near three degrees in length."

The reporter signed himself merely *"C.M."*

Whatever this object was, its motion rules out meteors; for it suggests control and steering, and some observational purpose, under control of some intelligent and unknown living entity, *not* of terrestrial origin!

A similar mysterious object was seen before dawn in summer 1949, in a state of western U.S.A.

Globe of light moving east to west in sky over Peckham,

then in Surrey. (Time: 1.7 p.m., Decr. 11, 1741). Similar object seen very high over Scotland and Solway Firth, also over York and Coventry. (Time: 7.45 p.m., July 29, 1750).

"Fiery thing like water-spout" seen over Rutland (5-6 p.m., Sepr. 15, 1749), and over Hatfield, Yorks., in previous years. It whirled and roared, frightened cattle and rustics, and took up water from river Welland, then passed over Seaton Hill and split and smashed oaks and trees in woods. It seemed to dart arrows of light into the ground. On January 1, 1751, this unknown object rose from the Mts. of Mourne, smashed trees, killed a woman on the ground, and unroofed houses, in radius of 15 miles, near Newry, N. Ireland.

Weird things like "two human bodies" rushed at each other, and lit up the "whole hemisphere" in the Midlands, for 4 seconds. Terrific speed and glare of light. (26 March, 1754, 10 and 11 p.m.)

Round ball with tail, emitting brilliant white light, as large as diameter of moon, seen over Amsterdam, and Chiswick (near London), where it descended like a helicopter. Altitude: about 66 miles high over Holland. (Time: 15 August, 1755, after sunset).

Cerulean blue object alarmed people, was not aurora, visible for 18 minutes, when it projected streamers of flame over Turin, Italy. A shock of explosion followed. (Jan 2, 1756, 4 p.m.) Luminous body in sky coincided with drowning of 200 cattle and 700 acres of land, at Ballinore, Ireland (January 21, 1756), when, in Scotland and Sweden at 10 p.m., the whole sky in east opened with fire and a pin could be seen on a ship's deck, in the unearthly light. Over Wetria, Sweden, luminous ball, as large as full moon, projected a searchlight, as it passed in straight line, east. This ball was also seen over Avignon, France, and sent out explosions, and rocket-flares. (Time: March 10, 1756, 6-10 p.m.)

At Köln, Germany, a body with a pencil of light hovered for an hour, from 7 to 8 p.m., and then vanished into space. It jetted an exhaust towards the north (March 10, 1756).

207

"Football of fire of immense size" came down from the sky over Colchester, Essex, and then ascended. (Time: Decr. 31, 1758, 8 p.m.) Thing like globe with conical tail passed, London, Cambridge, Scotland and Ireland. Twice changed course, and seemed to burn in an enclosed frame, with no vapours. Vanished at speed of 30 miles a second! Conical object of great speed passed over Edinburgh. (Time: 9 p.m., 26 Novr., 1758). It liberated three satellite discs and vanished!

Object like tennis-ball passed from Mendips, Somerset, to Essex, at high speed. Bluish light, moved downwards in curve, then vanished at the horizon. (First seen: 6 p.m., October 10, 1759).

Sphere of fire travelled in circle with light so strong that it cast a shadow in bright sunshine, over New England, U.S. (10 a.m., 10 May, 1760). A noise came from it, and oddly enough was heard sooner at the middle of the course it took than at the beginning!

Ball of fire seen travelling against the wind, at Whitby, Yorks. (Nov. 3, 1761, at 6 p.m.)

Town of Bideford, Devon, lit up on a Sunday, at 8.50 p.m., by strange object like "twisting serpent", descending gradually from sky. Visible for 6 minutes, in dazzling light. Vanished slowly. (Decr. 5, 1762).

Glowing ball—not a meteor—projected red beams of light from clouds, on a sunny day, over Chelsea (Sepr. and October, 1763).

People in Oxford, in the year 1769, had another cosmic surprise when, from 7.15 to 7.45 p.m., on October 24, there suddenly appeared in the sky what looked like a "house on fire"!

Two years before, the people of Oxford were startled by this "house on fire in the sky", and the same, or another cosmic "house on fire" frightened men living at Coupar Angus, in Perthshire.

Here is a report of this remarkable spectacle, which appeared in a Scottish newspaper of September 1767:

"On the water, at Isla near Cowper Angus (*sic*), a thick

dark smoke rose and then dispelled to reveal a large
luminous body like a *house on fire*. It presently took a
pyramidal form and rolled forwards with impetuosity,
till it came to the water of Erick. It rushed up this river
with great speed and disappeared a little above Blairgowrie. It caused an extraordinary effect! In its passage
it carried away a large cart, and bore it many yards over
a field of grass. A man riding on the high road was carried
from his horse and stunned. He remained senseless for a
long time. It destroyed half a house, but left the other
half behind, undermined. It also destroyed an arch of
a new bridge at Blairgowrie, immediately before it
vanished."

Is this a remarkable case where a strange cosmic visitant,
or interplanetary machine, actually came out of the sky and
moved very near the ground, in this far-off year, 1767? Who,
anyway, may call this weird and blazing object a meteor, or
even a meteorite?

Strange ball of light passed with slow motion, apparently just above noon, eastwards, and vanished. (Over
Hertford and Waltham Abbey, May 8, 1775, 8.30 p.m.)

Rotating object, like a vortex with "infinitely high
speed and circular motion", badly frightened people in
London, for 15 minutes, after dusk, 18 June, 1782.

A startling cosmic body appeared over the terrace of
Windsor Castle, on August 18, 1783. It was watched by Tib-
erius Cavallo, F.R.S. He called it a "most extraordinary
meteor".

He wrote:

"North-east of the Terrace, in clear sky and warm
weather, I saw appear suddenly *an oblong cloud* nearly
parallel to the horizon. Below the cloud was seen a luminous body. . .It soon became a roundish body, brightly lit
up and *almost stationary*. It was about 9.25 p.m. This
strange ball at first appeared bluish and faint, but its
light increased, and it *soon began to move*. At first, it
ascended above the horizon, obliquely towards the east.
Then it changed its direction and moved parallel to the
horizon. It vanished in the S.E. I saw it for half a minute,

209

and the light it gave out was prodigious. It lit up every
object on the face of the country. It changed shape to
oblong, acquired a tail, and seemed to split up into two
bodies of small size. About two minutes later came a
rumble like an explosion."

Other observers said they saw it over Deptford as a large
luminous body with tinge of blue at the edges, and appearance of electrical fire. It moved vertically at first and seemed
to change size and form. It left behind globules of fire
extinguishing themselves like the stars of a rocket. It seemed
as large as two full moons, and the ray it emitted lit up all
around in its glare. The archdeacon of York also saw it, and
horses in the fields trembled. Soon after, he heard two great
explosions. It was seen after 9 p.m. over Hartlepool, and in
Ireland appeared as a parabolic body with a vividly red and
blue and luminous tail.

A globe with rotary motion round its axis, and of
uncommon magnitude, passed very high in the sky over
Edinburgh, and was seen in south of England, Ireland,
Ostend and Glasgow, where it lit up the streets like day.
It glowed like incandescent iron. It was seen on the same
day, over Glasgow and Edinburgh. (Time: 18-20 August,
1783, 9 p.m.) On August 30, 1783, a singular ball with a
cone lit up the sky over Greenwich, and was seen to have
another blazing ball parallel to it. It expelled *eight satellite
discs*. Motion not rapid. It vanished south-east from
Greenwich Park, at 9.11 p.m.

Elliptical ball, rising and descending in sky, vanished
behind clouds. (Over Edinburgh, 8.30 p.m., June 21,
1787). In 1785, Edinburgh saw a sphere with conical
appendage, making her streets bright as day. (Time:
9 p.m., Dec. 26, 1785.) The same flying saucer was also
seen over Chelsea, Plymouth, Newcastle-on-Tyne, and
Dublin.

Queer body like "an apothecary's pestle, or cylinder,"
suddenly appeared from a cloud, over Alnwick, Northumberland. It appeared to fork, and split into two half-
moons, with streamers of light. Vanished after 5 minutes.
(Sepr. 10, 1798, 10.40 p.m.)

People in the year 1799 saw some peculiar things in the sky:

> "On Sep. 19, all England saw, at 8.30 p.m., a beautiful ball blazing with white light, and which passed from N.W. to S.E. It moved rapidly with a gentle tremulous motion, and noiselessly. The light cast by it was very vivid, and a few red sparks detached themselves from it. . .On Nov. 12, something like a large red pillar of fire passed north to south over Hereford, and alarmed people in the Forest of Dean, some miles away. Flashes of extremely vivid electrical sort preceded its appearance, and at intervals of half an hour, several hours before. This was at 5.45 a.m. . .On this night, the moon shone with uncommon vividness, when, between 5 and 6 a.m., bright lights in the sky became stationary. They then burst with no perceptible report, and passed north leaving behind them beautiful trains of floating fire. Some were pointed, some radiated. Some sparkled and some had large columns. . .The general appearance was terrifying, particularly to fishermen of Hartlepool, then out at sea. . . Seven days later, Nov. 19, at 6 a.m., folk of Huncoates, Lincolnshire, were alarmed by vivid flashes lasting 30 seconds, from a ball of fire passing in the sky." (*Gentleman's Magazine*). (Were these balls, "saucers"? *Au.*)

A strange story is told in the "Histoire de l'Académie Royale des Sciences" (Paris, 1766, "Histoires et Mémoires"), of an event that was reported to the Academy by Monsieur de Rostan, member of the economic society of Berne, and the medico-physical society of Basel. It occurred on 9 August, 1762; and I may draw attention to the fact that the phenomenon is related to one of those very mysterious, or spindle-shaped, fusiform bodies, seen in both U.S. and English skies in the 19th century, and since 1949:

> "On that day, he was taking the sun's altitude with a quadrant, at Lausanne, on Lake Geneva, when he noticed the sun give out a very faint pale light. He thought it was caused by the vapours of Lake Leman; but when he focused a 14-foot telescope, fitted with a micrometer, to the sun, he was surprised to see the eastern side of the sun *eclipsed* about three digits, and shrouded in a nebulosity which environed an opaque body by which the sun was eclipsed. In two and a half hours, the south

side of the said body, whatever it was, appeared detached from the limb of the sun; but the limb, or, more properly, the northern extremity of this body, which had the *shape of a spindle*" (Author's italics), "in breadth about three of the sun's digits and nine in length, did not quit the sun's northern limb. This spindle kept continuously advancing on the sun's body, from east towards the west, with no more than about half the velocity with which the ordinary solar spots move; for it did not disappear till the 7th September, after having reached the sun's western limb.

"M. de Rostan, during that time, observed it almost every day, that is, for near a month; and by means of a camera obscura he delineated the figures of it, which he sent to the Royal Academy of Sciences, at Paris. The same phenomenon was seen at Sole, in the bishopric of Basel, about 45 German leagues north of Lausanne. M. de Coste, a friend of Mons. Rostan, focused an 11-foot telescope on it and found it to be the same spindle-like form as M. de Rostan, only it was not quite so broad, which probably might be that, owing to growing near the end of its apparition (appearance), the body began to turn about and present its edge. A more remarkable circumstance, is that at Sole, it did not answer to the same point of the sun as it did at Lausanne. It therefore had considerable parallax; but what so very extraordinary a body, placed between the sun and us, should be is not easy to divine.

"It was not a sun spot, since its motion was much too slow; nor was it a planet, or comet, for the shape of it seemed to prove the contrary. In a word, we know of nothing that we can have recourse to in the heavens that may explain this phenomenon; and what adds to the oddness of it is that M. Messier, who constantly observed the sun, at Paris, during the same time, saw nothing of such an appearance."

Rostan took an early photograph of this unknown object, with his camera obscura. It is obvious that this space ship(?) must have been between the sun and the earth, out in space. He sent a print of the photograph to the Academy of Sciences in Paris; but it was not reproduced in their Memoirs, nor is it known what happened to what must be the earliest photograph ever taken of a flying saucer!

There was also reported to the Académie des Sciences, by
its correspondent, Monsieur Saussure, professor of philosophy
at Geneva, a queer and unexplained event of which he was
an eye-witness, on 3 August, 1763:

> "At about 5 p.m., on that day, I was passing over the
> first bridge at the Rive gate (Geneva), whose moat, or
> fosse runs immediately into the lake (Leman), when I
> saw several persons attentively staring into the moat. I
> stopped. . .and saw that the water of this moat had appar-
> ently risen, and seemed to have reached its highest point
> of ascension; for I did not see it rise any more. A moment
> after, I saw it fall very sensibly. I then went down into
> the bed of the moat and carefully noted the point to
> which the water had descended onto the rocks which sup-
> port the piers there, and which were then uncovered.
> As best as I could, I measured the difference in the height
> between the point to which I had seen it fall in level
> and that where I had seen it at its highest: four feet
> nine *lignes*. The water had taken 15 minutes to cover this
> difference in heights. At its second oscillation, when I had
> been forced by a new rise in the water to climb out of the
> moat, the water, on rising, covered a distance of four feet
> six *pouces* nine *lignes*, in 10 minutes; but in falling again,
> it descended only four feet two *pouces* nine *lignes*, and
> that in 12 minutes. In the third oscillation, it did not
> rise more than two feet eight *pouces* nine *lignes*, and in
> eight minutes. It then fell very slowly, and not expecting
> anything further of this curious nature, I went away.
> "However, I stopped at the barrier of the moat, and
> the water seemed to be still. The sentinel there told me
> that, before his arrival, there had already been a rise and
> fall in the water of the moat; but less than I had myself
> seen. The weather the day before had been very warm and
> there had been a considerable storm at 3.30 p.m., in
> Geneva; but at the time of the phenomenon only a few
> drops of rain fell and the wind was very light, and south-
> westerly."

Now, in Lake Geneva there are what are called *sèches*, or
spates, or freshets, from the feeding of the waters of the Rhone
and the Arve, by snow melting in the Alps; and, on the second
day after the phenomenon in the moat, the banks of the lake
had seen such a spate, but it was not more than three and a

half inches, and higher up (near Geneva), still less. Saussure did not think that the *sèche* was the cause of the phenomenon in the moat, and all the people along the banks of the Arve said they had seen no rise whatever in the water likely to have caused the phenomenon in the moat.

It is very curious that, in August, 1953, at Grafton, West Virginia, synchronising with the appearances of flying saucers near this region, a phenomenon very like that reported by Saussure as happening in the moat at Geneva, in August, 1763—exactly 190 years earlier—puzzled the officials of the local water reservoirs. They could not account for heavy losses of water in the night, when, three times, the level of the water in a million-gallon reservoir fell several inches, the fall being equivalent to a fire hydrant being opened at full cock. (There was no fire anywhere that night, and the police were baffled to account for the mystery.) Elsewhere, in this book, I have noted that observers on a lake in Ontario allege that they have seen midget men on a saucer land on the lake and siphon in the water through a green hose!

An immense body like a very large moon with a black bar across it terrified the people of Hull, England, who were called by others to rise from bed to see it between 12 midnight and 1 a.m. on June 19, 1801. It gradually formed itself into five smaller bodies, shining brilliantly, and they gradually faded out, leaving behind a *vividly lit sphere!* All the time it was visible, a faint bluish light surrounded the sphere. When it vanished, the sky appeared as serene as on a fine summer's evening.

In the same year, on July 14, at 9.30 p.m., Montgaillard, France, was astonished by a strange object in the sky. It first appeared as a "common cloud some 18,000 yards long and about half as broad. It then took fire, burning with a pale flame, bluish at the edges. This splendid glory lasted 15 minutes. After an interval, the fires were rekindled, for about 9 minutes, then extinguished, again re-appearing a third time.

Who knows what this amazing "cloud" really was?

Another of the conical saucers startled London, in broad day at 9 a.m., on July 17, 1806:

"It was apparently about a quarter the size of the moon's diameter, but more brilliant than Venus. Its course was swift and horizontal, and from its conical tail sparks shot out. We entreat our correspondents in the country to communicate to us their observations on the course of this large and singular meteor (*sic*). . .On October 14, a similar phenomenon lit up, at 8 p.m., a very large area of the countryside round Swansea, S. Wales." (*Gentleman's Magazine.*)

A brilliant thing in the sky, like a rocket, but not "flying faster than a bird", flew over Middleton Cheney parsonage, Northants, Eng., in the evening of Dec. 22, 1807. Its course was N.E. from S.W., and horizontal, and it vanished before reaching a hill. It was not more than 30 yards above the ground, and suddenly vanished, with no sparks.

What was it that John Staveley, of Hatton Garden, London, saw, in a thunderstorm, on 10 August, 1809?

He was so astonished that he wrote to the "Journal of Natural History and Philosophy and Chemistry":

"I saw many meteors moving around the edge of a black cloud from which lightning flashed. They were like dazzling specks of lights, dancing and traipsing thro' the clouds. One increased in size till it became of the brilliancy and magnitude of Venus, on a clear evening; but I could see no body in the light. It moved with great rapidity, and coasted the edge of the cloud. Then it became stationary, dimmed its splendour, and vanished. *I saw these strange lights for minutes, not seconds.* For at least an hour, these lights, so strange, and in innumerable points, played in and out of this black cloud. No lightning came from the clouds where these lights played. As the meteors increased in size, they seemed to descend."

Impious as the suggestion may seem to the orthodox astrophysicist of our own day, I would whisper in someone's ear that this was *not* the behaviour of any sort of meteor, but a form of flying saucer!

Again, in Switzerland, on 15 May, 1811, numbers of people at Geneva, among them members of the faculties of science at the local university, saw the following phenomenon:

215

"At 8.35 p.m., that night, there was a sudden flash of light in the sky, preceded by a whizzing in the north-west. A kind of serpent of fire appeared, bent back at the west end, like the letter S; then it spread out in the lower part. It then took the shape of a horse-shoe and nearly of a parabola. We watched it for seven minutes by our watches, when a cloud hid it, at the moment when it was slowly advancing to the west. The brightness diminished, and as it vanished, two very bright lights in points were seen, and at the lower branch of the parabola, the other on the same branch, near the summit of the curve. To the eye, it seemed twice the height of the Jura mountains. One eye-witness, with a telescope, said the most luminous was not homogeneous, but of separate parts. For a long time, it was practically stationary. It was also seen at Paris, at a height of probably $24\frac{1}{2}$ leagues high ($73\frac{1}{2}$ miles). No explosion came from it." (*Recorded by Professor Pictet of Geneva*).

The reader will have noted that this serpentine type of flying saucer had appeared in England, in the 18th century.

So far, in this singular narrative of cosmic visitants over the earth, it will be noted that the reports of what seem to be extra-terrestrial machines of some unknown type and origin have been confined mostly to the skies over the British Isles and Western Europe. But now at the turn of the 18th century a strange object appeared in the skies over Baton Rouge, Louisiana, U.S.A. It was on the night of 5 April, 1800, when a body *the size of a large house*, estimated to be 80 feet long, passed about 200 yards above the surface of the ground. It was brightly lit, but emitted no sparks. It had a "colour like that of the sun seen near the skyline on a frosty evening":

"As it passed over the heads of amazed spectators, the light cast by it onto the surface of the ground was little short of sunbeams, though, looking another way, the stars were visible. It moved rapidly from the south-west, and in 15 minutes had vanished in the north-east. As it passed, heat was felt on the ground. Immediately after it vanished there came a violent rushing sound and a tremendous crash carrying with it a sensible earthquake. Trees in a forest were found burnt or split."

This phenomenon *might* have been an aerolite of the sort which, in 1908 and 1944 fell with devastating effects in Siberia. But it might also have been *something else!* The data are capable of at least two interpretations.

In spring, 1825, a weird and brilliant object, like a "Pruning-hook", and apparently 20 feet long, was seen for 70 minutes in the sky over Poland; while on November 13, 1833, a long, luminous body, like "a square table", and emitting a long trail of light, was seen in the zenith, over Niagara Falls.

In the 19th century, sketches and photographs were made of strange objects seen in the skies by either professional astronomers or lay observers. For example, in March, 1870, the captain, F. W. Banner, of the British ship "Lady of the Lake", saw, in the north Atlantic, a remarkable object of the "flying saucer" type.

Here is an extract from his log:

"March 22, 1870, in Lat. 5° 47' N., Long. 27° 52' W. (the position would be west of the coast of Rio de Oro, N.W. Africa, *Author*), my crew reported a strange object in the sky... I saw it... It was a 'cloud' of circular form, with an included semi-circle divided into four parts, and a central shaft running from the centre of the circle and extending far outward and curving backward... The thing was *travelling against the wind*. It came from the south and settled right into the wind's eye. It was visible for half an hour, much lower than other clouds, and was lost to sight in the sky as dusk came on. I drew it." It looked like a half-moon with a long shaft radiating from the centre.

Now note: In March, 1950, an exactly similar object was seen in the sky over St. Matthew, South Carolina, U.S. The man who saw it said: "It was like a half moon with a tail in it!"

In 1883, amazing photographs were taken by the director of the Astronomical Observatory at Zacatecas, Mexico. He photographed hundreds of strange objects apparently crossing the disc of the sun, but really nearer the moon, in daylight. They took the form, in one case, of a weird object shaped like *a five-pointed star with a dark centre.* This happened on two days, 12 and 13 August, 1883. (I here reproduce one of the days, 12 and 13 August, 1883. *Note:* That *dark centre* is a feature of some of the flying saucer machines seen over the U.S.A. in 1948-50!

This director and astronomer was Señor José A. Y. Bonilla whose observatory was 2,505 metres (2 miles, 337 feet) above sea level. At the time, he was investigating sun spots. At 8 in the morning of 12 August, 1883, he was amazed suddenly to see pass, apparently across the disc of the sun, a little luminous body. He photographed it on the film, or plate used to take pictures of the solar spots. It traversed the sun like a nearly circular shadow.

His report is very interesting:

> "I had not recovered my surprise when the same phenomenon was repeated! And that with such frequency that, in the space of *two hours*, I counted up to *283 bodies* crossing the solar disc. Little by little, however, clouds hindered the observation. I could not resume the observation till the sun crossed the meridian, and then only for 40 minutes."

He counted 48 of these singular bodies in a very short interval of time. They were moving from west to east, but slightly inclining towards the north and south of the sun's disc. These peculiar objects seemed to be dark and black. Some were perfectly round. Others were more or less stretched out. They became luminous when, on leaving the solar disc, they crossed the field of the lens of the camera. They passed at very short intervals, in ones and twos, taking at the most a second to cross the solar disc. Fifteen or twenty passed almost at one time. It became difficult to count them. "I was able to fix their trajectory across the solar disc by noting their entry and exit, on the paper that served to photograph the sun spots. A clockwork mechanism adjusted the movement of film and paper to the apparent diurnal movement of the sun on the celestial vault.". . .

> "I photographed most of these strange bodies in pro-

jection and profile. Some appear round or spherical, but one notices in the photographs that the bodies are not spherical, but irregular in form. Before crossing the solar disc, these bodies threw out brilliant trains of light, but in crossing the sun they seemed to become opaque and dark, against its brighter background. The negatives of the photographs show a body surrounded by nebulosity and cloudiness and dark trains of lines."

Bonilla thought that when these strange bodies crossed the sun's disc they lost their brilliance by absorption of ray-emission in the actinic light of the sun. This diminished their photogenic power.

Next day, from 8 a.m. to 9.45 a.m., he saw 116 of these mysterious bodies cross the sun's disc. He telegraphed to other Mexican observatories at Mexico City and Puebla, but these bodies were not observed there. Probably this was owing to what is called parallax (apparent displacement of an object caused by an actual change in the point of observation).

The mystery of these weird bodies in space still remains unsolved. But it is unlikely that they were insects, birds, or dust in the upper atmosphere. Bonilla believed that these bodies were actually *travelling in space near the earth*, but not so far as the moon. He based that theory on comparative observations of the moon and planets in relation to the earth.

Unknown apparitions seen in the sky, long before the days of terrestrial aeroforms, airships, or airplanes, puzzled observers in the U.S.A., and seamen of the Bermudas, the waters of the latter "vexed islands", being the location of the unsolved disappearances of British *air* liners, referred to elsewhere, in this book: *

> *1880:* A thing, in the sky, appeared over Madisonville and Louisville (Kentucky), and seemed to be surrounded by machinery, and with a ball or sphere at either end. It descended, then ascended, under control, in the daytime, vanishing at night.

---

* Dirigible airships were built, in France, by the Tissandier brothers, and by Renard and Krebs, in 1884, but were merely in the pioneering stage. Also, in 1912, it was still too early to speak of "brightly lit airplanes", or other terrestrial aeroforms speeding in the skies. *Au.*

1882: The British steamer, "Salisbury", 800 miles off Ascension Island, S. Atlantic, saw in the sea a "huge object showing two lights. As the steamer approached, the mysterious object was seen to be 800 feet long. It slowly sank. There were sounds in it of working machinery.

1885: A singular triangular object was seen in the sky over Bermuda, and trailing things, like grapnels, hung under it. It descended, then ascended, and passed out towards the ocean.

1909 (March): Narrow, oblong object with powerful light seen in sky over Peterborough, Eng. Sounds of motor. (*N.B.* Airplanes then merely in pioneer stage). Same object seen also in skies from Essex and Midlands to Wales. Object must have had a speed of 210 miles an hour to have covered this distance in one night. Welshman said it was tube-shaped, and he saw "creatures like monkeys emerge from it." (This part of the story was not confirmed!)

1912: At Porto Principal, Perú, in January, a "ship in the sky", appeared over the town at tree-top level. It was shaped like a large square globe, but matched with no known type of terrestrial airplane or airship.

1913: A strange shadow, like that of an unseen body, was thrown onto the clouds over Fort Worth, Texas. (*N.B.* The same phenomenon was seen over Tisbury, near Salisbury, Wilts, in 1912).

1929: Object like large 'plane flying at 100 miles per hour, seen by British steamer "Coldwater", 400 miles west of Virginia coast. (No transoceanic flight known at the time).

I may also draw attention to the frequency with which these mysterious objects, capable of controlled ascent and descent, have taken the form of a *wheel*. Modern scientists point out that, if radiant energy, in any form, were harnessed to interplanetary machine propulsion, the best form of the vehicle, at any rate in outer space, would be that of a *wheel*. Ever since 1760, there have come from seamen singular stories about such wheels.

Wheels rotating in the sea were seen at least eleven times between 1848 and 1910:

> British Association told (1848) of a ship in the Arabian sea approached by "two rolling wheels of fire, which exploded with a crash and shivered the topmasts"; "H.M.S. Vulture" saw a wheel revolving in the Persian Gulf (1879), when a queer oleaginous substance was in the sea. Two "enormous rolling wheels" were again seen, in the sea (1880), accompanied by a phosphorescent gleam on the waters. (British India Company's "ss. Patna"). A vast mass of fire rushed from the sky, blinding the seamen and narrowly missing the British barque, "Innerwick" (1885), in mid-Pacific, long. 170° East. An enormous wheel—luminous body—passed high in the sky over the eastern coasts of the U.S. (1894), and emitting a brilliant white light, and a noise. For the third time, a vast wheel was seen rotating in the Persian Gulf ("ss. Kilwa", 8.30 p.m., April 10, 1901). A similar vast wheel, with no phosphorescence, was seen by a British steamer, and it revolved in the Gulf at Oman (1906). (Same phenomenon seen in Malacca Straits and China Sea, 1907, and 1891). A Danish skipper saw such a vast revolving wheel, *under and then on the surface of the China Sea*. (1909, June 3, 3 a.m.) It had a hub, and was illuminated. Similar phenomenon, in form of horizontal wheel of light, above water, seen August 20, 1910, in S. China Sea (Dutch steamer, "Valentijn").

It was noticed, in the Gulf Oman, in July, 1906, that vivid shafts of light from these vast revolving wheels passed right through the observing British steamer, without any interference. No report says anything about human or humanoid entities in any controlling part of these mysterious wheels. Were, or are they invisible? Were, or are they, in some cases, automata or robots?

None of the reports which I have seen say the phenomenon was otherwise than eerily silent, when in or on the sea, but, as stated above, the luminous wheel seen over five eastern states of the U.S. in 1894, was *not* silent.

It may be observed that a vast wheeled vehicle, rolling from planet to planet, might be forced to enter the earth's atmosphere in order to avert a terrific explosion, caused by some loss of control of the terrific energy used. In such a case, submersion in the ocean might produce a cooling effect, while the rotation was proceeding. No one knows! It is stated that there are stories of such wheels, still revolving, which have been seen to rise from the sea close to ships which have observed them. But, sometimes, they do *not* rise from the sea! (*Vide supra* "Innerwick".) What is odd is that these rotating wheels have been seen between the Equator and about 20° N. latitude, in an area stretching from the Gulf of Persia and the Arabian Sea, to the Indian Ocean, the South China Sea and the North Pacific. None know why this is so, and no alternative theory of the origin of these strange wheels has ever been advanced.

On the night—a very torrid and moonless one—of August 25, 1953, which, by the way, was, oddly enough, the month of strange and mysterious phenomena in the west and east of England, elsewhere mentioned in this book, a lady, Mrs. W.A.C., who lives in a house, with grounds close to Coyote Pass, Hemet, Calif., was suddenly awakened by a brilliant light, as she lay in bed:

> "I at once rose, and, outside, found that the whole half-acre round my house was intensely illuminated. I slipped on a dressing-gown and rushed out onto the terrace. Right opposite me was a huge disc which was slowing down, and becoming stationary. As I saw it, almost as if it had seen me, it suddenly accelerated and crossed over the hills towards Winchester. The light seemed to spotlight our place, and came from a ring surrounding a disc which was then stationary. The main disc had a kind of crumpled silver surface."

Once more, I, the author of this book, draw attention to this weird aeroform as that of a probably hostile visitant. It has been several times referred to in this book. I strongly suspect it has a radiant heat beam that has caused four fires on the night of 21 August, 1953, in the west of England.

On the moonless night of October 25, 1953, a bizarre adventure befell a high school boy of 16, Jim Milligan of Santa Fé, New Mexico, U.S.A. It is fortunate for him that he was not severely burned. Let me summarise the story, which appeared in the "New Mexican", of Santa Fé, N.M., a week later:

> It was on a Sunday, at 9.30 p.m., no wind blowing, when, as the boy, driving his car, reached a lonely park, something which looked like a piece of metal suddenly sailed right in front of his windscreen. He jammed the brake on hard, fearing a collision. But the object landed in some bushes on the roadside, close to a fence and bank. He got out of the car, and gingerly approached the thing, whose colour was like that of dull gun-metal. It was shaped like two boat-hulls, one affixed to the other, about 10 feet long and 5 feet wide. The boy put out his hand to touch it, but it reared up and climbed swiftly over a wooden fence. No odour and no jet of smoke or flame was seen, or smelt. Then the thing took off in a steep ascent towards Santa Fé. The boy arrived home, "shaking and white in the face".

In this region is the famous White Sands proving ground, where the U.S. armed forces have many highly secret devices and guided missiles; but Brigadier-General G. C. Eddy, commanding officer of this dépot, does *not* think that the mysterious object came from the proving ground. He says: "I know nothing whatever about this incident".

, Was this mysterious object of some unknown exploratory type linked with the flying saucer phenomena? What invisible, or hidden entities manned it? Or was it just a sort of robot? Its behaviour is oddly suggestive of that of a moth or butterfly on which a hunter was about to creep! Again, was it a device sent forth by some non-terrestrial space ship and equipped with something in the nature of "repulse radar"?

The boy says that when it took off from the bushes it made a sound like that of a model airplane engine, but not so high-pitched.

It is as mysterious, but in a different category, as the phenomenon met by a Royal Air Force Flight-Lieut. on August 24, 1953, when, at heights ranging from 4,000 to 6,000 feet he was bothered by swarms of wasps seriously interfering with vision through the windscreen. Wasps normally do not fly at this great height; but it has been noted, though never explained, in the past, that insect swarms unaccountably coincide with the appearances of comets or other cosmic phenomena. I have an account of swarms of gnats at Oxford, Eng., in June, August and September, 1766, at a time when a mysterious light with streamers was seen for some hours, in the sky, in the *southern* part of the horizon—hence, could not have been the aurora borealis—vanishing to the south, at 11.15 p.m., and leaving luminous vapour behind.

CHAPTER X

SPACE SHIPS: THE MOON, MARS AND VENUS

It was near the close of the 18th century when several men, in London and Norwich, saw strange lights on the moon that *appear* to indicate that our satellite was being used as a stop-over place, in flights of observation to the earth. A sort of cosmic Clapham Junction! The famous astronomer, Frederick William Herschel, who discovered the planet Uranus and its satellites and the satellites of Saturn, was looking through a 20-foot reflector telescope, on 22 October, 1790, when he saw, in time of total eclipse of the moon, many bright and luminous points, small and round. But "the brightness of the moon, notwithstanding the fact that it was in eclipse", did not permit him to view the phenomenon long enough to locate these points on the lunar surface.

He wrote to the Royal Society:

"We know too little of the surface of the moon to venture a surmise of the cause and remarkable colour of these points."

But, on 7 March, 1794, Dr. William Wilkins, of Norwich, was amazed to see a light *like a star* on the dark part of the moon's disc.

This is what he said:

"This light spot was far distant from the enlightened (*sic*) part of the moon and could be seen with the naked eye. It lasted for 15 minutes and was a fixed and steady light which brightened. It was brighter than any light part of the moon, and the moment before it disappeared, the brightness increased. Two persons passing also saw it."

Dr. Wilkins was not alone in his observation; for, away in London, a servant of Sir George Booth, Bart., said that, at 6 p.m., on this night, "when the moon was a quarter old, he saw a bright light like a star in the dark part of the moon".

Herschel had previously seen more of these lights on or near the moon, in 1783 and 1787. He thought they might be from volcanoes. But it is remarkable that these mysterious bright spots were seen on the moon, in November, 1821, *three times in succession, when they seemed to move with the moon,* and on four other occasions.

Rankin reported to the British Association, in 1847, that he, too, had seen luminous points on the moon in an eclipse. Later, in the 19th century, Cape Town Observatory reported a white spot on the dark part of the moon, and also three smaller lights. In 1896, one, Mr. W. R. Brooks, director of the Smith Observatory, U.S., said he saw a round dark object pass slowly across the moon in a horizontal direction.

When his report appeared, a Dutch astronomer, Muller, said that he had seen the same phenomenon in April, 1894, and a German astronomer wrote to the *Astronomisches Nachrichten* stating that he and three other people had seen a body, apparently six feet in diameter, apparently traversing the disc of the *sun*, which it took an hour to cross. The same object had been seen by these observers 15 minutes before it reached the *sun's disc*, and an hour after it had apparently left the sun's disc.

But it must be admitted that we reach the limit of insolubility when we read the report made to an astronomical journal, in 1912, that Dr. F. B. Harris saw, through a telescope, an intensely black object on the moon that he estimated was 250 miles long and 50 miles wide! "It was like a crow poised, and I think a very interesting and curious phenomenon occurred on that night!"

Since I advance the theory that our moon has been, and still probably is used as an advanced observation base, in regard to our earth, by mysterious cosmic visitants connected with the flying saucer phenomena, I may note that it is singular that all these centres of illumination are in the north-west quarter, or quadrant of the moon.

In March, 1877, an astronomer, in England, reported a brilliant light on the lunar disc, which was *not* the reflection of the sun's light. It was in the lunar crater, Proclus, and another bright spot appeared, that month, in or near the lunar crater, Picard. On March 27, 1877, night of a lunar eclipse, "a ball of fire" (to quote the *Astronomical Register*), "of the apparent size of the moon was seen at 10.50 p.m., seemingly dropping from cloud to cloud, above the earth, while a light from the mysterious object flashed across a road near the observer"!

Our ancestors in the 18th century, and earlier, were not exactly all fools or visionaries; and it is hoped that these comparative observations at widely sundered dates may convince *some* that these reports are not the vapourings of "mystic cranks".

An Australian radio research expert, Dr. F. E. Martyn, predicted, in 1951, what has now become almost a newspaper commonplace: That, before '1961, satellite earths, controlled from our own planet, and based some 25,000 miles up beyond the stratosphere, will be used for scientific and military purposes. He says this is no fantasy, but something that will certainly be achieved. It will become as commonplace as is now radio or television. The satellite earth may be rocket-propelled, and remain stationary over some part of the earth from which it has been fired out into space. It will carry instruments for relaying data back from outer space to earth, and by television and radar. On such a satellite vehicle, says Martyn, we may dump the radioactive and very dangerous waste products from atomic pile plants—that waste which has been dumped into the Irish Sea off Sellafield, the British Government's atomic station in Cumberland, and which, despite the heavy lead containers in which it has been sealed, has made a large area of the Irish Sea dangerous and lethal for perhaps a thousand years to come.

Martyn is a Fellow of the august and exclusive British Royal Society, founded in 1663, and he is chief scientific researcher in the Australian Radio Research Board. Every American knows that the American War Departments have blue-printed satellite earth-vehicles of this type. But what about the even more advanced rocket, or atomic ship *to the moon?*

I am cynically amused at the ingenious and very "calculated" (November 5, 1953) circulation boost of London's latest
daily newspaper. It is stated that the editor has applied to an
interplanetary society for two tickets on the first terrestrial
space ship to leave for the moon, which trip, it is inferred, is
only just round the corner. He will offer the two free trips to
his readers at the small expense of five words, and at some un-
stated time in the very hypothetical future. Whether the pro-
prietor or editor of this new daily is also planning to follow up
the original offer with free fire and cosmic lethal ray insurance
to the two beneficiaries with reversion to their heirs or assigns,
is better known to either than to myself.

Dr. Percy Wilkins, (Bexleyheath, Eng.) and Mr. John O'Neill
(N.Y. Herald-Tribune), in 1954 discovered a 20-mile-long
bridge, of "natural origin". spanning a mountain-barrier in
the lunar Mare Crisium plain. Sunlight is seen streaming
under it. Recently, in the lunar crater, Eratosthenes, quick-
growing vegetation, of H. G. Wellsian type, has been observed.

Interplanetary societies and space ship prospectors rather
airily tell us that, in 50 years, or even before, someone from
earth will land on the moon. They omit to tell us how the
lethal cosmic radiation in outer space is to be overcome—
radiation which one scientist computes would require a
sheathing of over *30 feet of solid lead* all round the space
vehicle! Those of us who are then alive, may, of course, know
whether that project will, or will not mark the culminating
point of 20th century mechanical science and engineering.
But this book, among other things, sounds a warning of strange,
and perhaps lethal things that may lie ahead. How if "others"
have been before us? Others whose forms may, or may not be
humanoid?

The moon has, they say, no water, though frozen air may
lie at the bottom of the lunar craters. Mars, too, has "little
or no water", but, although air and water are the necessities
of human life, as we know it, who is to say that life cannot
exist on a near-waterless planet?

228

I have been told by a correspondent, in Arizona, that there is a little animal (*jaculus jerboa*) in the deserts of that state and of Colorado, which makes its own water from the metallic oxides it eats in those arid spaces where rain may not fall for years. How can we *know* that on other planets there may not exist forms of life—humanoid or not—which can make their own water, in this synthetic fashion?

This little rodent, which is cousin to a similar species found in North Africa's waterless wastes, and allied to the North American kangaroo rat, has, like its North African relative, a special organ that extracts hydrogen from its food, and oxygen from metallic oxides it eats. It synthesises them, as H_2O, or water, within its body!

One side of our moon we never see, except for an edge revealed by "libration". Again, how do we *know* that our moon has a rotation corresponding to the diurnal rotation of the earth? We do *not*! For all we *know* the moon does not revolve on its axis; but, by centripetal, or gravitational field force is whirled round our earth like a bucket at the end of a rope. Usually, it is said, the moon rotates round the earth in 27 hours, 43 minutes odd, though the intervals of time between successive new or full moons are two days longer. One British astronomer, in order to prove this paradox of the rotation of the moon, in which we never see the other side, used a string, fixed with a pin, to which a pencil was attached. He says this method *proves* that a body rotating at the same time as it revolves, or progresses in a forward direction, always presents the same side to the centre—the earth. Does it? All I can say is that I, and others, have never been able to see, from such a device, why *all sides* of the moon, and not merely the same side only, should not successively be presented to the earth, if the moon rotates on its axis as does the earth.

It is no more understandable than the conventional scientific dogma that solar heat rays, in the form of radiant heat waves —and not electro-magnetic waves—are transmitted from the sun through a vacuum where the temperature is the alleged absolute zero of outer space—minus 490 degrees Fahrenheit—

229

in which all molecular movement ceases. But if this theory of the transmission of solar heat rays, as heat rays, were true, a vacuum flask would be an impossibility. And we know that that is *not* so!

May it not be, then, that what our sun transmits through the void of space is not heat, as such, but electro-magnetic wave radiation transformed, by some electrical reaction, into heat in the upper regions of our atmosphere?

Dogmas and dogmatisms have, or should have, no place in science, where they cause the discard of facts and mysteries which do not square with theories that become obsolescent. *But to return to the moon*: Is it so lifeless as many astrophysicists assert?

I summarise more than a century of remarkable phenomena seen on the moon:

> *October 20, 1824*: At 5 a.m., Gruithuisen, of Holland, a selenographer, saw a light on the dark part of the moon. It vanished, re-appeared six minutes later, and again vanished. Until sunrise, at 5.30, the light flashed intermittently.

> *January 22, 1825*: A light shining from the crater, Aristarchus, was seen by two British officers of "H.M.S. Coronation", in the Gulf of Siam. They saw light project from the moon's upper limb, and vanish, when a similar smaller light was seen on another part of the moon.

> *April 9, 1867*: Thos. G. Elger reported to the *Astronomical Register*, that, in the English sky, he saw a dark part of the moon suddenly flame out with a light like a star of the 7th magnitude. This was at 7.30 p.m. At 9.30 p.m., it faded out. "I have seen lights on the moon before, but never so clear as this." Vol. 20 of the *Register* adds: "Near the crater, Birt, on the moon, is an object shaped like a sword, and there are a group of three hills in an acute-angled triangle connected by three lower embankments, and a geometric object, shaped like a cross, in the lunar crater, Eratosthenes. In the lunar crater, Gassendi, are angular lines, and on the floor of the crater, Littrow, are seven spots in the shape of the Greek capital letter, Gamma." (*N.B.* These

peculiar formations were also seen on the moon on January 31, 1915.)

May 13, 1870: Lights variously numbered, by English observers, as 4, 27, or 28, were seen in the crater, Plato. (Were they signals, or landing lights for flying saucers? *Au.*) As to signals, it was observed that, as one of these lights on the moon increased in brightness, another diminished. Then another light alternately shone and faded out, as if responding to the touch on switches of some mysterious lunar operator of electric battens of lights!

Night of Feb. 20, 1877: Monsieur Trouvelot of the Observatory of Meudon, near Paris, saw in the lunar crater, Eudoxus, in the north-west quadrant of the moon,* a fine luminous line, like a luminous cable drawn across the crater.

March 21, 1877: C. Barrett, a British astronomer, saw a bright light—*not* a reflection of the sun—in the lunar crater, Proclus.

June 17, 1877: Professor Henry Harrison, in New York State, saw a light on the dark part of the moon which looked like a reflection from a moving mirror. Frank Dennett, in England, saw, at this time, a minute point of light in the lunar crater, Bessel.

Nov. 23, 1877: Dr. Klein reported to the French scientific journal, *L'Astronomie:* "I saw a luminous triangle on the floor of the lunar crater, Plato. It may have been reflected sunlight". (But *was* it? *Au.*)

1877: On the night of Klein's observation, observers in U.S.A. saw mysterious flakes of light moving from all other lunar craters towards the crater, Plato. These lights, as Klein noted near Paris, France, formed into a triangle of light on the floor of Plato.

Between February 21, 1885 and December 19, 1919, the phenomena seen on the moon in various lunar craters, comprise reddish smoke; a curved object like a wall; a new object in the centre of the illuminated orb; a black area whitened; something "like luminous cable" in the crater, Aristarchus;

---

* The north-west quadrant of the moon has been the location of many mysterious signals in the course of a century.

two lights on May 11, in 1885 and 1886 (a curious synchronism!); intense black spot with white border; black wall in Aristillus; black spot in centre of Copernicus; object black as ink on rim of crater, Aristarchus; a shaft of light projecting from a limb (seen by astronomers in the Azores and Paris); a red shadow; an intense black spot in craters, Lexall and Littrow.

The scientific evidence about the moon's atmosphere sometimes conflicts. For example, the spectroscope seems to show that the moon and Venus have no atmosphere; but the occultation, or obscuring of light, from the stars, by both the moon and Venus, attest that *both* have an atmosphere! Phenomena observed in eclipses of the moon have been unexplained. Walkley, an astronomer of Clyst St Lawrence, Devon, Eng., reported to an astronomical society, that, on May 10, 1848, in an eclipse of the moon, he saw the lunar "surface most beautifully illuminated". It was tinged "deep red, and the moon was as perfect with light as if there had been no eclipse whatever". Later, in 1878, two observers in New South Wales, Australia, witnessed an astounding phenomenon on the moon. Says one of them, H. G. Russell, F.R.A.S.:

"Both G. D. Hirst and myself were in the Blue Mountains, above Sydney. I was looking at the moon when I saw a large part of it covered with a dark shadow quite as dark as the shadow of the earth projected in a lunar eclipse. I could not resist *the conclusion that it was the shadow of no known body!*"

I have suggested that the moon may be, and long has been a stopover place for what we call flying saucers, or space ships. What evidence have we for this revolutionary assertion?

Look at what follows:

Sep. 7, 1820: Many observers in France saw, in a lunar eclipse, strange objects moving in straight lines. They turned in the same straight line, and all were separated by uniform spaces. Their movements were in military precision. (*Arago's Oeuvres at Annales de Chimie.*) (These mysterious objects seemed to be moving close to the lunar disc. *Au.*)

Aug. 7, 1869: Professor Swift, of Mattoon, Ill., saw, during a solar eclipse, objects cross the moon 20 minutes before the totality of the eclipse. In Europe, Professor Hines and Professor Zentmayer reported to *Les Mondes,* a Paris journal, that they also saw these objects, and they seemed to march in straight and parallel lines. *The Journal of the Franklin Institute* says that some of these objects moved in one direction across the moon, each division moving in parallel lines.

1874: Vast numbers of black bodies crossed the moon. (*Monsieur Lamey, in l'Année Scientifique, 1874.*)

April 24, 1874: "I saw an object of so peculiar a nature that I know not what to make of it. It was dazzlingly white, and slowly traversed the disc of the moon. I watched it after it left the moon's face." (*Professor Schafarik, of Praga, now Czecho-Slovakia.*) On Sep. 27, 1881, Col. Markwick, in South Africa, said he saw near the moon an object like a comet, but moving rapidly. (*Journal of the Liverpool Astronomical Society.*)

April 4, 1892: A Netherlands astronomer, Muller, saw a dark round object slowly pass across the moon's disc, in a horizontal direction. W. R. Brooks, of Smith Observatory, U.S.A., saw an identical phenomenon in 1896. Its apparent diameter was one-thirtieth of the moon's diameter, and it crossed the moon's disc in 3-4 seconds.

1899: Luminous object seen moving on the moon. It was close to the moon and travelling across it. (Seen at Prescott, Arizona, by Dr. Warren E. Day, who reported to the U.S. Weather Bureau, in March.) G. O. Scott at Tonto, Arizona, saw the same object close to the moon, on 7 March.

Nov. 15, 1899: An enormous "star", white, then red and blue, was seen moving like a kite in the sky, near the moon, at 7 p.m. Observation over Dourite, in Dordogne, France.

May 10, 1902: Many highly coloured things, like little suns, were seen moving high in the sky in the region of the moon. "It beats me what they were!" (*Col. Markwick, S. Devon, to a British astronomical journal.*)

Nov. 26, 1910: In the eclipse of the moon something like

227

a superb rocket left the moon. It was seen at Besançon. (*La Nature, France.*) On the same date, the *Journal of the Brit. Assocn. for the Advancement of Science* reported that a luminous part had been seen on the moon during the eclipse of the moon.

Jan. 27, 1912: F. B. Harris, in a report to *Popular Astronomy*, Eng., said: "I saw on the moon an intensely black object about 250 miles long and 150 miles wide, like a vast crow poised. . .clouds then came between it and my telescope. An extremely interesting and curious phenomenon must have happened."

Aug. 29, 1917: A bright object was seen moving on the moon's disc. (*Bulletin de la Soc. Astron. de France.*) On the same date, the Bulletin reported that the same bright object was seen close to the moon and travelling with it.

*   *   *   *

A recent observation, on a lunar mountain ridge, by Professor Harvey Nininger, of the American Meteoritic Museum, in Arizona, caused the Professor to pay particular attention to two peculiar craters. And it may be noted that the location of these craters is in the same western sector of the moon, noted above. He thinks these craters were produced by a meteor hitting the moon at 30 miles a second, and boring a tunnel 20 miles long through a mountainous lunar ridge. Nininger suggests that this tunnel would give the first men to land in the moon shelter from any meteorites buffeting the surface of the moon, whose presumably "airless" surface offers no protection from cosmic projectiles. Of course, this theory of the causation of a lunar tunnel is just as plausible —in default of proofs to be found only when a moon-, or space-vehicle actually lands from earth, there—as the other theory that mysterious visitants to the moon may have bored this tunnel.

The moon may be very far from the Hollywood conception of an assemblage of frozen crags and pits, dead craters and icy mountains, over which the sun shines in a cobalt sky down on an airless lunar atmosphere, where nothing lives, or has ever lived, in the long ages of time. Whether the Grand

Cham of the Moon will emerge from some vast underground world in the bottom of one of those craters, in the lunar north-western region where, as previously remarked, so many mys-terious signals and strange geometric shapes have been seen, and prepare a splendid reception for the first arrivals from the dominant planet, earth, our posterity *may* see!

Our earth-men may be regarded as gods, in the way that the Quechuas of Inca Perú and the Aztecs of the old Mexico regarded the barbaric Spaniards from Cortes' caravels, or the bandit Pizarro's conquistadores riding their Castilian jennets into the plaza of old Cuzco, to the spanging of the arquebuses and the flames from the muzzles of matchlocks. Or, from radar televisors, there may be flashed back to earth a dramatic pic-ture of fearful and suspicious space men, whether or not they are in humanoid shape, from some other world, bringing to bear on the earth-ship from old Terra some deadly ray gun, or heat ray annihilators, housed below in some vast lunar cavern!

As to what may be on the other side of the moon, which we do not see, and whether some sentient form of life dwells there, no one yet knows. It presents an incalculable element in the fateful story of the first personal contact of earth-men with the moon. Yet, as it is the destiny of man ever to aspire to enlarge the frontiers of the known, and to thrust back the great darkness looming over the unknown and the mysterious, the motto of *ad astra*, to the stars, is bound to entail unknown and tremendous possibilities, in the adventures of the space-voyagers of the future many of us will not live to see.

Now, a word about the biotic conditions on Mars. The conventional astronomers' theories, British and American, visualise the most primitive form of plant life, lichens and mosses, and a fauna of insects, or, at most, some form of biped far lower than the ape. But remarkable Russian researches, in 1948, in the observatory at Tashkent, and, in 1950, at Alma Ata Observatory, in the region of the Pamirs, have established certain probable facts about Mars which render obsolete several theories, hitherto cherished by orthodox astronomers. These researches, largely by Mr. G. Tikhov of the U.S.S.R. Academy of Sciences, and Mr. N. Kucherov of the Kazakh Academy of Sciences, have founded the newer science of astrobotany, and have made untenable the notion that the vegetation of Mars consists only of lower orders of plant life, such as lichens and fungi. On the contrary, there is reason to suppose that plants like those of earth exist on Mars, and, he thinks, on Venus!

In 1900, when Mars was comparatively near earth, in one of the planet's fifteen-year periods. Mr. Tikhov photographed the planet through the immense telescope-tube of the 30-inch refractor telescope in the Pulkhovo Observatory. He wanted to find out the colour and physical properties of the various formations on Mars, and he used red, green and yellow light filters in photographing Mars. When he compared the Mars photos with terrestrial photos of ice and snow, made with the same filters, he concluded that, in winter, the polar caps of Mars consist of snow, and in summer, or, at the melting period, of ice. Hitherto, some scientists had held that the polar caps of Mars might be frozen carbon-dioxide.

Tikhov also deduced that the wide canals on Mars actually exist, and are of the same colour as the dark Martian areas, the latter usually being deemed to be humid regions of vegetation. He finally concluded that the Martian "canals" are possibly belts of vegetation, dozens of miles wide, which may stretch along streams of water. The water may flow either in channels, or underground.

On May 13, 1940, he made new observations on Mars, again using the Pulkhovo refractor telescope, but with an object glass 15 inches in diameter, and a focal distance of 5 mètres. He used red, green and blue filters. On that day, it was the season of mid-winter in the southern hemisphere of Mars, and mid-summer in the northern hemisphere. He observed that, in the photographs of Mars' southern hemisphere, the dark areas were greenish-blue, while, in the northern hemisphere they were brown. He, therefore, theorised that there is on Mars vegetation which loses its foliage in autumn, and also vegetation that, in winter, and probably in summer, is *blue*. The light blue Martian vegetation is related to the winter green plants in the colder regions of our own earth.

In 1948, Tikhov and a group of scientists observed Mars from the Alma Ata Observatory in Russian Central Asia. When they used infra-red rays, or "black light", to photograph the spots on Mars which are supposed to be belts of vegetation, the pictures came out very dark, whereas terrestrial vegetation, when so photographed, is light-coloured, like snow. This optical phenomenon suggests that the climate of Mars is much more severe than that of the earth, and that the plants of Mars absorb and do not reflect the infra-red rays—solar radiant heat—of the sun.

Astrobotanists in Russia now proceeded to study the optical properties of plants in the high mountains of the Pamirs, in Central Asia, and in sub-arctic regions of the earth. They found that coniferous trees and plants absorb the infra-red rays of the sun much more than deciduous plants, while, in summer, their rate of absorption of these rays is about half as much as in winter. That is, plants adapt themselves to warmth and cold by reflecting, or absorbing the infra-red rays in sunlight.

Now, as is known, the red and infra-red rays of the sun are absorbed by the chlorophyll, the constituent of plants that gives them their green colour, and when the light-reflection of plants is split up, or decomposed by the spectroscope, it is seen that the area occupied by the red rays in the spectrum is missing, indicating that the plants have absorbed these rays. But, when the reflections from the dark area of Mars are split up by the spectroscope no such area of absorption of red rays is found. Why is this?

The answer is suggested when the reflections from plants and trees of the earth's sub-arctic regions, or of high mountains, are tested for chlorophyll absorption. It is found that the area of absorption is either absent or barely perceptible. A plant lives largely on the assimilation of carbon-dioxide from the atmosphere, and this power of assimilation comes very largely from solar energy, or radiation, acting on and absorbed by the chlorophyll. In a very cold climate, or at a great height, the plant absorbs not only the red and infra-red rays, but the adjacent bands of orange, yellow, and green in the solar spectrum; which bands provide another one-third of the solar heat.

The conclusion is, therefore, that, on Mars, plants and vegetation exist in conditions very like those in the earth's sub-arctic regions, or in high mountain areas, and that, as said above, Mars' climate is a very severe one. One can also see why the plants in Mars are of a light or deep blue colour. On Mars, the plants absorb the red, orange, yellow and green rays of the solar spectrum, and reflect the light and deep blue and violet rays. This means that the predominant colour of vegetation on Mars may be light and deep blue and violet; and also that the Martian plants contain chlorophyll as do the plants of earth, and are not merely a lower order of lichen and fungi.

If, then, there are plants on Mars like those on the earth, it is not unreasonable to infer that Mars has animals, and even intelligent beings, and that, as the redness of the planet denotes advanced age, those intelligent beings may be farther in the scale of evolution than men on the earth, always, of course, assuming that there has not been a severe retrogression caused by a cataclysm in the past of Mars. Moreover, since the climate of Mars is more severe than that of the earth, it may be that, in the conditions of the Martian winter, they may live underground. The Martian day is about 41 minutes more than that of the earth, and its year about 321 days longer.

And if either of the satellites of Mars—there are two—obeys the limit of the French mathematician, Roche, and has always the same face turned towards the master-planet Mars, then the period when it may disrupt and rain down in frag-. ments on Mars, must, since Mars is probably farther advanced in age than the earth, be considerably nearer than the kindred cataclysm is to earth. If beings of advanced science and intellect live in Mars, then they have long ago had a tremendous incentive towards constructing a space ship, or aeroform.

The Project Saucer scientists of the U.S. Air Force made a rather remarkable *volte face* (in late summer 1948), about life on Mars:

> "Astronomers largely agree that Mars is the only planet in the solar system capable of supporting life. The Martians, faced by the loss of oxygen and water, slow as it is, may have constructed underground cities, or evolution may have developed beings who can withstand the rigours of the Martian climate. . .Or the race, if it ever existed, may have perished."

As in the Moon, strange phenomena have been noted on Mars:

> *1862*: Sir Norman Lockyer saw a "long train of clouds" on Mars, so did Sacchi, four days later, when he saw a spot on the planet.
>
> *1873* (June 17): A bright object was seen to issue from Mars, and explode in the skies of Austria, Hungary, and what is now Czecho-Slovakia. Dr. Sage, in England, watching through a telescope, saw this luminous object issue from the red disc of Mars, and in five seconds explode over the earth. "It seemed. as if Mars were breaking up under the force of the impulsion of this object, and dividing into two parts. The concussion of the firing was sharp." Mars then in opposition to the earth. (*Journal of the British Association*.)
>
> *1892* (August 3): Mars in opposition. At Manchester, and Loughborough, Eng., rapid flashes, not aurorae, seen on Mars. On June 10, 1892, something "like a small searchlight" projected beams from Mars.

In February, 1936, I had occasion to be in correspondence, at a time when I was acting as London and European editor of a popular scientific journal in Chicago, with Professor Robert Damion, an astronomer then living at Cannes, on the French Riviera.

He wrote to me:

> "This winter (of 1936), I happened to be in the Montagne du Cheval Blanc, which is located in the Provençal province of Basses-Alpes. On several moonless nights, I saw a strange phenomenon. In the vault of the

sky close to Mars, a queer bluish light quite suddenly flamed up. It lasted forty seconds, but recurred at *regular intervals.* So powerful was this light that *one could read a book by it.* Now, this has happened before in France and has been seen by astronomers. It was seen from Lyons, S. France, in 1928. What do I think it was? I am sure that Mars was trying to signal to us, and by means we know not. If these were signals, we cannot answer them. Why? We have no searchlight projector that could flash a signal even a tenth of that vast distance, separating us from Mars. It would need a lens, alone, weighing 2,000 tons!

There have been other apparent and mysterious signals from Mars. On Novr. 24, 1894, Professor Pickering, at Lowell Observatory, saw a self-luminous body above the unilluminated part of Mars' orb. He thought the body was about 20 miles from Mars; but whether it was a cloud, or not, he could not affirm. Again, on the night of Dec. 7, 1900, a fountain of light played for 70 minutes on the orb of Mars, and Pickering was dumbfounded. He said it was "absolutely inexplicable." He thought he detected a code in the lights: Long and short flashes, and a norm in the intervals of the lights, from which there were variations of $\frac{3}{4}$, $1\frac{1}{4}$, and $1\frac{1}{2}$.

Pickering appears to have felt certain that Mars was trying to signal the earth. He also reported "many geometrical figures, seen on Mars, that could not have been just produced by nature." Marconi, in the early days of wireless telegraphy, received inexplicable signals that he thought came from Mars. Recently, too, the Japanese astronomer, Dr. Sabeki, who reported what he thought might be "an atomic explosion on Mars", also, saw, very brilliant flashes lasting several minutes, from Mars, and had reception of radiation of apparently artificial origin, like Martian signals. From time to time, there have been reports that electronic signals, clear and distinct sounds with a weird modulation, have been received simultaneously at widely separated places on the earth. These mysterious sounds increase or fade as Mars approaches or recedes. Various geometrical figures have been reported seen on Mars: Geometrical configurations of vast size, equilateral triangles, a cross in a circle, replaced by other figures; and, in 1907, and again in 1924, a vast octagon replaced by a five-. pointed star. Twice, on Oct. 24, 1864, and on January 3, 1865, red lights were seen on opposite sides of Mars.

Lowell had also observed the flashes on Decr. 7, 1900, and the fountain of light playing on Mars. He found in them a code of long and short, something like this, in a sort of metre: ∪ ∪ — ∪ — o. (Here the sign ∪ represents thirds, the *dash* unity, and the *o* half-unity.) At this time, the famous physicist and inventor, Nikola Tesla said he had received on his wireless apparatus, in New York City, vibrations he thought came from Mars. They were "a series of triplets".

Of course, there is not a shadow of proof that these three signals came from Mars.

In passing, I may make reference to Martian fantasy-stories current in mystic quarters of the U.S.A., since some reader is likely to ask if I have heard of them. The stories can neither be proved nor disproved, and must be believed or not. It is alleged that, in the past, space men have landed on the earth, when forced to do so from a disabled space ship. They waited, it is alleged, in mysterious and very ancient, vast caverns in the earth, of which they have knowledge, and which were constructed by "Elder men" who were very advanced scientists, and who, long years ago, left the earth to escape the poisonous radio-activity of the sun. Here, in the deep caverns and tunnels, the Martians expected the arrival of a space ship which they knew would be sent; since, on Mars, news had been received of their stranding! It is said that these Martians had an "orchid-coloured complexion", and looked much like men on earth; but, that, in Mars, there are other races quite different from these Martian space men, who are a race of light blond men; like the Nordic races of the earth. This blond, or orchidaceous complexion belongs, it is alleged, to a caste of "hereditary space men". At 12 years of age, the blood is drained from the young potential space men and replaced with synthetic fluid. This is done, because, out in space, these Martian space men are exposed to radiations different from those on their own planet, and more harmful than any known to men on the earth.

This synthetic blood, it is said, holds in suspension the "heavy metals of radiation", so that they may not settle in the bones and tissues and become poisonous and eventually lethal, in radio-active form. Periodically, the Martian space men are given new supplies of blood free of radioactive poisons, and immunized. The old blood is centrifuged, and reprocessed to rid it of the poisons acquired on space travel! The Martian space men's "circulatory and eliminatory systems are artificially arranged to suit low and zero gravity met in space, and on different planets." It is further alleged that these Martian space men are not really indigenous to Mars, but have lived there many ages.

It is also added that some of the mysterious visitants in the flying saucers are *not* Martians, and that no one knows who they are, or whence they come; for they surround themselves and their machine with a shield of rays impervious to exploratory beams of radar, and refuse to answer signals!

Then, Venus, rotating in an orbit much nearer the sun than our own planet, or Mars, has excited conjectures and stories, ranging from zoot-suited golden-haired men, "five-foot six inches tall with swastikas on the soles of their feet to two-and-a-half-foot midgets".

We do not *know* if Venus has any inhabitants; or, if she has, how advanced in scientific knowledge they may be. Sir Harold Spencer Jones, the British Astronomer Royal, says that "life is still going on and may exist in unfamiliar forms"; and he theorises that if there exist beings whose organisms have silicon cells, instead of carbon cells, silicon being very widely distributed and found in the stars, then such beings might be able to endure temperatures like that on Venus. However, it is safe to say, in view of some of his statements in the U.S.A., in 1953, that he would at once point out that we have no proof that such silicon beings exist on Venus, or anywhere else. H. G. Wells's Martians, we know, made aluminium direct from clay scooped by them from the London deposits, and the gleaming aluminium could be seen pouring in a steady stream from machines tended by whistling robots. Actually, of course, such a process on earth would be very costly and troublesome.

The U.S. Project Saucer reviews the possibility of life on the planet, Venus, where, it states, "the atmosphere seems to consist mostly of carbon di-oxide":

> "With deep clouds of formaldehyde droplets, and there seems to be little or no water. Yet, scientists concede that living organisms might develop in chemical environments which are strange to us. Venus, however, has two handicaps. Her mass and gravity are nearly as large as the Earth. (Mars is smaller), and her cloudy atmosphere would discourage astronomy, hence, space travel."

I may offer one or two comments: "The cloudy atmosphere of Venus," to which Project Saucer draws notice, might not be impenetrable to rays, of which many remain unknown, in the still unexplored octaves of invisible radiation beyond the red and violet ends of the solar spectrum. One may point out that radio-magnetic devices and radar have very recently been applied, by British universities, and the scientific research department of the U.S. Navy, to the exploration of nebulae in the Milky Way—a thing that would have been deemed impossible and fantasy before the year 1939!

Let us summarise a few of the Venusian mysteries:

1823 (May 22): "Webb reported seeing an unknown shining object near the planet, Venus." (*Nature*, vol. 14. *Vide* Webb's "Celestial Objects".)

1852 (Sept. 11): "People in Staffordshire saw, in the western sky, a bright shining disc visible between 4.15 and 4.45 p.m. It vanished, then re-appeared." (*British Association Journal.*) Lord Wrottesley, who at that time had an observatory at Wolverhampton, said this shining disc seemed relatively near the moon. Others say it was very close to Venus.

1855 (August 11, night): Observers report seeing in the sky, over Petworth, Sussex, a strange red disc rise slowly, diminish slowly in brightness and be visible for $1\frac{1}{2}$ hours. "From it were projections like wheel-spokes or stationary rays." Venus was then 2 weeks from her maximum brilliance.

1867 (May 30) and *1869* (May 2): Observers with telescopes, at Birmingham and Northampton, focused shining objects of various sizes, visible for 80 minutes, blue and fringed on one side, close to Venus. They were moving at various speeds, and not all in the same direction. All seemed to have "hairy appendages, following a very bright body." Time: 11 a.m. A remarkable light seen on Venus, in May, 1869. It vanished. At Radcliffe Observatory, Oxford, a strange object in the sky was seen hovering, and then moving, changing its course thrice. Visible for 4 minutes.

1871 (August 1): Coggia, in "Comptes Rendus", reported that he saw a splendid object in the sky over Marseilles, It was red, seen at 10.43 p.m., moved east slowly until 10.59, then turned west and vanished. Venus was three weeks from maximum brilliance.

1884 (Feb. 3): Brussels Observatory saw extremely brilliant point of light on Venus. Niesten, an astronomer, saw it, on Feb. 12, but some way from Venus. *3 July*: Over Norwood, N.Y., bright sphere, with a ring round it, and dark lines, like a central construction. On *Aug. 17*, a man at Rochester, N.Y., saw a brilliant point on Venus. On *26 July*, at Köln, on the Rhine, a bright sphere, of the apparent size of the moon, ascended from the earth remaining motionless for 20 minutes, and then ascended till it disappeared in space.

1892 (May 8): A shining point seen on Venus, some way from her pole. *13 August*: Professor Barnard reported, in the *Astronomisches Nachrichten*, that he saw some unknown object close to Venus. On the same day, in a town in New York State, a boy lost his fingers when a brilliant body, which he saw fall from the sky, exploded.

1895 (August): A wonderful glowing sphere was seen in the daytime skies over Ireland. Venus then being at the peak of her brilliance.

1909 and 1910 (Dec. 22): A bright light seen passing over Boston Harbour, Mass., was mistaken by a policeman for an airship, though none then existed, capable of a transoceanic trip. This object swept the skies over

Worcester, Mass., with a kind of brilliant searchlight, and hovered over the town. It was seen, again, two hours later and, in the sight of hundreds of excited people, vanished over the sea, southwards. At 6 p.m., next night, a strange light shone in the sky and behind it was an outline of some long, black object moving at high speed. It was said to have been seen nine times over Marlborough, Mass. Three huge and powerful lights from some mysterious thing, speeding over the country, were seen at various parts of the U.S. *Jan. 14, 1910*: A mysterious white thing was seen in bright sunshine over Chattanooga, Tenn., and vanishing in the south-east. It came back on the two following days. *Decr. 24, 1909*: At night, a luminous thing rose above the skyline, moved slowly southwards, and at 8.50 p.m., turned round, vanishing at 9.2 p.m. (Venus was then in the south-east in the early morning.)

1916 (July 31): At 11 p.m., a bright object was seen exploring the sky at Ballinasloe, Ireland. Visible for 15 minutes, then went north-west, and hovered for 45 minutes, returning to the first spot. After 4 a.m., when Venus rose as morning star, it vanished.

To some people, considering the data above, there may be nothing very improbable in the assumption that, granted Venus or Mars has beings capable of interplanetary voyages, they may use the moon as a stopover; and, *if* so, may know of each other, may have exchanged information, and have developed some remarkable surgical and radiological technique to overcome radioactive poisons in lethal zones they cross—black cosmic spots which probably exist in space and may cause something more than a headache to the pioneers of terrestrial voyages in space.

Any space men, from our own earth, who may land on the moon, say, in 50 years' time, would do well to think out beforehand some method of conciliatory approach, in order to avoid some lethal encounter with "previous visitors", whose suspicions, or opinions of the ways and manners of earthians may lead to very dangerous encounters. For, *if* these lights on the two planets, and these moving orbs and discs in the skies, seen in the course of around 200 years past, *are* really space

245

ships, or preluding their departure from planetary stations, it is certain that their science and mechanism will be far in advance of any we know. To them, we may appear merely as children playing with very dangerous toys of science, and children needing a powerful lesson!

One may summarise the more or less agreed orthodox scientific opinions on Mars and Venus.

Venus: Slightly smaller than the earth; not known to have any moons; radiometric observations made in U.S.A. observatories, in 1922, indicate that the dark part of the planet may emit cosmic heat; ultra-violet light photos, in July, 1927, and Pickering's observations in Jamaica, suggest a rapid rotation which Pickering believes may be in 68 hours; but others think that Venus, turning always the same face to the earth, rotates in about 225 days. *Habitability*: St. John found no absorption lines in Venus's solar spectrum, indicating the presence of oxygen and water vapour; but, here, it may be pointed out that the visible surface of the upper layer of the planet's cloud stratum is all we can see, at present, and we do not know if considerable amounts of oxygen and water vapour may be below the dense screen of the upper clouds. Life of some kind is *not* ruled out.

Mars: Becquerel of the Académie des Sciences, Paris, thinks that as the Martian atmospheric pressure is above the maximum tension of water vapour, water as a liquid can easily exist on Mars. Living matter could easily absorb carbon and solar energy for existence. Mars' protective layer against ultra-violet radiation is more efficacious than earth's layer of ozone. He believes it has a vegetation and fauna, and that the vegetation changes from blue-green, in summer, to yellow-brown in autumn. Thermo-couple data confirm this. Dr. Kniper, of Chicago University, in 1950, theorised that Mars may have insect life, and that, both on Mars and Venus, life is not necessarily only lichens and moss, but may include intelligent animal life. Dr. H. Strughold, professor of space medicine (U.S. Air Force School of Aviation Medicine), is not positive that intelligent life may not exist on Mars; but inclines against that theory.

Taine, the U.S. mathematician, thinks that *Saturn, Uranus and Neptune*, with atmospheres of methane, ammonia, and hydrogen, and great gravitational pull, may have evolved "intellectual *crystalline* beings, scorning the idea of intelligent entities on the 'oxygen-poisoned earth' "!

CHAPTER XI

HAVE THE FLYING SAUCERS
EVER LANDED?

The question posed above is one that can have hardly gone unmarked or uninvestigated by the air and security author-ities in Great Britain and the U.S.A.

If entities from these space discs or ships have actually landed, then the questions at once arise: Have they secret bases or landing grounds on the earth; who are their terrestrial contacts; and who are people who allege that they have either been eye-witnesses of the saucers' landings on this planet, or have spoken to or otherwise communicated with these mys-terious and elusive beings?

It may be assumed—by those who have considered the evidence assembled in this book, especially that part drawn from the annals of old Rome—that, whoever these entities may be, and whencesoever they come, they *must*, in the last 2,500 years since the date of their last recorded appearance in our skies, know a lot about our planet, and its scientific and cultural evolution. They have been eye-witnesses of two of our global wars in 20 years. This evidence of past appearances was set down by men not knowing the significance of what they observed, deeming it portents from the gods; and it needs no great effort of the imagination to divine why the occupants of flying saucers, or space ships, would probably choose remote places for their landings.

As I write these lines, I am informed by a well educated American who lives in Los Angeles, Calif., that, in summer 1952, he knew an American scientist and physicist who had been given, by high authorities in Washington, D.C., the job of preparing a report, to be submitted to a high authority, in Novr. or Decr. 1952, which details and evaluates eye-witness stories of close-up observations on strange discs, or unknown craft from outer space which have landed on mountain tops, or in desert regions in North America, in recent years. But, again, this report will *not* be made public.

My correspondent adds:

> "I believe that dark bodies exist in our solar system, not perceptible by astronomers in observatories, but on which sentient and intelligent life exists, I think that the visible planets, such as Venus, have 'etheric doubles', where exist, *not* spooks, or discarnate entities, but living beings of human type, imperceptible by our senses, or such instruments as we have, except the radarscope".

To which many will retort: Who knows? Who can prove, or disprove such assertions, at this time? It is true that *one* type of the saucers—the "Foo Fighters", seen at close quarters by U.S. war pilots, over the Rhine area, of western Germany, in 1944 (*Vide* pages 21-37 *supra*)—appear to become alternately visible and invisible in a very brief interval of time. Certain mystics, in the U.S.A., also assert that *some* of these space ships, not always discoidal in shape, come from galaxies whose immense distances from our own system are measured in hundreds of thousands of light years. In these cases, no material object, as we know it, could cross these immense voids and unimaginable distances, but are "teleported", or transported, as "thought-patterns", into our terrestrial atmosphere, where their rate of vibrations is converted to our own wave-lengths, and become visible and tangible to our human senses. The body of the operator, "being of etheric matter", is, say these mystics, teleported as easily as the space ship itself. They are *where their consciousness is*. The operating entity thus teleports himself and his ship without crossing any spatial interval.

Who knows, or can know? But it seems probable that there are also types of saucers which come from some point in space within or near our solar system, and which, hence, must cross space by means of which we have no knowledge, and which may transcend our own aeronautical science. Certain quarters in the U.S.A. have asserted that "Etherian visitors", in some of the saucers, "have largely succeeded in containing lethal, radioactive emanations from exploded atomic bombs within the earth's own ionosphere; so that the earth can herself have the benefit of the devilish juice made by nuclear fissionists, prostituting their scientific knowledge to the purposes of military powers, behind whom stand an unseen camarilla and the great unrepresented who decree all wars, and, alone derive benefit from them. "So", they say, "earth herself will get the worst effects, and the radiations be blanketed off from outer space."

Short of actual landings of flying saucers, I have singular reports of *attempts or contemplated landings*:

> *October 26, 1951*: "An engine-driver on the footplate of a transcontinental train, on the Australian East-West line, was startled, at 4 a.m., when a strange object in the sky lit up the track with full moon illumination. It moved swiftly, came lower, and seemed to examine the train, and even to be contemplating a landing in the nearby desert! Then it flew off." (*Melbourne newspapers.*)

> *November 29, 1951*: "I was on Route 5, of the U.S. highway near Madison, Ind., after dusk, hunting ducks along with two friends. On a sudden, in clear sky, was a thing emitting a vapour trail seen like white steam in the cold air. One of my friends put up his gun as if to shoot, and pointed at the strange object, which had stopped dead, right over us. It was motionless for two seconds, and then, as if it had observed the man with up-raised gun-barrel, it shot forward at a fantastic speed, which it soon reduced. It now turned on edge, banked, changed course, and we saw it to be round, with top, arched and streamlined. Three times it banked, and came much lower, as if contemplating landing. But it seemed to change its mind. The setting sun was reflected from its white, metallic surface. No sound was emitted, and, when banking, it gave the impression that it was cutting off fuel until it had changed course, when it shot forward with arrow-like velocity." (*Walter McBride, of Shoals, Ind., U.S.A.*)

The above would appear to have been a space ship emanating from some very material planet, as perceptible as our own.

> *July 29, 1952*: "A man, white as a sheet, walked trembling into a police station at Enid, Oklahoma, and told the

desk-sergeant, Vern Bennell, that it looked as if a saucer had swooped down on him with the intention of abducting him! The man was Sid Eubank, employé of a sales department of a photo studio, at Wichita, Kansas, aged 50, Eubank told the sergeant:

" 'I was almost swept from my feet on the highway, last night, when a *huge* flying saucer swooped down at terrific speed and stood directly over me, on U.S. highway, No. 81, between Bison and Waukomis, south of here, Enid, Okla. The object appeared suddenly out of the night and the tremendous pressure it exerted threw my automobile off the road. It was a huge round ball and stood right over me. Then it completely reversed direction, vanishing in a few seconds in the west'." (*Oklahoma newspapers.*)

One wonders how many cases of mysterious disappearances of men and women, in 1948-1952, might be explained as "TAKEN ABOARD A FLYING SAUCER MET IN A LONELY PLACE"? Fantastic as the suggestion sounds, it is by no means impossible. I would draw attention to the remarkable observation made by the U.S. merchant steamer, "Gaines Mills", at 7.50 p.m., on Wednesday, December 5, 1945, when five U.S. Navy "Avenger" type torpedo bomber 'planes, went out from the Naval Air station of Fort Lauderdale, Fla., on a routine flight. Fourteen men were in these bombers, and no one, from that day to this, knows what became of them, or their 'planes, after they had flashed a radio message that they were 200 miles out at sea off Miami, to the north-east. The sea was combed by U.S. warships and and the air by Navy 'planes. The five bombers were of a very buoyant type and carried efficient life rafts. To add to the already baffling mystery, one of these rescue 'planes, a big Martin bomber, with a crew of 13, also vanished without trace, while hunting for the missing five "Avengers".

Now, at 7.50 p.m., on the same Wednesday night. Dec. 5, 1945, the ss. "Gaines Mills" radioed that *she had seen an explosion high up in the sky*, and, yet, in the next morning, neither searching 'planes, nor warships, rushed to the spot, found any trace of wreckage, or oil in the sea.

Suppose these missing U.S. warplanes had been intercepted by a hostile, or curious flying saucer? Suppose that resistance had been offered? Suppose that one of these interplanetary craft can project a ray which can hold motionless and suspended in mid-air even the most powerful bomber? Suppose that it was one of these vast craft which flashed out the mysterious code word *Stendec*, when the British airliner, "Lancastrian Star Dust" vanished four minutes before she was due to land at the airport in Santiago de Chile? (*Vide* page 139 *supra*). For what spot far out in space, for what world not ours, was the word *Stendec* intended?

A very mysterious affair in the Straits of Malacca, on Feb. 4, 1948, is recorded in the *Proceedings of the Merchant Marine Council*. A dying radio operator on a Dutch steamer, "Ourang Madan", sent out an S.O.S.: "Captain dead, in chartroom. . . whole crew dead. . .I am dying. . ." Rescue ships reached the spot and found it was true. Men lay dead on deck and below; but what was weird was that every face on deck was *upturned to the sun* with a look of horror, eyes staring, and mouths agape. The ship's dog, dead, had its teeth bared. No sign of injuries was on the bodies, but when a tow line was attached to the ship, the rescuers had to beat a hurried retreat. Flames belched out of the hold, and in five minutes, the "Ourang Madan" was hurled into the air by a terrific explosion. *Why was every man's face, on deck, upturned to the sky?*

I would go even farther back to the year 1900, and the still unsolved mystery of the missing men in the Seven Hunters' Lighthouse, of the Flannan Islands, a most lonely light out in the North Atlantic, 19 miles from the almost equally remote island of Lewis, in the Outer Hebrides, Scotland. This lighthouse stands on a cliff of gneiss, 150 feet above the sea. The relief ship was overdue, owing to storms, and when she arrived, the relief men found the entrance door shot and barred, and could get no answer to their repeated hails. Forcing a way inside, they found the lighthouse empty, the clock stopped, no fire lit—it was mid-winter and cold—and not a trace of the four men, who should have been inside. The slate log

had a last entry, dated Dec. 14, 1900, and all the big lamps
were trimmed and the lenses cleaned. Only one thing was
missing: the oil-skins and sea-boots of two of the men. The
slate log recorded that a storm had died away on Dec. 14.
Later, it transpired that the captain of a passing steamer told
the Scottish Lighthouse Board that he saw no light on the
Seven Hunters on Dec. 15, the inference being that the men
had mysteriously vanished between Dec. 14 and 15. *How?*

If a tidal wave had suddenly swept over the lighthouse—
as stated, it was 150 feet above the sea—and washed the men
into the sea, how came it that the sea-boots and oil-skins of
the other two men still remained in the lighthouse?

They did not talk of flying saucers in 1900; but, as this
book has shown, such visitants appeared in the skies over the
lands and seas of the British Isles, long before and after 1900.
Naturally, one can have no shadow of evidence to offer that
there is any connection between the two things, in the nature
of cause and effect; but no man will be hanged for wondering
if. . . . ?

We now come to sensational reports of eye-witnesses who
say they have seen saucers landing, but who do *not* allege that
they had any communication, whether by word of mouth,
stop-watch-timed, or by telepathy or gesture, or any other
method. The earliest report is of an event happening on the
night of July 2, 1950, and I cite this remarkable and circum-
stantial story from a factory and house magazine, "The Steep
Rock Echo", of Sepr. 1950, and by permission of the Editor,
Mr. B. J. Eyton. It is an organ published by the Steep Rock
Iron Company, Ontario, Canada. Mr. Eyton says: "I have
been unable either to verify or disprove this story; but about
the time it was told and published in our magazine, men
working in the mines, here, at Steep Rock, saw a flying saucer
at night, and people in the nearby township of Atitokan told
the local press that they had seen them in a region between
Fort William and Port Arthur, a range of some 140 miles.
In fact, one night, the telegraphers of the Canadian National
Railroads wired to each other to look out for a strange object

in the skies, until it reached here. Then it turned back. Everybody is sure he saw a flying saucer that night."

Here is the story published in the "Steep Rock Echo" Sepr.-
October 1950:

"In the dusk of July 2, 1950, I and my wife had drawn
up our boat on the sandy beach of a tiny cove in Sawbill
Bay, where we had gone fishing. Cliffs rise on all three
sides of the cove. Small trees and bushes concealed us
and our boat from the sight of anyone overhead, in a
'plane,' had there been one round that evening. We had
snacks and a thermos flask of tea, and, as the dusk was
drawing on, we talked of going home. Suddenly, the air
seemed to vibrate as if from shock waves from a blasting
operation at the local iron mines. I recollected, however,
that the mines were too far away for that. I had an intui-
tion to climb ten feet up a rock, where was a cleft that
gave onto the bay.

"I was amazed at what I saw. As I peered through the
cleft, taking care to make no noise, I could see out on
the bay a large shining object, resting on the water. It
was in the curve of the shore line, about a quarter of a
mile away, across the top end of some narrows. I got down
from the cleft and sped back to my wife. She was startled
as I came running up. 'Why what on earth is the matter?'
she asked. 'Come and see if you see what I see', I said,
grasping her by the arm. 'And make no noise or show
yourself.' I drew her by the hand to the cleft. We both
peered through it.

"The shining thing was still resting on the water. It
looked like two saucers, one upside down on top of the
other. Round the edge were holes like black ports, spaced
about 4 feet apart. We could not see the underside, because the bottom of the thing was resting either on the
water, or close to it. On top were what looked like open
hatches, and moving round over its surface were ten little
figures. They looked queer, very queer. Rotating slowly
from a central position, and about 8 feet up in the air,
was a hoop-shaped object. As it rotated, to a point directly
opposite to where my wife and I were peering through
the rock-cleft, it stopped, and the little figures also stopped
moving. Everything now seemed concentrated on the little
opening through which we were peering. We were about
to duck down, as we thought these midget figures might
see us and take alarm, when, on the opposite side of the

253

cove, a deer appeared, came to the edge of the water, and stood motionless.

"We again peered through the cleft in the rock. The little figures and the previously rotating circle were aligned on the deer. But now the circle moved to the left. We ducked down, counted twenty, and took another peep. The thing was gyrating and the figures moving; but the deer didn't seem to trouble them. We ducked down, supposing that a ray had been projected towards the rock from the thing on the water. May be, the rock was a barrier and kept it off us.

"It looked as if the whole machine were worked from a central point below the circling ray. The operator was a midget figure on a small raised stand. He wore what seemed to be a red skull cap, or perhaps it was red paint. The caps worn by the others were blue. I should say the figures were from 3 feet 6 inches to 4 feet tall, and all were the same size. We could not see their faces. In fact, the faces seemed just blank surfaces! It was odd that the figures moved like automata, rather than living beings.

"Over their chests was a gleaming metallic substance, but the legs and arms were covered by something darker. These figures did not turn round. They just altered the direction of their feet. They walked on the angle, or camber of the surface of the disc, and the leg on the higher side seemed shorter; so that the compensation—real or apparent—provided against any limp. As I looked, one of the midgets picked up the end, or nozzle of a vivid green hose. He lifted it, while facing one way, and started to walk the other way. And now the air hummed in a high-pitched note, or vibration. May be, water was being drawn in, or something was ejected. I do not know if something was being extracted from the water of Saw-bill Bay.

"Next time we peered through the rock-cleft, we found that all the figures had vanished, and the machine was about 8 feet up in the air. I noticed that the water of the lake, near where the thing had rested, was tinged with colour combined of red-blue-gold. The disc I reckoned was about 15 feet thick at the centre, and some 12 feet at the edges. It tilted at an angle near 45 degrees . . . Now, there came a rush of wind . . . a flash of red-blue-gold, and it was gone, heading northwards, and so fast that my eye could not follow it. It was now quite dark. We decided to call it a day, and got into our boat and went out into the bay where the saucer had rested on the water. I had aligned two trees to estimate its size, which, I think, was 48 feet. I went back there again, on another day, and as we came through the narrows, I heard a rush of wind, and again something flashed above and beyond the trees. What it was, I could not see. My wife was scared. She said she would never go there again.

"A day or two later, I spoke to a friend at the mine, and told him what I had seen. He suggested we both go to the cove on a fishing trip. We had cameras, but after we stationed ourselves at the rock-cleft for three evenings running, nothing happened; and on the last evening, we moved quickly along the shore. We patrolled the bay for three weeks, when, one evening, as we were in our outboard motor-boat, and a strong wind was cutting across Sawbill Bay, chopping the water, *we saw the disc!* It was in the same spot. I surmise that, as the wind was up from them, they could not hear our motor chugging. I swung her round into the wind, and my friend got the cameras out. But it is difficult to hold a motor-boat into the wind on choppy water, while trying to take a photo. Indeed, the wind was so darned cold, that my fingers went numb, and I could not manage both the helm and a camera. The boat see-sawed up and down so much that my friend could not focus the camera.

" 'And now,' said he, 'I've seen what you saw, and see!'

"But before we got close up to the saucer, I saw the little figures vanish into the hatches. They had seen us! The rotating mechanism vanished, and the hose reeled in like a flash of green lightning—so fast did they work! There came a regular blast of air and the saucer whizzed off like greased lightning. But my eye was quick enough to see that a little figure, close to the water's edge, was only half-way back to the hatch. He must have operated the end of the green hose, or suction pipe. . . Our own engine stalled and then ran hot; so we got home late, and our wives were terrified. We had to promise never to go saucer-spotting again!"

Mr. Eyton, the editor of "Steep Rock Echo", says that a fisherman at Steep Rock, Ontario, was in Sawbill Bay, one night, when he saw something like a meteor race down from the sky and vanish towards the bay. Later, the fisherman noticed a curious, fluorescent sediment, greenish in colour, in one of the inlets of the bay. No fish would bite, in any part of this bay where the green scum was. He wondered if the green scum were derived from some mineral deposit; but he did not think of flying saucers! Another fisherman heard a whiz in the sky and saw what he took to be a shooting star flash across the bay. He, too, saw green scum on the water, and many dead fish in it.

On July 11, 1952, Herr Linke, mayor of a German city, and escaper from the Soviet Zone in Germany, swore an eight-page affidavit, which was communicated to Western Intelligence officers, that he and his step-daughter, aged 11, had seen at Hasselbach, close to the Western German border, a "50 foot saucer, like a large oval warming-pan". It emitted green and red colours, and had alighted in a glade in a forest:

> "Round its sides were two rows of ports. . . .and a conning-tower on top, 10 feet high. . .Standing by it, were two figures, one carrying breast-light, in shimmering metal dress, and bending down studying something on the ground. . .Hearing my daughter call from the road, the figures swiftly clambered up the sides of the object, vanished into the conning-tower. . .a vibration rose to a roar, the machine rotated, and a device like a cylinder, on which the object had rested on the ground, receded into its body. Round it a ring blazed into flames, and rotated. It whistled over the tree tops and ascended in the direction of Stockheim, across the hills and woods. A shepherd, George Derbat saw it from a mile away. He thought it was a 'comet'. Also, a night-watchman at a saw-mill saw it. Where the thing had rested was a depression in the soil. I never heard of saucers while I was in the Soviet Zone."

Here follows a story of possibly startled entities on a flying saucer who fired a light-projectile, or put a harmful ray on an intruder:

> "On the night of August 19, 1952, a scoutmaster, D. S. Desvergers, of West Palm Beach, Florida, got out of a car to investigate a strange light in a glade of woods in the Florida Everglades. He came on a thing like half a rubber ball, 3 feet thick, and high in the centre, so that three men could stand erect inside. (Other accounts say the object was 30 feet wide, and tapered to 3 feet on the rims, and that 8 men could have been housed in it.)

256

Round the object was a phosphorescent glare. He was seen, and the entities fired at him a ball that floated slowly at his face. (Another account says that the ball was like a Roman candle.) It singed his hair and face, and burned holes in his cap. Desvergers says he 'was blasted'—whether by fear or fright. U.S. Intelligence officers questioned Desvergers, but nothing further has been said. *(Summarised from the Los Angeles Examiner and New York and Chicago newspapers,* some of which add that police found Desvergers wandering in the woods, overcome, and complaining that a dreadful stench accompanied the ball of fire.) Deputy Sheriff Partin found later that the grass in the glade was scorched." *(From Miami and Charleston newspapers.)*

Here are two more American reports:

"Herbert Long, of Kutztown, Penna, says that, on August 31, 1952, he saw a flying saucer land 50 feet from a Pennsylvanian highway, and that he sketched it. From Watkins Glen, New York State, comes a report that three men swear that they saw a saucer plunge into Seneca Lake." *(New York and Philadelphia newspapers.)*

A dreadful stench was also the remarkable feature of the next adventure which occurred in the dusk of a September night, in 1952. Location was the lonely region of Flatwood Hill, West Virginia, country of scattered farms and thickly wooded hills:

"Half an hour after sunset, on Friday, 12 Sepr, 1952, two boys, Eddie May (13), and Fred May (12) excitedly told their mother they had seen a saucer land on the top of nearby Flatwood Hill. Mrs. Kathleen May, the mother, her five small sons, and a young National Guardsman, Gene Lemon, set off for the hill-top, and in the dusk of the starry evening, saw, near a tree a thing 'like a half-man, half-dragon, 10 feet tall, with red-orange-face, and green body. It seemed to glide over the grass towards them, the body all a-glow.' The whole party fled in terror, increased by an overpowering stench from the visitant. Back in the village, they 'vomited for hours'. On the same evening, there had been reports of lights and mysterious objects in the skies in that region, and local people said they had seen a silvery disc, jetting a red exhaust, rush at high speed, slow down, and then land on the hill-top. The object that landed had a high-pitched whine and pulsated, and the horrible stench may have been some powerful and irritant gas that it emitted and which encircled the landing-place. The saucer is said to have been a large sphere, and some say noise of working mechanism came from it. It is surmised that the 'dragon-like' entity was wearing a space suit and had landed and was returning to the sphere. Mrs. May later said that it was 'lit inside and had what seemed to be large and terrible claws'. (Grapnels?) A local editor who went to the hill-top, with five other men, all with shot guns, came onto the hill-top an hour later, and saw that something had landed there, left a depression in the soil, and had thrust aside bushes and stones. These men fairly reeled backward from the stench! There were also skid-like marks between the tree where the 'monster' had stood, and the site of the disc. All the May party had to be treated for shock. The 'monster' has been sketched, and appears to have been a very large truncated cone, resting on a smaller cone, with a round, transparent window in front. It projected two small, but piercing blue beams. It was the smaller cone that, apparently, looked like half-man, half-dragon. May be, the 'monster' went back to the disc; for it was not again seen. It is also said that, after the incident, 'a strange white substance' was picked up where the disc had rested, and sent for analysis to a laboratory at Charleston, S. Carolina. (If so, as in the case of the British Air Ministry (*Vide* page 100, *supra*) nothing has been revealed, nor has the U.S. Air Force said anything about its investigation of the Flatwood Hill incident.)

"The local police, however, admit that, on the day of the incident, a fleet of pear-shaped objects, dull-red, white, and gleaming had been seen flying in formation over the region, and had hovered in mid-air, ascended vertically, descended, then flew level, and that three of the strange objects had crashed in the dense woods. Yet the U.S. Air Force authorities declined to explore the woods! It is also said that the disc on the hill-top had been seen to flash a red light which pulsated in a pungent mist." (*Collated from Washington, N. Carolina and Va. press.*)

One has the impression that, here, was some entity clad in a giant's space suit and equipped to withstand differential pressures and a gravity and atmosphere, unlike the unknown world from which it came.

On Sepr. 2, 1952, Pietro Gian Monguzci (or Monguzzi), an

Italian draughtsman, and his wife were climbing the Bernina
Alps, south of the Swiss Engadine, when, at a height of about
10,000 feet, they saw something that Monguzzi reported to the
authorities:

> "My wife and I saw a saucer landing on a glacier in the
> Bernina Alps. It touched down for a few minutes, and
> there emerged a figure in human shape, wearing a sort of
> *diving suit.* The figure got out of the saucer and walked
> round it, as if examining it. Then it re-entered the saucer,
> which took off without a sound at breath-taking speed.
> It vanished north, over the Swiss Rhaetian Alps. I took
> a photograph of the saucer and its pilot."

France has also a story of a landed saucer. On 28 October,
1952, a *douanier* (Customs officer), Monsieur Gabriel Gachin-
ard, told a Monsieur Guieu, of the journal "Ouranos", about
an incident previously reported to the newspaper *Provençal*:

> "At 2.5 a.m., on 27 October, 1952, after the air mail
> 'plane from Paris had taken off for Nice from the air-
> drome of Marignac, where I am stationed in the customs
> sheds, I was in the urinals, washing my hands before
> taking a snack in our guard-office. I left the toilette and
> was crossing the airdrome, and halted, for a few moments,
> by some flower pots. Suddenly, I saw, like a shooting star
> fallen from the sky, an engine which was standing out-
> side the cement trackway (*piste de roulement*), where
> the 'planes stand before taking off. It is railed off, slightly
> to the left of where I stood. I put down my snack on the
> flower pots, and walked 50 mètres (164 feet) towards it,
> where I could make out the engine. It was 5 mètres (16.4
> feet) long and 1 mètre (3.3 feet) tall. It had portholes,
> from which came a pale light which pulsated on and off.
> I can't say what colour it was; for it was always dark.
> From this distance of 50 mètres, I saw sparks fly from
> its rear. Then the machine took off in very swift fashion,
> much more quickly than it had landed. In 2 seconds, with
> a noise like a small 14 July firework (*petite fusée*), or
> small rocket, it soared up, and I saw no more. Returning
> to the track control station, I found the time was 2.15
> a.m. (local). I 'phoned the control tower; but they had
> seen nothing. I have sketched this machine."

A farmer, Nello Ferrari, aged 41, made a remarkable statement to the police of Modena, a stately Italian cathedral city, 180 miles south-east of the Bernina Alps.

Ferrari said:

"It was 10 in the morning on Novr. 30, 1952, when I was walking around my farm. Suddenly, I was terrified to see, hovering over me in the sky, a disc about 130 feet wide, and I guess only 35 feet above my head. It was ringed with a red mist. In a few moments, as I was gazing at this big disc, which looked gold and copper in colour, its top part split open, so that it looked like two discs, one on top of the other. There emerged three figures of human shape with their faces half-covered with masks. I heard a loud noise from inside the disc, and then I saw a cylinder around 15 feet long emerge from the opening. The three beings spoke in some strange tongue, one word of which sounded to me like *warren firg unch!* Then they all went back into the disc and the top part lowered itself onto the bottom part, like a clam. The disc now rose straight into the sky with a sound like a flock of pigeons, and in a few seconds vanished into space."

Close to Melbourne, Australia, is an industrial suburb known as Sunshine road. On the night of 12 October, 1952, two lads, Jim McKay, aged 18, and Jim Robinson were out strolling when there came, *not* high up in the air, a terrible whistling sound, and there hurtled straight towards them a strange object coloured red and blue. The two youths were terrified and raced for shelter, as the thing whizzed overhead. "Not a flash of lightning," said an Australian Weather Bureau official. The two lads swore that it was a saucer come to take them aboard!

A being like a "flying man", apparently not terrestrial, was reported to have been seen, at 2.30 a.m., June 18, 1953, by three people, Mrs. Hilda Walker, Miss Judy Meyers, and Howard Phillips, all of them on a torrid night, sitting out on the front porch of a tenement house, 118, East Third Street, Houston, Texas. Here is what Mrs. Walker told the *Houston Chronicle*:

"'About 25 feet away, I saw a huge shadow cross the lawn, and at first thought it was the reflection of a big moth in a nearby street lamp. But the shadow seemed to bounce up into a pecan tree. We all looked up. It was the figure of a man with wings like a bat. He was dressed in greyish, tight-fitting clothes, and he swayed for half a minute on the branch of the old pecan tree. Suddenly, the light faded slowly and died out, and the figure vanished. Then we heard a loud swoosh over the tree-tops, and something like the white flash of a torpedo-shaped object was seen. The bat-man was wearing a black cape, and had quarter-length boots. I saw him plain, and he had wings folded over his shoulders. All round him was a dim grey light.' Mr. Phillips says the bat-man was wearing something like the uniform of a paratrooper, and was encased in a halo of light. 'I thought all the folk who talk of saucers were crazy, now I don't know what to believe. I saw it, whatever it was'."

Entities from another type of saucer were the subject of a report by two miners, on June 20, 1953, to Sheriff Captain Fred Preston of Marble Creek, Calif. The miners, whose adventure drew large, but disappointed crowds to the place, are John Black, and John Van Allen. I summarise reports from various American sources, newspaper and others:

"The miners were working in a titanium ore mine at Marble Creek, and on May 20, and again on June 20, 1953, saw a strange silvery object composed of two large discs of metal, 12 feet wide, and 7 feet thick, land on a sand-bar, 100 feet from them. The object was cambered, and on its crown was a 'plastic observation dome'. A being, like a man 4 feet tall, human in look, with hair and broad shoulders, descended a rope ladder from the machine which rested on four metal retractable legs. The being wore a long parka (coat), reaching to below the knees, and had a hood thrown back from the head. He wore 'sort of gabardine trousers', tied at the ankles. He took a thing of gleaming metal with flat round bottom, flared out like a section of a cone, drew water, and went back to the machine, inside which something took it from him. Seeing the watching miners, the object took off in a flash over the trees. Miner Black says he had found two camp-fire sites near the sand-bar, rocks still warm, where these beings had made fires. They had left five-inch long footprints. He found his compass spin wildly, and thought it was caused by an invisible disc near. He has seen them seven times, and always on the 20th day of the month. 'The discs resemble two soup plates fastened together, and convex. They travel soundlessly, and slip sideways between trees of a wood until altitude is gained. The little man he saw, on June 20, wore forest-green trousers, and very flexible-toed shoes of dull black. He had a green cap, black hair, good looks, fair skin, and walked stiffly, and it seemed as if he had not been much in the sunlight. The disc rested on a projecting cylinder. When he raced for the thing, the little man put his foot onto a step, and climbed into the saucer through the bottom. He went in as far as his knees, and then raised his legs. Then the landing-gear came up, the disc hung in the air a few seconds, and went off at an angle of 45 degrees, with a hiss. No rivets seen; but there was a window on the top side, through which Black could not see from outside. Black waved his hand as the saucer went off, and it seemed to wobble in reply."

A correspondent tells me that, on July 20, 1953, 200 people turned up near the sand-bar, but no saucer-men turned up. The two miners are said to be abstainers, and very indignant at talk about "Buck Rogerish comics and bourbon and rye whisky".

Has anyone ever got inside a flying saucer?

If Mr. Truman Bethurum, a mechanic of California, engaged in road construction work, is to be believed, he is the one man who has achieved that success, one night, just before dawn, in July, 1953. But exactly as in the case of another gentleman, Mr. George Adamski, of Palomar, Calif., he has overlooked one trifling "fourth dimensional" obstacle. Both men say they have met entities in saucers who have the power of metamorphosing themselves from our own three dimensional plane of visibility to a fourth dimensional plane wherein they are normally invisible, being entities of a planet of some etheric order of matter whose wave-lengths are of a dense matter of the order of invisibility. That is, of matter not our own. Both men see no contradiction in asking these entities to convey them—men of our order of visible matter—to a world which is etheric and invisible, and inhabited by beings who are invisible—to us!

But, how, apart from corporeal dissolution, does either of these men suppose that this wonder of a visit by invisible `saucer to a fourth dimensional world in space can be achieved *for him?*

I, as before, summarise this story from various Western American newspapers and journals:

> "On the time and date stated, Mr. Bethurum, asleep inside a truck, parked on State Highway No. 91, some 70 miles west of Las Vegas, Nevada, alleges that he was awakened by people talking outside. The stars were still in the pre-dawn sky, when Bethurum arose from his uneasy seat in the cab, and called out: 'What's goin' on here?' Outside, he saw eight little men grouped spookily in a semi-circle. Mr. Bethurum suspected that there must be a saucer parked nearby. 'What about my going aboard her?' he asked the little men. He does not say how they understood him; but says they took him to the saucer. It will be noted that he was not struck by any paralysis ray, as Mr. Adamski says *he* was, when incautiously approaching *his* saucer from Venus. Mr. Bethurum was led down a corridor past several closed cabin doors, right into a room fitted up like an office and lounge. A very pretty lady confronted him. She was some inches shorter than the men, and had a 'Latin appearance'. She told him she was captain of the saucer, and a long and highly confidential talk followed. It appears that the little lady was not at all anxious to inform Mr. Bethurum about herself, the crew, or what the saucer was doing in Nevada."

One rather odd thing was mentioned by Mr. Bethurum: That the lady spoke English in rhymed couplets!

> "She said the disc, called a *scow*, came from a planet behind the moon, named *Clarion*, where all is mental and spiritual progress, and an Arcady without war or strife. The crew, who spoke an unknown tongue, were in a grey-blue uniform, but only a few came ashore on the earth, at a time. Mr. Bethurum saw no one else in the saucer. The lady-skipper wore a black skirt and red blouse, was 4½ feet tall, and was a grandmother with two grandchildren, *not* on board the saucer."

However, Mr. Bethurum did not leave the saucer quite scatheless:

> "He told someone that he brushed against the exterior of the saucer—convex, and like a silver dollar—and at

263

the laundry, later, it was found that large holes, as if caused by acid, had been eaten in his coat and trousers. The lady said they had many flying saucers, all skippered by women, and a crew of 32 men in each."

This seems to imply that *Clarion* is a matriarchal planet.

"The *scow* had no power motor, but flew in an up-and-down motion, or in steps, along lines of magnetic force. Said the lady to Mr. Bethurum: 'I may take five people from earth to *Clarion*'."

Mr. Bethurum told the newspapers that he had eleven meetings with the saucer from *Clarion*. He had another meeting:

"Mr. Bethurum and his foreman boss were eating hot dogs and drinking hotter coffee, in a desert café in Nevada, one evening, when, on a sudden, there entered a mysterious woman, in dark glasses, accompanied by eight little men. A flustered waitress took their orders for, she thinks, cakes and lemonade, and came across to whisper to Mr. Bethurum. Whereupon he went across to the visitants' table and said: 'Ma'am, we have met before? Say, ain't these the little guys from *Clarion*?' At this very moment, Mr. Bethurum's boss went outside, he said, to keep an eye on where the visitants might go. Whether or no the *Clarion* lady, seeing the sudden exit, suspected that the boss might be looking for a police highway patrol, they all got up, and, in military precision, walked to the exit and vanished *into nothingness!*"

And that was that!

He has not seen the *Clarion scow* since, but hopes for another encounter. "The U.S. War Department men have been to see me about it, but mum's the word all round", he adds.

No doubt about it; for another Californian gentleman who alleged that, in 1952, he spoke to a golden-haired five-foot-six man from Venus, by telepathy and gesture, timed from a quarter of a mile away by stop-watch, naively complains that, when *he*, later, invited two official gentlemen from U.S. Governmental intelligence departments to come and see him and his Venusian planetary exhibits, those bored gentlemen listened intently, but registered no surprise on their poker and blasé faces.

A young gentleman, from Virginia, tells me that these stories of encounters with saucers are running all through California like a prairie fire. In England, people are asking why none of these startling things happen *here?*

To them, I suggest attention to the news story following:

> "Police and firemen returned to Llanberis reporting that their searches for a mysterious object, seen on the slopes of Snowdon, on July 31, 1953, have been fruitless. Police say no aircraft is reported missing." (*London newspapers' reports, August 2, 1953.*)

What, on Snowdon, might attract flying saucers?

In February 1939 a research engineer reported that he was overcome with a sudden vertigo, while he was prospecting on the slopes of Snowdon, N. Wales. He thought the cause was radioactivity, and he sent samples of the rock, which he believed induced the vertigo, to a certain chemical company's laboratory. There may be uranium deposits on Snowdon; but I know that the results of the analysis were never revealed.

Perhaps less evidential are the stories following: A woman in an Oklahoma (U.S.) township says that, "many years ago", she was travelling in a Conestoga wagon, and on a roadside in Missouri, listened—she was then aged three—to a talk between her father and an old roamer who hove in sight, when the coffee and hardtack were ready for breakfast in the woods:

> "He was an old man and he told my dad that, about 40 years ago (may be, in the 1880's), he, the old man was a lad and had gone hunting in the hills, where he saw a round thing settle down from the sky on the bald top of a mountain overhead. He was frightened, but that did not stop him from climbing up the mountain to see who it was. 'It stood in the clearing of some woods, and was like a big silver ball.' Soon, a piece of the top slid back and two things came out. Said the old man: 'They wuzzn't as tall as me; but, sure, wuz nice-lookin' folks. Hadn't much on their purty bodies and legs, that's sure; but the gal wuz as purty as a filly on a medder in the spring a-foolin' round an' raisin' the passions of an old spavined stallion, and then kickin' her heels and dashin' off. They tried to talk to me, but neither on us could understand what the other said. I was too scared to say

265

much. Then they stepped back into the ball, slid back the lid, and the ball went up into the sky till it was lost to my eyes. Yep, it's the doggone truth I'm tellin' yo', though smarties round this location say I alwuz was loco'."

There have been unconfirmable reports of alleged landings of saucers, one in the deserts of Australia, the other in lone woods in Ontario, Canada. Also, somewhere in the Andes: "Vast space ships, a mile long", are alleged to have landed.

A man in Oregon wrote a letter to a friend of mine in Oklahoma, about what his son, a U.S. marine on the way to his dépôt at Fort Pendleton, overheard, in Decr. 1951, at the famous observatory at Palomar, Calif., site of the world's largest telescope:

> "I, and another marine, were chatting to one of the Palomar professors, when a friend of his arrived from Berkeley, Cal. He, too, is a professor. They began talking, and we listened in to what we were not supposed to hear. The Palomar man said that the U.S. Federal Bureau of Investigations had forbidden the publication of astrophysical photos taken at Palomar. 'Why?' asked the other. 'Well, they show things which the U.S. Government think it wiser people should not know. They might cause panics. There are pictures of jet 'planes chasing flying saucers, and disintegrating in mid-air. There are data about strange changes in the atmosphere, and the effect on other planets of radioactive emanations after the explosion of atomic bombs. I have heard, too, a strange story that a landing-field has been found in one of the Australian deserts, whose origin is unknown. The Australian Royal Air Force authorities are said to have cordoned off the area, and no one is allowed in there. They are trying to find the origin of the landing-field, which they do not believe was made by any terrestrial being.' "

I have a friend in Australia, whose son is an officer in the Australian Air Force. He passed my inquiry to his son, who replied:

> "A space ship *could* have landed in one of our deserts; for they are just one hell of a place, and there are plenty of blank spaces. If Mr. Wilkins can find out the supposed date of the landing, I should be interested."

I do not know the date. Some time later, in 1952, my friend wrote that he wondered if the alleged unknown landing-field were one of those made in World War 2, at the time there was a trek from Darwin, in N.W. Australia, when the Japánese bombed it from the air.

In June, 1952, I got a reply: "Our Australian Air authorities, when shown your report about an alleged landing-ground of a flying saucer, or space ship, said:

"We have no comment to make."

So? My reply is: "Then have you something you wish to hide from the public, that is not concerned with security matters?"

Walter Winchell, the well known columnist, stated:

"June 30, 1952: Scientists at Palomar Observatory, Calif., are supposed to have seen a 'space ship' land in the Mojave Desert, in May last. Four persons stepped out, took one look, and went off again. The U.S. Army may officially announce it in the fall."

Needless to say, the U.S. Army made no such announcement at *any* date!

Evidently, there are people in the U.S.A. who believe that flying saucer entities have kidnapped human beings! In July, 1953, one, George Sodder, of Fayetteville, N. Caro., put up a billboard, on which was the following announcement:

"I offer $5,000 for information about the fate of five children, mysteriously snatched away from a burning house, on Christmas morning, 1945. The parents escaped, but at first they believed the children had perished in the flames, supposed to be caused by faulty wiring. But no remains were found in the ashes. A 'bus driver says he had seen balls of fire thrown on the roof."

Other reports, confirmable or otherwise, have reached me. They are fairly sensational, but probably would not come within a British High Court's rules of evidence:

"A little man from a saucer is being tenderly cared for in the 'incubator room' at San Diego, while cadavers of two saucer pilots are being dissected by surgeons of the

U.S. Army-Air Force (Medical Division). A Californian air pilot told me that, in 1942, he had been right inside a giant saucer, and seen giant fly-wheels sheathed in metal-skins, and found that the motive-force came from electro-static turbines, whose fly-wheels create an electro-magnetic field of force, creating tremendous speeds. The little saucer men have a smaller bony structure than earth-men, but the bones are proportionally heavier, and their stomachs smaller." (*Mr. Joe Rohrer of Pikes Peak Radio Company, at a Chamber of Commerce luncheon, in Pueblo, Colorado, on July 22, 1952.*)

Letter from a correspondent in Oklahoma, to the author of this book (July 24, 1952): "On a business trip to San Francisco, last week, I met a nice reliable fellow who has heard from a pal in the U.S. Air Force, that they have captured a little fellow, three feet tall, from a forced-down saucer, and are keeping him alive in a pressure chamber, somewhere in California. He comes from another planet, and was one of three others killed in a crash caused by radar, in an Arizona desert, in 1950. They are showing him pictures and teaching him to read and write, and understand."

I offer no comment on the following stories:

"*Buffalo Evening News*, 27 August, 1952: A man at Lamberton, N.C., says a thing 8 feet long and 6 feet wide, landed in his yard after knocking bricks off his chimney. A man about 2 feet 6 inches tall came out and stood by the thing. 'I asked him if he was hurt. He scrambled in, and it went away with a whistle and a whiff, and loud noise.' "

"Three saucers are known to have landed, and one of the inmates stepping out, died on his own doorstep. The space visitors can't get acclimatised to our atmosphere. The U.S. Government are deliberately confusing folks and hiding the truth." (*Mr. S. Farwell, special agent of the General Electric Company, speaking at a Rotary luncheon, in the Hotel Sherston-Gibson, at Los Angeles, Calif., on 29 August, 1952.*)

In March, 1953, Mr. N. Bean, a research engineer, startled listeners at a Rotary Club affair, held at Miami Beach, Florida, by stating:

"I have personally talked with a truck driver who hauled a forced-down flying saucer from New Mexico to a place in Ohio. The driver told me that the U.S. authorities have been unable to find a way to open the saucer. But I can't accept as positive that little men have been found in saucers; though, on March 31, 1953, I saw a whole squadron of saucers, in formation, over Golden Beach, near Miami, Fla."

A radio announcer in another state swore that' one night he heard a "mechanical-like voice" speak on his radiophone. It said:

"Say, bo, I'm talkin' to yeh from the planet Venus·"

Then, at Monticello, Indiana, on August 2, 1953, it is alleged that:

"Folk, here, saw for an hour on the beach (*sic*) a flying saucer, after it had landed. It came exactly a year after the Monticello Chamber of Commerce put out an invitation." (*Press reports in U.S.A. Middle West newspapers.*)

This sounds like a publicity "stunt", and whether it inspired the incident following, I am unable to say:

October 8, 1953: "Yesterday, in New York City, a high, thin voice interrupted a radio show which was boosting a book on saucers. It said: 'You earth-men will soon be annihilated, and your planet, unless you stop talking about flying saucers. I am speaking from a space ship over Los Angeles, Calif.' Later, the same voice came on the air, saying: 'I am over Salt Lake City. You cannot see me, but I can reach you easily. If you saw my hideous face, it would scare you to death'. The radio concern and author and publisher deny any knowledge of this affair." (*Various New York City newspapers.*) *N.B.* It is an admirable coincidence that the unseen speaker should have spoken over the air by using a private telephone number of a National Broadcasting Company's producer, which number is *not* listed in the N.Y. telephone directory. Also, the publisher, some years before, had issued a book by a well known Hollywood character, who subsequently admitted publishing a book about little men from Venus, which he was badgered, by the U.S. magazine *True*, into admitting was a hoax.

CHAPTER XII

THE SHADOW OF THE UNKNOWN

In England and France, and in the U.S.A. and Canada, in the years 1951-1953, peculiar and very disturbing phenomena have been recorded, and not explained, although they certainly have not gone without inquiry by the military and scientific branches of Air Ministries, Air Forces, and security and defence departments. I do not think, however, that terrestrial agents of war departments are actually involved.

These phenomena have taken the forms of blasts from the skies, often preceded by strange flashes of light, the latter suggesting that suprasonic power jet 'planes, passing the sonic barrier, may *not* be the causative factors. They have, also, in England, in 1953, and in the U.S.A., both in 1953 and earlier, taken the form of mysterious fires, in forests and on hills, of remarkable "heat ray" character; of sudden interruptions to power lines, in Middle Western U.S.A., and of the blowing up of factories known to be concerned in processes figuring in the making of nuclear fission and thermo-nuclear (atomic and hydrogen) bombs (where sabotage has not been discovered); of the dropping in England and France of unknown substances from the skies; and of a long series of unexplained accidents to British and U.S. jet 'planes, besides mysterious disappearances of civilian air-liners, and military 'planes and personnel.

Let us look at the power line mysteries:

> *April 1952*: Sudden and mysterious black-out of an electric power line system in north-eastern Ohio, followed, two days later, by an unexplained black-out of a power station at Evanston, Indiana, which lasted two hours. Experts and scientists and police puzzled. In Ohio, the power came on as suddenly as it went off. High line patrols went over the line, foot by foot, every piece of

apparatus concerned was tested and re-tested, but found in perfect order. Charts from recording instruments were studied, but gave no clues. The power line company were unusually honest and frank. "The only logical assumption," they say, "is that *some object or foreign substance came across the line and grounded it out;* but we have not the slightest clue to what it was, nor the faintest idea why the power went off, nor why it came on again".

In Ohio, and also, it is believed, in Indiana, just before, or about this time, mysterious objects were seen in the sky.

What happened late in August 1953, one night, to the large reservoirs of the water department of Grafton, West Virginia?

"Three times in one night the water supply took a drop of several inches in the million-gallon reservoir. It was the equivalent of a fire hydrant being turned wide open, except that no such hydrant operated. Water officials call the phenomenon 'gremlins', and the police worked on the case, with no result" (*Information to the author from Mr. Gray Barker of Clarksburg, West Virginia*).

My readers should compare this mystery with what happened on Steep Rock Lake, Ontario, in late summer 1950, when midget entities from a saucer were seen by two people to be "hosing in water". (*Vide* chapter XI, pages 252 *et seq.*)

There were the phenomena of green balls, seen by many observers, some of them airmen and scientists, speeding through the night skies of Arizona and New Mexico, in January and Novr. 1952, and characterised by a spectral band of 5,200 angstroms, close to the green of burning copper. Copper, it may be noted, is not found in meteorites:

Jan. 1952: Three green fire balls seen high over Taos, New Mexico. One hung motionless over U.S. Hill on the Santa Fé highway, in the twilight, burning bright yellow flame for 10 minutes, then vanishing. A second green ball swayed to and fro, in the sky over mountains near Taos. A third, at 10 p.m., shot across the sky and vanished. Three days earlier, airport at Santa Fé airdrome saw strange illuminated object come into sight. Immediately, airport lights were switched on, and the object at once climbed at a steep angle and remained motionless, very high, for 25 minutes. At Gallup, N.M., just before dawn, strange shining objects moved at high speed, stopped, and remained motionless in the solar disc.

Nov. 2, 1952: Green ball larger than full moon, and much brighter, exploded in tremendous paroxysm of light, *with no sound*. Dr. La Paz, director of meteorics, University of New Mexico, U.S., says that these green balls are *not* electrostatic phenomena, nor meteorites. (Similar green balls seen in 1948 in south-west U.S., and 50 of them in 1950, over eastern states of the U.S., and over Puerto Rico, W.I.)

At Tucumari, New Mexico, U.S., a ball of fire flashed out of the sky, on a January night, and, immediately afterwards, a big tank, found to be neatly pierced, released 750,000 gallons of water which destroyed twenty buildings and scattered sheet steel all around. One theory is: uranium green balls have been discharged by mysterious, but friendly saucer entities, in order to clear up dangerous radio-active emanations after the detonation of atomic bombs. Another theory is that they are composed of "contra-terrene matter", that is, matter of an etheric type very different from matter as we, on earth, know it, and when such projectiles strike terrestrial objects terrific explosions result. It will be seen that this theory envisages hostile non-terrestrial space ships, operating high in our own stratosphere! One might, perhaps, presume that they violently object to etheric stresses set up in space by atomic and hydrogen-tritium bombs detonated here—or by the latest sonic-barrier-passing jet 'planes. The ready laughter or derisive smiles of our own official scientists may be met with one question: "What do *you* really *know* of the effect of the immense lethal and uncontrollable energies which you liberate in these insane experiments, and how they may react in the voids of outer space; or do you know *all* about suprasonic-speed phenomena?"

We now come to other mysterious phenomena, which have caused one man's death, not many miles from where this is written by the author of this book, and that, in November 1953. They are violent shock-waves, blasts from the skies following the passing of suprasonic jet 'planes over the sound-

s

barrier. They can and do concuss houses and villages, and cause deaths. *But* there have been occasions, in England and overseas, when a *preceding violent paroxysm of light*, followed by the blast of sound, makes one wonder if *something other than the suprasonic 'plane* may be the causative agent!

> *April 1950*: Major Johnson flew a new suprasonic 'plane (jet F.56), nine miles high over Ohio. In a power dive, he passed the sonic barrier. On the morning of his test flight, a terrific explosion shook Dayton, Ohio, blew out windows and rocked buildings. At Wright Airfield, 7 miles away, bad shocks were felt. A strange incident followed: Before noon, *next day*, another blast came and was heard over a range of 30 miles. Birds vanished, leaves fluttered from trees. At 3.30 p.m., same day, a third blast came, followed by a fourth, 12 minutes later. On that day, Johnson made another power dive, and it was noticed that a blur of vapour, like a ball, enveloped the jet's dive. On the ground, a terrific shock wave followed. In the afternoon, came another blast, 25 minutes after the jet pulled out of its dive."

Now consider this: The time lag of these sky-blasts is *very* peculiar. It ranges from 50 seconds to *several hours*: but the riddle of how an *onde de choc* (shock-wave) of the speed of sound, or even more, could arrive *hours after the jet's dive* is not explained. Unless a jet, going at such a vertiginous speed, sets up stresses in the ether of outer space, from which those stresses return the blasts, hours later!

One may, in this place, make the comment that *all* these mysterious phenomena may not necessarily be caused by flying saucers, or non-terrestrial space ships, but may arise when our solar system, on its long voyages through the voids of infinite space, may enter regions of differential ethers and strange cosmic phenomena. We do not *know*; we can merely conjecture. Yet there are incidents which seem to involve the deliberate intervention of hostile agents of some unknown, or humanoid character from outer space:

> *Summer 1952*: A violent explosion in a big Ford tank, in a Michigan township, wrecked property, and was *unexplained*; a flash of flame wrecked a store in another

town in Michigan .(*unexplained*); over Guam Island, mid-Pacific, a 'plane suddenly exploded in mid-air, and five men were killed (*unexplained*); over Ohio, a 'plane suddenly fell 2,000 feet, but did not crash. Experts were mystified as to the cause.

July 1952: A strange silvery object was seen high in the sky over San Anselmo, Calif. Five minutes later, there was an unexplained crash of a quite airworthy 'plane, five miles away, at Nicasio, the pilot being killed. The U.S. Navy Office cannot account for it. (*N.B.* The logical fallacy of *post hoc ergo propter hoc* might be involved if one linked these effects with one cause. One would need a series of events and phenomena of the same type in order to establish a theory of causation. *Au.*)

"A brand-new power station in a middle western state suddenly blew up with violence. The place has been heavily guarded, and it is known that the power was used for processing parts of atomic bombs. Neither the police nor the F.B.I. can find any proof of sabotage. The thing is a mystery." (*Letter to the author from a man living near the works, which he did not locate.*)

August 29, 1952: El Toro Marine station, U.S., felt a violent blast that shook buildings. *No 'plane was up at the time.* The epi-centre of the shock was not *on* the Marine base, but seemed near it.

April 11, 1952: "Two hundred pumps in the Coolidge Area, Arizona, were badly damaged when electric motors, driving them, suddenly and unaccountably changed the direction of their rotation. Electrical engineers, rushed to the region, were mystified by the sudden change of polarity in the motors, or of the current feeding them." (*Los Angeles Times*)

October 6, 1953: Dreadful explosions shook the "ghost town" of Boroloola, thousands of miles from any centre of population, and in the "abo" country of the N. Australian Territory, on the Gulf of Carpentaria. There was a "rumble" travelling east at terrific speed. Time 4.50 p.m. Aboriginal blacks badly frightened. Officials baffled to explain the phenomenon. (*N.B.* No jet or suprasonic aircraft are in *this* lonely and savage region.)

Regarding *some* of the incidents, above, occurring in the south-west, west and middle west of the U.S., one may note that saucers have frequently been seen in the skies, by day and night, of those regions. The phenomena may import that some suspension of the normal physical laws—sabotage may be ruled out, in these cases—occurs, and that flying saucers, when hovering over plants, or approaching them, may interact with motor fields. Another theory is that what are called "drifting ether-energy nodes", when they enter an area, may have these mysterious effects.

May we dare, however, the "impious" supposition that, far beyond our earth, *something*—we know not what or whom— is affected by etheric stresses set up by our scientists' machinery, and resents them by showing that *they*, too, can blast with their spatial artillery? Remember, too, that, without dropping one bomb, a squadron of 50 or 70 of these new terrestrial suprasonic jets—they need not even be manned—could wreck a city below, cause chaos and set up panic flights. Might not that unknown entity determine to stop the nuisance from us by causing explosions, making our 'planes collide or crash, or even disintegrate in the skies—these things have actually happened, by the way!—by using some lethal energy, or by picking off the pilots? Who, yet, really *knows*?

Butler, in his "Erewhon", visualised a state in which death was decreed to scientists and inventors. Of course, a fantasy and paradox—but consider the following:

> "Dr. R. D. Zentner, American atomic scientist, said today (June 20, 1952), that physicists now have devised a 'contamination bomb', which can scatter radioactive particles over a wide area. A glider, pulled by a 'plane, will sow it. Says this gentleman: 'With it we can force the evacuation of a city and make whole areas uninhabitable for years'."

How far we have gone down the satanic road to hell is clear in this man's statement, which is one more evidence of the fact that none of these official "scientists" trouble to make even the most perfunctory apology for blasphemy such as this. Does this man suppose that America will have any monopoly of such a device? On this side, we have also the type of Ministry scientist who hypocritically shrugs his shoulders, saying: "I hope our atomic bombs and thermo-fusion weapons will never be used." Man has now become a god, and plans to destroy himself, and his world, and all that therein is.

What a degradation all this is, and how it would have appalled men in the older school of science, such as Kelvin, Faraday, Rutherford, Tesla, Russel Wallace, Huxley!

Here are a few items about what has been happening in English skies, in 1953:

> *Novr. 27, 1953: A violent blaze of light* in the sky, followed by a terrific blast, was heard and seen over a wide area of north Kent. The blast caused a deep trench to collapse, suffocating an excavator in it. Police and firemen spent 5 hours in digging the unfortunate man's corpse out of the débris, at Shorne, Kent. Buildings in nearby villages were rocked, farms damaged, and, in one case, coals from a live fire were thrown out of a grate. *No jet 'planes were up*; but a postmistress at Cobham, six miles from Meopham, says that, before the explosions —of which there were two—*she heard something in the sky like a machine.* Police baffled to solve the mystery.

> *Decr. 1, 1953:* A mysterious explosion over a table in the dining-room of a house at Littlehough, near East Grinstead, Sussex, is the biggest topic of talk here. No one was hurt; but what was strange was that, though a substance like thick glass, that crumbled, was found in the room, yet not a window or glass object in the house was broken! *Whence came this mysterious substance?* East Grinstead people rule out poltergeist phenomena; but say flying saucers were seen in the sky near, and that the substance came from them, and perhaps fell down the chimney. It is a mystery. (*N.B. Readers should compare the above with what, in this book, is reported of a substance that fell in Essex, from the sky, and which was taken away for analysis by the police. The Air Ministry have never revealed the result of the analysis. Author.*)

> *Decr. 3, 1953:* Flaming streaks seen rushing through the skies over the Midlands, at height of about 3,000 feet. They disintegrated noiselessly and police and firemen have searched for fragments of what fell. A mysterious object like a silver ball was seen high in the sky, and visible for 8 seconds. The President of the Royal Astronomical Society, Prof. Herbert Dingle, cannot explain the phenomenon. The phenomenon was also

seen in north London, the Home Counties, and South-
end, Essex. Some accounts say that a noise like an aircraft of the 1914 type was heard.

What caused the appalling tornado which swept across
Russia, on August 24, 1953, and devastated the ancient city of
Rostov? The wind lasted three minutes and cut a swathe 300
yards wide, devastating the citadel and mediaeval churches.
(*Lady Kelly*, speaking on the B.B.C. Russian programme.)
The Soviet Government puts a ban on the publication of news
like this; but it may be compared with the really appalling
devastation of mile on mile of forests, farms and roads, over
a crow-flying distance of 135 miles, and diameter of 50-85
miles, from the town of Thurso, to south of Balmoral, in
January 1953, when there was a synchronism with disastrous
tidal floods on the east coast of England, and in the Thames
estuary. Cause: may be natural and purely meteorological;
but it seems that, in both cases—and the wind in Scotland, at
the time, reached the Mexican Gulf hurricane force of 120
miles an hour—there may—who knows?—have been synchron-
ous detonations, in Russia and U.S.A., of hydrogen bombs,
blasting out terrific heat and radioactivity.*

In this book, I have spoken of the apparent hostility of
some types of flying saucers, particularly of the weird aeroform which has an insulated and non-rotary fusiform, or
cigar-shaped centre, around which revolves a singular ring,
like the rings round the planet, Saturn. This ring is drawn
out into an ellipsoid in order, as photographs taken over
California show, to release satellite discs. It would be interesting to know whence this queer saucer comes, and who or
what is aboard it.

Consider the following:

February 16, 1952: Five mysterious explosions occurred
in an orange grove (a strange place for them, surely!),

___

* It was noted by Colonel W. Shields, a naturalist, that at Lynmouth,
scene of the disastrous flood and freshets, black salmon, which are
seldom seen, all took up a position in the centre of the river, as if
foreknowing what was to happen, and making ready to go upstream.
(*Told to the London News Chronicle*).

near Riverside, Calif., and débris was hurled 500 feet in the air. At the time, strange objects were seen in the sky. What was called "a huge meteor" exploded over Virginia, and, both there and in North Carolina, "a big shaking noise" was heard in the air, and "cows jumped up and down". An observer says that, when the explosion occurred, he saw a "silver, arrow-shaped object in the sky, travelling at an ungodly speed". U.S. Air Force men say the object was *not* a guided missile.

In another chapter of this book, I remarked on a singular periodicity of exactly *one month*, in the case of an alleged landing of "saucer-men", at Marble Creek, Butte county, California (May-June, 1953). This curious periodicity, accompanied by the phenomena of mysterious fires and of a very weird sky phenomenon is also to be noted in connection with some unexplained incidents in the Cotswold Hills, near Stroud and Cheltenham, Gloucestershire, in July and August 1953.

I set down the reports in order of occurrence, though their possible linkage seems not to have been noted by any save myself, who happens to be a native of the region: On *July 21*, 1953, at 2.45 a.m., a night patrol policeman, a G.P.O. mail van driver, and a parson, the Rev. G. T. Haigh, vicar of Oakridge, near Stroud, Glos., all saw, high in the sky, a strange, white bright light, from which a ball of fire seemed to be dropping. The phenomenon was visible for five minutes, and, hence, was hardly a meteorite, or meteor. The vicar, who was driving his car, at that very early hour in the morning, on a lonely hill road that runs north from Stroud to Birdlip, on the Cotswolds, wrote to me—though it must be stressed that he, the Rev. Gordon T. Haigh, who is a distinguished scholar —M.A., and M.Litt.—does not advance any theory as to the nature or origin of the phenomenon. He tells me he runs an amateur radio transmitting station and is interested in scientific matters:

> "I was descending at some speed, in my car, over the hills from Birdlip into the Camp, which you know as Eagle Pitch. Time about 2.25 a.m., on July 21, 1953, when I suddenly became aware that the dark and moonless

night was illuminated by a strange light, hidden from me by the overhanging trees, that outshone the moon at its maximum. On breaking clear at the dip, just before the Camp, I saw a long vertical column of light, in length about a quarter of the distance from the zenith to the horizon. Below the vertical column, and sinking slowly to the ground, was a flaming light which I, not unnaturally, took to be a crashing 'plane. (But it was not that!) The column of white light remained, slowly fading, and above the falling bright, yellow-red object, with a space of non-luminous sky intervening. I would not agree that the vertical column was 'white-hot'; it was luminous and looked like a slow-motion comet, or a somewhat mystical inverted candle, in the darkness. The burning lower object appeared to drift slightly to the right from beneath the vertical column, and gradually continued until it passed below the level of the nearby banks and tumps alongside the winding road into Bisley. The road, as you know, is very winding, and so it is difficult to keep an exact orientation and sense of compass bearings.

"I looked in all directions, for the light had been just due south of me at first, to see if anything was burning on the ground. To the west, towards the Slad road, and Sheepscombe woods, there was a light, rather faint and fading, in the sky, and thrown from an unseen source. This may have a bearing on the falling object, but, on the other hand, it may not. So certain was I that a large 'plane had fallen in flames, that, on getting home to my vicarage house at Oakridge, on the other side of the Stroud Valley, I rang up the Stroud Police, and found that a member of their own force and a civilian had already reported the phenomenon. Lights were still on at the local R.A.F. 'drome, though all exercises had ceased at least 40 minutes before I witnessed the mysterious spectacle. About 30 minutes after my report, a 'plane took off, flew round, and touched down again 20 minutes later, doubtless taking a look round to see what could be seen. I understand the 'drome was told immediately. I have heard nothing further, but it may well be that you are onto something worth following up, though where it all leads to I do not yet see."

Mr. Haigh sent me a sketch of what he had seen.

What was this vertical column of light? No one knows; but I would draw attention to the strange fact that this almost identical phenomenon was witnessed 90 years earlier by Monsieur de Rostan, and reported to the French Académie Royale des Sciences at Paris*:

> "On 23 March 1763, there was seen west of Lausanne, Lake Geneva (Lac Léman), half an hour after sunset, a *light in the form of a vertical column*, which, at the height of about 10 degrees, was bent so that its upper part made with the horizon an angle of about 35 degrees, and with the lower part an angle of 125 degrees. This curved part was not more than 3 degrees long, and the whole phenomenon was about 2 degrees broad, and was terminated at either end by a point. The colour of this phenomenon was very near to an orange-yellow and was much weaker at the two ends and at the edge, one easily distinguished the colours, despite a rather clear cloud which horizontally cut the luminous column in two places. It constantly followed the movement of the sun, and the entire phenomenon lasted about 30 minutes, and before disappearing became a very clear red. This detail is drawn from an observation made by M. de Rostan and communicated to the Academy".

It may be pointed out that the R.A.F. controller of Aston Down station, whence the night plane was sent up after the Rev. G. T. Haigh, the policeman, and the G.P.O. mail van driver had reported what they had witnessed, denied that any jet 'planes had been up at the time, or that the mysterious phenomenon had anything to do with Véry lights.

Exactly a month later, on August 21, 1953, 29 British, Belgian, Dutch and German youths, and one Australian girl were roused from sleep at a youths' hostel on Cleeve Hill, which is also located on the same Cotswold Hills, about 18 miles north from the Sheepscombe and Stroud region, by a mysterious fire in a shed where they had parked their bicycles. Rain was then falling in torrents. They found that 29 bicycles had been burnt to fragments. (*Note*: steel can be fused only at a temperature of 2,800 degrees F., and no such enormous temperature can be generated by a wood fire in the open. Compare with this what happened on the trestle-bridge over

* Histoire de l'Académie Royale des Sciences. MDCCLXIII. Observations de Physique Générale De l'Imprimerie Royale, à Paris.

Salmon River, Oregon, in 1947, where, also, were mysterious forest fires).

On the same night as the fire outside the hostel of the Youths Hostels Association at Cleeve Hill, two other mysterious fires occurred, and in no way can any of these three fires, whatever the solution of the mystery may be, be attributed to the "mere pranks of small boys". For one thing, country boys whose fathers have to get their living from the land do *not* engage in arson. I cite a newspaper report:

> "On the same night as the fire in the hostel shed at Cleeve Hill, Glos., two other mysterious fires broke out on two different farms, about four miles from this hostel, and located near Winchcombe, a picturesque Cotswold village. These fires caused damage and loss of thousands of pounds. In one case, five tons of hay suddenly burst into fire in a barn on the farm of Mr. C. Forty, of Coates Mill Farm, Winchcombe. No sooner were firemen fighting this blaze than an alarm came that another mysterious fire had broken out in a Dutch barn on the farm of Mr. T. F. Mayor, a quarter-of-a-mile away. Here, 80 tons of hay were destroyed in their bales, and two steel tractors and farm implements. The farmers mounted a fire-watch; but neither they nor the police have been able to solve the mystery, let alone discover a perpetrator."

I have been unable to ascertain from the organisers of the Youth Hostels Association what theory, if any, they have as to the cause of the fire at Cleeve, though they admit that the whole property would have been destroyed but for the exertions of the local wardens and the members staying there that night. Presumably, these Youth Hostel organisers are as baffled as were the police and farmers; and the police of Gloucestershire remain as much baffled as were their U.S. counterparts, the F.B.I. of Washington, D.C., in the case of the Salmon Bridge and forest fires in Oregon.

Was there a linkage between the phenomenon witnessed by the Rev. Gordon T. Haigh, and these mysterious fires, all on the Cotswolds? Suspicion may be strong; but proof is wanting.

I have to state, however, that I ran into a sort of rubber

wall in my persistent attempts to obtain from a quarter most concerned any comment on the mysterious cause of the fire, and on an absurd story that, according to one not very reliable London Sunday newspaper, the pranks of small boys were to blame. I suspect that some very exalted official Government authority had pronounced that "MUM!" should be the word.

Before passing on, I may note that mysterious fires also occurred on farms in Sussex, Cornwall, and Essex, in October and November 1953:

> *October 10, 1953*: A farmer and his wife, at Halse Town, near St. Ives, came home to find a fire in their kitchen, not lit by them, an easy chair alight, and, a mile away, 5 tons of hay were in flames in a lorry.
> *November 7 and 9, 1953*: The police were unable to solve the mystery of fires on farms in Sussex. A fire-raiser, unknown, is at work on farms in mid-Essex. At Tolleshunt d'Arcy, a building 150 feet long was in flames, and a few hours earlier, other fires occurred on farms at Sandon, Tollesbury, and Hanningfield.

The periodicity of the saucer phenomena caused an aircraft company's principal, at Los Angeles, Calif., to write to the *Los Angeles Examiner*, in mid-July 1952:

> "I am amazed at the increasing audacity of strange, disc-like objects seen in the sky over Los Angeles airport control tower. For four nights running, they've been seen at the same time (between 7 and 8 p.m.), and the same place. On the last occasion, three of them hung poised for five minutes by the clock."

Some of these mysterious aeroforms seem as material as our own aircraft of a third dimensional world; but others, as noted before, suggest emanations of an order of matter of worlds of another "etheric type" than our own. In this connection, the theories of Dr. Meade Layne, of the Borderland Research Scientific Association, of San Diego, Calif., are interesting, but, of course, not at this time capable of scientific proof.

He says:

> "There are in space, an infinite number of particulate ethers, of enormously dense matter, interpenetrating each

other. Just as there are sounds we cannot normally hear, or rays in the invisible angstroms of the solar spectrum we do not see, so there is matter we cannot touch, because of its high vibratory rate, or density. These worlds of ultra-dense matter support life forms with cultures and civilisations of their own, and among them are beings of races who journey throughout the solar system, and even beyond it. They are the 'Guardians' for whom the problems of space and time, gravity and cosmic radiation do not exist as they do for us. The space craft are weightless, and the magnetic fields of the molecules do not merge, and use is made of magnetic interplanetary tides, by a principle of resonance."

One does not see how physicists can complain of these mystic-sounding theories, when they have themselves reduced the world of the atom to a metaphysique of Kantian philosophy. He thinks that:

"The saucers fly on magnetic meridians, and, owing to their imperfect charting over the earth, there may be occasional forced landings. The first small discs, which were forced down, came from a way-station on the moon, but they have mother-craft which hover above the upper limits of our atmosphere. The satellite discs seldom undertake interplanetary voyages."

Most people will recall the violent earthquakes in the Ionian Isles and in Turkey, in summer 1953, when, in August, 1,000 people were killed. Are there going on in the deep-lying strata of our earth, crumblings of strata and geophysical changes dependent on causes which may lie far out in space? Causes which may produce internal pressures, alterations of equilibrium, earthquakes, volcanic eruptions, sudden elevations of volcanoes where none existed before, alterations in etheric pressures and gravity-thrust, and phenomena triggered off by hydrogen and atomic bomb explosions?

Seismologists and physicists may smile at what seems fantasy, but consider what is set down below:

1952: Suddenly arising from the bed of the Pacific, a new 1,000-feet high volcano, "Didicas", growing at the rate of 50 feet a month, spouting a two-mile high plume of smoke, gases and flames (38 miles north of Luzon, in the Philippines). Overnight, a volcano rose in a Mexican maize paddock, blotting out a large area, and becoming a mountain; in East Pakistan, a large area is sinking into the sea, accompanied by Krakatoa-type bombardment, and forcing evacuation of 40,000 people; in mid-August, a cone of a new volcano rose, and in six weeks reared a summit, 1,500 feet above the Pacific, in the uninhabited island of San Benedicto, 780 miles south of the U.S. Navy electronic station of San Diego. Dr. R. Dietz, U.S. Navy geologist, says this new volcano is the first in the Hawaiian basin in historic times, and may point to a major change in the earth's crust. On 20 Sepr., a submarine volcano, 320 miles south of Tokyo, erupted and blew up the survey ship, "Kaiyo Maru", with 5 scientists, and crew of 22. Wreckage only was found after an air-sea search of 90 hours. On 27 Sepr., violent explosions came from the sea in the middle of the Channel Islands, and earth tremor was felt, lasting 22 seconds as recorded at the Maison St. Louis Observatory, at Jersey. No one could explain the mysterious submarine explosions which sent people, in Guernsey, from their beds out into the street, in their pyjamas.

Who can say if scientific entities, on board the flying saucers, are aware of these phenomena, know they are related to other cosmic phenomena, and are here to observe and explore the earth?

The year 1952 has been remarkable for mysterious substances which have been seen, by police and others, in England, France and the U.S.A. in the act of being dropped from unknown objects in the skies. I have already referred to the phenomena in England:

> *July 22, 1952*: Mrs. Leo L. Barucha, of Lincoln, Nebraska, saw a "black sphere about the size of a soft ball" land in a field, and emit a thick greenish-yellow smoke. It disintegrated, and her children poured water on what was left. The sediment of this unknown substance was handed to a geologist at Nebraska University, but he could make nothing of it.

> *Sepr. 21, 1952*: Over Tangier, and Marakesh, Morocco, unknown objects in the skies startled many people. A disc appeared whose speed was estimated at about 25

285

miles a second(!). It became elongated into an ellipsoid, when west of Neffik, Morocco, stopped momentarily over Casa, and explosions came from it. No apparent retardation, or change in its trajectory followed the explosions, nor was its illumination affected.

Night of Sepr. 21: Mlle. Noelia Senegas, dental operator, at Aix-en-Provence, S. France, says she saw:

"A thing like a very brilliant metal cigar, emitting a long trail of light, or an exhaust, which diminished over a distance about eight times that of the object, which was as long as the apparent diameter of the moon. It changed course from NNE. to SSW., and must have made a very large turn (*virage*). It was very silent, too slow for a meteor, and I saw it at 7.25 p.m. on 21 Sepr. 1952. Some people say they saw it emit sparks, and that it was variously coloured."

October 17, 1952: Monsieur Yves Prigent, surveyor-general (*surveillant*), of Oloron College, in S. France, saw, high in the sky, "a sort of armada of different forms and colours, from which were emitted a rain of white filaments". He reported as follows:

"The sky was clear, the objects, shaped like a cigar or cylinder, and their height might have been 10,000 mètres (six miles), or more. Their apparent diameter (to the eye) was about 2 mètres (6.6 feet). When I looked at them through binoculars, they appeared like red central spheres surrounded by a clear yellow light, like the ring of Saturn. My wife looked independently, and with no prompting from me, said they looked like the red sphere of Saturn, encircled by a yellow ring. As these weird cigars advanced in the sky, they left in their rear a rapidly forming train of flocculent substance, which scattered in the air and took the shape of a veil of long filaments. I am unable to say whether the threads, later picked up on the ground" (*Vide* next paragraph. *Au.*) "necessarily came from these cylinders. I had some of the filaments in my hand, later; but I do not say the filaments are what we call *Les fils de la Vierge*, or *Les fils de Marie* (free-floating webs of spiders)."

These mysterious filaments seemed to emanate from the front of lead-coloured cylinders, and similar matter seemed to link the saucers in pairs.

October 29, 1952: Over Gaillac, in the white wine country of the Garonne, north-east of Toulouse, mysterious
objects in the sky, very high up, were seen by gendarmes
to drop a material like steel wool, *but found to be of
unknown character.* It fell upon trees, bushes, and telephone wires where it hung for two hours, *and then
evaporated into nothingness!*

Let it be said at once that this mysterious substance was
assuredly *not* floating webs of spiders, of the sort called by
French and Belgian peasants "Virgin Mary threads". Prigent,
above, says that what he picked up looked like asbestos threads,
but was not, drawn out, and offering a certain resistance to
tractive effort. It vanished little by little, with no trace, but
could be set on fire, when it would burn with a flame like that
from cotton wool. It seems that, owing to its progressive disappearance, nothing was left for analysis.

No one knows what purpose this mysterious saucer substance
served; but it is of importance to find that something like this
has previously fallen from the skies, as the following reports
show:

> *Daily Oklahoma,* 11 Novr., 1951: A farmer of Anadarko,
> Okla., found in his 20-acre field a thick covering of strips
> of metallic leaves, from $\frac{1}{2}$ to nearly 5 inches long. They
> looked like tin, but Monnig, a specialist on meteorites,
> said the metal was of no known meteoric origin. A local
> sheriff found no signs of footprints in the field.

> *Denver, Colorado*: Late in October 1951, unknown
> matter fell from the skies, but resembled no known
> meteoric substance.

> *Kansas City*: Dec. 11, 1953, strips of "foil", 200 ft. long,
> $\frac{1}{2}$-inch wide, found in fields. Topeka Air base denies any
> connection. Phenomenon has happened four times in U.S.

> *New Haven, Conn.*: Glowing ball from sky bursts
> through sign-board, then whirls over hill $\frac{1}{2}$-mile away.
> Copper and copper-oxide left behind. (Aug. 1953).

> *Numerous falls,* from the sky, of both incandescent and
> non-incandescent material have been seen, in the U.S., in
> the shape of cosmic bodies; yet no trace of the material
> has been found in the surrounding territory.

> *France*: In the Forest of the Meuse, near Robert-

Espagne and Magneville, on 16 June, 1952, woodcutters saw what looked like "an immense parachute" falling from the sky. They heard a noise of metallic type, and trees crackled; but when the gendarmerie made a minute search of the woods and the country round about, nothing was found.

U.S. and England: Mysterious "foamy" substance found in Ohio river, near Wheeling, W.Va., became black in warm room (April 10, 1953). On October 15, 17, 18 and 20, 1953, similar substance, found in rivers in Bucks., Northant, Sussex, Beds., Suffolk and Middlesex, theorised to be "detergents", but of unknown origin. (Who, or what is "syphoning water" in earth's rivers? *Au.*)

I cannot close this chapter without again drawing attention to the mysteries of accidents to jet 'planes, *not* to be explained away as carelessness and inefficiency of personnel, and the unsolved disappearances of both military 'planes and commercial air-liners:

1950 and 1951: In U.S.A., there occurred a strange series of mysterious accidents to jet 'planes, a squadron of which crashed in the skies of Ohio, while others caught fire in the air, or exploded later, or even disintegrated in mid-air.

March 1952: British Wing-Commander J. Baldwin, an ace of the second World War, when he shot down three German 'planes on a raid over London, and swooped down on Rommel's car, near Caen—hence, he was not a man easy to kill—was on a reconnaissance flight, over Korea, for meteorological purposes, when his jet 'plane failed to come out of a cloud. Mystery never solved. (About this time, a U.S. carrier in Korean waters, had sighted a strange object in the skies.) Baldwin's colleagues, flying with him, failed to discover what had befallen him. Baldwin was a master of his machine.

June 9, 1952: British Air Vice-Marshal Atcherley, commanding the 205th group, Middle East Air Force, set out in an amply fuelled meteor jet from the Suez Canal zone for Cyprus, 300 miles. Last radio signal came three minutes after take-off. He never arrived, and a two days' sea-air search, dawn to dusk, revealed nothing.

May 15, 1952: While British Royal Air Force investigation of a very long series of jet 'plane disasters, was proceeding, the whole U.S. Air Force 123rd First Bomber Squadron was ordered to be grounded at Manston airdrome, Kent. There had been a series of fatal accidents to Thunderjet 'planes, crashing in sea or on land. The ban was lifted, and, two days later, a Sky Blazer, U.S. jet was seen to dive suddenly, 2,000 feet up, and to disintegrate 20 feet above the runway. "There was an explosion and mass of flames." On the same day, a British Vampire jet suddenly crashed over Hensham, Cornwall; while, off the Yorkshire coast, wreckage was found of another meteor jet, lost in a flight. No trace of the pilot was ever found.

February 2, 1953: A York transport aircraft, with 33 passengers and 6 crew, vanished on the Atlantic, on a trooping flight to Jamaica. On the day after its start, a radio man at Gander airport had an S.O.S. which ended abruptly. Sea and air search found nothing, and an official Court of Inquiry, in London, could find nothing to explain this mystery of the lost air-liner, which was airworthy, and operated by an experienced crew. "Cause unascertainable", said the Court, in London.

May 2, 1953: A British Comet (jet) air-liner met a mysterious disaster, immediately after it had taken off from an airdrome at Calcutta. Its speed was 500 miles an hour. Suddenly, it caught fire in the air, disintegrated, and crashed, the wreckage being strewn over an area of 5½ miles. An investigator from the British Ministry of Civil Aviation, Mr. J. H. Lett, said that lightning had *not* struck the Comet, nor had it come into collision with another 'plane, nor was there the slightest evidence of faulty materials, or bad workmanship. *BUT HE FOUND THAT IT BROKE UP IN THE AIR, AFTER STRIKING SOME HEAVY AND UNKNOWN BODY!*

Novr. 17, 1953: U.S. paratroop 'plane, over Fort Bragg, Calif., hits "invisible body", crashes, 15 men killed, only survivor stating 'plane hit something, in air, "sounding like two automobiles in collision."

Apart from any actual collision, *what was this heavy and unknown body?* No one knows! Yet, as such terrestrial areoforms are stages on the way towards future terrestrial space ships, has some mysterious cosmic entity a purpose in possible causation of disasters, such as this at Calcutta?

T   289

Who, I must be forgiven for asking again, *knows*, or can, *at this time, know?* Yet, all this talk about golden-haired men in zoot suits, animated with the most friendly spirit, not willing or able even to kill an anopheles mosquito, and as unaggressive as a new-born lambkin, does not fit very well into the pattern of *some* of these mysterious events.

CHAPTER XIII

INTERPLANETARY TRAVEL :
THE RED LIGHT

Many of the riddles presented by these weird and elusive
cosmic aeroforms are of importance in relation to our own
terrestrial problems of the conquest of space and space-travel,
which is far from "just round the corner."

No one knows why some of the discs are noiseless, and why
others emit distinct sounds. Nor do we understand how some
of them can attain the fantastic speed of 5 miles a second,
as the Washington (D.C.) airport radar and the theodolite
calculated, when the saucers were seen for a long time over
that airport, and even cruising high over the White House,
in 1952! That riddle seems to be connected rather with a
fourth dimensional plane of existence than with phenomena
of our own normal third dimensional world.

I here give some theories of a well known engineer, Mr.
Frederick G. Hehr, who lives at Santa Monica, Calif., and
who was in touch with me, in 1952-53:

Says Mr. Hehr:

"Three-quarters of an hour before sunset, on a June
day in 1953, I had a unique experience. Twice in one
day I saw saucers, and witnessed a whole squadron of
them go through various manoeuvres, lasting ten minutes.
I was seated in the park, here, on the water front, chatting
with a lady, idly watching a cloud-bank, above the ocean
to the west, and which streamed inland over the mountains. Where it lifted over the mountain-edge, there was
a fairly constant, but shifting set of holes. Unluckily, I
had just exhausted my camera-film, when I noticed a brilliant white bar, with perfectly sharp contours, which was
exactly horizontal, in one of the cloud-holes. It was joined
by another, which simply appeared. Then others appeared
in other holes. Now, one of the first took off in the line
of sight and dwindled very rapidly to nothing. It returned
the same way, in about 10 seconds. I think it had been up

291

to Santa Barbara, and back, and I reckon its speed was around 7,500 miles an hour (2.083 miles a second). Now, they all formed a diamond pattern round a somewhat diffuse object, which lasted several minutes. A curious manoeuvre followed, as one after another suddenly disappeared from its station, and, at the same moment appeared somewhere else. At first, they each returned to their stations, and, later, jumped all over the holes. The round central object had vanished.

"Now, one after another, they just switched off and were gone, and the whole show had vanished in a few seconds. Later the same evening, I saw one hanging beneath the moon. I watched it till I entered my house. I dashed for my binoculars, but, when I came out, it had vanished without trace. It looked like two Jupiters, closely coupled.

"My conclusions are, (1): The objects are material, fairly large, say, 50 metres' span. Nothing immaterial will show such sharp outlines, or be so exactly reproduced. The ratio of their span to their thickness is as about 6 to 1. (2): They control gravity; since they hang so perfectly still. (3): They have no inertia; since nothing could withstand changes of speeds from 7,500 miles an hour to nil, without apparent acceleration or deceleration, and avoid vaporisation. (4): Their motive power may be derived from hooking into magnetic energy, or currents.* (5): They are manned by intelligent beings of a human order. They have human foibles, as is shown by their small errors and corrections and tendency to show our military authorities that a superior genius is at work. Their flathatting in such locations proves that. Being inertialess, they just go, or do not go. Their lack of weight and inertia make it possible for them to attain tremendous speeds with small power, as our terrestrial aeroforms cannot attain, without tremendous power. (6): They are not what we call 'space craft'; for they probably would not function in space. Such craft have more compactness, and usually show some cone of ejection, and change in colour with changes in altitude, and/or acceleration. Of the latter, both the ball and shell form have been seen quite often.

"It is intriguing that the show I saw was right over the hush-hush naval test station for guided missiles, at Point Mugu!

* Obviously not the classic magnetism of the 19th century—*Au!*

"Now, their instant speed and stops and their speeds in between make them invisible, when in lateral motion.

"I have other reports from people I know well. Here are a few. Freda owns a house in Topanga *cañon.* One night, she was wakened by the flapping of a blind. She got up, looked out, and saw a silver bar hanging in the sky, quite near, *with a pendulum movement,* a slight movement. It hopped around, here and there. It would vanish, then return, as if quartering the neighbourhood, looking for something. Her description tallies with mine, except for the pendulum swing, the slow speed, and its slight rounding at the corners. A number of people have seen a round object showing different lights and colours, moving fast through the clouds, by day or night, the closest description being from a friend of mine who saw it over the sea, in daytime. He says: 'It was like a large ball, mostly silvery white, with flattened top and bottom.' (Vortical indentations).

"Another friend came down to the San Joaquin Valley and bought gasoline from a station, north of Fresno. He saw the attendant keep looking all over the sky. 'Looking for saucers?' asked my friend, jestingly. The unexpected answer came: 'Yes, the darned things have been flying round here lately, every day.' But there were no reports in the newspapers. Mine, also, were suppressed.

"In 1903, an old man told me of many future things I should live to see. I should see radio, television, aeroplanes, submarines, and three world wars which would destroy our civilisation. He described the flying saucers and space ships, their owners and their purpose here. . . In one year, I have had more than 20 independent sightings of a shell-like space ship, seen all over the globe.

"Here, on the west coast of the U.S., are certain 'mystery spots' in which gravity and light are distorted. They appear to be aligned in a straight path, having an average distance of around 50 miles. I know of other cases of this phenomenon in many other states of the U.S., and there are at least two in England. Now, a curious fact emerges:

Saucers and space craft seem to follow the lines of these mystery spots, as if they were beacons! They also often make right-angle turns where such lines intersect.

"It is curious how unobservant most people are.* While

* Same in England! *The Author*

I was watching the saucer show, there were thousands of people along the coast road and on the beaches; yet only I and my lady friend saw the saucers, and she, only because I pointed them out to her and told her what to look for. They were between us and the sun, but very much brighter than the clouds irradiated by the sunshine, and straight in outlines. If you visualise a piece of tantung or stellite, 1½ inches long and ¼ inch thick, ground rectangularly and highly polished, you have a near approximation to what I saw".

It is curious that Mr. Hehr mentions stellite, which is a hard, brilliant alloy of 75 parts of cobalt, 25 parts chromium, with a proportion of tungsten, or molybdenum, produced by melting these constituents together in an electric furnace, at more than 1,500° C. It is in two grades, one being used for high-speed cutting tools, cutlery and surgical instruments, or for scraping hot scale off billets; the other, as a nitric acid resistant material, and used in machine parts subject to wear, for drilling equipment, and in the oxy-acetylene blow-pipe and the electric arc. One may theorise that an alloy of this sort may actually be used in the construction of these weird aeroforms.

Mr. Hehr considers the question which has perplexed many people. How do these visitants pass through the air at fantastic speed, and yet create no major disturbance in our atmosphere?

"I think there is a progressive dematerialisation and rematerialisation of matter inside a field of force which encloses the saucer. Or, a structure so loosened that molecules of air pass through without noticeable friction. Or, again, the air may be scooped up, rendered weightless and inertialess within the force-field of the saucer, and, so, passed around it and re-deposited, without addition of energy, or loss, in the rear of the saucer. It has been stated that the space craft have often noticeably shaken airplanes that have passed so near them as nearly to be in collision. Their speed is often far less than that of the saucers, at low altitudes."

"I was told in 1903 that a third world war may wipe out our civilisation, and that an older race on Venus is taking measures to re-establish a new and better order in the shortest possible time. The saucers have been taken out of storage, and are now being tested, in order to train crews in their handling. When the atomic bombs begin to fall, these extra-terrestrial aeroforms may be used to salvage what is good in our civilisation, either persons or things. The target-date for the start of the third war will probably be in 1960, the re-establishment of peace in 1965. In between, there may be little active war, but five years of chaos and total anarchy."

All one can say is that it is quite impossible to evaluate such predictions; for this old planet of ours has been so threatened with annihilation, from the days of early Christians anticipating the "coming of the Sun of Man riding the clouds in glory", right through the early and later middle ages, and in the 16th, 17th, and 18th centuries, not to speak of the 19th century, that one is prepared to wait and see, and to suppose that a good many thousands of years, yet, lie before our planet, which the Jupiterians in "Captain Stormfield's Visit to Heaven," had, with derision, to use a large telescope (or was it a high-powered microscope?), to find on their colossal map of the universe! I am prepared to relieve of the burden of unwanted bank balances and gilded stocks and shares anyone contemplating running to the Andes, the high Himalayas, or the central highlands of Guatemala, for safety in the imminent wrath to come! I may also add, that quite a number of people have been less conservative than Mr. Hehr; since they have predicted the end of all things terrestrial in 1953!

There arises the fantastic query several times referred to, in this book: Are there, among these saucers, entities from, what some call etheric worlds, or the invisible doubles of planets, or from the visible worlds we see with the naked eye, or the reflector-telescope? The question is hardly likely to arouse much interest in the minds of the average scientists who measure and weigh, and heap up mathematical equations. And yet, the higher ranks of scientists have called in the metaphysical system of Kant in order to formulate a temporary theory about causation in the world of the atom!

There are mystics who ask us to visualise a universe of units of varying orders and density, in which time corresponds to motion, in which units oscillate according to their order of density, governed by their law of motion. This theory appears to imply that there exist "invisible planets" of some fourth dimension, from which may come to our own third dimensional earth space ships and satellite discs, moving at any speed they desire through fields of matter offering no resistance to their mass and motion. That is, that there exist "doubles" of the visible planets. It must also imply that these beings have devised some unknown method of insulating themselves and their crafts and aeroforms from the lethal cosmic radiation in space.

How could they do this?

Not by using the heaviest metal, lead, with its very heavy atomic weight, but by, in some mysterious way, closing up the electro-magnetic fields of atoms and molecules, so as to impose an impervious shield to the penetration of dangerous rays. It is also implied that these invisible beings from the planetary "doubles" are not spooks or ghosts, but entities of another order of living matter. Even the metals of which their aeroforms are constructed are alleged to be, as it were, some isotopic form of our own terrestrial minerals, like copper and aluminium. And when this type of cosmic entity enters our own atmosphere, it must have the amazing power of transforming itself and its aeroform into our own third dimensional form of matter, and back again immediately. Whether these transformations are indicated by the sudden changes in the gamut of lights, shown by some of the saucers—red, blue, green, white, yellow and amber—no one can say.

But, however one may regard these theories—and there is some observed basis for them, as this book has shown— one must again stress that the so-called etheric visitant is *only one* of the types of saucers entering our atmosphere, and scanning our earth, and that there are at least 20 other types which come from some unknown bourne, in space, of an order of matter akin to our own.

But exactly what for these weird things, whether they hail from worlds in our own dimensions of space-time-matter, or from "etheric worlds" have come here, and are appearing, in our skies, so much more frequently than in the long past, no one can say. For the solution of this most portentous riddle of our age, we must simply wait and see, bearing in mind that, whether motivated by fear or not, some of them are very definitely hostile!

We have yet to find out what are the mysterious substances that disintegrate, which have been dropped from saucers hovering over the U.S.A., and France, in the last five or six years. What purpose is being served by these mysterious substances dropped to the ground? If we knew that, we might have a clue to their purpose in exploring every part of the earth. On the face of it, the mysterious type of cosmic entity concerned has no desire that any terrestrial chemist, or metallurgist shall discover the nature of this strange exploratory substance.

The tremendous problem of the source of propulsion of the flying saucers is of great importance to the pioneers of terrestrial space-travel. It seems obvious, that we, on this earth, have discovered no source of power which could drive aeroforms at miles a second—even if we had the men who would not be blasted to atoms by the appalling stresses involved!

The difficulty that confronts space travellers from the earth has presumably been overcome by flying-saucer entities. (I make the assumption that they are not terrestrial). With all the talk of atomic-powered vessels, it is still not known how to release atomic energy that is controllable! The heat emission from our atomic piles is not powerful enough to drive such vessels, while that from the atomic bomb is terrific and beyond control. If rocket-propulsion be used to propel and power space ships, it is true that, as it works by recoil and not by driving force, it would probably be efficient in space beyond the earth's field of gravitation. But a rocket-propelled ship to the moon, with a motor that could generate power enough for a speed of 25,000 miles an hour, necessary when once the ship has escaped the pull of the earth's gravitation, is not yet in sight. Also, the cost of the fuel is prohibitive.

Moreover, if such a rocket-ship were manned, the acceleration at the start would be, very likely, fatal to all on board.
No one knows how, or whether cosmic rays could be used
to drive such a ship. If one attempted to approach the speed
of light—which, by the latest calculations, is rather more than
186,325 miles per second, *in vacuo*—then, according to
Einstein's theory of relativity, matter would be converted into
energy at such a speed. If this be so, it seems to follow that
space voyages outside the solar system, where light years are
the units, would see the volatilisation, or ethereanisation of
space vessels, and all in them, speeding at the velocity of
light! The corollary follows that the mysterious 'Foo
Fighters', seen in 1944, must be etherian beings, or belong to
a totally different order of entities from any we know. They
must be living in a band of invisible wave-lengths, in a world
totally invisible to us on this earth!

Besides nuclear fission, or cosmic rays, there exists another
problematical source of power, such as the discovery of such
a reactive force as anti-gravity. In theory, it would render a
space ship weightless, and allow of the generation of fantastic
speeds without resistance. I have been told that the U.S. War
Departments are, at this time, working on a "magnetic principle, or device" that may develop such speeds.

Still another possible source of propulsive energy is suggested by the peculiar properties of the rare metal known as
germanium which, when combined with nitrogen, converts
sunlight into electricity. (But, of course, here arises the question to which no physicist or astronomer seems to have paid
any attention: In the theoretical vacuum of outer space, with
its theoretical absolute zero of temperature where all molecular
movement ceases, will the space ship find an electro-magnetic
radiation from the sun that does not contain heat as such,
since heat *may* be the transformation of negatively charged
electron particles, or waves, encountering positive charges of
electricity in our own upper reaches of the atmosphere? *If*
the change into electricity is independent of red and infra red
rays in the solar spectra, the chemical combination *may*
work!)

It may be noted, here, that germanium is a very rare greyish-white metal found combined with argyrodite, and a few other very rare minerals. Argyrodite, again, is a steel-grey and very rare mineral of metallic lustre, which is a combination of silver, germanium and sulphur. Germanium was found in 1886 by the German chemist, Winkler. It is bivalent and quadrivalent. The famous Russian chemist, Mendeleef, discoverer of the periodic system based on the atomic weights of materials, which, in chemistry corresponds to Bode's astronomical Law in regard to missing planets, called germanium "ekasilicon". And, at a time when it had not been found, predicted that it would be found. As one has said, it is of very rare occurrence on the earth.

But is it common on other worlds, in or outside our own solar system? Do any of these flying saucers, whose types are varied, come from a world where some metal like germanium is common, as is iron on the earth, and is used as a source of propulsive energy? If so, do they use it to activate motors in their space vessels, where propulsive energy is created from sunlight in space?

André Fernand Roussel, who developed the dipolar vortex theory, of the ether-whirl of electricity, magnetism and radiation of matter to explain the self-perpetuating rotation of the earth and other planets, is the author of a book titled: *The Unifying Principle of Physical Phenomena*. His theory is that the earth and all the planets have an electron negative, or electro-magnetic field. This field, it is theorised, could be used to provide power to start off a space ship to go from planet to planet, using the electro-magnetic field of force of each planet, in turn, and so need no other fuel.

Do any of the cosmic visitants use this force—assuming that such fields exist?

Roussel's theory is that the field is generated by a rotary spiral motion of the ether at the core of our sun. The spiral whirl creates and spreads a rotary field that reaches out far beyond the planet Pluto, on the bounds of our solar system. The extent and range of this rotary field of Roussel—which, it is to be supposed, is duplicated by other suns in the stellar universe—is apparent, when one recalls that Pluto, discovered in 1930, lies beyond Neptune, is computed to be 4,650,000,000 miles from the sun and has a diameter about twice that of earth, and a year equivalent to 300 of our years. These rotary fields are, in Roussel's theory, geared so that, at each pole of a planet, one flow of ether-energy streams in from the north, and another from the south pole. Both form a "stirring mechanism", or rotary field that "blows" through the crust of each planet, as through that of the earth, and keeps the planet rotating on its axis, like a gyroscope.

Again, one may ask: Are these rotary fields of energy (if they exist), "tapped" by any type of flying saucer?

There are other problems of the space ship.

For example, what about the effect on the human system when men are, or may be, one day, hermetically sealed in such a craft? A recent Hollywood film of a voyage to the moon by rocket-ship makes a great play on the difficulties met with, out in space beyond the earth's gravitational field. Men are shown letting go their hold on seats, to which they were strapped, and floating weightlessly and helpless in the inside of the ship. But nothing is shown, in this film, about how the problem of eliminating breathed-out carbonic acid gas is dealt with. If this oxidation process continued, the men in the ship would be asphyxiated, just as surely as they would be in a sunken submarine beyond the reach of help from divers and salvors. It is one of the many minor problems, of course. Nor is anything shown in regard to the circulation of the blood, when once the pull of earth's gravity has been removed. Little things of that sort are below (or above?) the attention of Hollywood!

I mentioned above (p.p. 241-2) the mystic fantasy, or story of Martian space men whose circulatory and eliminatory systems had to be adjusted, in some mysterious way, in order to enable them to function in conditions of low or zero (no-) gravity.

Then, again, the problem of orientation on a voyage to some far more remote planet than our moon has to be faced, in conditions when radar guidance from the earth may not be available. All these and many other factors have to be taken into account, together with another danger revealed by the Smithsonian Institution at Washington, D.C., in 1934. It was found that, if it were not for the belt of atmosphere above the earth, all life would be wiped out by rays from vast "stars of death". There are "blue stars" in space that emit death, or lethal rays, which are screened out by a layer of ozone, high in the earth's atmosphere. This unknown cosmic factor suggests possible dangers arising from the explosion of thermo-fusion (hydrogen), and thermo-nuclear, or atomic fission bombs, which may rupture a protective belt. These "blue stars" are said to have a surface heat of 36,000 degrees Fahrenheit, three times as hot as our sun; but the "blue stars", on the other hand, have been found to give off few or none of the sun's beneficial type of ultra-violet, or heat or infra-red rays.

When all these and many other factors—many still unknown—are taken into account, one gains a very lively notion of the problems perhaps already solved by the mysterious entities aboard the flying saucers!

APPENDIX

Since this book has been set in type, a number of mysterious phenomena and unexplained incidents have happened, or been disclosed, both in England and in the U.S.A. I summarise them:

Mid-February, 1953: A curious story is being told by an official in an official attorney's office concerned with tracing lost persons, in Los Angeles, Calif. Two strange men, 6 foot 6 inches in stature, temporarily engaged by the director of this legal inquiry bureau, have recently disappeared. About January 20, 1953, these men, said to be emaciated, not very well clothed, bluish-green in complexion, and with prick ears like those of certain breeds of dogs, were given a job, in this Los Angeles department, to help in tracing lost and missing persons. They were so efficient that they astonished other investigators by tracing missing persons in a fraction of the customary time. It is also alleged that, one day, one of these two men leant over the steel top of a filing cabinet, and, with his curiously curved hand, scored an indentation in the steel at least $\frac{1}{2}$ inch deep! I am informed that it was noted that these two men had strangely curved wrists and hands, which appeared jointless and different from the histological structure of human beings. They said they came "from another planet", and, about the middle of December 1952, had landed from a small flying saucer, in the Mojave Desert, some 200 miles east of Los Angeles, and learnt to speak English by listening (presumably in outer space?) to broadcasts of radio and TV! The Federal Bureau of Investigations, in Washington, D.C., sent agents to investigate this affair; but, when the agents arrived in Los Angeles, the strangers had vanished. The indented steel was sent to a metallurgical chemist, who said that, to produce such indentations, would require a force of some 2,000 lb. to the square inch! It is also added that traces of more than a dozen unknown elements were found in the dents. The F.B.I. agents are said to have sent a secret report on the affair to Washington, D.C. Obviously, this story can neither be proved nor disproved, and the indented steel has been locked away. (*Communicated to the author, by a correspondent in Los Angeles, Calif., who insists on anonymity*).

Author's comment: It is difficult to know what meaning to attach to the story above, about the "unknown ele-

303

ments" in the indentation of the steel. All one can say is that, *if* this story is not merely a hoax, these visitants had bodies not like our own, but metallic in a way unknown to the terrestrial human physiology.

February 22, 1953: An ex-Australian Air Force officer, and his wife, sitting on the verandah of their house, at Adelaide, South Australia, were startled, at about noon, when, on a sudden, there shot out of the sky two rapidly rotating discs, a short distance apart. They got closer to the ground, then ascended and vanished. The officer rushed into the house for his binoculars. A few minutes later, the discs re-appeared, approached each other, almost met, and then one disc banked into a steep climb and went out of sight. When he looked for the other disc, it had vanished. A man at Elwood, Australia, reported the same phenomenon in late summer, 1953.

March 10, 1953: A woman at Brisbane, Queensland, Australia, saw at 1.30 a.m., a cigar-shaped thing with fluorescent lights gleaming inside it. It passed noiselessly across the skies and disappeared.

July, 1953: A loud explosion startled a miner, Harold Adams, at Toms Creek, near Coeburn, Va., U.S.A. Going into a field, he found a grey, putty-like substance which burnt his fingers. Nearby was a curious container like ivory, which he touched with a stick, and, throwing the stick into a brook, it burst into flames, exploded and cast water over many yards. Police impounded the substance, which a chemist said was metallic sodium. But how came it to fall in the middle of a field? Military 'planes do not carry this chemical, relatively uncommon and dangerous.

Sepr. 3, 1953: A mysterious, very large and luminous object flitted in the air around Bedford Park, Cleveland, Ohio. A youth of 18, named Cashman, told the police that "it threw a branch of a tree at him. It made "a humming noise", hovered motionless, and then whizzed off. It re-appeared in the park, two days later, and "threw a rock at young men who approached it". The mystery has not been solved. Some of these youths were injured.

November 3, 1953: Boys and their headmaster, at a Roman Catholic school at Denton, Gravesend, saw at 4 p.m.—an hour later than a strange object seen on a radar screen of a Territorial Army unit, at Lee Green, about 18 miles away westward—a strange thing very high in the sky, emitting bright flashes intermittently, while it remained stationary for half an hour. It then moved eastwards towards the European continent. The Air Ministry explanation that this was merely a weather balloon does not explain how a balloon could remain stationary *for half an hour* and emit flashes.

November 10, 1953: A newspaper in Bridgeport, Connecticut, reports that "three men in black", believed to be agents of the Federal Investigation Bureau, or secret service agents, called on a man in that town, and sternly ordered him to shut down a journal, "Space Review", organ of a body called the "International Flying Saucer Bureau". The newspaper says that these agents also caused the organisation itself to be closed up, and the membership dispersed. The man says he was so frightened that he could not eat or sleep for three days after. It is alleged that the man proposed to quote a prediction of the famous French doctor and astronomer, Michel de Nostradamus, buried at Saint-Remi, Bouches-du-Rhône, in 1566. It is also added that this prediction was that "a third world war would break out soon, and that a big space ship would land", in the U.S.(?), "to aid terrestrials." The newspaper also imported that information about flying saucers from all over the world had been circulated by someone to the F.B.I. While some quarters in the U.S. protest at "an invasion of liberty in a free country", others speak of "mischievous vaticinations" that might cause hysteria and panic among badly fused elements of the American population, as actually happened in faked broadcasts in Tokyo and Ecuador, alleging that men from Mars had landed in the earth.Also, be it noted, in Gt. Britain in a fatuous and mischievous B.B.C. "Goon Show" flying saucer spoof, in early December 1953, at a time when flying saucers had previously been reported in English skies, I merely cite this Connecticut story, making no comment on it; except to draw the reader's notice to the previous item of February 1953, in which the F.B.I. are also alleged to have conducted an investigation into a saucer story. Another U.S. newspaper says that the Connecticut man told a reporter that he expected to be called to Washington, D.C., on a prolonged visit to some mysterious U.S. Govt. official. It is not *generally* supposed that the man is about to be appointed as first American ambassador to Mars or Venus.

November 15, 1953: A thing like a silver sphere went above and behind a Meteor jet plane flying over Yorkshire, Eng. It was seen to descend lower in the sky, swinging like a pendulum, and then moved off at terrific speed. (*N.B.* Saucers with this curious pendulum movement have been seen more than once, high in British and U.S. skies in previous years. This book mentions several such incidents). The R.A.F. admit inability to find "a natural explanation" in five per cent of all saucer incidents investigated.

November 18, 1953: Two U.S. Air Force pilots soared up to an altitude of 17,500 feet, over Ohio, in order to obtain a close-up view of a mysterious bright red object. When they landed to report, authority threatened them with a court-martial if they talked to press or public about what they had seen. As it is unlikely that these pilots would have investigated a secret weapon or device, what is the U.S. Air Force trying to hide from the public?

Novr. 22, 1953: At Bookaloo races, near the famous Woomera range, C. Australia, 350 out of 353 pedigree homer pigeons entirely vanished, radioactivity after hydrogen (?) bomb explosion being suspected.

November 29, 1953: Fire damaged hundreds of tons of hay and grain at two farms near Redcar, Yorkshire, Eng. Damage was said to be £7,000. (*N.B.* These fires had previously happened, in very mysterious circumstances, in the Cotswolds, Essex, Sussex, and in Decr. on Sir Winston Churchill's estate at Westerham, Kent. (*Vide pages 279-283, supra*).

November 30, 1953: U.S. Air Force sets up 33 special cameras, in 33 states, to break down light and determine if it comes from tangible, or intangible objects in the skies. The U.S. Air Force headquarters, Wash., D.C., reveal that they have coloured cinema pictures of flying saucers flying over Utah, in 1952, and cinema photographs of saucers seen to fly into a "huge object over the Gulf of Mexico". These latter photos were taken by observers in a U.S. bomber 'plane. A well known U.S. airplane constructor, Mr. Martin, predicts that, by 2,000 A.D., earth will have achieved a flying speed of *7 miles a second!* He does *not* say where will come the men who can survive the terrific gravitational forces involved. The Canadian Royal Air Force sets up a flying saucers bureau in Toronto.

December 6, 1953: An hotel worker at a place near Racine, Wisconsin, on the western shore of Lake Michigan, reported to the police that four strange men in green dresses and caps with red stars came ashore in a rubber life-boat, and asked him where was the nearest airfield. He refused to say, and they got into their boat and went to another craft, about 200 yards off-shore. Coastguard vessels patrolled the lake, and Air Force 'planes searched a wide area north of Chicago. At the end of the hunt, General R. M. Woodward, Illinois Director of Civil Defence, called the report a "fantastic hoax". (*N.B.* Apart from the unlikely fact that a man who has to get his living would be so foolish as to try to hoax the U.S. State police and security forces with a silly story, and invite a long gaol sentence, Chicago correspondents of mine write that there are unconfirmable rumours that these four strange men wore a dress like that of "midget saucer men" seen on a lonely lake in Ontario, in early July 1950. *Vide* chapter XI, p. 254.)

December 12, 1953: Five people see, in daylight, at 6.40 p.m., a "splendid object in the sky, like a large electric globe, tapering to a point", travelling from the north, eastwards over Black Rock, Victoria, Australia. It vanished over the horizon.

December 15, 1953: While the Italian railways declined to carry in their freight vans parts of the diabolical cobalt bomb which is said to treble the devastating powers of the "ordinary" hydrogen tritium bomb, and to be capable of making areas uninhabitable for centuries, newspapers in Berlin report that Soviet Russia has, on a new branch line of a railroad north of Lake Balkhash, in the province of Akmolinsk, in Russian Central Turkestan, a secret, heavily guarded establishment for the manufacture of these Satanic cobalt weapons. Vast hydro-electric power stations and a secret airdrome are associated with this strictly "forbidden" region. One would not wonder if this region is surveyed by the mysterious flying saucers. (*N.B.* Naturally, or unnaturally, Russia cannot hope to keep to herself a "good thing" like this; for, beyond a doubt, the *rival* combines are all earnestly engaged in preparing something bigger and better that will render *all* the planet uninhabitable for 10,000 years to come! *Au.*)

Dec. 16, 1953: A mystery of the air: Four Meteor jet 'planes flew into thick fog over Waterbeach, Cambs., Eng., after taking off there. In a few minutes all the jets crashed, without collisions. Two pilots had to bale out, and one was hurt, after crash landings. These jets came down, three in Cambs., one in Suffolk. The singular official explanation was: "These jets all ran out of fuel". (*Vide* January 11, *infra*).

Now compare with the following:
   Right through 1950 and 1952, in the U.S.A., there were a phenomenal series of accidents to jets and military air trans-

port, and commercial 'planes. There seems a very singular pattern in the mysteries, which I will outline in a moment.

Summer 1950: Three new type jet 'planes took off from a military aerodrome near Washington, D.C.—over which, that summer, literally squadrons of five-miles-a-second flying saucers caused a furore in the radar room of the big commercial airport at Washington. On a sudden, all these three jets crashed into Chesapeake Bay, near Washington, and for no apparent reason. One pilot only survived, and could give no explanation, but said: "The 'planes just suddenly stopped". One jet was salvaged from the bay, and examined; but the U.S. Air Force never revealed the conclusions.

August, 1950: Over Indiana, U.S., four of a flight of 8 jets suddenly all crashed at the same time. Official "explanation" was that ice had formed over the intakes of the jets and shut off the air supply; *but* several U.S. Air Force pilots immediately declared: "Impossible! The jets were not high enough for ice to form over the jet intakes." The pilots were suddenly silenced. No subsequent jet crashes were revealed to the public.

1952: Three commercial 'planes, either taking off or coming in to land, at Newark, N.J. airport, within a few months of each other, fell into congested areas, two of the 'planes' crashes causing great loss of life, on the the 'planes' crashed causing great loss of life, on the ground. Public protests finally caused the airport to be closed. No satisfactory explanation of the crashes was ever given. All that was said was that the 'planes, for "some reason", went out of control and crashed.

Incidental Pattern: These 'planes were all of the latest type, or carrying cargo, or personnel of exceptional value, skill, or special knowledge. It is to be noted, too, that all are stages towards terrestrial space craft. Is "something", from outer space, trying to discourage experiments or accumulation of data?

December 17, 1953: Householders and their terrified families, of Claremont square, Islington, north London, rushed into the streets in the early morning, informing the metropolitan police that there were strange reverberating noises in their houses which shook violently, as if by earthquakes. (*N.B.* To attribute this phenomenon to air-locks in pipes, or to water-cocks is wholly unconvincing; but, although proof is obviously impossible in the establishment of a causative link, it must be pointed out that mysterious phenomena, like flying saucers were, at this very time, reported by soldiers and airmen over London and Kent. I am also well aware of the logical fallacy: *Post hoc ergo propter hoc! Au.*)

December 23, 1953: At 8.38 p.m., a great explosion was heard all over south and west London. Police were baffled. (*N.B.* There is *no* proof that any 'plane at this time passed the sonic barrier in flight. Phenomena of this sort *might*—proof is not at present obtainable—arise from differential "etheric stresses" met by the solar system on its voyage through space. It is, also, nonsense to say, as did one London newspaper, that pilots are not aware when they are passing the sonic barrier. The facts are that, as they approach the barrier, the tremendous compression of the air feels like a wall; but in *passing* the sonic barrier, the strange effect becomes one of relative smoothness in flight. On passing *out* of the barrier, the effect of wall-like resistance is again felt by the pilot. *Vide* mystery, *infra*, of January 3, 1954. *Author*).

Christmas Eve, 1953: The night express from Auckland, New Zealand, crashed through a flood-damaged bridge over the river Wangaehu, with loss of life of 166 people. One theory is that the neighbouring volcano of Mt. Ruapehu, 9,000 feet high, had erupted, burst a wall of ice in a crater, and injected millions of gallons of water into the river Wangaehu, whose terrific force broke the concrete pillars of the bridge.

(*N.B.* Apart from the fact that North Island, N.Z., an area of vulcanism, has a natural instability in the crust of the earth, disequilibrium may also arise, as in the case of *some* of the mysterious blasts in England, from some cosmic cause, or perhaps from differential etheric stresses. In some quarters, it has been urged that these crustal disturbances, and the increasing tempo of disintegration of lower-lying strata of the earth are being observed by *some* of the types of flying saucers. *Au.*)

January 1, 1954: An experienced pilot, Captain D. Barker, of the A.N.A. airline, saw a very strange object, in the sky, above the Yarra Valley, Victoria, Australia, at 10.15 a.m., and visible for 12 seconds. "It was huge, had a speed of about 700 miles an hour, was well below the minimum altitude for normal craft's safety, was shaped like a metallic mushroom, shot off shafts of light as though it had been made of celluloid, and had what looked like an observation car under it. I am sure it was of solid metal, and very definitely was *not a Convair* air liner. It flew into clouds for a second or two, then sank down to an area of clear sky, and its colour changed from clear plastic to sky-blue. Size at least four times as big and speed ten times as fast as a DC.3." Other observers said the strange thing "seemed to have a transparent glass-like dome." A year before, an A.N.A. pilot over Mackay, Queensland, saw a similar object in the sky. Captain Barker adds: "Its main body was elliptical, with a long shaft of the length of its body, slightly curved, with a sort of control tower at the end."

January 1, 1954: Race-goers at Hanging Rock, Victoria, Australia, saw a round silvery disc hanging stationary and noiselessly in the sky for 2 minutes. Then it turned on edge and vanished.

Same day, at 2.30 p.m., observers at Box Hill and Melbourne, Victoria, Australia, saw something high in the sky—and *not* a balloon—shaped like a queer box which was turning over and over slowly. Suddenly, something like a ball of vapour dived on the "box" at terrific speed at an angle of 45 degrees, and both objects vanished. Later, a thing like a sphere trailing vapour flashed at vertiginous speed across the sky to the east. At 3.17 p.m., same day (Jan. 1, 1954), over Hampton Beach, Victoria, and very high in the sky, a "clear plastic-like object, like a dish, rushed across the skyline." At 8.45 p.m., on the same day, a huge silver object of unknown origin was seen at other places in Victoria, Australia, coming down to a height of 300 feet trailing a streamer of vivid red-blue flame, and then vanishing at amazing speed, until it was seen as if to dip downwards towards a high hill.

January 2, 1954: In the cellars of the splendid hôtel de ville, of the ancient town of Arras, Pas-de-Calais, N. France, there was found a mediaeval manuscript which escaped the bombardment of the German artillery, in the first world war. The chronicler says: "In this year of our Lord, 1461, on the day of All Saints (Novr. 1), there flew high in the sky over the town a strange thing like a ship from which streamed fire." (*N.B.* In France, Louis XI had just been crowned, the "cannon of battery" was in use for sieges (a sort of mediaeval culverin), and across the Straits of Dover, in England, Edward IV was on the throne, while, on Towton Moor, some 33,000 men lay dead after an internecine battle of the Wars of the Roses, and most of the old English aristocracy had been extirpated. *Au.*)

January 3, 1954: About 200 sheep were found drowned in dykes on the Isle of Grain, and on the marshes near Gravesend. They seemed to have stampeded in terror. What was very singular was that the sheep, in every case, stampeded in a *westerly* direction. (*N.B.* While there is no proof that flying saucers were the cause of this stampede, it must be observed that birds, such as pigeons, and sheep are very sensitive to appearances in the sky. The *same* phenomenon happened, in similar conditions to those of January 3, 1954, at 8.30 p.m., on January 15, 1869, near Swaffham, Norfolk, when "something seen in the sky, and mysterious explosions," not of meteoric origin, stampeded hundreds of sheep; on Novr. 20, 1887 and Novr. 3, 1888, over an area of 210 square miles in Berkshire, and simultaneously on farms *not* contiguous; again, on Novr. 10, 1888, in the night, in the Thames Valley on farms scattered over an area of 70 square miles; yet again on the night of Novr. 13, 1888, over a region in the Thames Valley, 220 square miles in area. The next morning, some of the sheep were found lying under hedges, panting in terror, and crowded into corners of fields on very widely scattered farms. On October 25, 1889, in the Chiltern Hills, and round Chesham, over a region of about 40 square miles, sheep in hundreds simultaneously burst out of folds and barns. The strange panic was contagious, though the farms and folds were miles apart. In one case, in Berks, on Novr. 20, 1887, the phenomenon happened at 8.20 *a.m.* In 1901, sheep similarly stampeded in the Thames estuary marshes. Apart from fog and mist, *to which sheep are accustomed,* it seems that mysterious cosmic phenomena cause the same disorientation and panic in sheep as one noted in the case of homer pigeons, in Australia, after the explosion of the hydrogen(?) bomb at Woomera, in summer 1953). Sheep, of course, like many birds, have a highly sensitive nervous organism, and are peculiarly susceptible not only to excitant and mysterious objects in the skies, but to high-pitched sounds. It may be noted that, as these sheep of the Thames marshes stampeded in a westward direction, whatever panicked them may have come in from the east or north-east from across the North Sea.

January 3, 1954: Mr. John W. Boyle, vice-president of the Victoria (Australia) branch of the British Astronomical Association, saw at 11 a.m., on this day (Sunday), visible for 30 seconds, what at first looked like a "piece of paper" blown by the wind, at a height of about 30,000 feet. But there was little wind, and the object resolved itself into something like aluminium rocking from side to side and flashing in the sunlight. Each time it flashed, a halo of purple shone round it. No vapour emitted, and no light of its own. If the object had been 30,000 feet up, he thought its speed might be 1,000 miles an hour, "five degrees a second", and its diameter about 60 feet. Mr. Boyle emphatically denies that what he saw was a cosmic ray balloon. He does not dismiss the theory that the object was interplanetary. "Anybody", he says, "who denies the possibility that these things may be visitors from other planets, is either very frightened, or just plain stupid. Some people as I've seen myself at public lectures, on interplanetary travel, become seized with screaming horrors if one talks of little men landing on the earth".

January 3, 1954: Weird spinning object, trailing an aluminium-like streamer (*Vide*, also, January 6, *infra*), seen by three women, over *Footscray*, Victoria, Australia. Time 8.30 p.m., high speed, cigar-shaped saucer flashed across sky of Victoria, was white, with blue flames, but no obvious propulsion unit. "Quite a common report", says Air Traffic Controller, in Melbourne, "and we can't find out what it is. Many of our staff have seen this thing". (*N.B.* He may like to hear that this "cigar-shaped object" has caused serious fires in both U.S. and England. *Author*). On the same night, an object like a rocket, with a blue trail, dropped 500 feet from the sky, vanished behind a belt of trees and came in sight again, in Victoria. (Melbourne airport has been choked with saucer reports).

January 5, 1954: The curious phenomena, here recorded, appear to have begun in Sept. 1953, and were very noticeable both before, during and after Christmas, 1953. In the wooded regions of Buckinghamshire, Eng., and close to the Chiltern Hills, mysterious noises, ranging in timbre and volume, from a persistent humming and deep vibration and throbbing to a sound like a motor lorry ascending a hill, or a 'plane "revving up its engines", or even to the noise made by a mammoth machine vibrating in a hollow, have maddened residents and kept them awake at night, it is peculiar that, of three bungalows on a hill-top at Chalfont St. Giles, Bucks., in this region, the middle bungalow has heard the mysterious noises only once, while the other two constantly hear it. The cause does not appear to be connected with telephone wires, water pipes, local factories, or engineering work, and the local authorities have given up the investiga-

tion as in vain. The Air Ministry denies that the phenomena
are in any way linked with any establishment under their
control. A similar phenomenon has been heard in Essex,
north Lincolnshire, and in south-west London and Surrey.
It has also been heard in deep-lying caves in chalk in Surrey,
and at the bottom of a Yorkshire coal-mine. There seems
also to be a subjective element, in that not all people hear it.

Previous records are of a sound like wagons rumbling
heard for 1½ hours at Bulwick, near Peterborough, July,
1830; the mysterious sounds called "Moodus" by N. American Indians, which seem to be subterranean, heard in
Connecticut, in 1791, 1880, 1891; strange noises in sky when
a luminous object was seen, over Piedmont, Italy, and the
Swiss Alps, and La Tour-d'Auvergne, Puy-de-Dôme, France,
1808; "cannonading in sky", heard continuously for a
month, all day, at Melida Island, Adriatic, 1822; similar
phenomenon at Gabes, coast of Tunis, N. Africa, July 1881;
steamship "Resolution" heard a cannonading in sky over the
Arctic, July 30, 1883; cannonading in sky heard in N. France
and Belgium, 1892, and 1893; same thing heard in Cam-
bridgeshire, Eng., in January 1869; at Comrie, in Perthshire,
explosions in sky, or rattling sounds, or ribbon-like flashes
in sky, sometimes accompanied by ground tremors, at many
dates between 1822 and 1894; great explosion in sky over
Colchester, Essex, February 1884.

January 6, 1954: Superintendent of Traffic Control, Dept. of
Civil Aviation, Melbourne, Victoria, Australia, appeals for
reports of unidentified aerial objects. "They are *not* a joke,"
he says. The same department officially releases reports of
saucers, seen between Novr. 1951 and July 8, 1953, over New
South Wales, Victoria and Queensland, observers including
air pilots, radio operators, airdrome and fire station officers,
control tower operators, and private men and women. Objects reported comprise: Illuminated cylinder, travelling at
tremendous speed (June night); bright lights, not stars,
travelling at high speed, horizontally (nights of May); silent
formation in inverted V-shape, at great speed, without
wakes; illuminated fishbowl-like object manoeuvring at
high speed round a DC.3 'plane, and then vanishing—no
other 'plane then up (night of May); light ascending at
terrific speed from 4,000 to 5,000 feet, also seen out at sea,
nine hours later, at 3 a.m., May 17, 1951; lights in the air,
not ground lights or from aircraft; brilliant light which pilot
tried to intercept, but it flew away from Lincoln bomber;
strange object seen over New Guinea (October 1953); round

disc with long trail, like that seen by Captain Barker on January 1, 1954. It shot across sky over Bendigo. *Not* a meteor. A.N.A. line pilots report saucers over Sydney, N.S.W., one pilot, Captain Jackson, stating that a thing with an orange light at tail streaked towards the coast at 11 p.m., re-appeared two minutes later, completely circled his 'plane as if to examine it, then again vanished towards the coast. "A nerve-racking thing", he said. "A definite object, but control tower radar missed it."

January 6, 1954: Captain Ivan Woolley, another A.N.A. pilot, reports an experience of the sort, elsewhere mentioned in this book, which has happened in France and U.S.A. When mowing his lawn at *West Footscray*, Australia, he saw queer things like brown scraps of thin metal float down from the sky. At a height of about 200 feet, these metallic filaments suddenly shot upwards at terrific speed. Definitely *not* from weather balloons. *Vide* Jan. 3, *supra.* (*N.B.* Novel feature of this incident is the apparent control of the objects from an unseen source).

January 7, 1954: The Australian Flying Saucers (unofficial) Investigation Committee report 20 sightings of saucers over Victoria, six being over Melbourne.

January 7, 1954: Miss I. M. Lutze, driving on road near Ballarat, Victoria, reports that, on October 7, 1952, 28 saucers dived at her car, then turned upwards and vanished. They were not in formation, but scattered, silver-white in colour, and a beautiful sight against a clear afternoon sky. Fearing ridicule, she did not report them before. They travelled slowly enough to be counted. Dept. of Civil Aviation at Melbourne, points out that flutter at edge of short range radar often prevents detection of saucers, while, on long range radar permanent "echo" patterns on the screen may cause them to be missed.

January 7, 1954: An unknown object like a disc with a wake of crimson light streaked across the N. French sky and fell with a violent explosion into the Channel off Dieppe. French military authorities deny that it was either a 'plane or secret missile. Houses were shaken over a wide area. The blinding flash, white, then orange, was seen 80 miles away, and for three seconds was like the noon-day sun at night. A French trawler, about 30 miles off the coast, said he saw "a tremendous bowl of fire flash over the sky in the direction of Dieppe. It left a wake of sparks."

January 8, 1954: "Terrifically bright object seen in north-west quadrant of the sky, at 9.45 p.m. Observer, Mr. Alan Brown of Hamilton, Victoria, Australia, says the object was like two saucers, the upper one inverted. Colour: bright orange. It left a vapour trail, visible for half an hour.

January 8, 1954: About midnight, Mr. R. Cobain, of Sale, Victoria, Australia, saw, low on the horizon, a strange object "corrugated on top", and flashing crimson lights. He called neighbours, and they saw the object change from crimson to a misty green, move up and down, flash crimson again, and vanish. It did not re-appear on the next night.

January 9, 1954: Capt. W. Booth, flying an A.N.A. 'plane, 100 miles north-east of Adelaide, South Australia, saw a strange object very high in the sky, moving erratically after sunset. It circled slowly, and went side to side. The first officer, Mr. Furness, said the object was straight ahead and resembled the silhouette of an aircraft circling slowly, 50 miles away, but the A.N.A. 'plane could get no nearer to it.

January 10, 1954: For several nights running, a mystery man with Herculean physique, has caused trouble in a memorial park garden, at Heanor, Derbyshire. In the morning, the keeper has found steel name-plates, half an inch thick, broken in a half or bent double, and a copper beech tree snapped in two at the thick bole. The mystery man has also wrenched a sundial from its base, torn up 20 rose trees and 100 wallflower plants, and given the impression that a mad bull elephant has been at large, stampeding in the night hours. Police cannot find him, and £5 reward offered for his apprehension remains unclaimed. (*Vide* the incident, *supra*, of the strange man who indented steel half-an-inch, at Los Angeles, mid-February 1953).

January 10, 1954: From 2.30 to 3.15 a.m., a bright planet-like object hovered, then moved swiftly, vertically, then sideways over Adelaide, South Australia. Four people watched it. Its colours ranged from white to deep orange. A bright pin-point of white light was seen to circle the object twice, at immense speed. The planet Jupiter was setting, but the swift sideways movement of the object was not that of the planet.

January 10, 1954: In fine weather and under a blue and nearly cloudless sky, the B.O.A.C. *Comet* jet airliner suddenly crashed into the sea off Elba Island, and near the too appropriately named "Calamity Point". A few minutes before the disaster, the *Comet* was in radio communication with other aircraft and sent out *no* distress signals, which may imply that the crash happened with strange suddenness. Italian fishermen say they heard three almost simultaneous explosions above a belt of cloud, and then "a silver object flashed out of the cloud and hit the water". Theories include a turbulence in a clear sky for which there is no explanation. Whatever happened, the extreme violence of the explosions is suggested by the small size of the fragments of wreckage picked up. Previous disasters of this recent type of "stratosphere airliner" comprise a sudden crash with loss of 43 lives to a B.O.A.C. *Comet*, at Calcutta, on May 2, 1953, and a crash, with loss of all aboard, of a Canadian Pacific *Comet* airliner, taking off near Karachi, India, on March 3, 1953. All *Comets* now grounded. Italian doctors reported that there were no burns on the bodies of the dead, found floating on the sea, but that their legs and lower part of the bodies were crushed up.

It was also found that there was no water in the lungs of victims found floating in the sea, the inference being that death took place before impact with the sea. Another significant thing is that only fragments of clothing on the upper part of the victims' bodies were found, which is an indication of the sudden impact on the victims of explosion-blast, or *onde de choc*. At Beirut, in Syria, the previous stopping-place, the authorities strongly affirm that there could have been no possibility of sabotage; since the airliner was under close observation. (Elba, in 1943, at the time of its invasion by the Allied Force, the scene of one of those phenomenal falls of ice, about two feet long, from the skies, which, from time to time, occur in the British Isles, in Europe and the U.S.A.)

Mr. Lennox-Boyd, the British Transport Minister, states, in Rome, on 19 January, 1954: "Of the 15 bodies recovered from the wreck of the *Comet*, and being presumably those of passengers sitting in the rear of the airliner, some of them appear to have been *struck from behind* by some sort of explosion. We must concentrate with great vigour on all possible causes of the disaster," he adds.

According to a Rome newspaper, Professor Fornari, pathologist of Pisa University, who made an autopsy of some of the victims of the *Comet* disaster, found no external signs of burns; but the internal injuries to the lung and heart tissues showed severe injuries, consistent with a sudden and violent explosion. Fishermen trawled up bits of the casing of the *Comet*; but as the wreck seems scattered over a region of the sea-bed, about 13 miles south-west of Elba, and lies at a depth of about 80 fathoms, a difficult task confronted the British Admiralty salvors from Malta. (*Vide* the disaster to Pilot Mantell over Fort Knox (Godman Airfield), Kentucky, on *January 7, 1948, a curious periodicity noted before, pp. 90-4 supra*).

January 11, 1954: Three U.S. Air Force Sabre jets were flying at night near Darmstadt, Germany, when something caused their pilots to bale out. What happened to the third pilot is unknown. (*N.B.* What is decidedly curious is that, here, as in the exactly parallel incident recorded in the English eastern midlands, on December 16th, 1953 *supra*, the U.S. Air Force, like the British R.A.F., says that *all* these jets "ran out of fuel"!)

January 14, 1954: The Department of Civil Aviation, Melbourne, Victoria, Australia, receives a letter enclosing a report from an unnamed French professor of science, who alleges that flying saucers in opposed cohorts will fight out the next world war, black Jupes, or Jupiterians on one side, and Red Martians, on the other, with our old planet as their football.

January 14, 1954: A disaster remarkably similar to that of the British *Comet* jet airliner, four days earlier, befell the airliner, *Cloudmaster*, of the Philippines Airline, bound from Manila to London. Stories of what happened are contradictory: (1) She had signalled that she was about to land at Rome airport, when, as she turned at a height of 500 feet, there came a "tremendous roar of the engines", and she skimmed over a block of buildings, and crashed in a field, sixteen passengers being killed. As the *Cloudmaster* hit the ground, a terrific explosion occurred in the 20-foot crater she had dug on impact. Rain was falling in torrents. (2) The Italian Ministry of Defence says that the *Cloudmaster* crashed suddenly at a height of 6,000 feet. At 11.44 a.m., the *Cloudmaster* had switched over to the airport traffic control frequency for landing, as directed by the Rome airport control, and gave her altitude as 6,500 feet. Thirty seconds later, the staff of the airport control tower, saw the airliner about to crash and heard the blast of an explosion. She appeared to have plunged straight to the ground, after a sudden violent explosion. Exactly as in the case of the *Comet*, the *Cloudmaster* had not had time to send out an S.O.S.

January 15, 1954: Four intelligent Australian aborigines rushed at 5 a.m. into the camp of an Australian prospector, Mark Mitchell, and his wife and excitedly woke them up. "Boss, we jist heard a strange whine comin' from the east, above them clouds thar. We heard 'planes often enough before. It fair screeched as it passed. Crikey, boss, what name that fella?" *Place*: Hart's Range, 100 miles from Alice Springs, in the Northern Territory, close to the Tropic of Capricorn, and the first saucer known to have been seen there.

January 20, 1954: The Royal Aircraft establishment for Research at Farnborough, stated that it had been found that the *Comet* jet air-liner, G-AIYV, which mysteriously crashed (*Vide* page 289 *supra*), at Calcutta, with loss of all 43 occupants, on May 2, 1953, had *not* crashed owing to lightning or explosion. Dr. P. B. Walker, chief of the structure department, at Farnborough, stated that examination of the starboard and port main planes of the airliner, and the tailplane, gave the impression as "if they had all been torn off by a giant!" Something very abnormal occurred. In the House of Commons, the Minister of Civil Aviation said that detailed examination of four *Comet* aircraft that had been grounded threw no light on the disaster to the *Comet* airliner off Elba.

January 21, 1954: "Ghost of crashed airplane pilot, at English séance, in 1950, warns of entities from Saturn voyaging to earth, and studying hidden scientific forces, who must not be carelessly approached by self-destroying earthians". (Letter in *Melbourne, Vict., "Argus".*) Australian Air Minister, Mr. MacMahon, says his government has sent, to be processed, in U.S., a telephoto-movie of a saucer seen over Port Moresby.

January 25, 1954: British War Office and Air Ministry forbid service men to tell public of saucer sightings.

January 27, 1954: Military and 'planes turn out in force when large unidentified object flies at 25 feet above Quantico (U.S.) air-base. Results: negative. Revealed that U.S. Navy Secretary, in 'plane in mid-Pacific, was 'buzzed' by a saucer. Strange red lights, flashing from sky, and bursting into red fountain-sprays near ground, worry U.S. defence authorities.

Summing up the flying saucer drama, which has been as tragic and singular in England, the Mediterranean, and the

318

U.S.A., as portentous in Australia, in the closing months of 1953, and early in 1954, one might hazard the unpleasant Wellsian conjecture that there may be sinister, or hostile forces of unknown interplanetary origin which seem determined to keep aerodynamic and future extra-terrestrial explorers well within the limits of the sub-stratosphere, and have demonstrated their intentions and power in lethal ways. *If* this is not mere fantasy, nobody can foretell what we may expect when, or if, we proceed to the construction and launching of satellite space vehicles, as planned by Mr. Forrestal of the U.S.A. Government, and thence, proceed to attempt a landing on the moon. One may have very grave doubts about the optimistic calculations that, before the end of this present tumultuous century, earth will at last have succeeded in landing on her satellite, the moon. Is there any astronomical or cosmic reason why certain air disasters have occurred in the month of *January*?

It may be a very long way off, yet, before England or the U.S.A. establishes a spatial protocol, and appoints the first ambassador from earth to the moon, or Mars, or some other world of which our astronomers have, at this time, no knowledge. *If* (and who can say?) there *is* a League of Worlds, we on earth have, as yet, no bright prospects of a seat on either the Council or the Assembly thereof. It is but too likely that those who come after us may find that man's road to the stars and the planets is paved with disaster on disaster. Before we arrogantly talk of conquering space, let us, without the aid of any official priest or scientist, first conquer ourselves.

The advice is thousands of years old, but we have never taken it.

BIBLIOGRAPHY

Among the many works and authorities cited in this book are the sources following:

ANGLO-SAXON CHRONICLE, THE

ANNALS OF DUNSTABLE.

ANNALES MONASTERII BERMONDESEIA.

ANNALS OF ULSTER.

ANNUAL REGISTER (Many vols. from 18th to 19th century).

L'ASTRONOMIE (Paris, France).

ASTRONOMISCHES NACHTRICHTEN (Berlin, Germany).

BARKER, GRAY: "The Saucerian", (Clarksburg, W. Val.).

BATEMAN, S. T. The Doom: Warning all Men to the Judg-
     ment (London, 1581).

BEE, JACOB. Diary (1689).

BELLAY, JOACHIM DU. Oeuvres (Paris, 1569).

BENEDICT OF PETERBOROUGH. Gesta Regis Henrici Secundum.

BOOK OF LEINSTER, THE.

BORDERLAND SCIENCES RESEARCH ASSOCIATES. San Diego, Cal.

BRITISH ASSOCIATION FOR THE ADVANCEMENT OF SCIENCE. Re-
     ports and Journals.

BRITISH ROYAL METEOROLOGICAL SOCIETY. Reports.

BRITISH ROYAL SOCIETY. Archives and Philosophical Trans-
     actions.

BRITTON, C. E. A Meteorological Chronology.

BRUNSWICK AND LUNEBURG CHRONICA.

CHASTELAIN, DOM PIERRE, Journal of, 1709-1782.

CHRONICON ANGLIAE.

CHRONICON DE LANERCOST.

CHRONICA VON MAGDEBURG.

CHRONICLE OF MELROSE.

CHRONICON SCOTORUM.

CLOUZOT, E. Histoire et Météorologie (Paris, 1907).

CRUSIUS, PAULUS. De Epochis seu aeris temporum (Basel, 1578).

DENESDE, ANTOINE. Journal (1628-1687). (Archives Historiques
     du Poitou).

DUNSTABLE, ANNALS OF.

DURHAM (DUNELMENSIS). *Vide* GRAYSTANES.

DUVAL, LOUIS. Phenomènes Météorologiques (Paris, 1903).

ETHELWERDUS, FABIUS. Chronicorum.

FABYAN, ROBERT. The New Chronicles of England and France (16th cent.).

FATE MAGAZINE. Evanston, Ill.

FINCELIUS, JOBUS. Wunderzeichen. . .von dem Jar, an MDXVII bis MDLVI (Jhena, 1566).

FLAMMARION, CAMILLE, Astronomical Works of.

FLORENCE OF WORCESTER. Chronicon.

FORT, CHARLES, Works of.

FOUR MASTERS, THE.

GAIMAR, GEOFFREY. Lestorie des Englis.

GENTLEMAN'S MAGAZINE. Many vols. in the 18th century.

GRAYSTANES, ROBERT DE. Historia de Statu Ecclesiae Dunelmensis (1320).

HALLEY, EDMUND, Astronomical Works of.

HELLMAN, M. G. Reportorium der Deutschen Meteorologischen, etc. (Berlin, 1883).

HENNIG, Doktor R. Katalog bemerkenswerter Witterungsereignisse von der altesten Zeiten bis zum Jahre 1800 (Berlin, 1904).

HENRY OF HUNTINGDON. Historiae Anglorum.

HERSCHEL, FRIEDRICH W., Astronomical Works of.

HOLLAND, RALPH M. Voice from the Gallery, and letter to author of this book, from Cuyahoga Falls, O.

IRISH MIRABILIA.

KNIGHTON, HENRY. Chronicon. . .Monachi Leycestrensis, and, also, The Continuation, by another hand.

LANERCOST, Chronicle of.

LYCOSTHENES (or CONRAD WOLFFHART). Prodigiorum ac Ostentorum Chronicon (Basileae, 1567).

MAGDEBURG, Chronicle of.

MATTHEW OF PARIS (*Vide* PARIS).

MILES, MATHIAS. Siebenburgischer Würgenengel (Hermannstadt, 1670).

NATURE. British scientific journal.

NICHOLSON'S MAGAZINE (London, 1809 and 1812).

OBSEQUENS, JULIUS. (Roman chronologist of 4th century A.D.) Prodigiorum.

OURANOS, Revue Internationale pour l'étude des SOUCOUPES VOLANTES et problèmes connexes (Bondy, Seine): Marc Thirouin; E. Biddle. (London, N. 20); This is one of the best and most scientific of flying saucer reviews.

PARIS, MATTHEW OF. Historia Anglorum.

PEMBRIDGE, CHRISTOPHER. Annals of Ireland.

PHILOSOPHICAL TRANSACTIONS OF THE BRITISH ROYAL SOCIETY.

PROJECT SAUCER (Vide U.S. AIR FORCE).

RALPH OF COGGESHALL. Chronicon Anglorum.

ROBERT OF READING. Continuator of Matthew of Westminster's Chronicle (1628-1687).

ROBERT, SIMON (notaire). Journal (Archives historiques du Poitou).

ROGER OF WENDOVER. Chronicon.

ROYAL IRISH ACADEMY, Transactions of.

ROYAL METEOROLOGICAL SOCIETY, Reports of.

ROYAL SOCIETY OF ENGLAND, Archives and Philosophical Transactions of.

SELLER, JOHN. History of England (London, 1696).

SHEPHERD, GEORGE. Climate of England.

SHORT, THOMAS. A General History of the Weather, Meteors, etc. (London, 1794). Very rare. Not in the British Museum.

SIMEON OF DURHAM. Opera Historica.

SPECULUM REGALI, IN KONUNGS-SKUGGSJA.

THANNER KRONIK DES KLOSTERS IN ELSASS.

TIGERNACHUS (O'BRAAIN). (Abbatis Clunensis). Annales.

TRIVETUS, F. NICHOLAS. Annales.

U.S. AIR FORCE. Project Saucer Press Communiqués.

WALTER OF COVENTRY. Memoriales Fratres.

WALTER OF HEMINGFORD. Chronicon.

WAVERLEY, ANNALES MONASTERII DE.

WESTROP, DIETRICH. Dortmünder Kronik (1550).

INDEX